D1578605

# *First Cosmic Velocity*

ALSO BY ZACH POWERS

*Gravity Changes*

ZACH POWERS

*First Cosmic Velocity*

G. P. Putnam's Sons

NEW YORK

PUTNAM

G. P. Putnam's Sons
*Publishers Since 1838*
An imprint of Penguin Random House LLC
penguinrandomhouse.com

Copyright © 2019 by Zachary J. Powers

Penguin supports copyright. Copyright fuels creativity,
encourages diverse voices, promotes free speech, and creates a
vibrant culture. Thank you for buying an authorized edition of this
book and for complying with copyright laws by not reproducing, scanning,
or distributing any part of it in any form without permission.
You are supporting writers and allowing Penguin to
continue to publish books for every reader.

LIBRARY OF CONGRESS CATALOGING-IN-PUBLICATION DATA
Names: Powers, Zach, author.
Title: First cosmic velocity / Zach Powers.
Description: New York, New York: G. P. Putnam's Sons,
an imprint of Penguin Random House LLC, [2019]
Identifiers: LCCN 2018044742| ISBN 9780525539278 (hardcover)
| ISBN 9780525539285 (epub)
Classification: LCC PS3616.O94 F58 2019 | DDC 813/.6—dc23
LC record available at https://lccn.loc.gov/2018044742

International edition ISBN: 9780593085844

Printed in the United States of America
1  2  3  4  5  6  7  8  9  10

Book design by Francesca Belanger
Photo credit: Maria Starovoytova/shutterstock.com

This is a work of fiction. Names, characters, places, and incidents
either are the product of the author's imagination or are used fictitiously,
and any resemblance to actual persons, living or dead, businesses,
companies, events, or locales is entirely coincidental.

*For my brother, Josh Powers, a lifelong space enthusiast*

"You know, the truth, even the most bitter truth,
is always better than a lie."

—YURI GAGARIN

# *First Cosmic Velocity*

# Baikonur Cosmodrome, Kazakhstan–1964

Nadya had been the twin who was supposed to die. But she lived, and it was her sister, the other Nadya, who'd departed. The Chief Designer placed his hand on this Nadya's shoulder and squeezed. He meant it to comfort her, but it had also become a superstition of sorts. The first time, at least, he had meant to comfort her. Since then, it was for his own comfort. No launch had ever failed following the gesture. This calmed him in a way the vodka never could.

The bunker walls were bare concrete. The control panel, a patchwork of different metals, unmatched switches, knobs, and dials like a hundred varieties of flower, faced the wall opposite the door. A half-dozen engineers manned positions at the console, and as many as that stood behind them. The Chief Designer knew only a few by name.

Had Nadya lost weight? He remembered her being meatier, muscles sculpted. She still trained back then, he supposed. No need for that now. Perhaps he simply misremembered. This was only the fifth time his hand had so much as grazed Nadya over the years of the program, once for each launch. Hell, he even managed to touch his wife more often than that. His wife and son, how long since he had last seen them? He looked at the countdown clock.

Some of the engineers called the Chief Designer *Medved* because they did not know his name, but also because of his breadth. The large scar on his head, too, befitted an animal. The gouge ran from just above his right eyebrow deep into the territory of his balding pate. He would never discuss its origins. Half his teeth were artificial, the incisors grayed like an old cheap saucer.

He slid sideways through the narrow space at the end of the control console to the bunker's periscope, a box of raw metal with goggles protruding from the side. The distance shrunk the R-7 rocket to toylike proportions. Only the top showed above the great tulip framework of the launchpad. The four metal buttresses, gripping the rocket like a vise, would not fall away until the thrust reached a certain level. The pad's design had been Mishin's. Or was it Bushuyev's? The Chief Designer could never remember.

Beyond the pad spread sprawling flatness, the Kazakh steppe like something from a nightmare, one where he would run and run but never seem to make progress. Downrange had become a grave-yard for spent rocket parts, dropped early stages, shrapnel from the occasional explosion. Not as occasional as the Chief Designer would have liked. Some of the younger technicians took trucks, vintage from the war, and searched for souvenirs. Mars had re-turned once with a piece of metal sheeting, the skin from a failed rocket, with a red slash painted on it like a wound. It was the tip of the sickle. He had searched for the hammer, Mars said, but the steppe was a big place. Or a non-place. After a certain point, a thing's vastness diminished its identity.

The Chief Designer did not look at the landscape, however. He scanned the sky, grimacing at the gray roiling over the horizon. He had received word of a storm surging across the steppe, the kind that would muddy the whole complex and postpone the mission.

"There's only so much of nature I can conquer at once," he said, speaking the words as if through the periscope. No one in the con-trol room heard him.

The mission had already been delayed once after a single

centimeter-long wire shorted out. Of the kilometers of wires, hundreds of vacuum tubes, and thousands of other little electronic devices, all it took was the tiniest glitch to ground the whole thing. The Chief Designer hated that faulty wire, sometimes he even hated the engineers who had installed it. In his more generous moods, he would congratulate the engineers on the foresight of the indicator light. Left unrepaired, even that forgettable span of wire could have destroyed the whole rocket. The fuse was always tiny compared to the explosion.

The Chief Designer squeezed back around the console. Mishin, or was it Bushuyev, handed him the bottle of vodka. No glasses this time. For the first two launches there had been glasses, so that a successful launch might be toasted. By the time those launches actually occurred, however, there was no vodka left. They had drunk it all in the waiting.

The Chief Designer gripped the bottle with both hands and gulped down a mouthful, like a man emerging from the desert, scared that the substance might turn to illusion if he did not down it fast enough. He passed the bottle to Mars at the communications terminal quickly, so that the liquid's rippling would not reveal the tremors shooting through his body. Mars took a sip and passed the bottle along.

The radio crackled with static. An exhaled breath. The Chief Designer shoved himself next to Mars and took the microphone.

"T plus one hundred," he said. "How do you feel?"

"I feel fine." The voice came small and tinny from the speaker. "How about you?"

A round of subdued laughter crested through the bunker.

The voice belonged to Leonid, crammed inside the little globe of the Vostok capsule perched atop the R-7. It was the first joke the Chief Designer ever remembered him making. At least this Leonid.

The other one had been trained to tell jokes, to be normal. More than normal. He was the socialist ideal incarnate. As if an ideal was something that could be trained into you. Sometimes the Chief Designer thought of them, the two Leonids, as the same person, but then that was the whole point.

Nadya slipped around the console to the periscope. She didn't press her face against it, but stood back, observing the small image of the rocket, fish-eyed by the lens. *Speaking of ideals,* thought the Chief Designer. How old was she now? Twenty-five? The original cosmonauts, the Vanguard Five, were all the same age, give or take a year. Nadya was the only one among them to achieve grace in a jumpsuit. Her blond hair so fine. He wondered what the other Nadya's hair had looked like in weightlessness. The first human in space, and no one had thought to take a picture. No one had thought to ask.

The only time Nadya's grace had failed her was the day before she was scheduled to launch. The little white dog Kasha, herself trained as a cosmonaut, had darted under Nadya's feet in the hallway. The Chief Designer had been there, along with Mishin and Bushuyev, walking from the training center toward the mess, discussing the logistics of launch day, though all of them knew the procedures so well by then that any recapitulation was pointless beyond even the usual levels of redundancy the engineers favored. Nadya seemed to rise up, over the top of Kasha, and then toppled to the beige-tiled floor. She looked down, her face seemingly stretched by surprise, not pain. Kasha sat beside Nadya, as if protecting her. Nadya hovered her hand above her knee and said simply, tragically, "It's broken." The Chief Designer remembered the electric shock those words had caused to pulse below his skin. That was his last clear memory of the first launch.

Now he stood, looming over the control panel like the rocket over the pad, both figures, to look at them, unlikely to ever leave the ground. His finger floated above the ignition button. Could he press it again? After the first launch, he had always pressed it himself. Whoever's finger did the work, though, the ultimate responsibility was his. It was his button, his rocket, his cosmonaut. No, he would not press it again. He would remove his hand, scrub the mission. He would stand on the scaffold of the launchpad as Leonid emerged from Vostok. He would welcome Leonid home like a son, though Leonid had never actually left the ground. Like Nadya. Like the Nadya who survived. What had her sister's hair looked like in space?

"We never think to ask the right questions," he said.

The Chief Designer mouthed the final numbers of the countdown: *pyat, chetirii, trii, dva, odin.*

He pushed the button, and the engines, all twenty of them, lit as one.

LEONID WATCHED HIMSELF launch into space. A small spark flashed at the base of the R-7, and then it grew, flaring so bright that the rocket itself was swallowed up. He worried something was wrong. Even though he had seen four previous launches, the fireball seemed impossible to survive, the rocket a matchstick igniting the sun.

He felt the rumble coming even before it rattled the bunker. It knocked him off balance. At breakfast that morning he'd only managed two bites of black bread. His brother, his other self, had eaten everything else. That was the first time they had seen each other in months, one of only a few times over the years. They had always trained separately, always pretending to be one and the same person. Leonid's brother did most of the real training, this Leonid learning just enough to appear capable, his main job to wait, to stay invisible until such a time as he was needed. Until today. Neither brother had spoken a word the whole meal. Now Leonid's breakfast would leave the very planet it came from.

The trusswork petals around the rocket separated and then fell back, a bloom of metal and flame. At first by fingerbreadths and then meters the rocket rose, and then it ate up sky, leaving whole lengths of itself behind as smoke. Leonid thought of a gray thread stitching blue fabric. The thread grew finer as the rocket drew away, until all he could see was a distant orange glow, fading in and out behind wispy clouds. The glow faded a final time and never returned to view.

The smoke trail thinned, feathering at the edges, and took up position in the sky as a narrow cloud. A tether without substance, carried across the steppe by the dry, hot wind.

Through the slitted window, Leonid could see the other bunker, the control room, about half a kilometer up the main road. The bunker looked like an anthill from afar, just a bump rising out of the dirt. All the other twins were there now, manning the controls, or like Nadya, just watching. Leonid was the last twin, and so this bunker was his alone. The other cots would remain empty. He'd spend the three days of the mission sleeping, eating the premade meals, and staring out the window at the unchanging scenery. He noted the clouds on the horizon. The storm would soon turn the complex into an edgeless field of muck, but he was grateful for the rain. It was the only movement he would be able to see through the window.

His eyes followed the smoke trail up to the vanishing point. He spoke his brother's real name, the one given by their parents, not the one the two of them now shared. Leonid knew that secret name, as did the Chief Designer, and of course Tsiolkovski. No one else, though. Not since Grandmother said goodbye and they boarded the train and Tsiolkovski spoke to them for the first time: "From now on, you are one boy, the same boy. Your only name is Leonid."

All of a sudden, that first statement was true. Leonid, in his tiny bunker with its crack of a window and uncomfortable cot, was the only Leonid on Earth. The bottom of the smoke trail lifted, breaking contact with the ground.

ENGINEERS SCURRIED AROUND the control room, giddy, always about to bump into each other but somehow never colliding. *Molecules in a gaseous state,* thought the Chief Designer. It was always like this after a successful launch, especially one with a cosmonaut on board. The tension of waiting was replaced with euphoric release. The technicians made short work of the post-launch checklist. *Systems were shut down, valves secured, inspections made.* One by one, the indicator lights on each control panel darkened. Mishin and Bushuyev gathered the fifteen thick volumes of technical data on the R-7, barely able to hold half each in their arms, and carried the books out to the Chief Designer's black Volga sedan. The driver offered to help load the volumes, but Mishin and Bushuyev declined. Sometimes it seemed as if they always had the books wrapped in their embrace.

The last person to leave the bunker, besides the Chief Designer himself, was Mars. Azerbaijani by birth, Mars's personal history had of course been rewritten to make him a proud son of Leningrad. He and his twin had quickly learned the accent, the local customs. Though they did not exactly look the part, no one had ever questioned their heritage. Mishin and Bushuyev took the Mars twins, one at a time, on tours of the city, but the Marses themselves ended up serving as guides. Through their studies, they had learned Leningrad better than even lifelong residents, navigating the streets without hesitation. That was how they trained, too. The Chief Designer recalled the simple assurance with which the other Mars would flip a switch. It seemed like such a small thing, a toggle of mere millimeters, but Mars had mastered that tiny gesture in a way the other cosmonauts never would. This Mars had shown the same confidence as his brother in the simulator, though he had spent far less time inside it. It pained the Chief Designer to see how much that confidence had been purged from him.

Mars leaned over the communications console, speaking in whispers to Leonid as *Vostok 5* settled into its orbit. Mars would stay there, mouth held millimeters from the microphone, until the capsule rounded the horizon and communications were handed off to other stations—Makat, Sary-Shagan, Yeniseysk, Iskhup, Yelizovo, Klyuchi, Moscow, Leningrad, Simferopol, Tbilisi, Kolpashevo, Ulan-Ude, Sibir, Suchan, Sakhalin, Chukotka, Dolinsk, Ilyichevsk, Krasnodar—where strangers would carry on impersonal conversations with Leonid, more concerned with inserting data into tables than speaking to the lonely cosmonaut. When the launch crew arrived back in Star City, Mars would head directly to the communications room, where he would remain for the duration of the mission, as he had done for every mission after the second, when his own twin had launched. Back when they still hoped to bring the twins home. More than once, the Chief Designer had thought he heard Mars's low voice ask, "Do you see him?" Mars's brother, though, had burned up on reentry. There was nothing left to see.

"Mars," said the Chief Designer, "it's time to go. We must make it to the plane before that storm arrives." He pointed through the wall in the direction of the approaching thunderhead.

Already the speaker fed back only static. Mars flipped several switches and silenced it. He had developed a hunch to his shoulders, as if he were always leaning down to speak into the microphone. His hair, thick and black, he kept cropped so close that scalp showed through. He often forgot to shave, his beard growing in far longer than his hair. Mars stood and left, snatching his cap from a hook by the door.

The Chief Designer took a final look around the bunker. Everything was off that was supposed to be off. He tucked chairs under the console. He picked up and pocketed a pencil someone had left behind. As tidy, he thought, as the inside of a concrete block could be. He turned to leave.

A figure shifted in the corner, amid shadows not so dark that they should have been able to conceal someone. The scent of cheap cigarette smoke wafted from the corner, sullying the air. Even though he did not believe in such things, the Chief Designer at first suspected a ghost. Certainly he was a person worth haunting.

"Here's to another successful launch, Chief Designer."

The woman emerged into the lit part of the room as if coalescing from the dark. She was part smiling face, the rest leather jacket, several sizes too big. The high fur collar rimmed her neck. Her hair was cut in a Western style, her makeup like something an actor might wear to portray a pharaoh. She dropped a cigarette, snuffing it out with her heel. The Chief Designer sighed. It was Ignatius, a writer for Glavlit, responsible for crafting every word written about the space program. She was the one who had decided to never use his name.

Two glasses of vodka balanced on the palm of her extended left hand. The Chief Designer took one and accepted her toast. The vodka was pure, obviously filtered many times, better than the swill he and the other engineers had been sharing earlier. He gulped it down. If he believed in such things, it would have felt a little like sealing a deal with the devil.

"Are you here for an interview?" he asked.

She laughed. Not once had she interviewed him, though many, many times she had attributed to him words he never spoke. The nameless Chief Designer of the newspapers orated grand statements of Soviet glory. Seldom did he speak about outer space.

"I simply wished to see the launch," she said.

"The bunker doesn't offer the best view."

"Everyone, even you it seems, thinks only of the ignition of the engines. You wouldn't need a roomful of people if it were as simple as that."

"Hardly simple. One day you should count the parts of the R-7."

"I'm not sure that I'm qualified to tell where one part ends and the next begins. At what division is a part of a part a thing itself?"

"Ask Mishin. Or Bushuyev."

Ignatius set her glass, still mostly full, on the launch console. The Chief Designer moved it to the communications console, something cheaper to replace should the vodka spill.

"Mars seems sad," said Ignatius.

"He's a melancholy sort."

"Only after a launch, which one might consider strange."

"Are you here to write about us or psychoanalyze us?"

"I'm here to write about the successes of the Soviet system. As such, I have a vested interest in the continuation of those successes."

"Are you implying something?"

"Your time in the gulag has made you suspicious."

"Your presence makes me suspicious." The Chief Designer turned and faced the wall as if looking through it to the launchpad.

"Chief Designer," said Ignatius, "we want the same thing. We both want glory."

"I don't want glory."

"You want the moon. What's more glorious than that?"

"Silence, perhaps."

Ignatius snatched her glass, splashing some of the vodka though not enough to do damage, and drank the rest in a single gulp. She held the glass up to the Chief Designer's face. She spun and hurled the glass at the wall, exploding it into a starfield of shards. The pop of the impact was followed by the delicate percussion of the fall.

"Glory is a fragile thing, Chief Designer. You may fool the Presidium, the military, even Khrushchev himself, but you don't fool me. What would I find, for instance, if I visited the bunker up the road?"

"A broom, perhaps, to clean this up."

"When I come to clean, it will be with more than just a broom."

"A threat?"

"I want only what you want, except I don't care who accomplishes it. The General Designer, perhaps."

"The General Designer is an ass."

"If we were to catalog offenses, I think yours would be more numerous." She held up her hand, fingers spread. "I count five. Four and a half, at least."

The Chief Designer stared at her. Only a few knew the truth. The twins. Mishin and Bushuyev. Tsiolkovski, of course, though he had vanished years ago. The scar on the Chief Designer's head throbbed.

"Don't get me wrong, Chief Designer. I have no desire to expose you. In fact, I'm the only person really on your side."

"I didn't ask for an ally."

She inspected her palm, her fingers still splayed. "So many of us don't ask for the things we receive. Someone more spiritual might call it fate."

Ignatius brushed bits of the broken glass into the corner with the toe of her boot. She opened the steel door. Its massive hinges groaned. Daylight peeked through, and a gust of wind carried in a cloud of yellow dust.

She said, "Hurry, or you'll miss your flight. See you in Moscow."

The plane would wait, though. That was one thing, at least, over which the Chief Designer retained a modicum of control.

THE LATCH CLICKED, and the door creeped open.

Leonid had been watching through the window as the motorcade approached from the control bunker and drove past. A fine grit of dirt plumed behind the cars. The service vehicles came next, technicians returning from the pad. A few people strolled alongside the road to personal vehicles parked at the edge of the launch complex. Within a few hours, no one would be near Leonid for kilometers around. He reminded himself that his brother was even more remote.

When the door opened just wide enough, Nadya slipped sideways into the bunker. She wore the gray suit all cosmonauts were forced to wear on launch day, flat and featureless except for the black trim along the mandarin collar, designed to look futuristic but accomplishing monastic instead. Her hair was pulled back in a bun, something she only did for public appearances, and only then when told to do so. There must have been a photo shoot following the launch. There had been ten thousand photos for every rocket.

"Where's the Chief Designer?" asked Leonid.

"He left."

"How'd you get the key?"

"I took it from his pocket. He's always so distracted before a launch." She looked at a corner of the room while she talked.

Unlike the other earthbound twins, she had never been trained in social graces such as eye contact.

The door closed behind her, and the lock clicked. There was no keyhole on the inside. Four folded cots leaned against the wall. Nadya took one and set it up beside Leonid's. She sat down, face hung toward the floor. The concrete looked like the moon, pocked and ashen.

"You won't return to Star City?" asked Leonid.

"I always end up there eventually."

She reached across the gap between cots and pulled Leonid's hand to her lap, massaging the faint scar on his forearm with her thumb. It was the same gesture her sister, the other Nadya, used to make after they first arrived in Star City, when the twins, still children, were split up and homesickness rose in waves each evening. That Nadya would go from bunk to bunk, soothing weeping to silence, only returning to her own bed after all the other children slept. Leonid's scar had been darker then.

There was no confusing that Nadya for this one, who was so much colder and more distant. Maybe this Nadya had once been the same as her sister, but the Chief Designer trained that out of her. For every hour Leonid had spent learning manners from Mishin and Bushuyev, and more recently with Ignatius, for every speech he was required to give to his reflection in a mirror, he knew the space-bound twins had spent just as much time inside simulators and centrifuges. That was how Nadya had lived her whole life up until the launch. She was merely meant to be another mechanical component of Vostok. A switch to flip the other switches.

The other Nadya had been barely more than a child when she launched. Leonid remembered himself then, face dotted with acne, his jawline softer, still shedding the shape of boyhood. Now his cheeks stubbled by lunchtime, and it required mathematical precision to shave the sharp features of his chin and cheeks without nicking himself.

Nadya, this one, hummed softly to herself, a song that never quite realized its own melody. She had taken to that lately, humming the same song as if relearning it from memory. The melody reminded Leonid of the folk tunes of Bohdan, his home village, simple songs about long-dead Cossack heroes.

"What is it," asked Leonid, "that song?"

The humming stopped.

"Please, go on."

She tried to start the song again, but the notes came out at random, as if she had not forgotten just that song but the whole concept of singing.

"I don't remember it," she said.

Leonid pulled his hand from Nadya's lap and rested it in his own.

"Tell me about my brother," he said.

"He's like you. More confident, maybe, but that's just the training. Tell me about my sister."

"She was very little like you."

The two of them often repeated this exchange when they were alone together. That was usually where it ended, but Nadya raised her face and looked Leonid directly in the eyes.

"What did she say to you?" asked Nadya. "I saw the video. Before she boarded the rocket, you were the last person she spoke to."

"She said she was glad she was the one to go and not you."

"Why would she say that?"

"She was your sister."

"What's a sister if you've barely seen each other in years?"

"She didn't have to see you to think of you. I still think of her now, and she's five years dead."

Nadya stood and paced the perimeter of the room, brushing her fingertips along the rough concrete walls.

"Let's go for a walk," she said.

"The door locks from the outside."

"One day, then. One day let's go for a walk."

## Bohdan, Ukraine—1950

**M**onday morning and the train didn't come. The villagers idled by the tracks, kicking at fat stones cascaded down from the mountain. Usually, when the train was late, they swept stones to kill time. There were not enough, though, to warrant the effort. No one could remember the last rains, anything more than a drizzle, strong enough to shake loose even dust from the craggy face of the mountain. The green of the forest had grown less vivid. The wet scent of the firs, once filling the valley like water in a pond, had faded to nothing.

By noon, it was clear that the train would not arrive. The villagers gathered their shed coats, dusty things that hung like sheets over their shoulders, and dragged their empty carts back down the rutted dirt road to the village proper. The tops of the homes, recently shingled by a crew of Russian carpenters, rose like gray peaks above the low trees of the valley's center. There were perhaps a dozen cottages in all, if one counted the church and the schoolhouse. Even in a village as remote as Bohdan, it was usually best not to count the church.

Leonid—then still known by his birth name—watched the empty carts parade by, wooden wheels clunking unevenly, the people that pulled them gaunt as the legs of horses. His brother, the younger Leonid, crouched in the brush on the other side of the road. They had planned to steal a sugar beet each from the carts as they rolled by, a practice tolerated by the villagers, who had themselves swiped beets from their parents like their parents from their grandparents before them. With no train, though, there was nothing on the carts to steal.

The twins should have been in lessons, but the small clapboard schoolhouse had remained empty since the teacher left with Russian soldiers some weeks before. When the teacher boarded the outbound train, she had paused on the top step, casting a long look around the valley as if she did not expect to see it again. The train chugged away, huffing out great exhalations of snow-white steam, gathering speed and distance, ascending the mountain through the pass where the steam blended with the mist and the train evaporated into the outside world. Grandmother had told the two Leonids that no one who took the train ever returned.

So for weeks there had been no school. The boys read from their tattered lesson books when Grandmother pressed them, but mostly they spent their time outside, exploring the forest or shadowing the villagers.

The swine squealed in their pens as the empty carts ricketed past, kicking up a fecund scent with short stomps of their hooves. Leonid remembered there being more animals, but that was the memory of a toddler, when everything seemed larger and of greater numbers. These animals were more like pets than livestock, spindly and with the shapes of bones visible beneath their skin. Nothing worth eating. The fattest had been sent out on the train months before. Like Grandmother said, what left on the train never returned.

Kasha, the village's lone dog, owned by no one in particular and fed by all intermittently, emerged from behind a log pile and marched alongside the carts. She was as tall as a man's knee, all leg and lean muscle, narrow-snouted, fur white like the steam from the train. In better times, the boys would have shared whatever food they had stolen, or the villagers would have dropped something for Kasha to eat. Still, the dog seemed happy, practically prancing as she walked. Her tail, though, hung limp behind her. Some injury, predating Leonid's memory, had robbed the tail of its motion.

The younger Leonid caught up to the procession and helped old Mr. Yevtushenko pull one of the carts. The left wheel was lopsided and snagged in the path's ruts once per revolution. The younger Leonid boy's strength didn't help much, but it was enough to keep the cart moving. The older Leonid looked for a place to help, too, but the other villagers had no trouble with their own carts. Maybe if they had been laden. He wondered why the villagers had not just left the carts at the top of the hill, so they would be there when the train eventually came. He wanted to ask, but he knew that no adult wanted the advice of a child. So he followed, not helping, saying nothing. Kasha trotted beside him.

The villagers parked the carts by the arid dirt patch that used to be a garden. They huddled as if they might unload the carts, scooping up empty space into buckets and barrows, and then carry the nothing home with them. Some of the villagers would climb into the hills and try their hand at hunting. It was not a village of hunters, though, so they rarely returned with more than a red squirrel, half exploded from the bullet that felled it. Grandmother told the twins stories of roe deer that used to fill the valley's forests and the feasts their meat used to provide. Those stories rang more like legend than memory.

From the hills, throughout the afternoon, the hopeful sound of gunshots sometimes echoed down from the hills, little pops like hammers on wood. In later months, the sound would become more ominous, emerging as it did from the barrels of Russian rifles.

That night after the villagers went home, the two Leonids climbed atop the cold gray roof of Grandmother's cottage, brushing aside the sere dirt deposited there by summer winds, and watched the wide crease of sky. Kasha scrambled up the berm at the back of the cottage and flopped between them. Long before they knew the stars had names already, they gave them names of their own.

## Moscow, Russia—1964

Leonid and Nadya descended the frail metal staircase pushed up to the side of the Tu-124, the sound of the jets still dying down even as they disembarked. Domodedovo Airport had just opened the month before, and did not yet show the wear of a single Moscow winter. Every other runway Leonid had ever seen was crisscrossed with black lines where the cracks had been filled in, black circles demarking repaired potholes. This runway, though, was flawless gray. Domodedovo's control tower rose like a stone slab from the tarmac, a giant's headstone. The jet fumes smelled acrid but also sweet.

After three days in the bunker at Baikonur, Leonid and Nadya had been retrieved by Mishin and Bushuyev in a timeworn Sorokovka armored transport. The cargo bed carried a Vostok capsule, bearing scorch marks as if it had reentered the atmosphere when in reality Mishin and Bushuyev had attacked it with blowtorches. The transport carried them hundreds of kilometers across the steppe to the supposed landing site. Once there, Leonid helped Mishin and Bushuyev push the capsule off the back of the transport. It landed with a hollow thud and sank into the damp dirt. They attached a parachute and allowed the wind to billow it open. Mishin and Bushuyev radioed the rest of the recovery team, who had no part in the deception. Who believed. Hours more of waiting, followed by a trip to an airstrip another several hundred kilometers away. Leonid found some small amusement in the fact that he had to travel so far to pretend that he had traveled even farther.

Ignatius waited for them on the tarmac at the bottom of the stairs. She wore a leather jacket with a fur collar, several sizes too large, though it was too warm for even a sweater. A black Zil limousine idled behind her, its door held open by a man dressed in a black suit. In the distance, just outside the terminal, a small crowd waited, and with them a military band playing the "Aviamarch." Nadya sang along in whisper, *"Ever higher, and higher, and higher we direct the flight of our birds,"* bobbing her head out of time with the beat. She must have heard that song a thousand times after her sister's launch.

"Comrades," said Ignatius, spreading her arms, "welcome back to Moscow."

"It's only been a week since we left," said Leonid.

"But you left the planet entirely. Certainly you deserve a welcome home." She smirked as she said this, turning to the car before Leonid could respond.

Other than for launches, he had only been away from Star City twice since he first arrived as a child, both for trips into Moscow, so that he might know the history and the monuments. Moscow did not feel like home, no matter how close to Star City it might be. But then, returning to Star City never felt like returning home, either.

The Zil's engine grumbled, and the car slid forward, wheels whirring across the tarmac, then through an ungated gap in the wire fence that surrounded the whole airport. A lone highway threaded away from Domodedovo, nothing much around it, forest and field and an occasional silo breaking through the canopy of trees. On maps, the area was marked with the names of towns, but Leonid saw no sign of them. No one waited for his arrival this far out, kilometers and kilometers from Moscow's center. He settled back into the plush leather seat. In training, he had been required to sit for hours in a mock-up of the Vostok capsule, the seat padded just enough to make tolerable the way it curled the body like a fetus. Young Giorgi called Vostok the *iron womb*. He seemed to have a nickname for everything and everyone.

Giorgi was the sixth cosmonaut, brought in later, the only one who did not have a twin, who prepared to both fly and return to Earth. He had no idea the cosmonauts he knew now were not the same ones he had trained with for years. He had no idea that his five closest friends were dead. Four dead, thought Leonid, with one who might as well be.

A black radio receiver was built into the back of the Zil's passenger seat. Ignatius fiddled with the knobs, cycling through static and squeals, until she found the robotic ghost of a voice. She tweaked the tuning until the voice came in clear. It was Yuri Levitan, announcing Leonid's arrival in Moscow, directing the populace to Red Square and telling them which streets Leonid would traverse on the way there. Levitan's rich voice, thick with a Moscow accent that Leonid still sometimes had trouble understanding, filled up the whole cone of the little radio's speaker, the loudest words, always Leonid's name, *Vostok*, or *socialist*, popping on each hard consonant.

The city began in fits and starts, buildings clustered instead of standing alone, the distance filling with the gray outlines of taller structures. Here and there, a group of Muscovites waited by the side of the road to wave as the Zil sped past. These people still wore an older style of clothes, not much different from the shapeless tunics and baggy pants that Leonid wore as a boy. Traveling from the outskirts to the city was like following a time line, the old ways evolving to modernity.

As the Zil entered the avenues of old Moscow, the crowds grew, though nothing like Nadya's procession years before. It seemed then as if all of the city's five million citizens had packed into Red Square, flooding the streets, slowing her car's progress to a crawl. Men pressed against the window and proposed to her. Parents, cheeks streaked with tears, held out babies as if Nadya might bless them. Children followed the car, sometimes for blocks, surely out of sight of their families. Nadya was the first, though, and the crowds had shrunk with each subsequent launch. Leonid, being fifth, had doubted that anyone would show up at all.

Two police cars joined the Zil, one leading, one following, their blue lights flashing but faint in the midday sun. Ignatius rolled down the side window.

"Greet your admirers," she said to Leonid.

He did not much feel like waving, but as soon as the window was down, his hand metronomed back and forth without him having to think about it, as if powered by the inrushing air. His training had included whole classes on how to emote. He could shake hands and bow and hug with professional acumen. He waved and waved. He imagined that his hand actually belonged to his brother.

The convoy passed behind the Kremlin, up to the short road that entered Red Square from the northeast. The police escort peeled off, one car in either direction. The Zil halted near Lenin's tomb, where an armed soldier opened the door from outside. Ignatius exited and Leonid followed. By the time he was standing, however, Ignatius had merged with the crowd that pressed toward the car from all sides. The whole of Red Square was paved or laid with brick, and the sound of so many people echoed back onto itself, amplifying every clap and holler and clomp of foot. A semicircle of soldiers held the crowd back, but Leonid felt as if he were about to be crushed. As a boy, he had seen landslides tumble unstoppable down the mountainside. Then Nadya was beside him, taking his hand and pulling him along. They mounted the raised platform in front of the mausoleum.

Khrushchev waited there with a small entourage, politicos and military officers, all huddled against the back wall, where they could not be seen from below. Leonid recognized one of the officers as Marshal Nedelin. He had been forced to learn Nedelin's face from photographs, but he could not remember why Nedelin was important. Leonid saluted, and Nadya followed suit a beat later. Instead of returning the gesture, Nedelin strode forward and gripped Leonid by each shoulder. Leaning close to Leonid's ear, Nedelin spoke, "A good show, son. A good show, indeed." He released Leonid and moved to Nadya, gripping her shoulders in the same fashion. She smiled, just slightly, and Leonid could not be sure but thought he saw the faintest red of a blush.

Khrushchev beamed at Leonid, a gap-toothed grin bunching his supple cheeks. Leonid had never met the man before, and was surprised by how short he was. The cosmonauts were not so tall themselves, but still Leonid looked down at the top of Khrushchev's head, the pate sprouting a few final wisps of white hair. Khrushchev embraced first Nadya and then Leonid, deep hugs of real affection. Leonid lifted his arms, but despite the many times he had been forced to practice hugging could not return the embrace. He patted Khrushchev's back instead.

"They're waiting," shouted Khrushchev, motioning in the direction of the crowd. He shoved Leonid forward. "You first."

The roar crescendoed as the peak of Leonid's cap came into view. By the time his whole upper half was visible, a sort of pandemonium took hold. Leonid was sure that the people were damaging their throats with such screams. The violence with which they waved their arms seemed sure to dislocate shoulders. Some hopped in place. He had expected a small crowd, but there were thousands, fanned out from in front of the mausoleum through the far reaches of Red Square. He scanned the faces for anyone he might know before realizing that the only people he knew were right there beside him or back in Star City. Maybe there was a chance to spy Ignatius, but she seemed able to disappear even within a closed room. His hand waved without him having to think about it.

Nadya took her place beside Leonid, and the roar exploded, louder still. She would always be the favorite. Russia's first daughter. The Soviet ideal personified. The only noise to which Leonid could compare this new cheering was the launch of a rocket. The platform trembled beneath him.

When Khrushchev finally took his place alongside the cosmonauts, the cheering had abated somewhat. He did not seem to mind that there was no new ovation for him. He smiled wide and squeezed Leonid's shoulder over and over. Several random generals shook Leonid's hand and then Nadya's and then waved to the crowd.

Khrushchev produced a slim felt-covered box from his inside jacket pocket. He opened the lid, revealing the glinting pentagon of a medal, Pilot Cosmonaut of the USSR. Khrushchev plucked the medal from the box as if picking a flower. It was such a tiny thing, thought Leonid, but Khrushchev held it up to the crowd as though it could be seen even from the far reaches of Red Square. Leonid had seen at least one person in the crowd with binoculars. Gripping Leonid by the lapel, as if he were about to take a swing at him, Khrushchev deftly pierced the pin of the medal through the fabric over Leonid's chest, in and then back out again, and secured the pointed end in the clasp. Khrushchev stepped to the side and took Leonid's arm and raised it. A new wave of cheering. Besides the man with the binoculars, Leonid doubted that anyone there knew exactly what they were cheering for.

Someone gripped Leonid's arm and pulled him away. It was Ignatius. She had changed clothes, and now wore the uniform of an air force officer, freshly pressed, the blue unfaded. He tried to identify the medals on her chest, an ostentatious showing, but he did not recognize a single one of them. Sometimes he thought of adding random strips of fabric and scraps of metal to his own uniform to see if anyone noticed. Ignatius continued to pull him down the steps. A black Volga sedan waited near the bottom.

"You have a winning smile, comrade," she said.

He touched his face and felt the smile there. He did not much feel like smiling. He willed his face to relax.

"I thought you were an agent of Glavlit," he said, "not an officer in the air force."

She tugged at the sleeve of her uniform. "You know better than any the importance of appearance. I simply . . . borrowed this uniform so I could blend in."

"It suits you more than it suits me."

She opened the door to the Volga. Nadya passed between them and entered the car first. Her uniform showed signs of wear, the fabric pilling, unable to hold a crisp crease. She had worn it for probably a hundred appearances. The uniform alone might have traveled farther than her sister's single orbit.

Leonid looked back over his shoulder. The crowd crested toward him, like it would overwhelm the mausoleum, sweeping away the car and him and Nadya and Ignatius and Lenin's waxy corpse. He wanted to join the crowd, blend his face with a thousand others. He wanted to be a blur. If he stepped into the throngs now, there was no way Ignatius could follow. He would shed his uniform jacket. He could hear in his head the sound of the medals impacting the concrete. But where would he go? Where could he? For a moment, he envied his brother.

"Get in the car," said Ignatius. "The public isn't done with you yet."

He stooped into the car and sat beside Nadya. Ignatius closed the door from the outside.

THE CHIEF DESIGNER was not allowed to display his medals, dozens of them at this point, stored instead in their original boxes in a footlocker back at Star City. He wore a plain tan suit and a white shirt with no tie, huddled with a few of the other engineers beside the platform, trying to accept the roar of the crowd as his own even though not one person there knew who he was. Sometimes his title ended up in *Pravda*, but never a name, and certainly not a picture. What a joke of a newspaper was *Pravda*. What *truth* did it ever report? Still, he was happy. The cosmonauts were like his children, and of what is a father capable if not pride?

Mishin and Bushuyev stirred beside him, grumbling something, one of them to the other, though he could not tell which had spoken.

"What is it?" asked the Chief Designer, but he saw the answer even as he asked.

The General Designer strode in front of the mausoleum, directly below Leonid, before all the cheering thousands. He was a tall man, equal in height to the Chief Designer, though only half as broad. His gray suit was cut wide in the shoulders, forming points like a hanger was still left inside. He shuffled his feet as he walked, barely lifting them for each step.

His gaze fixed on the Chief Designer. Mishin, or was it Bushuyev, muttered a curse and the two walked away. The General Designer stopped and faced the Chief Designer, standing much too close.

His breath, tinged with the meaty scent of a recent meal, blew across the Chief Designer's face.

"Another success," said the General Designer, shouting to be heard over the crowd and the band that played an endless loop of "Aviamarch."

"Nothing less," said the Chief Designer.

"But what's next? Surely even you must grow weary of these endless orbits."

"The Earth has been orbiting the sun for all of human existence, and no one complains about that."

"I think you equate your own complacency with that of everyone else."

"Of all the things I've been called, this is the first time I can add *complacent* to the list."

The General Designer leaned in and spoke the Chief Designer's real name, a name he should not have known.

"You won't long be the only star in the sky," said the General Designer, "nor the brightest."

The Chief Designer grasped the upper arm of the General Designer and pushed him away, holding him at arm's length.

"The Americans are already there," said the Chief Designer, "and that's the only competition I care to consider."

"As do I, comrade," said the General Designer. "But ask yourself, are you really the one in the best position to win it?"

The General Designer shrugged off the Chief Designer's grasp and strode back in front of the mausoleum. He stepped into the crowd on the other side. The Chief Designer watched his head bob in and out of view until he lost sight of it.

Mishin and Bushuyev stepped forward.

"What a *dolboeb*," said one of them.

"Doesn't he have a point?" asked the Chief Designer.

"You're a Soviet hero, Chief Designer. Until the General Designer's rocket launches, until his capsule reaches the moon, he's nothing but a pretender."

"We pretend, all of us," said the Chief Designer, and then to himself, "that the only ones who know my name should be adversaries."

He thought just then of Leonid. Not the one here on Earth, but the one still in orbit, the one whose every breath drew him nearer to the last. That was a real hero. One without body, survived only by his name.

The cameras flashed as soon as Leonid entered the room. He paused just inside the doorway and blinked away the spots, only to have the first round of flashes followed directly by another. The photographers, snapping pictures every few seconds, stood along the back wall of the room. In front of them, in low wooden seats, sat the reporters. The seats looked as if they had been made for children. Leonid's hand waved without him having to think about it.

Ignatius entered behind him and ushered him to a seat beside the podium. At least a dozen microphones blossomed from the podium's top, many labeled with letters from other alphabets. Nadya lagged in last, looking around as if she had entered the wrong room. She took the seat next to Leonid.

A man Leonid did not know took the podium first, talking about the space program as if he were somehow involved with it, though Leonid did not think the man was one of the Chief Designer's engineers. Certainly not one important enough to be speaking in such grand terms. The man pontificated about the importance of conquest and about the exceptional dedication of the individuals who made it possible. He spoke of the pride of the nation as if it were his own personal emotion. He seemed to be able to pause and smile just before every camera flash.

"It's now my honor," said the man, "to introduce to the world one of the heroes of the Soviet Union, the fifth cosmonaut to leave the surface of the Earth and to safely return."

The cameras popped again from the back of the room as Leonid took the podium. He had spent most of his life preparing for this moment, but none of the training had included the flashes. He felt dizzy and blind. Leaning forward, he went too far and bumped his chin into one of the microphones. Ignatius squirmed in her seat. The sight of her discomfort somehow comforted him. He laughed and flashed a grin. A grin he had rehearsed in the mirror every night for months—his *signature expression*, Ignatius called it. His lips felt both strange and familiar. He rubbed his chin where it had bumped the microphone.

"I guess," said Leonid, "I'm still not back to being familiar with the feel of gravity."

Members of the Soviet press laughed, and then a moment later so did the international reporters.

"Let me start by saying how honored I am to have been part of this historic achievement of the Soviet Union."

Leonid followed the script of his introductory remarks, words that he had rehearsed nearly as much as his grin, rehearsed to the point of meaninglessness. He did not even recall the content of what he spoke. It had taken him only a few readings to realize that there was not much content to it, anyway. When he had expressed this concern to Ignatius, she laughed. "You're not supposed to say anything," she had said, "just something."

Now Leonid snuck another glance at Ignatius, leaning her

elbows on the low table beside the podium, watching him, and she nodded her approval.

He inflected the right words of the speech. The *gloriouses* and *exceptionals* and *superiors*. He had read the speeches of the previous cosmonauts, and he knew these same words had been spoken at similar podiums many times before.

The first, expected questions came from the Soviet reporters. Leonid related the made-up details of his life, from his name to his parents to his home commune, where his parents had worked the land and exemplified communist ideals before untimely deaths. He could barely remember his real parents, and sometimes even he confused the stories with the truth. His name, even that was false. About the only truth he uttered was the fact that he was Ukrainian. He suspected that if not for his accent, of which he had never been able to completely rid himself, the Chief Designer would have insisted on changing his heritage as well. When Ignatius took over his publicity training, just a few months ago, the first thing she had done was give him speech lessons. He could hide his accent for a time, but it always reemerged the longer he spoke. Eventually, Ignatius had accepted it and said the Soviet people would, too.

The first international reporter asked a question in what sounded like French.

Ignatius translated, "What is it like to be weightless?"

"At first like falling," said Leonid, "and then you float."

It was the answer Nadya had given, the other Nadya, the one who rode that first rocket and died. Mars had communicated with her the whole time she was in range of the radio receiver, chatting as if the two of them were at a cocktail party, not separated by thousands of kilometers. The transcripts of those conversations had been used by all the other cosmonauts, the twins who remained behind, to describe space.

"What did the Earth look like?" asked a German.

"One is struck by the size, of course," answered Leonid, "but also by the smallness. I could see so much more of it, the whole thing in a matter of hours. And all around it is boundless space."

An American spoke next, "Does the Soviet space program have plans for the next mission?"

"I think that our engineers and cosmonauts will undertake the next mission when it is necessary."

"Were you lonely?" The question was asked in Russian, but Leonid recognized the accent: Ukrainian. "In orbit, did you feel alone?"

Leonid did not have a rote answer for the question. It had not come up in practice with Ignatius. He did not want to look at her, but he could sense her gaze on him.

"It's unbearably lonely," he said, "but one must remember that while Vostok is small, the whole of the Soviet people travels with you."

Ignatius practically leapt up from her seat and clapped her hands once.

"Thank you all for your time," she said, leaning into the microphones. "We must transport our cosmonaut to his next appointment."

The cameras flashed again. Ignatius nudged Leonid out a door on the opposite side of the room from where they had entered. It led to a narrow hall lined with stacks of dusty chairs, the same child-sized chairs used by the reporters. Lightbulbs caged by metal grates protruded from the ceiling, but only every third or fourth shone. The dim illumination textured every surface as if in gray felt.

Ignatius slapped Leonid on the back. "Brilliant, comrade! You're a born star. And that last answer couldn't have been more perfect even if I'd scripted it myself."

"Your lessons haven't gone unlearned," said Leonid.

Nadya entered the hallway and sat on one of the small chairs. She swayed in the seat. She did that sometimes. Leonid had asked her about it. Imagining weightlessness, she had explained. The motion made her seem like a child. She faintly hummed a simple melody.

The man who had introduced Leonid came into the hallway next. Ignatius offered a familiar but not overly friendly greeting. They talked just above a whisper, too soft to hear from even a meter away.

"Do you think," Nadya asked Leonid, "that the Soviet people are still with him, now that the Soviet people think he is you?"

Ignatius glanced back and then pulled the door to the press room completely closed.

"Nadya," said Leonid, "I don't think they were with him even before. Never."

Though he did not know where it led, he followed the hall toward the doorway at its distant end. Nadya rose, hurried to his side, and went with him. Faint sunlight framed the doors through the cracks and a bright gash split them down the middle.

## Star City, Russia—1964

The radio room was located behind a steel door twenty centimeters thick. To open the door, Mars twisted the dial, larger than his hand, through the sixteen digits of the combination. He stopped on the final 27, and then cranked the wheel, a device that looked as if it had been borrowed from the bridge of a galleon. The lock *thunked* and unlatched. Despite its mass, the door glided open as if weightless. Mars pushed it closed behind him with only the tips of his fingers. A final thread of light shot through the gap and then all was dark.

Mars fumbled along the wall to the light switch, placed at more than an inconvenient distance from the door. The padded walls sucked up all sound, so this period between closing the door and lighting the room felt purgatorial, a kind of nonexistence. How the twins in space described their experiences.

Orange-white light flickered from the overhead lamps, revealing the radio console, more than three meters long, but the only thing on it was a keypad, a single red button, a small round speaker, and a microphone on a metal gooseneck, all situated just left of center. Mars keyed in the code to activate the system. The speaker crackled, fizzed with static, whined like a sick dog, and then settled into mostly silence, broken only by the occasional pop of interference.

As Mars's ears adjusted to the faint sounds, he picked out something like humming amid the ambient hiss.

He pressed the red button and spoke into the microphone, "Leonid, is it you?"

"I never learned music."

"I can tell."

Leonid hummed again, an atonal tune, if it could even be called a tune, a sound somewhere between singing and mumbling.

"What do you call it?" asked Mars.

"Shit," said Leonid.

Mars laughed. He pressed the red button and laughed again so Leonid could hear it.

"You made a joke," said Mars. "Did you ever joke before?"

"I've been practicing. I'm not sure whether it's to amuse myself or to try to elicit a laugh from the empty space all around me."

"Any luck so far?"

"I feel dull and space remains silent. You know, none of the training prepared me for the silence outside Vostok. The capsule itself will make noise, the flow of air, creaks, several thuds that I was sure were the sound of the thing coming apart. But from outside, absolutely no noise. It's like the anechoic chamber, but a thousand times more quiet. I guess it was just as quiet in the chamber, but there was still something outside. Could it be psychological? Did I know, even in the silence, that the microphone in the chamber connected me by wire to a room just a few meters away? What connects me now? Some incorporeal wave of cosmic energy, beamed from you to me and back again. Even if I were small enough to worm my way through a wire, I couldn't ride the infinitesimal crests of the waves that connect me to the planet."

"We're with you, comrade."

"I know, I know. I simply regret that I'm not also with you."

WITH TRAFFIC, the trip from Moscow to Star City had taken the Chief Designer almost two hours. The sun glared in the side window the whole time, and he had sweated through his shirt. His driver apologized over and over about how long it was taking, as if the man were actually an automaton programmed to speak just that one thing. As if the driver controlled the route of every car on the road. While the Chief Designer had spent much of his life casually shuttling to and fro in aircraft, a simple car ride left him exhausted. At least in a plane he could get up and move about. The plasticky scent of the car's interior coated him like a slick.

Star City's campus had grown from a small huddle of low buildings to a sprawling complex complete with several towers. The dormitories came into view first, thirteen stories high, bare bricks of concrete and glass, the concrete already turning a shade of dirty brown. These three towers seemed to sprout from the middle of the forest. As the car got closer, the whole campus came into view, lower buildings arranged according to no plan that the Chief Designer could decipher, laboratories, offices, training facilities, and a few structures he had never entered and had no idea what they might contain. He would have to ask Mishin and Bushuyev, but if the Chief Designer was honest, he did not much care. He tried to ignore what he did not absolutely need to know. It was easier that way.

The whole complex grew lush with trees, left unfelled at the Chief Designer's insistence, the only clearing a long quadrangle on the other side of the dormitories from the main training facility. The original plans had called for clear-cutting the whole area. The Chief Designer, though, had spent too many years in the treeless tundra. He argued that technology was not meant as a way to escape nature, that space exploration was not about leaving the Earth behind, but that humanity would one day fill the cosmos with what Earth had to offer. His driver parked the car in the billowing shadow of a tree. The Chief Designer got out and stretched, flexing the kinks out of his legs.

He tracked Mishin and Bushuyev down in the training facility, where young Giorgi—attached to so many wires and tubes that he seemed more machine than human—ran on a treadmill. The muscles of Giorgi's bare chest pulsed with each pump of his arms. His hair, even during the most strenuous training, kept a perfect part, as straight as the white line on a blueprint. His stride was casual, his breathing even.

"How long has he been going?" asked the Chief Designer.

Mishin and Bushuyev exchanged a glance.

One of them said, "We stopped keeping track after an hour."

"An hour!"

The Chief Designer looked back at Giorgi. Maybe he really was a machine. But even better. None of the Chief Designer's machines functioned nearly so well.

Giorgi saw the Chief Designer and waved, raising the tangle of wires attached to electrodes on his arm. He smiled around the clear plastic tube clutched in his mouth. Giorgi was always grinning, and the expression only grew the harder he ran. On the monitor, the Chief Designer watched Giorgi's pace increase while his heart rate remained the same. Giorgi's feet struck the rubber track toes first, his calves bouncing him back up as if they were loaded with springs. *Tap tap tap tap tap.* His steps landed with the consistency of a metronome.

The rest of the equipment rested unused, metal frames like the bones of prehistoric beasts. The gyroscope, which looked like a cross between a medieval torture device and a model of the solar system, rings hinged one inside the other, the innermost jutted with handles and footholds to secure the cosmonauts as technicians set the whole contraption spinning along several axes at once, dominated the center of the room. Its only function was to test how a cosmonaut handled dizziness. A circle had been cut in the carpet around the gyroscope's base. It had proved much easier to clean vomit from bare concrete than from the fabric of the carpet. Giorgi, though, had never been sick even once during the training.

The room had three white walls and one, opposite the door, covered with a detailed mural depicting the faces of the first four cosmonauts and a glorified version of the R-7, the painting much prettier than the actual rocket, like the propaganda illustrations Ignatius distributed to the press. There was already the outline of a fifth head, which the Chief Designer assumed would soon become that of Leonid. The mural had been Giorgi's idea and was the product of his own talents. On his first day at Star City, he had entered the training room, looked around once, and declared, "What a drab place! Chief Designer, surely you'll let me beautify it for you." The Chief Designer *hrmphed*, not agreeing but not outright forbidding it. That was enough for Giorgi, who the next day, when he had a free minute in the rigid training schedule, managed to acquire paint and brushes and laid the first few streaks of color in a room that for half a decade had been nothing but white and gray. The scent of fresh paint merged with the room's usual stench of sweat.

There was a time when the whole room would have been full of cosmonauts in training, each strapped in and wired up, surrounded by a hive of buzzing technicians. The original five cosmonauts, sometimes their twins, and then Giorgi, yet to launch and twinless. The Chief Designer's youngest and best cosmonaut candidate yet. The Chief Designer regarded him like a son, loved him like he had no one else since . . .

"He reminds me of Nadya," said the Chief Designer.

Mishin and Bushuyev exchanged a look.

"He's certainly as capable physically," said one of them.

"Though his personality," said the other, "is considerably warmer."

"Did you never meet Nadya's twin?" The Chief Designer whispered this.

Mishin and Bushuyev went rigid. They had known the other Nadya better than anyone, and it was taboo to mention the twins outside of the private depths of the Chief Designer's office.

"She was like that," said the Chief Designer. "If sadder."

He gazed at one of the unoccupied treadmills.

"Giorgi is ready," said the Chief Designer.

Mishin and Bushuyev visibly relaxed.

"Yes," said one of them.

"But our ship is not." Pain flared in the scar on the Chief Designer's head. He ground his artificial molars together until it subsided. "We need a launch in six months, before the General Designer can ground-test Proton."

Mishin and Bushuyev tensed again.

"But, Chief Designer," said one of them, "we don't even have half a rocket assembled."

The other, "Not to mention the issues with the ablative heat . . ."

The Chief Designer snapped, "Don't tell me what we can't do."

Giorgi looked over. He faced forward again and ran faster.

"Let's not argue in front of the children," said the Chief Designer. "Giorgi may be ready, but we're not ready for him. Ignore the heat shield. Just get me a rocket assembled in six months."

Mishin and Bushuyev leaned in. "We don't have a twin to pilot it."

"Not for Giorgi, but we have a whole roomful of twins we have yet to use."

Giorgi whipped a towel from the treadmill's railing and dabbed at his brow, though there was not enough sweat there to see from across the room.

THE KENNEL ERUPTED in a chorus of yips when the Chief Designer entered. A few of the dogs were running free while the rest poked their noses out of the grated doors at the front of their cages, four-by-four squares stacked along the back wall. The earthy scent of dozens of dogs crowded the air. The attendant, sitting at a low metal desk, a book spread open in front of her, looked up slowly. She leapt to her feet when she recognized the Chief Designer.

Years ago, he had visited every day, but when people replaced dogs as the first cosmonauts, his attention had been necessarily diverted. Now he saw the dogs only rarely, when his guilt seemed too much to bear, the pain of his scar throbbing, and he knew that the dogs would show him affection undiminished by time. The three uncaged dogs circled him, jumping up and putting their fore-paws against his thighs. Laika, Strelka, and Kasha, the daughter of the original Kasha, who was brought to Star City with the Leonid twins—how many years ago was that—by Tsiolkovski, back when Tsiolkovski still visited.

"Chief Designer," said the attendant.

He could not remember her name. He was not even sure that she had been the attendant the last time he'd visited the kennel. Nadya and Leonid spent much of their time caring for the dogs, every free moment it seemed, and one of them was usually here. But they would be away for weeks.

Bending down, fighting against the ache in his bad knee, he

pulled the three dogs into a squirmy embrace. They licked at his neck and face, panting sour breath. He released them and laughed. He scratched each behind the ears in turn. Kasha ran to the corner and returned with a length of rope, knotted on each end. She dropped it in front of the Chief Designer. He picked it up and slung it back to the corner. The three dogs darted after it, wrestling over the prize. Kasha emerged from the scrum victorious and trotted back to the Chief Designer, Laika and Strelka jostling for position behind her.

Falling back into a seated position, the Chief Designer allowed Kasha to climb up onto his lap. She dropped the rope and twisted her head to gnaw on the knots with her molars. Her fur was pure white and thick all over, hiding her thin frame in an illusion of bulk. The Chief Designer could have lifted her with one hand.

Most of the dogs had twins in the cages, not blood relatives but animals that looked enough like one another that they could pass for identical in black and white photographs. Kasha did not, though. She had never trained to go into space. That had been the intent when Tsiolkovski brought her mother. The original Kasha was the first, in fact. But no twin could be found for her, except maybe this Kasha, her daughter. Mishin and Bushuyev, who nabbed dozens of strays and not a couple unattended family pets, could find nowhere in Moscow another dog so perfectly white, none with a tail that curled up over her back like a sickle.

In the early days, this Kasha, still a puppy, had free roam of Star City, a couple times turning up in clean rooms to the angry shrieks of engineers. She even flew with the Chief Designer to the first launch. He remembered Nadya, the one who should have died, sitting on the floor in the corner of the control bunker, wedged up against two walls at once, her bandaged left leg extended straight out in front of her. She hung her head and sloped her shoulders—the only time the Chief Designer ever saw her with poor posture—like she was crying, but the stony façade of her face never broke. Kasha, who had been sniffing around the control console, saw her there, sat, and cocked her head. It was just as unusual for Kasha to be still as it was for Nadya to slouch. Kasha took tentative steps toward the corner. She nosed Nadya's knee, licking the bandage exactly twice, and then stepped back as if considering the taste. Her tail wagged, a great fan of fur, and then she laid down, resting her head on Nadya's thigh.

The Chief Designer almost cried then, and had nearly missed liftoff as he composed himself. He almost cried again now, remembering it.

Laika and Strelka curled up on either side of him, and he ran a hand down each of their backs. Kasha continued to gnaw at and slobber on the knots. The Chief Designer looked at the cages, at the little black noses that poked out of the grates like buttons, but he tried not to look too hard. He did not want to see the twins of these dogs at his sides, the ones who would be, like five humans before them, sentenced to die alone, hundreds of kilometers from the nearest living thing. He did not want to see them for the same reason he had difficulty looking the human cosmonauts in the eye. To do so made him feel like an executioner, stopping by the cell of the condemned.

"I'm not a heartless man," he said to Kasha.

The dog lifted her head from the rope and considered him.

"I did what had to be done." The scar on his head throbbed.

The attendant asked, "What was that, Chief Designer?"

The Chief Designer lifted Kasha off his lap, stood, rising on creaky joints to his full height, and brushed away some, though not all, of the white fur that clung to his pants.

"Prepare Laika, Strelka, and their backups for training," said the Chief Designer.

"Training?"

"I believe that's your function here."

"Forgive me, Chief Designer. I didn't realize there was a mission planned for the dogs."

"You're the first to know." The Chief Designer felt the coldness in his own voice and forced himself to soften it. "Mishin or Bushuyev should have the old training regimen, if it's no longer contained in your own files."

"Yes, Chief Designer. Thank you."

All the dogs barked goodbyes as the Chief Designer left the kennel, all except Kasha, sweet, sweet Kasha, who regarded him with the concern of a mother, an expression both worried and proud. "She's just a dog," he spoke to himself, but he knew it was only half of an argument and not a belief.

## London, England—1964

Leonid felt weighted down. As if the wool coat of the uniform had not been heavy enough, now it was festooned with such an assortment of medals and ribbons as he had never seen before. The Order of the Hero of the Soviet Union. The Order of the Hero of Socialist Labor. Pilot Cosmonaut of the USSR. Many more medals he could not name and a dozen ribbons of similar anonymity. Even the ones he knew he often mixed up. Long ago, his boyhood slouch had been trained out of him, but he felt bent forward by the weight of the symbols on his chest. The medals *tinked* together as he walked into Earls Court. Beside him, dressed in the same clownish regalia, Nadya inspected the far corners of the room, oblivious to the hundreds of reporters gathered there.

They had been to so many cities on the tour that Leonid often forgot which crowd in particular he was addressing. First it had been what seemed like every city in all of Eastern Europe: Minsk, Tbilisi, Riga, Tallinn, Budapest, Warsaw, Prague, Sofia, Bucharest, even tiny Tirana. Then they crossed the imaginary line to the West: Rome, Paris, and now London. He had learned a little English as part of his training. This would be the first time since they left the East that he understood what anybody was saying to him without Ignatius providing translation.

From outside, Earls Court was a massive structure, and it seemed somehow even larger on the inside, soaring ceilings and broad spaces broken up only by widespread columns and the free-standing walls that divided the exhibitions. The Soviet exhibition presented a caricature of Russia, as if everyone worked on a communal farm or built rockets. The whole rest of society was absent. A nation of farmers and scientists. Suspended from the ceiling in the center of the exhibition was a large device, supposedly the Vostok capsule, but instead of the simple orb of the actual Vostok, this one was done up as much as Leonid's uniform. Giant fins swooped toward the back of the conical ship. Convoluted antennae sprouted from all over like saplings. The surface was so shiny Leonid was sure it had to be plated in silver. A crimson hammer and sickle took up one whole side of the fuselage.

Leonid was greeted by British dignitaries, including the Queen and a boy he assumed to be a prince. The boy almost gaped at Leonid, and only stepped forward with a gentle shove from the Queen. Leonid knelt and shook the boy's hand, a small thing like the paw of an animal. The boy grinned, revealing a row of lopsided teeth. Leonid smiled back, and a camera flashed. He stood, saluted the Queen, and made his way to the dais in the center of the room, directly under the fake Vostok.

There were about two hundred reporters crowding the dais, as Leonid estimated it. Before the tour, he had never been around so many people all at once. If someone had told him that there were tens of thousands in attendance at his first appearances, he would have believed them. Any number more than a handful seemed to him countless. Now, though, after dozens of such events, he was beginning to recognize the size of a crowd for what it was. Afterward, Ignatius would always give him an estimate, then jot it down in a notebook she kept in a pocket of her leather jacket. Leonid's estimates usually aligned with hers.

He stepped to the cluster of microphones atop the podium and addressed the crowd in halting English. His arm lifted into a wave without him having to think about it.

"Greetings from outer space to our friends in Great Britain."

Dozens of cameras flashed, but he hardly noticed them anymore.

The usual barrage of questions followed: *What does weightlessness feel like? What does Earth look like from space? Were you scared?* On to the more specific questions. *Can you describe the launch process? How do you navigate the capsule? What is the next mission? When can we expect the next launch? Who is the next cosmonaut?*

Leonid gave all the rehearsed answers, Ignatius helping with the English when he got stuck on a word. The same answers he had given to reporters across the whole continent. The words felt even more meaningless in a language not his own.

The questions petered out, like the drops of rain at the end of a storm. Leonid recalled watching Nadya's press conference in London years ago. He had huddled around the small television in the barracks with the other twins at Star City. The questions to her came in torrents that seemed like they would never cease. She answered in clipped, awkward phrases, always in Russian. An interpreter, standing so close to Nadya that she held equal share of the podium, translated every question and translated back every answer. Leonid did not know why Nadya would not answer in English. She had always spoken it much better than him. It would not be until her return to Star City that Leonid found out that she was not the Nadya he had known, but her twin, trained to pilot *Vostok 1*, not to answer questions from foreign press. Leonid still felt guilty that he had not known right away.

A reporter in the third row asked a question, but Leonid had not been paying attention.

"Could you repeat, please?" he asked.

"What does it feel like to be a hero, not just to your own country but to the world?"

"I am no more hero than any Russian worker."

That was the rehearsed line. Ignatius, standing just to his side, smiled.

Leonid continued, "And I am less hero than some."

He looked at Nadya, standing by the dais, still looking around the hall at the many wonders of the Soviet Union, tractors and plows and spaceships, toiling workers with insane grins stretched wide across their plastic mannequin faces. Ignatius pulled him by the shoulder away from the podium, and offered a quick thanks to the press. As they moved toward the exit, Ignatius leaned close and whispered, "A fine improvisation, comrade," but she did not sound like she meant it.

THEY TOURED LONDON followed by a cadre of photographers. The color of the sky reminded Leonid of winter in Star City, but it was not cold at all. It smelled different, too. Passing the Thames, salt and brine wafted with the mist. Leonid had only first seen the sea the previous week, and now here was that smell again. It was a smell like catching the sunset back in his home village, when it fell right in the V of the valley, as if the light funneled directly to the core of the Earth.

Sometimes the photographers would ask Nadya and Leonid to stop in front of a landmark. The cosmonauts posed, backs bolt-upright, chins slightly raised, Leonid flashing his smile. Nadya would try to pull her face into a shape other than a scowl. The picture snapped; they moved on.

Leonid did not recognize any of the places where they took photos, though he found many of them beautiful, the architecture a far cry from the Soviet utilitarianism of Star City. Things here felt old, as if wandering the city was actually touring a memory. In the Eastern nations, tours had always focused on factories and modern museums. Here, though, and in Paris and Rome, every other building they paused to inspect was a church, some small and old and others massive and older still, surfaces adorned with angels and saints, swathes of stone interspersed with colorful windows depicting even more angels and more saints. Back in his home village, the church had been made of old stacked logs and capped by a thatched roof, later shingled by a team of Soviet carpenters. The only decoration was two branches left over from the church's construction, tied together in the shape of a cross and hung over the unraised altar. Over time, the crosspiece had gone aslant, slipping halfway through the binding. The shape that remained was more mystic rune than crucifix, but no one ever thought to repair it. Probably by now the twine had rotted to nothing, leaving just a vertical stick nailed to the wall.

The front of Leonid's thighs throbbed with dull fatigue. The sidewalk they followed sloped up, not much, just enough to make the change in elevation known. They stepped from the narrow lane into a paved expanse on the other side of which soared an ornate, domed church, far larger than any place they had visited so far.

The tour guide led them alongside the church, explaining in English what it was and its history. Leonid listened just closely enough to pick up the name of the place, St. Paul's, and that a *cathedral* was a special sort of church, he assumed like a *sobor*, though it looked nothing like St. Basil's. They passed into the church through an entrance on the side of the building, through a narrow hallway that forced them to progress in single file, and then an open space burst before them. The ceilings vaulted high above, domes and panels painted with massive renderings of biblical scenes, columns and arches gilded. There was no flat space to be found, no inch free from image, but instead of feeling crowded, the ceiling soared higher and higher, the figures painted there as far away as the faintest pinprick of a star. Leonid wished he had visited this place before he had to describe outer space in interviews. This sensation, he was sure, was as close as he would ever come to understanding what his brother had experienced in orbit.

He sat down on a bare wooden seat near the altar while the rest of the tour group moved toward the nave. The photographers snapped a few photos of Leonid from a distance, and then hurried on. Nadya was still their favorite subject, even though she never smiled for the camera.

A man emerged from one of the cathedral's many corners and stopped to stare at Leonid. The man wore a black jacket over a dark red shirt with a Roman collar. This was a priest, Leonid realized, even though the vestments were different from the only other priest Leonid had ever known, back in the village, before the priest was taken away.

Leonid looked up at the ceiling again, scanning his eyes slowly across every surface as if reading sentences in a book. When he looked back down, the priest was still staring. Leonid made direct eye contact and felt the heat of a blush on his neck and cheeks, and then the weight of the cap still on his head. He had forgotten to remove it when they entered. He snatched it off, fumbling the brim in his fingers. The cap slipped free and fell to the checkerboard floor, landing on the gold button on its side, pinging out a sound that resonated through the whole cathedral. The priest grinned, an expression that squeezed his ample cheeks into a series of folds.

Tugging down the bottom of his jacket, the priest slid sideways into the narrow space between the chair rows and shuffled toward Leonid, taking a seat right next to him.

"I am sorry for my hat," said Leonid.

"Oh, you speak English?" said the priest.

"Some."

"Don't worry about the hat. We have so many tourists come through here, we would exhaust ourselves trying to remind everyone who forgot to remove their hats before entering. Anyway, I should apologize to you for staring. I'm particularly fascinated by space exploration. The Americans, I was fortunate to meet them when they came to London. It was arranged in advance, but I never expected to see a Soviet in a church." The priest slapped his thigh. "I can't believe it! Stumbling across a cosmonaut just sitting by my altar."

"Not only me," said Leonid. He flicked his thumb toward the nave, where the rest of the tour group stood in a semicircle around the guide. Nadya lingered several steps away, staring off in a direction opposite from everyone else. "The first human in space admires your church also."

The priest's face went agape, but he quickly composed it. The man was older than Leonid had first thought, fine lines like shatter marks at every place where his face creased. These were smoothed somewhat by the ampleness of the priest's flesh, rounding the hard edges of age. His eyes were like those of a child, still able to find wonder, still seeking it.

"Can . . . can I meet her?" asked the priest.

"I will introduce you," said Leonid.

The priest turned from Nadya and gazed up at a mosaic above the altar, depicting a man even Leonid knew enough to recognize as Jesus.

"Before that, can I ask you a question?" asked the priest. "I've been curious about it. It's said that everyone in Russia is atheist. Can there really be a whole nation without God?"

"You are priest, yes? I know of confession. I tell you this, you must keep it secret, yes?"

"I'm the Bishop of London, so yes, a priest."

Leonid started to jump to his feet, to follow the protocol for meeting a foreign dignitary, protocol that had been drilled into him for years. He jammed his shin hard against the chair in front him and fell back into his seat, wincing. The Bishop gripped the sleeve of Leonid's uniform.

"No need for formalities, son," said the Bishop.

Leonid rubbed his shin, sure that he could feel the lump of a bruise already forming.

"And we have no formal confession in our church," continued the Bishop, "but I can promise, man-to-man, that I won't share what you speak."

Leonid made himself sit upright, ignoring the pain that still shot through his leg.

"Church is dangerous," he said.

The Bishop laughed, a hearty guffaw that seemed out of place in the sanctuary. Several nearby tourists looked over, and kept looking, talking too loudly among themselves about the strange pair in the seats, the priest and the soldier. They did not seem to recognize either of them. The farther west Leonid traveled, the fewer people knew of him, and he found this was not something he minded.

"All the churches closed," said Leonid to the Bishop. "The buildings were destroyed or used for other things. In my city, the old church was used to store food. Very cool inside, yes? Good for . . ."

"Preserving?" offered the Bishop.

"Yes! People do not worship with no churches, but some still believe. It was not just buildings. Fewer young people. But old people still believe. They believed for too long just to stop."

"And you?"

"I think it would feel nice to believe."

"But you don't?"

"It would also feel terrible."

"Why is that?"

Leonid patted his shin where he had banged it. "I hit my leg on many things already."

Leonid smiled, and not the practiced smile he used for photographs, but a natural one, like sometimes happened when he took Kasha out into the grassy quad to play when the weather was actually warm. This priest, no, this bishop, was full of warmth, like a father, or how Leonid imagined a father should be. How, in his earliest memories, Leonid remembered the man who was his father, a large figure with the face of his brother, but an older version of that face. And when Tsiolkovski used to visit, more like a grandfather than a father, but still. Leonid always felt that without a figure with the rank of father, he was missing something, missing this warm sensation he felt now, a rush that spread from his chest to his face and upturned the corners of his mouth.

The Bishop smiled back, but stared into Leonid's eyes as if waiting for more, as if the joke were not a real answer. And Leonid knew that it was not. Ignatius had trained him to dodge real questions with humor. When the truth could not be revealed, the only option was charm. Leonid stopped smiling.

"If I feel I want to believe," said Leonid, "then to believe would make me feel right. God is not important then, just the sensation I get from choosing to believe. Is this not bad . . ."

"Logic?"

"Yes, logic. This is bad logic, yes?"

"Faith is based on feelings for so many people, and so many people trust feelings. As if feelings were a thing, something you could pick up, like a smooth, white stone in the black dirt by a roadway. But science has shown us what feelings are. Chemicals in the brain. It feels good to believe, so people believe. It feels good to pray, so people pray. When someone says they feel God in their hearts, what they actually feel is a chemical in their brain."

"Are you sure you are Bishop?"

"I have the outfit and everything." The Bishop tugged at his collar. "My point is not that faith is bad, but that faith based only on emotion leads to an ignorant kind of faith. There is a term in English, *blind faith*. Too many people let the fact that belief feels right mean that it absolutely is right, but that kind of belief is what led to every terrible thing ever done in the name of religion. Crusades and pogroms and inquisitions.

"These people had faith without doubt. But doubt is strength, and not just for the individual, but for Christianity. Nothing here on Earth is perfect, not even a church. It's our duty to God to try to be more perfect each day, to make the church more perfect each day. If we assume that we're right, that we must be right and can't be wrong, then it becomes impossible to improve. Feelings of belief must be coupled with a logical consideration of the faith. Feelings alone are not enough."

"I have never seen a logical reason for faith," said Leonid. "I am sorry. I do not mean to offend."

"No, no. This is just the kind of conversation that I think should happen more often. Of course, a priest in the pulpit can't tell his congregation to doubt everything he tells them, but we need more dialogue like this. You're not wrong. The Bible is full of miracles, but when was the last time you witnessed one? But look who I'm talking to." The Bishop made an exaggerated motion of tapping his forehead. "You're a man who has traveled to the heavens themselves. A miracle, if there ever was one. But with blind faith, we never would have done it. Humanity would remain stuck to the ground. In both the literal and metaphorical sense. Do you know metaphor?"

"I do not know the word."

"Flying in space is literal. Ascending to heaven is a metaphor."

"I think I understand. Feelings, then, are . . . metaphor?"

"Yes, yes! I wish we had more time." The Bishop pointed back toward the nave. "Your party is leaving without you."

Leonid jumped up, narrowly avoiding another bash to his shin.

"Come, Bishop," he said. "Let me introduce you to Nadya."

The pair hurried down the center aisle, oblivious to the tourists they brushed past. Above them rushed the angels and saints. *As if in orbit,* Leonid thought.

The Bishop and Nadya shook hands, and the photographers' flashes filled the whole cathedral.

DEPARTING THE CATHEDRAL, Ignatius walked with the tour guide, ahead of Leonid and Nadya. The photographers brought up the rear. The tour guide was a younger man, maybe thirty, with some portion of noble blood, an earl or a marquess or a viscount, a title bourgeois even by the standards of the West. He sported a wavy coif of brown hair that assumed a pleasing shape without seeming to require much effort at styling it. Ignatius said something that made the guide laugh. They walked closer than should have been comfortable. The guide glanced at Ignatius, then glanced away. Ignatius glanced back, then away, then back again.

"I think they're flirting," said Nadya.

"I never imagined Ignatius to be capable of such a thing."

"What's there to be capable of?"

"I used to flirt with your sister."

Leonid had not meant to say it. The words just came out. After weeks of interviews in which every word had to be carefully chosen, it felt like utter freedom to actually share an uncensored thought. He looked at Nadya, but she did not seem to react.

"I wasn't very good at it," he said. "Yuri was much better. Even Mars."

Nadya said, "Maybe that's why Yuri is married and you're not."

"I've lived in a box for my entire adulthood. Who would I marry? One of the dogs?"

"Strelka does seem rather fond of you."

"She's too much of a barker. And was that a joke? Since when do you joke?"

"I thought we were flirting."

"See? I told you I'm not very good at it."

He did not add that Nadya was a poor flirt herself. Never once had her expression cracked, their exchange lacking the kind of mirth that passed between Ignatius and the guide. But he could not blame Nadya entirely. He had not meant to flirt with her. As close as he felt they had become, it seemed perverse to treat her the same way he had her sister. Despite appearances, no one who met them both could ever confuse the two Nadyas.

"Ignatius tried to convince me to marry one of the other cosmonauts," said Nadya.

"Who would you choose?"

"You're the only tolerable one."

"Yuri always fancied you before he married. He, Mars, and Giorgi are all great men."

"Great and tolerable are unrelated qualities."

"I'm honored that you would rather spend time with me than marry a great man."

"Why do you see yourself as so different from the others?" Nadya's tone lost whatever little playfulness had tinged it before.

Leonid glanced back. The photographers raised their cameras. He smiled. Flashes. The photographers fiddled with their cameras, and Leonid turned back to the front. Ahead, Ignatius and the guide leaned their faces near to each other as if sharing a secret.

"I know we're all pretending," said Leonid, "but I feel the other twins could actually have done it. They could have been real cosmonauts. They understand the crowds as more than just faceless noise. Can they believe for even a moment they're legitimate? That the praise belongs to them and not their departed siblings? Maybe they can. Maybe they're more like their twins than I'm like Leonid. There's a reason he was selected for flight and I was held in reserve, even though I'm older."

"Older by minutes."

"But shouldn't those minutes have meant something? Shouldn't I have recognized my mother's frailty, and known, even by instinct, that it was my duty to protect my brother when his birth sapped the last of her strength? As Grandmother tells it, I came out wailing and my brother without a sound. The last thing my mother heard was my infant screech, the last thing she saw my scrunched face. And she never saw my brother's face at all."

"Fortunately, the face is the same." It seemed like a joke, but Nadya's tone did not change.

"Are we the same? Are any of the twins actually like the other? Talking to you isn't like talking to your sister. I would never have said these things to Nadya. The other Nadya. I wouldn't confuse the two of you if you'd ever been in the same place. And no one could confuse me for Leonid. He's a hero, and I'm just his shadow."

"Heroism is simply opportunity."

"And I missed mine."

"Since my launch, since I missed it, I've often thought of opportunity. I hope that it comes more than once in a lifetime."

"Even though it came only once for our twins."

The hotel loomed in front of them, a redbrick front with white stone trim, five stories high and several times as long. Posh Londoners came in and out of the lobby, greeted and wished well by bellhops in funny red uniforms. No funnier, Leonid supposed, than his own, though definitely redder. The sound of a train rumbled in the near distance.

Leonid and Nadya posed for a few final photographs, backdropped by the hotel's great wooden doors. Leonid thanked the photographers in English. Several firm handshakes were exchanged, pats on shoulders. One of the photographers lingered near Nadya, spinning the rings on his lens back and forth, before drawing himself away. He turned back, raised the camera, and clicked off one final photo, this one of Nadya only. Her expression was less guarded, the usual stony set of her face relaxed, like Leonid saw her sometimes when they were alone together, and he remembered her sister, and thought then that maybe none of them were all that different from their twins, except in circumstance and the luck of survival. The photographer pressed his lips into a bashful smile, bowed his head, turned, and almost fled around the corner.

"I think you have a fan," said Ignatius in English.

The tour guide chuckled. Leonid translated for Nadya.

"At least this one didn't propose to me," Nadya replied.

Ignatius translated for the guide, who laughed again, a fine and honest laugh, Leonid thought. He liked this gentleman, and thought maybe of inviting him for a drink at the hotel bar. Leonid had endured nothing but formal interactions for the whole of the tour, and the thought of casual conversation with a friendly stranger seemed supremely appealing. His thoughts were interrupted by Ignatius's hand on his shoulder.

"You two should get some rest before dinner," said Ignatius.

"What about you?" asked Leonid.

"I still have energy left to burn." She hooked her arm through the crook of the guide's elbow and led him into the hotel. The bellhops closed the great doors behind them.

"Her energy is admirable," said Nadya.

"Do you think she'd care that I had a drink at the hotel bar?"

"I think she'd forbid it. Fortunately, she'll be otherwise occupied for at least the duration of a drink."

"Will you join me?"

"I've never drunk, and I don't plan to start today. I need to lie down for a while, anyway. You're right, it takes too much energy to play the part of hero."

She hooked her arm through his, and they entered the hotel. Inside, they parted. Leonid found the bar while Nadya took the elevator all the way to the top.

## Bohdan, Ukraine—1950

A short way up the north rise of the valley, the forest cleared in a near-perfect circle. The ground there, sere and pebbly, tolerated only the shortest weeds, a sparse spattering of green. Trees rimmed the perimeter like a fortification. Wind gusted in from the south, carrying unfamiliar scents from beyond the mountains. At night, the clearing was the best place to view the stars.

The children of the village played a game of Dragon, forming a line, hands on the shoulders of the child in front of them, running. The line's leader circled around and tried to catch up with the child at the back, the head of the dragon chasing its tail. There was not much to the game besides that. It mainly served to kick up the dry dirt, which glommed to the children's sweaty skin and clogged the weave of their homespun clothes. Kasha sat in the shade near the edge of the clearing, barking from time to time as if to offer encouragement. Whenever the line neared her, she would leap up and join the chase for a lap or two, her limp tail flopping behind her.

The older Leonid was at the front of the line. He quickly circled back around and tagged Mykola, a boy with shocks of wiry hair and a round face. Mykola muttered a curse as he took over his place as head of the dragon. He was too young to be cursing. Had his mother been around, she surely would have struck him. But cursing had become a common occurrence. The Leonids heard the adults of the village using words aloud that before had been relegated only to whispers.

The younger Leonid was now the dragon's tail, and Mykola could not catch him. Every time Mykola got close, Leonid would dodge. When Mykola began to anticipate the dodges, Leonid would simply feint, dodging in the opposite direction as if he could read the older boy's mind. Usually a round of Dragon lasted a minute at most, but this one went on for many minutes and seemed no closer to completion. All the children panted. One of them in the middle stumbled, fell, and dragged the rest of the line down with her. At the last moment, Mykola dove after Leonid, the tail, and out of the shoulder grip of the older Leonid behind him. The dive broke the twin rules of Dragon: *hold on* and *remain held*. Even cheating, Mykola had not come close.

The older Leonid slipped free of the grasp of the child behind him, avoiding falling with the rest of the line. The Leonids were the only two left standing, the only two with clothes not streaked with a fine grit of gray dust. Mykola cursed again, pushing himself to his knees. He dropped back into a seated position.

He said to the Leonids, "If your grandmother didn't eat all the food, then maybe the rest of us wouldn't be too hungry to run."

"What did you say?" asked the younger Leonid. He stepped forward.

"Easy," said the older Leonid.

Grandmother had kept her roundness even through the lean times. The Leonids knew, though, that she had thinned just like everyone else in the village. She simply had more girth to begin with.

"Maybe you two hoard food, too," said Mykola. "But I don't think you'd be able to get even a scrap away from that fat b—"

The younger Leonid lunged at Mykola, knocking him onto his back. They grappled and threw errant punches and disturbed the dust into a cloud around them. The older Leonid rushed over and groped for his brother to pull him away. One of the older girls, Oksana, did the same from the other side. As they pulled the fighters apart, Mykola flung one last wild punch, finally connecting with Leonid's face, but not the Leonid he had intended. The older twin palmed his cheekbone and stumbled back. Everyone else stood stock-still. The only motion was Kasha, circling the scene of the fight, whimpering.

Mykola looked shocked. He muttered a curse.

The younger Leonid trembled, deep rouge rising on his cheeks.

"You *upizdysh*," he said, and formed his fists into clubs. He started forward.

"Stop," yelled the older Leonid.

All was still again. The younger Leonid spat.

"Go fuck your mother," he said to Mykola.

The older Leonid leapt forward and slapped the younger across the cheek. Several of the other children gasped.

Mykola stood and stalked away. "I'd say the same to you, but you'd have to dig her up first."

"Mykola," said the older Leonid.

Mykola stopped but did not turn around.

"If you ever mention my mother again," continued Leonid, "I won't be stopping my brother, but helping him."

Mykola entered the shadow of the trees that rimmed the clearing. Kasha trailed at his heels. The younger Leonid rubbed his cheek where he had been slapped. The older placed his hand on top of his brother's.

"Forgive me," said the older Leonid.

"That really stung," said the younger. He smiled.

The brothers laughed, and then the other children joined in.

They re-formed the line to continue the game of Dragon, the Leonids adjacent in the middle. Eventually, one of the twins would be forced to chase the other.

GRANDMOTHER HADN'T EVEN looked at them before she asked what happened. The twins stood inside the doorway, smeared with gray-black mud. This type of filth was not unusual, so she could have only been referring to the older Leonid's eye, already swollen half shut and turned a putrid shade of purple.

"Mykola," said the older Leonid.

Grandmother turned from the stove, her face set in a grimace. Her dress hung loose. Everyone's clothes hung loose.

She said, "That boy's an ass."

"Grandmother!" said the younger Leonid.

"Get yourself cleaned up," she said. "We'll eat shortly."

A pot on the stove steamed, and that's what it smelled like: steam. The stews they ate had been gradually lightening in color, now just water with a few frail vegetables tossed in.

The twins stripped off their dirty clothes in the corner, and then each grabbed a rag from the basin and wiped himself down. A small gash had opened under the older Leonid's eye, and the water stung. He donned clothes somewhat cleaner than those he had shed and took a seat opposite his brother at the old pine-topped table. The surface was covered with dents and scrapes.

"It'll be a few minutes more," said Grandmother.

Leonid could not imagine what difference a few more minutes would make in the quality of the stew. One might as well drink warm water and eat the vegetables raw.

"Have I ever told you about the man our village was named after?" asked Grandmother.

Grandmother only had one story, the life of Bohdan Khmelnytsky, from which she plucked and repurposed snippets. She had told every snippet, though, a dozen times. The twins could have told all the stories themselves.

This did not stop Grandmother from telling one of the stories again.

"BOHDAN ZINOVIY MYKHAYLOVYCH KHMELNYTSKY joined the Cossack army when he was still barely a boy. He'd been a scholar before that, studying with the Jesuits in faraway lands. He could have gone anywhere in Europe and done anything he wanted. In the face of all that possibility, he came home and became a soldier. And not a very good one, at least not at first. He was captured and enslaved by the Turks in his first battle, but that's not the worst of it.

"He was then still fighting with the Poles, long before he rebelled against them. Along with his father, he traveled with the Polish forces to Moldavia, where the Ottomans had amassed a vast army. The Ottomans then were the greatest force on Earth, as mighty as the Soviets now. The Poles and the Ottomans hated each other, but I don't know why. I don't know that they were really much different. The Ottomans were heathens, to be sure, but are the Catholics any better? Of course, we have no religion. That's what the Soviets tell us. But we used to, and it was neither in service of the Turks' god nor the Catholics'. Of course it's more similar to the Catholic god. Or it was, when we still had religion. Before it was all declared false. I think even then Khmelnytsky didn't believe. How else could he have picked one side only later to betray it? He was a pragmatist. Do you know what that means? He did the thing that was most beneficial to him in the moment. But it turned out not to be. It turned out to cost him more than a bruised eye."

She thrust her cooking spoon toward the older Leonid's injured face.

"On the day of Khmelnytsky's first battle, only five thousand men had turned out for the Poles. Barely a regiment, much less an army. The Turks, on the other hand, had over twenty thousand, more than four times as many. I wonder what Khmelnytsky saw looking over the battlefield, if he could see from his place within the ranks that his own force was so much smaller, or if his perspective was skewed. I wonder if he thought he had a chance. Because he didn't, despite the fact that he took his first steps toward becoming a hero that day.

"The Turks advanced, or the Poles did. I don't remember and it doesn't matter. Who throws the first stone is less important than who throws the last. And the last stone was definitely from the sling of a Turk. Among the stones thrown in between, one felled Khmelnytsky's father. They'd been battling side by side, holding their own, fending off wave after wave of attackers. His father, a skilled swordsman from whom Khmelnytsky learned the same skills, greeted each approaching Turk with the edge of his blade. Turkish bodies piled up in front of him, and a similar, if slightly smaller pile formed in front of his son. The Turks had to climb over their dead comrades to even mount an attack. But all around the Khmelnytskys, the Polish lines faltered, the outnumbered Polish soldiers not so deft with their swords. They fell, one by one, until the younger Khmelnytsky's flank was revealed. A new swarm of attackers came from his side to join those who advanced from in front. Even the best soldier couldn't fend off so many shimmering crescent blades. Khmelnytsky was wounded and fell. Even from the ground, even with part of his body split open, he kept on fighting. When he grew too weak to raise his sword, he slashed the enemies' ankles. Then his father sprung to his side, defending his own flank and Khmelnytsky's as well. He plucked a second sword from the clawed grip of a felled Turk, and extended one in each hand

and swung them like the spokes on a wheel. The Turks who tried to get close lost their heads or were chopped clean in two. But they kept coming, and the pile of defeated enemies grew so high and dense he could no longer move. The Turks climbed over this wall of their fallen brothers, dozens of them from all sides, and pounced on Khmelnytsky's father, and rent the swords from his hands and broke his fingers and his arms and beat him until all that was left of the man who had been Khmelnytsky's father was a shattered, bloody lump. From underneath a pile of dead Turks, Khmelnytsky could just peek out through a gap in the tangled limbs, watching his father fall, and he memorized the events, and he muttered 'Goodbye, Father,' and his consciousness left him.

"He awoke later under the night sky. His wound had been bandaged, the gray cloth stained through with red in the shape of the branch from a fir tree. Slowly, the memory of his father's death came back to him, but he did not cry. He knew already, from the language of the men around him, laughing and telling stories he could not understand, that he had been captured. He began to plot then, blood still seeping fresh from the stitched wound on his chest, how to enact his revenge. He saw, in the distance, his escape. He did not then know how far away it was. He did not know the patience it would require. But if it was one thing that allowed him to become a hero, it was his patience.

"The stew is ready."

Grandmother ladled the clear broth into three wooden bowls, filling the last with less and keeping that one for herself.

## London, England—1964

Officially, the cosmonauts did not drink. But Mars had started sneaking vodka into Star City even before his brother's launch, and had then somehow found a source for Scotch after his homecoming tour. It was rare to find Mars without a glass in hand. The radio control room was about the only place he stayed sober, and then only for those few days while there was a cosmonaut in orbit, sometimes for a day more, when Mars would talk to the silent capsule hoping for a response even though the air had already run out.

So Leonid was unofficially familiar with Scotch and recognized some of the bottles behind the hotel bar even if he did not know their names. He selected the green bottle with the yellow label. The bartender poured the glass near full. Leonid stared at the oily sheen swirling on the surface for a while before taking a sip. Usually, back in Star City, they downed their alcohol in one great gulp. He had never really considered the flavor before. Taken slowly, it did not burn so much. It did not catch in his throat.

After his second drink, he was joined at the bar by a pair of American travelers, a slim man and a sleek woman, who recognized him from his picture in the newspaper, or at least recognized his uniform. They introduced themselves, but he forgot their names immediately. He had trouble understanding their inflected English. Every other word seemed to be a mispronunciation, and they laughed so much that every sentence was broken in two by a chuckled pause. Leonid was fairly sure they were already drunk. Maybe their diction was usually as good as the Queen's, but at the moment slurred.

The woman ordered a round, pointing at Leonid and asking the bartender for "whatever our comrade here is drinking." Three new glasses arrived, filled to the lip with Scotch. Leonid raised his glass, unsure if the Americans would clink their glasses with his, but they did. He took some small comfort in this shared tradition. The couple downed their drinks in one long pull, so Leonid did the same. As soon as they set the empty glasses down, fresh drinks arrived for all three of them.

"Your flight finished about two weeks ago?" asked the woman.

"Yes. I have traveled since then. I feel I have traveled more since I returned than I did in space."

"Have you been to London before?" asked the man.

"I am only ever in Russia, except for launches. I was born in Ukraine. A communal farm."

"Any brothers or sisters?" asked the woman.

"Yes." Leonid closed and opened his eyes. The lids felt heavy. "No. No brothers or sisters. That is how I think of my fellow cosmonauts. We have spent much time together. As family."

"We met John Glenn," said the man.

"Well, we were in the same room as him," said the woman.

"He's so quiet. Like you." The man squeezed Leonid's shoulder. "But also like you, he has a sort of presence about him. Maybe it comes from seeing the world as something small. Literally seeing it. There are what, ten of you who've shared that perspective?"

"Nadya met Glenn and Shepard in America."

"You know her?" asked the man. "But of course you know her. It's just hard to imagine her as an actual person. Like with the President. Or Khrushchev in your case."

"I know Khrushchev, too, but not well. Nadya is in this hotel."

The woman looked up, as if searching for Nadya above them. Leonid looked up, too, which set the ceiling atwirl. He wobbled on his stool. One of the Americans, he did not see which, reached out and steadied him. Leonid lowered his head and braced himself against the bar. The surface felt frigid. Was the air here conditioned? He looked around for vents, but had trouble bringing anything farther away than the bar top into focus.

"I'm sure you're tired of this question by now," said the woman, "but can you tell us what it's like to fly into space?"

"Hmmm?" said Leonid. He twisted his head to see her and blinked until her face unblurred. "Ah, it's a great thrill, the ride up on the rocket. It's as if the whole Earth trembles, and then you pull away from the ground, but the trembling doesn't stop. At last, the engines cut off, and you float up against the straps of your seat. Only then do you dare a peek out of the little round window, filled with black sky and the orb of the Earth, blue strung with white clouds."

This was a paraphrase of Nadya's description of space, the other Nadya, the one with whom he used to flirt. Her description, amended by the cosmonauts to follow, was used by the twins back on the ground to describe spaceflight.

"It sounds like quite an adventure," said the man. "What about the rocket? What is it like? We've seen a model of the capsule here in London, but it's suspended from the ceiling and we couldn't get a good look."

"If you can keep a secret, comrades," said Leonid, "I'll tell you. The capsule is quite a bit simpler than that. What you saw is the product of artists, not scientists. The real thing is more like a great metal volleyball. You play volleyball in America, yes?"

"I believe we invented it," said the woman.

"Excellent, excellent. We play in Star City, when there is time. Outdoors when the weather is nice. Giorgi's always organizing a game of volleyball. The capsule is like that, like a volleyball."

"Who's Giorgi?" asked the man.

"Who?" asked Leonid.

"You just mentioned someone named Giorgi."

"Ah, yes. He's a colleague. One who likes to play volleyball." Leonid laughed and tried to smile, but he had difficulty feeling the shape of his face. He was not sure if the muscles had moved at all.

"What about the inside of the capsule?" asked the man. "Is it really like in films?"

Leonid shook his head. "I haven't seen American films. It's not like the spaceships in Russian films, but not so different, I suppose. If you were to look at the inside without a manual to instruct you, it would be the same sort of nonsense they make up for fiction."

The woman placed her hand on Leonid's wrist.

"If you ever make it to America," she said, "we must take you to see a film."

"Let us!" Leonid raised his glass, almost slopping the little bit of remaining Scotch onto the bar.

"How do you pilot the capsule?" asked the woman.

Leonid realized she looked a little bit like Nadya. He could have confused the two in a dark room, or outside at night. The man, though, looked like no one. He looked specifically as if he was supposed to look like no one, every feature of average size and nominal placement. Maybe instead of no one, the man looked like everyone, a twin to all of humanity.

"The capsule," said the man.

"Ah yes. There's Chayka."

"What's that?" asked the woman.

"It's the attitude con—"

"Greetings." A clipped voice came from behind them.

Leonid turned. It was Ignatius. He noticed that half of her jacket's fur collar was flipped up. He reached back to adjust it, but she brushed his hand away.

She asked, "Who are your friends, Leonid?"

The couple did not turn around to face her.

"We just met here at the bar," said Leonid. "I'm afraid I can't recall their names."

The couple did not offer them.

"I hate to cut your conversation short," said Ignatius, "but you must prepare for your next engagement, Leonid. Let me pay for your drinks."

"They're on us," said the woman.

"Very kind of you," said Ignatius. "Please note that there's a mirror behind the bar."

The man and woman had been looking down, but now they lifted their faces and met the reflection of Ignatius's gaze. Leonid looked between the three of them. He was the only one to move at all.

"You know my face," said Ignatius to the Americans, "and I know yours. It would be best if we were never to see each other again. Come, Leonid." She gripped his elbow and guided him away from the bar.

In the lobby, she pulled him into a nook where a black telephone hung from the wall. Her expression did not change, but she locked her eyes on to his. He glanced away under the intensity of the stare, but she did not relent. After a few seconds, he looked back.

"You're not to drink in public," she said. "You're not to talk to anyone you don't know unless I'm there with you."

"You sound like a mother." Leonid had been enjoying his time at the bar.

"How would you know what a mother sounds like?" asked Ignatius.

The irritation left him as if spilled. Whatever enjoyment he had felt was replaced in an instant with melancholy. His face, still mostly numb, slackened. He looked down to a corner of the alcove.

Ignatius placed her hand on his shoulder, a gentle touch, comforting.

"Leonid," she said. "Those weren't new friends you made at the bar. They were American agents. Spies."

Leonid kept staring at the corner. "Surely you're wrong."

"Did you not notice that the conversation shifted from English to Russian?"

Leonid thought back. The transition had been so seamless, the couple's Russian so perfect.

"Don't feel too bad," said Ignatius. "I'm fairly sure that they drugged you. Did you tell them anything?"

"I think I was about to."

"Then let us celebrate the good timing of my arrival. Next time, the drinks are on me."

Ignatius placed two fingers on his chin and turned his face to hers. She was smiling, lips pressed a little too tight. He recognized the expression from Grandmother, one he had always identified as concern mixed with happiness at having something to be concerned about. Ignatius had her own agenda, yes, and he did not trust her. He could not. But she was an ally, which might turn out to be more reliable than a friend.

Ignatius led him back to his room and instructed him to take a shower. As he undressed, he found a slip of paper in the inside pocket of his uniform jacket. The paper was folded into a perfect square. He spread the creases and tried to read what was on the inside. He could not make it out until he realized it was in Ukrainian, not Russian. A street address in Odessa. The bottom was signed in neither Ukrainian nor Russian, but English. *Hope to see you soon! —Your Friends from America.*

## Star City, Russia—1964

Nadya and Leonid were scheduled to arrive back in Star City within the next few hours. It was the longest Nadya had been away since touring with Mars four years ago, and the Chief Designer was surprised each time he realized she was not around. Over the past five years, rarely had a day gone by that the Chief Designer did not stumble across her, always in the unlikeliest of locations. She would be leaning in the hallway when he emerged from the wash, or pushing a broom around the training room, which was already swept several times a week by the custodians, or walking one of the dogs out of a sterile lab, where even people, who shed considerably less, were required to wear smocks and caps. Whenever they went to Baikonur for a launch, it took hours of convincing before she would leave Star City without Kasha in tow. The Chief Designer wondered what would happen without the dogs, if Nadya would just wander away.

But no, she was coming back. That strange woman whom he had practically raised since childhood. He tried not to admit the relief he'd felt when it was her sister and not her who launched, but . . .

No, no. All the cosmonauts were like his children. He admitted to himself, usually only in the enveloping dark of night, that he had cared less for the surviving twins. He had spent limited time with them, left their minimal training to Mishin and Bushuyev. The surviving twins had not sacrificed themselves for the cause. But he could not blame them. They were all victims, and of the Chief Designer's own crimes. In his most honest moments, he knew what held him back with the twins, even if he could not always admit it. They were living reminders of his failures.

That was what now held him back with dear Nadya, the Nadya who survived. He lacked faith in his own endeavor. *Faith*, he thought. He ground his artificial teeth. Any store of faith he once possessed had rotted right out of him. Years and years ago, when rocketry was at most a pastime and a hope and ultimately a fall. Faith was an old concept, anyway.

The Chief Designer stepped out of his office and found not Nadya but Giorgi in the hallway, dragging a sofa. The young cosmonaut greeted the Chief Designer loudly, then returned to his task.

"Do you need help?" asked the Chief Designer.

Giorgi paused in his efforts. "I can manage, sir. Is there anything I can help you with? You seem concerned."

The Chief Designer smiled. Besides the other Nadya, Giorgi was the only one who ever noticed his moods. At least the subtler ones.

"No, Giorgi, I'm fine. Or I one day will be."

Giorgi proffered a jaunty salute. "I promise that today will be a good day, sir. I'll see you at the party."

He crouched, grabbing the arm of the sofa, and backward shuffle-walked down the hall with the sofa in tow. He sang a song, "Kalinka," as he went.

> *Wee red berry, red berry, red berry of mine!*
> *In the garden, a berry, red berry of mine!*
> *Ah, under the pine tree, the green needled pine tree,*
> *I lay me now down to sleep,*

*swinging and swaying, swinging and swaying*
*I lay me now down to sleep.*

GIORGI BUSTLED from room to room around the dormitory, hanging makeshift decorations from the exposed pipework that ran along the ceilings. For ribbons, he had salvaged the straps from old harnesses, the ones once used to simulate weightlessness, before Mars, on the second mission, told the engineers that dangling from wires was nothing like being weightless at all. Giorgi borrowed the yellow seatbelts from the centrifuge and shredded to strips a piece of silver insulation that the Chief Designer did not have the heart to tell him cost thousands of rubles. Giorgi cut up an old Soviet flag, weather-beaten and faded from crimson to pink. After he was done decorating, only white napkins remained in the commissary, the favored blues stolen, sliced, and suspended from the frame around the front doors.

The staff arrived in the mess hall only to discover that lunch had not been prepared. In addition to commandeering the napkins, Giorgi had sent the cooks home in order to claim the kitchen as his own. He prepared dozens of slabs of gingerbread in the Tula style, some filled with jam and others condensed milk. Any hungry engineer who grabbed for one was met on the knuckles with the backside of Giorgi's spoon. *For later,* he said, and sent them to the pantry for bread and whatever else they might be able to eat with it.

In the common room, he set each table with several bottles of vodka from Mars's stash. Giorgi had not seen Mars in several days, so the vodka was technically stolen, but Giorgi would pay for it and apologize. No one ever stayed mad at him for long. Every glass he could find in all of Star City surrounded the vodka bottles, like each table was a sprawling crystal palace with a Babelian spire in the middle. He poured himself two swallows and flipped the glass to his mouth, tossing the liquid straight to the back of his throat.

His guitar and balalaika were leaning in the corner, already tuned, waiting to be plucked up and strummed for vodka-soaked sing-alongs. The balalaika, a contrabass, was comically large, taller on end than Giorgi, the triangular body more than half that wide. For a laugh, Giorgi would hide behind it so all that could be seen were his arms, as if the instrument played itself.

Giorgi had been painting a new mural on the back wall of the common area, an idealized spacescape with the long curve of Earth in the lower left corner. Above it, as in the training room, the faces of the first five cosmonauts were rendered with stunning detail. Stunning not just for their likenesses to the actual people, but for the fact that Giorgi had painted each of them from memory. The paint of Leonid's face still glinted with the last traces of wetness. There was a space to the right of the portraits large enough for another. Mishin, or was it Bushuyev, had joked that Giorgi was saving room for himself. But that space was now filled with the first lines of a poem Giorgi was writing, painted in elegant calligraphy:

*The clouds are moving in the wrong*
*direction, I assume toward something*
*interesting.*

The first black stroke of the next line was painted, but did not offer a hint as to what letter it would become.

The door to the common room creaked open, and Mars squeezed through the smallest possible gap that would allow him entry. His skin, already dark by Russian standards, seemed swaddled in ashy shadow. Under his eyes, squinting, the color faded to deep purple. Each of his steps was barely more than a stumble. He took in the glass- and-bottle-filled tables and threw up his arms.

"Here it is!" he said. "Dammit, Giorgi, can't you ask before you take?"

"Can you not hide yourself away when I seek to ask you something?"

Mars dropped his arms. From the nearest table he selected the tallest glass and filled it almost to the rim with vodka.

He said, "At least you didn't take the Scotch."

"You have Scotch?" said Giorgi. "I couldn't find it."

"And you never will."

"Have you been sleeping?" asked Giorgi.

"No. Does it show?"

"You're either fatigued or dead but walking."

"I'm not sure I could tell the difference at this point."

Mars took a tiny sip of vodka, like a bird dipping its beak into a puddle.

"What's the party for this time?" he asked.

"Nadya and Leonid will return anytime now."

"Has it already been four weeks?"

"It has!"

"But that's impossible. I talked to Leonid just . . ." Mars stopped mid-sentence and brought the vodka to his lips. Instead of his usual sip, he sucked up a whole mouthful. He swallowed and said, "I have to go."

"The celebration starts in an hour. Make sure you get here on time or everyone else will finish your vodka before you get a chance to refill."

Mars replied with a quiet *da*, but he did not seem to hear what

Giorgi had said. He left the common area, taking a sip of vodka for each step.

THE CHIEF DESIGNER thumbed through a new report on the ablative heat shield, probably the fiftieth such report he had read, all of them saying one of two things: either the shield burned away too quickly or it burned away too slow. Whichever the defect, the result was the same. Vostok could not reenter the atmosphere. Any capsule that made the attempt would flare, then fizzle to a spark, leaving no trace of the cosmonaut trapped inside. Leaving no trace of Nadya . . .

A frantic series of knocks startled the Chief Designer out of a daze. He realized his eyes had been closed. The knocks came again, faster and louder.

"Enter," said the Chief Designer.

The door kicked open, and Mars practically fell through. He looked ill, skin sagging, dark marks like bruises beneath bloodshot eyes. He held a tall glass half-full with what was either water or vodka.

"It's been four weeks already," he said. "Four weeks! Is that really true?"

"Since the launch? Yes, Mars, it's been four weeks." The Chief Designer pointed at the glass in Mars's hand. "Have you been drinking the whole time?"

Mars did not seem to notice the jab. "No, I was in the radio room. I've been talking to Leonid."

"Shut the door," snapped the Chief Designer.

Mars turned and found the door still open wide behind him. He fumbled for the knob and then pushed it shut.

The Chief Designer said, "Show some discretion, man. I'm happy to put up with your drinking. I know that I've put you in a terrible position, but if anyone outside the inner circle ever found out, there—"

"You're not hearing me," said Mars. "I've been talking to Leonid this whole time. I always lose track of the days in the radio room. There are no windows, no clocks. I thought less than a week had gone by, but it's already been four, and Leonid's still there. I spoke to him not an hour ago, before he passed out of range of the transmitter."

"Come, Mars, that's impossible. There's only air enough for five or six days."

"I know, I know. I know all this, but either Leonid is still alive or his ghost can operate Zarya."

The Chief Designer tried to process what Mars was telling him. It had to be a mistake, or some sort of cruel joke. Mars had been drinking, as was often the case. Maybe he was trying to be funny, to trick the old man. Maybe he was too drunk to realize just how terrible a joke it would be.

"This is no time for jokes," said the Chief Designer.

"When have I ever joked?"

The Chief Designer knew it was true. If Mars had a flaw, it was over-seriousness. The only time his personality ever warmed was in the radio room. He had been affected much more than the others by the death of his twin, even though the two Marses had been chosen at a younger age and separated for their unique training regimens earlier than the rest. They met maybe twice a year, in secret late at night, so that this Mars would know all that the other one did. They did not speak before the launch. They were supposed to be the same person, after all. What use would it be to speak to oneself?

At first, the Chief Designer considered the deception a necessary caution, the next logical step in Tsiolkovski's original plan. But no, he could not blame Tsiolkovski. The Chief Designer alone bore the blame. Looking at Mars now, the Chief Designer knew he had mistaken cruelty for caution. He recalled a time when Mars would flash moments of great humor, but that was years ago, a memory of a different version of this person. No, this Mars never joked.

"I'm sorry," said the Chief Designer, "but you must understand this is hard to believe."

"Come talk to him yourself."

"When will he be in range?"

"A half hour, maybe."

"Nadya and Leonid will be back by then, and Giorgi's party will have started. Come find me."

"Yes, Chief Designer." Mars turned to leave.

"And, Mars . . ."

"Yes, Chief Designer?"

"I'm sorry."

"For what?"

The Chief Designer only lowered his head in response. Mars walked out. Could he possibly be right? Could he have been talking to Leonid this whole time? And if so, what did Leonid's survival mean?

On his desk, the Chief Designer found the heat shield report still open, chart after chart printed on page after page. A decade and they still seemed no closer to a solution. It was so easy to make something burn, so much harder to make it burn how one wanted.

THE MOMENT NADYA and Leonid walked in the front door of the dormitory, Giorgi was there handing them glasses filled with vodka. Leonid looked back to Ignatius, who had entered behind him, and she nodded that it was okay to drink. Engineers and technicians lined the halls, clapping and backslapping as the cosmonauts passed by, following Giorgi to the common area. The sounds of the party erupted from the propped-open doors, the bright din of a dozen overlapping conversations, laughter, a bellowed song, clattering glasses. The facility was usually so quiet, it felt to Leonid now as if he were someplace he had never been before.

A great cheer rose up when he and Nadya entered the room. Leonid did not recognize many of the people, those who had trained his brother and who all thought that he and his brother were the same person. His first week back would be spent learning new names and shared histories. Learning how to pretend to be someone else. He made his way through the room one awkward hug at a time. It was fortunately too noisy to have to talk to anyone. His hand broke into an unconscious wave.

The Chief Designer waited at the back of the room. Mishin and Bushuyev were nearby, but otherwise he was given wide berth, a semicircle around him the only free space at the party. He smiled when he saw Nadya, and hugged her. She did not hug him back, but Leonid saw her lean against the Chief Designer, letting him support some of her weight. Then the Chief Designer was in front of Leonid, gripping him by the shoulders. He looked into Leonid's eyes, held the gaze for too long to be comfortable, and then nodded once. The hug that followed was firm but brief. Mishin and Bushuyev came over and shook Leonid's hand.

The Chief Designer took a glass from Mishin or Bushuyev—they stood so close Leonid could not tell whose hand had been holding the glass—and raised it.

"A toast," said the Chief Designer.

His deep baritone overpowered the din of the party. The gathered engineers, technicians, even custodians and the people who served the meals in the cafeteria, stopped talking and turned to find him. All raised their glasses toward his.

"To all our cosmonauts, past, present, and those yet to come. They are our people's greatest heroes. Let us drink to their success, and to ours as well. To our cosmonauts!"

The room replied, "To our cosmonauts!"

And just like that the first round of drinks disappeared.

"I hope I'm not too late." A voice, almost as booming as that of the Chief Designer, came from the hall. Two men in dark suits, fine suits, much nicer than anything worn by any of the engineers, stood on either side of the doorway. The men exuded an air of intimidation, standing out at Star City like tourists. Between them was a smaller man, older, completely bald on top of his head and what hair there was around the edges pure white. It was Premier Khrushchev.

Several of the engineers who were also in the military snapped to attention. Ignatius snaked through the room and emerged on the other side of the crowd with a glass for Khrushchev. He took it, raised it, responded to the Chief Designer's toast, threw the glass to his face, and gulped down the contents. He handed the empty glass back to Ignatius.

"Where's our newest hero?"

Leonid raised his empty glass above the sea of heads. "I'm here, Mr. Khrushchev."

"Come forward, son. Our public appearance didn't allow me enough time to truly thank you."

Leonid pushed his way from the back of the room to the front, a slow, elbowed procession during which the silence grew more awkward. Someone coughed, and then someone else, and then it was as if a minor plague swept through the room, afflicting every fifth or sixth person with the irrepressible need to clear their throat. Leonid emerged into the space that had formed around the door. Khrushchev gripped him by the shoulders, like the Chief

Designer had before, and looked into his eyes, but unlike the Chief Designer, Khrushchev had none of the sadness in his expression, just pride. Fatherly, ignorant pride.

"You've risked yourself," said Khrushchev, "for the sake of our whole people. There will be statues"—he pointed to Giorgi's mural across the room—"and paintings. Your likeness will appear all across the world. But the greatest mark you've made is in the hearts of our people."

Ignatius, who Leonid had not seen move from her place beside Khrushchev, produced a full glass of vodka and handed it to the Premier.

"Refill your glasses," said Khrushchev, "and drink to our newest Soviet hero and all those who've come before."

Khrushchev, with his free hand, took Leonid by the wrist and raised his arm. The engineers, who had silenced even their breaths while Khrushchev spoke, now cheered, clapping or banging the bottoms of their empty glasses on tables. Vodka bottles channeled among a stream of hands, and the soft sound of pouring was soon joined by renewed chatter, the conversations that had been interrupted by Khrushchev's arrival resumed.

Leonid had a fresh glass of vodka in his hand. He was not sure how it got there or where it came from. Khrushchev touched his glass to Leonid's.

"Before I leave," said Khrushchev, leaning in close, "you must tell me all about it."

His expression had gone from fatherly to childlike. He walked into the crowd and started shaking hands.

KHRUSHCHEV'S UNEXPECTED ARRIVAL ended the party early, at least for the Chief Designer. Instead of sharing drinks with his staff, he stopped after his first and shadowed Khrushchev around the room. Khrushchev engaged each cluster of people he came across, asking everyone what they did for the program. The Chief Designer could not hear all that was said, especially as the noise of the party grew, which it seemed to with every drop of vodka consumed. Whatever Khrushchev was saying, it always seemed to be accompanied by him pointing up at the ceiling, or through it, as if he needed to remind those he was talking to as to the location of space. Space, though, was in every direction, so no matter where one pointed, even straight down, straight through the hellish heat of Earth's core, there on the other side was near-maybe-infinite space. The hardest part of reaching the cosmos was conquering the animal instinct that still insisted, in spite of rational knowledge, that the Earth was flat.

After half an hour, the Chief Designer retreated to the quiet of the hallway and waited. Giorgi came out shortly after, handed him a glass of vodka, and then returned to the party. Giorgi always seemed to be more aware than everyone else, able to notice a single person leave a crowded room, able to sense that person's desire for a drink. Still so young, but the Chief Designer already thought of him as a great man, the cosmonaut who would lead them into the future, the first human to walk on Mars . . .

But no, that was just a distant dream. In his mind, the Chief Designer emphasized the word *dream* more than he did *distant*.

The sound of Giorgi's guitar came from the common area, strumming out a quick beat, and then Giorgi sang, a high, strong tenor. The Chief Designer could not make out the words, but based on the laughter that ensued, he assumed the song was the usual *chastushke*. Giorgi seemed to know an endless list of short, humorous, often risqué songs. His performances had become a staple of Sunday nights at Star City.

Soon the staff was clapping and singing along, raising a ruckus that was terrible and wonderful at the same time. For a man like the Chief Designer, who had been harnessing explosions most of his life, such controlled chaos was a comfort. He thought about going back in, ignoring Khrushchev and simply enjoying the sight of his staff's celebration. He did not think he could be an actual part of it. For him, there had been nothing yet to celebrate, only half victories presented as complete to the public, to everyone except those who survived and a few besides. The Chief Designer noticed that his glass was empty. He had finished the vodka.

A single bark came from behind him in the hallway. Nadya walked with Kasha toward the Chief Designer. Kasha's tail, arced up and forward so that the tip pointed at her back, jostled back and forth. Each of her steps was half bounce. Her tongue dangled out of the side of her mouth, like she was making faces, and her lips, such as a dog has them, curled up in a grin at the base of her long snout. She jumped up and placed her legs on the Chief Designer's thigh. He leaned down, fighting against the creak in his left knee, and scratched Kasha behind the ears and under the chin.

"And who is this?" Khrushchev spoke from the doorway to the common area. "I didn't know you kept a pet, Nadya."

"Not a pet," said the Chief Designer. "This is one of our dogs. We've trained them for spaceflight."

"A dog in space?" asked Khrushchev. His round face scrunched all across with wrinkles. "What for?"

The Chief Designer stood. "I'm glad you ask!"

He felt his voice change, taking on an artificial cheeriness. It was a tone he had learned from the ware sellers in the less prominent streets of Moscow. The very streets where they had hunted the stray dogs for the program, all of the dogs except Kasha.

"We'll use the dogs," said the Chief Designer, "to test our new multi-person spacecraft, Voskhod."

"A new spacecraft?"

"Yes, Mr. Khrushchev. It will be the next phase of the program, leading directly to the ultimate goal of interplanetary exploration."

"I've heard you talk of other planets before, but I didn't realize we were so close."

"There are still obstacles, Mr. Khrushchev, but dogs such as Kasha here will help us overcome them."

"Little Kasha will be a Soviet hero!"

"Not Kasha herself. We have other dogs trained for the mission."

"Nonsense. Look at her. She'll be the perfect symbol of our progress. Pure white like fresh snow, sweet and innocent."

"I must—"

"When will this mission be launching?"

"We need about six months to prepare the craft."

Nadya had crouched and drawn Kasha back, holding her close. Khrushchev regarded them, his mouth pursed and eyes narrowed.

"Can you launch in five months and a half? How perfect would it be to launch on the anniversary of the Revolution? Let's launch on November 7."

"Of course, as long as you're fine with me requisitioning additional resources, it should be possible to—"

"Wait, Chief Designer. I have an idea. Use my dog as the second cosmonaut. He's a similar size. How thrilling would it be to have him in space. I mean thrilling for the Soviet people to see Byelka in space."

The Chief Designer could not follow all that was being said. "Pardon me, but a squirrel?"

"*Byelka* is my dog's name, Chief Designer!" Khrushchev smiled like a proud parent. "Byelshenka."

"Our dogs have been trained for years, most more than even Kasha. And not all dogs are able to handle the stresses of spaceflight."

"Nonsense. Just give the little fellow a sedative if you have to. I'll let you take him for two weeks before the launch. I suspect he can be prepared in that time."

"Of course, Mr. Khrushchev." The sound of the salesman had completely drained from the Chief Designer's voice.

"Byelka and Kasha, the four-legged heroes of the Soviet Union." Khrushchev gestured to an invisible headline in front of him. "Yes, Chief Designer, I like this very much. Take whatever you need to succeed from the General Designer. He'll be notified to cooperate in full."

"Yes, Mr. Khrushchev."

"This is very exciting. Very exciting."

Khrushchev summoned his bodyguards and walked away down the hall.

Nadya asked, "Will we really launch Kasha?"

"I don't know if we can avoid it."

The Chief Designer looked down and saw tears in Nadya's eyes. She had never, as far as he knew, cried in front of anyone. He had doubted until right then that she was capable of crying at all.

THE CHIEF DESIGNER unlocked the door to the radio room, entered, and locked it behind him. He flipped on the light and jumped back at the sight of Mars already at the console.

"You were here in the dark?" asked the Chief Designer.

Mars looked up at the overhead light, blinking his eyes deliberately. "I didn't even notice. It's been several days since I last slept. I think I thought my eyes were closed."

The Chief Designer rested his hand on Mars's shoulder. "After this you'll sleep, yes?"

"I don't want to leave him alone."

"I'll take the next two orbits, and Mishin and Bushuyev after that."

"I'll try to sleep."

"It doesn't look like you have a choice. Your eyes are barely open even now."

The Chief Designer turned on the radio console. The gentle hum of its electronics filled the quiet of the room.

"It's risky to talk to him, you know," said the Chief Designer. "The Americans are surely listening, not to mention the operators at our own stations. Are you using encryption?"

"Zarya is functioning properly."

"How's Leonid doing?"

"You know the twins. It's as if they talk in riddles sometimes. Leonid is as much a part of the machinery of Vostok as the switches and wires. Now for the first time he has time to think about who he is. His existence is no longer limited to only training and action. He's a machine manufacturing a philosophy based on the very limited life he's lived."

"You're starting to sound like a philosopher yourself."

"I've let myself become trapped up there with him."

The radio crackled. Underneath the static, a faint organic sound repeated. It grew stronger and clearer. A human voice. It asked over and over, *Hello?*

"Hello, Leonid. It's the Chief Designer."

"Is Mars not there?"

"I'm here, too," said Mars.

"I've been saying hello," said Leonid, "for several minutes. I forgot to note the time when we last lost communication, so I didn't know when I would again be in range. Also, I've begun to distrust the clock. It wasn't made to run for so long."

"The clock is fine," said the Chief Designer.

"That's good to know. It'll save me several dozen *hellos* on the next orbit. All of my supplies are limited, and I suspect I have only so many greetings at my disposal, as well. With infinity literally all around me, the idea of shortage is one that's difficult to deal with. It's not that I don't have everything I could possibly ever need, it's that I can't reach it. I remember being a boy, very small, unable to reach something on the table. What possibly could I have been reaching for? The memory of the thing is gone, but I remember wanting it so badly. I remember my short arms. I remember lifting up on my toes, pushing against the floor with them as hard as I could. I was young enough to believe that my will alone would let me achieve the goal. The goal of reaching the forgotten thing on the table.

"Do you know what my brother did? He pushed a chair up to the table and climbed from it to the top and got the thing I wanted. He dropped it down to me. I don't remember the thing, but I remember my brother standing there, and I thought he was so tall, but we have always been the same height. He was no taller, even though he could reach farther.

"So I wonder. I think these things to be out of reach, the resources I need to survive and all the *hellos* I have yet to speak, but perhaps I've just not yet thought to use a chair. The infinite is infinite, but the extent of our reach is ingenuity. I strained against my limitations, but my brother knew to ignore the limitations entirely. My brother, how is he?"

"He just returned home today," said the Chief Designer.

"To Bohdan? How's Grandmother?"

"No, he's barely closer to Bohdan than you are. He returned to Star City."

"Tsiolkovski was the first to tell us Star City was home, but I was never able to convince myself entirely. Here, in my little metal ball, I feel more at home than I ever did there. No offense intended, Chief Designer."

"This doesn't offend me at all. Most days, I, too, wish to leave Star City and return to my actual home. Months go by when I don't see my wife or boy."

"You have a family?"

"I'm supposed to be only a title, *Chief Designer*, so my family is a secret, even from my staff. I figure there is no harm in telling you. Not because of your . . . situation, but because you have proven, for even longer than the other cosmonauts, that you can keep a secret."

"And me?" asked Mars.

The Chief Designer placed his hand on Mars's shoulder. "You, Mars, are too sleepy to remember any of this tomorrow."

Mars brushed the Chief Designer's hand away with an emotive flare.

"I'm not so feebleminded as that," said Mars.

The men laughed, but not loudly or for long.

Leonid spoke into the silence that followed, "Can I share a secret of my own?"

"Of course, Leonid," said the Chief Designer.

"I don't remember her name, my grandmother. She, too, is only a title."

"Tsiolkovski told it to me when he brought you here. I made a point to remember. I felt that I should honor her sacrifice at least that much."

"Do you think my brother remembers her name?"

"If not, and if he ever asks, I'll remind him."

"Will you remind me now?"

The Chief Designer leaned close to the microphone and whispered her name.

AFTERNOON GAVE WAY to evening and the staff filtered out of the party. Glasses lay sideways and overturned on the tables, even on chairs and the floor. The whole room reeked of spilled spirits. The only ones left were the three cosmonauts, Nadya, Leonid, and Giorgi, sitting on the floor, leaning against Giorgi's mural on the back wall of the room. Kasha curled in Nadya's lap. Nadya hummed a simple melody, and Giorgi sometimes pitched in a harmony.

"Let's play table tennis," said Giorgi.

"I can't even stand," said Leonid.

"That'll make it easier to defeat you."

"You say that as if you've had difficulty defeating me in the past."

"But you at least offer more of a challenge than the rest of them."

But the real challenge had come from Leonid's twin, who would play with Giorgi on breaks from their training. Because of this, Mishin and Bushuyev had unveiled a new table tennis table in the windowless common room of the dorm where the earthbound twins resided, half in hiding, half in waiting. By that point, it was only Leonid who still lived there. Nadya would visit almost every day, but she had taken up her sister's old dorm room. Mars lived in his brother's. Valentina and Yuri had moved out into real homes long ago. They had left this life behind, escaped in a way Nadya and Mars seemed unable. Leonid envied Valentina and Yuri that.

So since childhood, Leonid had spent his days waiting for Mishin and Bushuyev to come take him to training. There was no set schedule that Leonid could decipher, his training days always a surprise. His brother would go into hiding, and Leonid would learn the things his brother already knew, though never quite as well. Much of Leonid's energy was spent simply remembering the names of the people his brother interacted with every day. Yes, he learned the controls of Vostok, but he knew he would never remember them well enough to pilot the thing himself.

In the meantime, he practiced table tennis for at least an hour a day, sometimes with Mishin and Bushuyev, sometimes against the wall, until he played well enough to pass for his brother in a casual match. Leonid admitted to himself that table tennis was one of his few actual pleasures. With the racket in his hand, concentrating on the ball, he was able to escape his own mind, projecting himself into the action so that the only part of him that existed was motion and response. As much as he might enjoy it, Leonid also knew that he was no match for Giorgi, who the Chief Designer claimed might have played in international competitions had he not joined the military.

"How about tomorrow?" asked Leonid. "I now have no official duties for the foreseeable future. Maybe I can finally practice enough to win."

"Tomorrow, then!" Giorgi picked up the nearest bottle and held it upside down. "I think we're out of vodka."

"The bottles may be empty, but I'm still full of the stuff."

Giorgi set the bottle on its side and rolled it across the room. Kasha leapt from Nadya's lap and trotted after it, catching up just before it impacted the far wall. She tried to bite the fat part of the bottle, but even with her mouth wide open her teeth clicked futilely against the glass. She bit the neck next, positioning her head to get a grip on it with her molars. Each time she tried to lift the bottle, it slipped free after it rose only centimeters off the ground. After a few attempts she stepped back, tilting her head from side to side, looking from one end of the bottle to the other. She went back to the neck, crouched in front of it, and latched her front teeth around the lip of the bottle's mouth. Without attempting to lift the bottle, she scuttled slowly backward, dragging it in Giorgi's direction.

"Such a clever girl," said Giorgi.

Kasha's progress was slow, almost painfully so. Leonid wanted to get up and help her, but he was still unsure of his ability to stand. And Kasha seemed so determined. He felt like she would be upset if anyone offered any help at all.

"Why do you think she does it?" said Nadya.

"What do you mean?" asked Giorgi.

"Chase after a bottle. Or a stick. What compels her?"

"Instinct, I suppose."

The bottle scooted, tinking against the floor.

"My father gave up church like everyone after the Revolution," said Nadya. "There was no church to go to anyway. I've heard that there were still priests in smaller towns and villages, but it was like they disappeared overnight in the city. My father, with no church to attend, who explained to us why religion was false, a silly superstition, he kept an icon in his dresser. He would mumble to himself. That's what he would call it when we caught him, 'mumbling.' But I heard him once before he noticed me, and what he mumbled was a prayer. I barely knew what prayer was, and it seemed strange and magical what he said. I knew the words, they were common enough, maybe not the word *god*, that one I had not heard used very much, if at all. 'Papa,' I said. He turned and saw me, and he blushed and I felt myself blush, too, like we'd both just discovered each other's most embarrassing secret. He told me he'd just been mumbling again, and I told him it was okay if he mumbled. Not long after that, Tsiolkovski came."

"Let's not dwell in the past," said Leonid.

It was dangerous to say too much around Giorgi, who did not know the whole truth about the twins. He was not even supposed to know that they had been recruited as children, but Mars drunkenly spilled that secret one night in front of Giorgi and a number of engineers, most of whom had disappeared from Star City shortly thereafter.

"There's no shame in celebrating our histories," said Giorgi. "Our past is the only sure cause of our present."

"All I meant to say," said Nadya, "is that sometimes I mumble myself. I don't know about god, but it's an instinct, of sorts."

"You two have been to the heavens themselves, so I'll trust your opinion on the matter of gods."

Leonid said, "One need not have been to space to know for sure there's no such thing as a creator. In fact, it's easier to see that from right here on the ground."

Kasha finished her bottle-laden trek across the room. She stopped, panted several times, and nosed the bottle to Giorgi's feet.

## Bohdan, Ukraine—1950

In school, before the teacher went away, the Leonids had been taught that there was no such thing as god. Science had all the answers, and it was hard to argue. If the magic that had allowed the fleets of warplanes to fly overhead could be explained by science, then the Leonids were sure that anything could. When such a plane carried their father away but failed to carry him back, it was not the failure of a miracle, or the triumph of an enemy's miracle—guns that could launch bullets from the ground halfway up to heaven—over their own. It was simply the science of a plane that it could not fly with one wing shot off. No false comfort in that, no false hope.

Sunday morning came, barely different from any other morning of the week. The boys woke and moved from their shared bed to the table, just a few steps away. Grandmother had laid out two pieces of dry, black bread, moistened just enough by a thin spread of watered-down butter to be edible. The boys ate the bread and drank a cup of water each. They were still hungry after breakfast, but they had gotten used to being hungry. Sometimes they would ask for another cup of water. Drink enough and it gave the illusion of being full.

The twins changed from their bedclothes to old pairs of pants, sturdy but threadbare at the knees, and donned their oldest, dingiest shirts. The fabric had always been a light shade of brown, but now it was threatening black. They put on their shoes by the door and were almost outside when Grandmother called them back.

"How about a prayer before you go?" she asked.

"You know we're not supposed to pray," said the older Leonid.

"Who says? Do you see a red soldier here with a gun and a book of rules making sure we follow each one?"

"But there's no god to pray to," said the younger Leonid.

"Maybe it's not who you pray to," said Grandmother, "but who you pray with that matters."

"Grandmother," said the older Leonid, "we have to go. They're expecting us."

"Go, go," said Grandmother, shooing them away like she sometimes did to Kasha when the dog tried to come inside. "I don't want to implicate you in my illegal activities."

The twins shuffled out, one after the other through the narrow front door. Grandmother sat with her elbows on the table, hands folded in front of her.

"Is it really illegal?" asked the younger Leonid once the twins were away from the cottage.

"Grandmother's right," said the older. "Who is there to stop her? Let her pray if she wants."

"But I don't want her to be arrested. Do you remember when they came and took Mr. Shvets away? It was the middle of the night and the whole village awoke to the sounds of Mrs. Shvets shouting at the soldiers. I remember Mykola standing beside her. He was silent, but weeping."

"When was the last time you saw a soldier? They only did such things when they first came, and then they left."

"What if they come again?"

"Grandmother's wise enough not to be caught praying if they do."

They walked the dusty trail between their cottage and the rest of the village, where the Tarasenkos lived. Mr. Tarasenko had injured his back the day before, in the middle of repairing their cottage's exterior wall, replacing rotted clapboards. Colder weather was just ahead, and now there was a hole right through the wall to the inside. As the twins approached, they could see the Tarasenkos waiting at the table, sipping hot drinks from mugs. Probably not tea. Most of the village had been steeping tree bark instead. No tea leaves had arrived on the train in over a year.

It was just Mrs. and Mr. Tarasenko in the cottage, both of the same generation as Grandmother. They had a son, supposedly a great friend of Father's, and like Father, he'd disappeared through the mountain pass on the train. What left on the train never returned. When the twins were younger, the Tarasenkos were frequent guests, arriving with sweetcakes and hearty laughs. Now, though they were still friendly, they seldom visited. But it was not just them. No one seemed to have time for things like that anymore, even though everyone had more time on their hands.

The Tarasenkos saw the twins through the hole in the wall. Mrs. Tarasenko rose from the table and greeted them outside. She was a small woman, shrunk even more in recent years, and her dress, yellowed and tattered, fell shapeless around her like a collapsed tent. Her smile revealed several missing teeth, black gaps in almost perfect squares. She led the twins around to the side of the cottage. The twins greeted Mr. Tarasenko through the hole in the wall, and he grunted in response.

"Don't mind him," said Mrs. Tarasenko. "He's just upset that he needs you boys to help. He's too proud to be grateful."

"I can hear you," said Mr. Tarasenko.

"It's good to know that your ears work better than your back."

She laughed, a cackle really. Mr. Tarasenko turned to her. The twins had expected anger, but he was fighting back a smile. He sipped from his mug and turned back to face the table.

"Thank you, boys," he said.

Mrs. Tarasenko showed the Leonids where the new clapboards could be found, and then instructed them in how to properly hang them. She and one of the twins would each support an end while the other twin hammered in the first few nails that held the board in place. The fresh wood of the new boards, sap still seeping out along the grain, looked as bright and yellow as a fresh-bloomed flower compared to the weathered gray of the old ones. The project only took an hour, the top of the sun just cresting the eastern mountains as they finished.

"It looks like we replaced one hole with another," said the younger Leonid.

"Better a hole that will keep out the cold," said Mrs. Tarasenko.

She offered them tea, but the boys declined. Neither drank tea, and certainly not the stuff that passed for tea anymore. When she opened the door, Mr. Tarasenko shouted his thanks from inside. The door slammed shut, shuddering the whole cottage. The Leonids worried that their work would fall apart as soon as they had completed it, but the cottage held together, like it always had.

THE LEONIDS WALKED home down the dirt path from the village. A dry scent kicked up with the dust. The route was not the most direct—it was a much quicker jaunt through the forest, where a trail had been worn by years of the twins' shortcutting. The village had been as quiet as the forest this morning, everyone holed up indoors. Maybe a few out trying their hand at hunting, up the mountain in the thicker forest, hoping to snare a dinner of stringy squirrel meat.

A long, low whistle came from the direction of the pass, rising in pitch throughout its duration. The train. It had been months since it last came. The older Leonid had almost forgotten the sound. As if choreographed, villagers emerged from their homes, tugging light coats over disheveled shirts. Gathering barrows, slings, and carts, they formed a line and marched in the direction of the station. The Leonids joined the procession next to Oksana. She carried a basket large enough for one of them to fit inside. Her face bore a wide scar on the cheek, a mark that the older Leonid did not remember from before.

The screech of the train's brakes carried over the trees, the pitch short and high. The twins knew this meant there was not much cargo. When it used to arrive fully laden, the sound of the brakes was more of a moan, as if the mountain itself griped against holding up the train's weight. The villagers ahead of them picked up their pace.

Shouts came from the station as soon as the brakes silenced. The voices were too far away to make out what was said. A few words carried through the trees, but still did not make any sense. Russian. The Leonids had learned some of the language before the teacher was taken away, but the words they heard now they did not know. The shouting stopped, followed by a series of pops, the sound like punctuation.

Oksana pulled the twins to the side of the road.

"Go back to your home," she said. "Go inside and stay there, and if anyone comes, let them in."

"Who's coming?" asked the older Leonid.

"Go now. Run."

From around the bend several figures came into view. In some places they seemed to sprout extra limbs. Rifles. These were soldiers, like the ones the Leonids remembered from years ago, like how their father had looked in his uniform, buried in the middle of all that equipment. The twins turned and ran, jutting off the main road onto the path through the woods.

Grandmother waited for them on the front step, wringing a cloth in her hands. When they made it to the door, she ushered them inside and had them sit at the table.

"What happened?" she asked.

"The train arrived," said the younger Leonid, "but soldiers got off. They fired their guns before we got close to the station. Oksana told us to run home, so we did."

"Good, good. You're to stay at this table. Even if a soldier comes to the cottage, stay seated. If they tell you to do something, do it. Do not raise a single word in protest."

"What's happening?" asked the older Leonid.

"All will be well. We just have to wait for the soldiers to leave."

Grandmother joined the twins at the table. Minutes passed and then time stretched into a blur. Grandmother fetched three cups of water, but no one drank.

Usually, the older Leonid could only sit still for so long. The energy pent up inside him would build and build until he could not contain it. Grandmother would be scolding him to stop fidgeting before he even realized he had begun. Sometimes he excused himself outside if only to run, to release the feeling of being trapped inside himself. But this type of sitting was different. Instead of filling him with energy, it drained him. He stretched his hearing as far as it could go, searching for the faintest noise in the distance, trying to deduce what was happening in the rest of the village by variations in the wind. Whenever he noticed his own body, all the muscles were tensed. He forced himself to relax, only to tense again as soon as his mind returned to listening. Even breathing became difficult, like when the air was thick and soupy in summer. But it was not summer.

The younger Leonid's posture betrayed no tension at all. The only sign that he was even alive was a nervous tapping of his foot. No matter how often Grandmother scolded him to stop, he could not still the tapping. Right then, she did not even comment on it. Her own fingers rapped out the same agitation atop the table.

It must have been hours. No one approached the cottage. The older Leonid felt his body unclench, muscles loosening. He took the water from the table and sipped it. It tasted of metal and sulfur. The same as it had always tasted, the only water he had ever known. He wondered why he noticed these flavors now. He sighed, and then his grandmother sighed. The younger Leonid kept tapping his foot. And then he stopped.

"Did you hear that?" he asked.

The older Leonid realized he had stopped listening for the approach of the soldiers. He forced the invisible arms of his ears out farther, past the walls and the surrounding forest. He heard nothing, though, except the ambient wind. "I hear noth—" he began, but then the sound reached him, a noise carried barely above the wind. One quick pop. It was fainter, but Leonid recognized the sound from before. A shot fired from a Russian rifle.

"Stay here," said Grandmother.

She went to the door and cracked it open, leaning her ear to the gap. She closed the door.

"They're coming," she said.

"But the sound was far away," said the older Leonid.

"Then there is more than one group of them. I heard steps coming from the path."

The older Leonid was not sure whether to believe her. Sometimes she had trouble hearing him speak from across the cottage. Outside, on windy days, she would often ask him to repeat himself two or three times before she finally understood what he said. She might have just heard the rustle of branches in the breeze.

A knock came on the door.

"Come in," said Grandmother.

The door opened, and the barrel of a gun jutted through, followed by the soldier who held it. After him came another gun followed by another soldier. The first soldier kept an eye on the table while the other used her rifle to poke through the items on the shelf beside the stove. There was not much there to see.

"Does anyone else live here?" asked the second soldier. She spoke in broken Ukrainian, with an accent that made her difficult to understand.

"Just the three of us," said Grandmother.

The soldier pointed to the twins. "Father?"

"He died in the war."

The soldiers looked at each other and nodded. They lowered their weapons.

The second soldier stepped toward the table and looked closely at the boys. She said a word in Russian.

"I don't understand," said Grandmother.

"The word, I do not know it. Two people who are the same."

"Twins," said Grandmother.

"Yes, twins."

The first soldier pulled out a notepad from one of his uniform's many pockets and wrote something down. The second soldier pointed to one of the full cups of water on the table.

"May I?" she asked.

"Yes," said Grandmother.

The soldier took the cup and gulped down half its contents. Water glistened on her upper lip. She licked it away. She returned the cup, making an extra effort to set it in the exact same spot from which it had been taken.

"Thank you," she said.

The soldiers left and shut the door behind them. Grandmother rose from the table, and refilled her cup from the urn. She downed the water in gulps even greater than those of the soldier. She tried to hide a burp behind her hand, but the boys heard it anyway. Resting one hand high on the wall and leaning forward, she sucked in deep, deliberate breaths. Even on the worst day, the Leonids had never seen her look so tired.

She returned to the table, and the three of them listened again for noises that might let them know what was happening in the rest of the village. But no noise came until the train whistle sounded, followed by the faint chugging as the train climbed the mountain back up the pass.

THE VILLAGE SAT silent and listless as the Leonids followed Grandmother down the main path. A few of the cottage doors gaped, swaying in the breeze, but no one could be seen inside, no voices were heard. Squirrels sometimes chittered from a tree branch, but the squirrels were few. Grandmother knocked on the door to the Shvetses' cottage. No answer. It was as if the train had taken everyone when it departed.

A little farther on, soft murmurs intruded on the silence. At first they sounded far away, but then through an overhang of trees the speakers became visible, a knot of them outside the Tarasenkos' cottage. Everyone who was missing from their own homes seemed to be gathered there. Beyond them, the hole in the wall, fixed not hours before, was back, the new boards pried away and missing.

"Why would they take the boards?" asked the younger Leonid.

Grandmother did not answer, edging toward the cottage with short steps. The other villagers watched her approach. She pushed through them to the wall and peered into the hole. She held her hand to her mouth as if to stifle a yawn. The Leonids peeked around her.

Mr. Tarasenko lay flat on his back on the floor, unmoving. His dingy shirt now sported three crimson blossoms, two over his stomach and one on his chest. The same color was dripped on the table, on one of the chairs, and in streaks across the floor. Red footprints surrounded the body like the steps to a frantic dance.

Grandmother pulled the Leonids away. The younger, though, wrenched himself free of her grip and leaned his head all the way through the hole. Grandmother released the older Leonid, and he gazed through the hole from a few steps away. One of the villagers sat with Mrs. Tarasenko on the straw-stuffed bed in the corner. Mrs. Tarasenko's hands were red, and her fingers choked a blood-soaked rag.

The older Leonid placed his hand on his brother's shoulder and drew him away from the hole.

"Careful, or you'll fall through," said the older Leonid.

They stood at the edge of the clustered villagers as Mrs. Kharms explained that the soldiers had seen the fresh wood on the wall and decided to take it. No one knew why. Mr. Tarasenko had risen to protest, but with his bad back stumbled forward instead, directly into one of the soldiers. The soldier reacted by releasing two shots into Mr. Tarasenko's stomach from only centimeters away.

"How do you know all this?" asked Grandmother.

"Mrs. Tarasenko was strangely calm when we arrived," said Mrs. Kharms. "In shock, I suppose. She told us the details as if she was talking about cooking."

She continued, explaining how Mr. Tarasenko had collapsed back onto the floor, like he was now, but still breathing, rubbing at his stomach like scratching an itch. That was how Mrs. Tarasenko described it, like an itch. He might as well have already been dead, two bullets in him and no doctor. The first soldier, the one who had fired, backed away, bumping into the door. Tears were in his eyes but he wasn't exactly crying. The other soldier, a higher rank, knelt over Mr. Tarasenko, lifting up his shirt to inspect the wound. He apologized several times. There was nothing he could do. He stood, sighted his rifle, and fired one shot into Mr. Tarasenko's chest.

"Mrs. Tarasenko talked about the expression on her husband's face," said Mrs. Kharms, "but I'm not sure I should say it with the children here."

"They're old enough," said Grandmother. "If they were not before today, then they certainly are now."

"Mrs. Tarasenko said it was the face he used to make, when they were younger and they used to . . ."

One of the young men of the village failed to stifle a laugh. A round of chuckles passed through the small crowd, Grandmother included.

"Then the soldiers gathered the two boards and left," said Mrs. Kharms. "All this over some crude hunks of wood."

"It's never as simple as that," said Grandmother.

"The boards were all they took from this cottage, but before you arrived, we were trying to inventory everything that was taken. All the carts we hauled to the train station. The plows from our fields. The goats. A few sacks of grain. If they had brought more sacks, I suspect they would have taken it all. We may not know everything that was taken for days yet, not until we go to look for something and it's not there."

"She can't stay here tonight," said Grandmother, pointing through the hole in the wall.

"Mrs. Shvets already offered her home. They have room for one more."

"It seems as if we are always making room," said Grandmother. "Come, boys."

She walked away, not down the path, but up into the forest, where the ground was bedded with leaves and the sun shone down in specks.

"I THOUGHT SOLDIERS were supposed to be heroes," said the older Leonid. They were deep enough in the forest that the Tarasenko cottage was out of sight. "Father was a soldier, and you always tell us how brave he was, but what's brave about shooting Mr. Tarasenko? Is that what Father did in other villages?"

"Your father never did such a thing," said Grandmother. "His enemy came with guns and tanks and planes, and if not for men like your father, they would've destroyed everything in their path. One of the villagers who returned from the war had been in Stalingrad. It was not even a city anymore after the battle there, just a pile of stones that used to be buildings. That's what your father fought against. If he ever killed a man, then it was a man who also wished to kill him."

"Stalingrad's far away. Why did Father have to go there, and why do soldiers from there come here?"

Grandmother slipped on a mound of brown leaves, stumbling up the slope. The younger Leonid reached out to steady her.

"Have I ever told you about the man our village was named after?" asked Grandmother.

Neither brother responded.

"After the Battle of Cecora, Bohdan Zinoviy Mykhaylovych

Khmelnytsky was captured by the Ottomans. He was sold to an Ottoman admiral as a slave, set to work on the oars of the admiral's boat. Forty oars, each manned by two slaves. The wound on his chest had healed, but on cold nights it ached, and it ached when he thought of his father. There were many cold nights. He lay awake on the wooden bench, an infinity of stars above him. When waves rocked the boat, they slid him to and fro, slivering splinters into his back. Each morning, the slaves pinched the splinters from each other's skin.

"Khmelnytsky was one of the few Cossacks, and they were forbidden from speaking to each other. How dizzying it must be to be surrounded by people but to still be alone. Instead of speaking, Khmelnytsky listened, picking up the Turks' language a word at a time, practicing the shape of the words in his mouth even as he rowed and rowed and rowed. Years of Khmelnytsky's life passed like this, uncountable splashes of the oar against the Black Sea. His skin darkened and his muscles turned to ropes like the ones used to moor the boat.

"The Ottomans were not a people to know peace. As often as not, Khmelnytsky rowed toward battle, archers arrayed along the sides of the boat, bows drawn, like statuary around a church. The old churches in large cities used to have statues of angels and saints. Khmelnytsky had seen these in his youth, not knowing that one day the statues would be of him.

"The admiral commanded his boat and dozens of others, and he usually led them to easy victories, overwhelming the small boats that seaside villages sent out in futile defense.

"It was early morning, the Black Sea as calm as a pond. The Ottoman fleet sailed straight for a small village, barely more than a fishing camp. It seemed like it would be a short battle and an easy victory. Two dozen skiffs launched from the village. The smaller boats weaved so quickly through the Ottoman fleet that the archers missed target after target, their arrows sliding like sleek divers into the water. The skiffs carried archers of their own, and the tall, proud Ottomans proved to be easy targets. The first archer felled on Khmelnytsky's boat collapsed across his lap, and he shucked the body overboard. More archers fell. The boat lurched, and then turned hard to port, carving a circle in the water. The rudder-man had been killed, his body left leaning hard against the tiller. More archers fell. All around, the Ottoman fleet scattered in different directions.

"Khmelnytsky bounded to the back of the boat, running in spite of the shackles around his ankles, and hauled the rudder-man out of the way. He gestured to the oarsman in back, just a boy, all long limbs and sinew, to take up the post. The boat straightened out, facing away from shore. The admiral, at the prow, screamed orders to his men and waved signals to the other boats. The admiral was a formidable military man himself and managed to regroup his boats into a defensive posture even as arrows slashed the air around him. He was about to organize a retreat when Khmelnytsky spoke, his voice ringing loud and deep. Months in the sun had creased the corners of his eyes. His hair, after the battle where he'd watched his father die, had gained early streaks of silver. It was impossible not to listen. He told the admiral to sail toward the beachhead, as fast as the oarsmen could manage, grouping bowmen at the stern to fire at the enemy skiffs. The admiral obeyed. By the time the Ottomans landed, the enemy boats were far behind, the bulk of the village's men on them. A small contingent took the village while the Ottoman archers held the beach, decimating the small boats long before they got close to shore.

"Imagine, a slave speaking such a thing to a man of prestige and power. Had Khmelnytsky spoken at any other time he would have been beaten. Maybe even slain. But Khmelnytsky waited for the right moment to act, as he would again later, and so the admiral listened. The Ottomans took the beach and then the village. Defeat had been turned to victory.

"That night the Ottomans dined on plundered food around great fires, and even the slaves were given a feast. Khmelnytsky's shackles were removed, and he was brought to the admiral's own table, allowed to eat with the officers. They patted him on the back and got drunk and told crude jokes that he could only understand the half of. He laughed with the others, I'm sure. Not because he understood the jokes. He laughed because he had not been in a position to laugh for so long. He had oared and oared and his only feelings were for his lost father, his only thoughts on learning the enemy's language. Imagine the release of being surrounded by laughter, of having to neither feel nor think. You are boys, so you cannot yet imagine the release of that first sip of drink after so long without.

"I think that's when Khmelnytsky remembered freedom. He'd lost so much, had been wounded deeper than the blade had cut him. If he hadn't asserted himself when the opportunity arose, he might have stayed a slave forever, oaring boats around the Black Sea for his enemy until the day he died. Freedom is the possibility of happiness, and there with fresh meat and flowing wine he remembered it.

"Back on the boat, he was allowed to remain unshackled. Before battles or landings, the admiral would call him to the prow and ask his opinion. Khmelnytsky's Turkish was almost perfect by this point, only a slight accent preventing him from passing for a pale Ottoman. He studied the admiral's maps, and from the prow saw every beach and inlet they passed. Over two years, he memorized the whole coastline of the Black Sea.

"You would think that the other oarsmen would have been jealous of Khmelnytsky's favored status, but he never forgot that he was a slave and spent as much time on the oars as anyone. He convinced the admiral to provide more and better rations, and the oarsmen were able to row harder for longer. After a battle in which half the bowmen were killed, Khmelnytsky sold the captain on the merits of unshackling all the oarsmen, so that they might take up the bows of fallen soldiers. This strategy turned a later battle from defeat to victory, and on that night all eighty slaves were invited to join the admiral around a high fire on the beach, where a dozen animals, spoils of the victory, were skewered on swords claimed from fallen enemies and roasted.

"The admiral and Khmelnytsky became great friends. At the end of each campaign, the admiral brought him home to his estate, where the admiral had twenty wives and was willing to ignore it when one of them seemed to favor Khmelnytsky. The two men would stay up late into the night, discussing the great philosophies of the world, arguing over the outcomes of ancient battles, debating the merits of Western and Eastern art. Every meal was a celebration, visited by Ottoman nobles and merchants and generals. These men came not for the admiral, but for Khmelnytsky, the slave.

"Sometimes he would fall silent in a conversation at the mention of a place he had once known. The admiral never failed to notice and understand. He would refill Khmelnytsky's drink and turn the conversation in a new direction.

"Who knows how many years his life went like this. Certainly not Khmelnytsky himself.

"Back at sea, as he oared, Khmelnytsky watched the coastline slip past through the round oar holes. Only that small circle was visible, but he started to recognize the features of the land, inlets and half-sunken stones, the wide mouth of a river, the delta beyond. It was the Dnieper. The land he saw was his home.

"Khmelnytsky dropped his end of the oar and strode to the prow. He took an officer's saber right from the sheath. The officer died by his own blade before he could even notice its weight missing from his belt. The admiral turned, saw Khmelnytsky, and smiled. Khmelnytsky nodded to the admiral, and then lopped off his head in one swift, sure stroke.

"Alone on the prow, he turned back. The other Ottoman soldiers were stunned, unable to react. Khmelnytsky nodded once to the other slaves, long since left unshackled, and without further instruction, they overwhelmed the soldiers, whom they outnumbered three to one. Not a single slave died in the mutiny. Few sustained even a scratch.

"The slaves were Poles and Cossacks and other sorts Khmelnytsky could not recognize. But all followed his command when he bade them row up the mouth of the river, against the strong current, to a small town that welcomed them with long docks. The men of the town, at the sight of an Ottoman boat, took up arms. Khmelnytsky greeted them by holding up the severed head of the admiral, offering no other explanation. The former slaves rushed off the boat, especially the Cossacks, explaining what Khmelnytsky had done, the words tumbling out too fast to follow, each version of the story a little bit different.

"When they looked around to find him, to thank him, to celebrate his very name, Khmelnytsky was gone. He had already passed through the town, stolen a horse, and set off in the direction of his family and his home. The former slaves would never see him again, but they would speak of him. They would speak of him to any who would listen."

"That's why he's a hero?" asked the younger Leonid.

"One of the reasons."

The twins had never left the village. The older Leonid wondered what it would be like to come home after such a long time away. Their cottage emerging in slices through the gaps in the thinning forest. What would he remember? What would he forget?

"Khmelnytsky was a hero, yes," said Grandmother, "but also a murderer. It's interesting how one man can be both."

## Star City, Russia—1964

The Chief Designer was halfway through the report before he realized he had not paid enough attention at the beginning to know what it was about. He knew all the terminology, of course, and he understood the equations, but why these terms and these numbers were relevant to him he could not begin to guess. It seemed as if half his time was spent reading reports. He wondered what he might accomplish if he were ever given time enough to actually act. Instead, he relied on the work of a hundred others, conducting them as if they were an orchestra and he the maestro. The Chief Designer did not know much about music, but he was impressed that so many people could all end something at the same time.

He flipped back to the beginning of the report, skimming the first page, hoping the words that would make it all make sense would jump out at him. He did not have time to reread the whole thing again. Six similar reports, each over a hundred pages, crowded the edge of his desk. If half his time was spent reading reports, the other half was spent responding to the authors, many of whom he had never actually met.

A small commotion came from the waiting room outside his office. He heard Mishin or Bushuyev—they sounded so much alike—talking fast, a hint of irritation in his voice. The commotion drew closer to the Chief Designer's cracked door.

"You can't go in! He's very busy."

The door slung open, and the General Designer loomed in the doorway, Mishin and Bushuyev, looking panicked, behind him.

"I'm sorry," said one of them.

"It's all right," said the Chief Designer.

Of all the people he would have preferred not to see, the General Designer held the pole position, but the Chief Designer had to admit that any distraction from the reports was welcome, even if the person of the distraction was not.

"Come in, General Designer. I'm sorry for the hassle. I asked not to be disturbed today, so Mishin and Bushuyev were just following my orders."

Mishin and Bushuyev offered a small bow of apology from the doorway, and then one of them pulled the door shut.

The General Designer took a chair facing the Chief Designer's desk.

"It's not Mishin and Bushuyev with whom I'm annoyed," said the General Designer.

"Since you're here, I'll assume I'm the source of your annoyance."

"I've been ordered by Khrushchev to assist you. Khrushchev himself! He showed up at OKB-52 and told me to put my projects on hold. I don't know how you managed it, and I don't care. I may not like you, Chief Designer, but I never expected you to cheat."

"First, comrade, what is there at which to cheat? This isn't a game. Maybe you still think it is because you have yet to risk the life of a single person. Maybe when all you do is perform test after test on rocket engines, you forget that the real test only comes when you affix a man to the other end of the rocket. Yes, what we do is a competition, but it's not against each other. It's not even against the Americans. We compete only against gravity. Gravity is my opponent, and only someone with an ego the size of the planet would dare to think that they're of the same interest to me as the stuff that holds the very Earth together.

"Second, comrade, your problem is with Khrushchev. I didn't ask him to approach you. If you have a complaint, take it to him."

The General Designer let out a bitter laugh. "Everyone knows you've cast some sort of spell on him. That man adores you, though it's never been clear to me why. What sway do you hold?"

"Not as much sway as you believe. If I had my way every time, OKB-52 would not exist, but here you are, and with a title superior to mine. As is the case with most who declare themselves victims, you're only a victim in your own mind. You've had nothing taken from you, and yet you declare loudly all your losses. There's a significant difference between losing and not having yet received. And didn't Tsiolkovski teach us all that the best way to preempt loss is with sacrifice?"

The General Designer dipped his head and rubbed a spot just above his eyebrow. He had been closer to Tsiolkovski than the rest of the Soviet rocketeers. For most of them, Tsiolkovski was like a minor god, but for the General Designer he had been like a grandfather. To mention Tsiolkovski was gamesmanship, the sort of cheating the General Designer had accused the Chief Designer of at the beginning of the meeting. Had it been anyone else, the Chief Designer might have felt ashamed.

"Have you seen him?" asked the General Designer.

"Not in years," said the Chief Designer. "I hear he's moved to a mountain. Like some sort of oracle. That's what we all thought he was, anyway."

"It was 1960, the last time I spoke with him. He was already . . . untethered. He'd stopped talking about space, fixated instead on selective breeding or something like that. It was hard to follow. It was hard to watch such a great man slipping. Have you received any letters?"

"No, but you were closer to him."

This denial was a lie. After Nadya's launch, Tsiolkovski had indeed sent a letter, shakily written in blue ink. The message was half incoherent, but here and there a flash of the old master shone through. For instance, Tsiolkovski had known without being told that Nadya's ship had burned up on reentry. He had begged for the Chief Designer to apologize to the other Nadya for him. The Chief Designer ignored the request. Apologies from Tsiolkovski were so long overdue as to be meaningless. And though Tsiolkovski had first found the twins, had viewed them as little more than lab rats to test the effects of space travel upon, it had been the Chief Designer himself who decided the twins' final fates. Tsiolkovski had less to apologize for than he believed.

The Chief Designer opened a report on his desk, the one he had been flipping through without actually reading.

"If you're to assist me," he said, "then here's what I need. Continue your projects, and if you have something that will help me, I'll ask for it specifically."

"You're asking me to continue?"

"I already have a staff, General Designer. I don't need a second one."

"Don't come to me later asking me to build you a rocket."

"As if I would trust any rocket that you built. Do you know why Khrushchev asked you to help me? It's because of his dog. He wants me to send his dog into space."

"Byelka?"

"You know it?"

"An obnoxious animal. I visited the Premier's dacha once and spent the whole time trying to keep the thing from mounting my leg. He wants to send it into space? Maybe you could leave it there."

The General Designer laughed, a short deliberate sound. The Chief Designer followed suit.

"I don't like you," said the General Designer, "but I appreciate that you didn't send Khrushchev to me. Assuming that's the truth."

"It is. You have an engine test for the Proton next week? Perhaps I'll visit, though I don't trust hypergolic fuels."

"You're afraid of them. Ours isn't an industry for cowards."

"Nor one for fools."

"And yet it seems to attract them. I suppose I'll see you soon."

"It's unavoidable."

"Gah! How little of our own fates we control. That mine should be bound with yours."

The Chief Designer stood, rounded his desk, and opened the dark-stained door. He waited there until the General Designer was out of the office and down the hall. Mishin and Bushuyev watched him from their twin desks, one on either side of the room. The Chief Designer slammed the door shut. The old solid wood thudded in a way that pleased him. A well-made thing performing as it should. It was a feeling, he realized, that he seldom enjoyed anymore.

MARS HAD MOVED a cot into the radio room. The cot was surplus from the army, Mars suspected from the end of the war, given to Star City before the dormitories were built, back when the cosmonauts slept in the gymnasium, separated from each other only by thin sheets hung from wires. Yuri's snores would echo through the room like the launch of a thousand rockets. Mars had thought more than once to smother Yuri in his sleep.

The cot, coming apart at the joints, creaked whenever Mars

climbed onto it, but if Mars lay still, the radio room descended into a kind of silence he had never known before. At least outside of the anechoic chamber. There, though, the silence was artificial. That silence was designed to drive a person mad if it could. The only ones ever to come out of it after an extended stay and still have their wits about them were Nadya, the one who survived, and Giorgi. The first thing Giorgi did after he emerged was play a game of table tennis, as if the *tok-tok-tok* of the ball did not sound a thousand times louder.

Mars tried to remember Leonid's four-week stint in the anechoic chamber. After he got out, Leonid seemed disoriented and talked only in whispers. The sound of a footstep could make him jump. He once said that food tasted different, as if sound affected his sense of smell. The loudest noise in the chamber was always one's own chewing.

And now Leonid had been in isolation twice as long as that. The second month came and went, and he still breathed and still spoke, and back on Earth, Mars took turns with the Chief Designer, Mishin, and Bushuyev to talk to him. The Chief Designer had forbidden any of them from telling the other Leonid. He said he did not know how the news would be taken. Leonid's grief had already come, and there was no use making him reprise it. Mars doubted the logic behind that decision, but what was one more secret to keep?

Mars almost never left the radio room, sleeping there even when one of the others was on shift. He did not explain why, and no one asked. He was not sure exactly why himself, but he had a suspicion. For every other twin, he had been the last person to speak to them. With Nadya, he had wished her luck before the radio blacked out on reentry. He had waited and waited, for hours after it was obvious she was lost, until the Chief Designer physically lifted him from the console. With Yuri and Valentina, he had pressed his ear to the speaker in order to hear the faintness of their last breaths. And with his own brother he had recalled memories that he had not thought of for years, back to an impossible time when they were still together.

Mars did not want to miss the last words of Leonid. He felt it was his duty to hear them. To the public he was a cosmonaut hero, but to himself he was the hearer of last words. That was his only purpose, the only thing he had left worth doing.

He rose from the cot and turned on the radio. A clock hung on the far wall, but he did not consult it. He had internalized the timing of Leonid's orbits and could place himself at the console within seconds of the first staticky *hello* from the capsule. The speaker crackled, like a type of echo that preceded the sound it mirrored, and then came Leonid's voice, raspy, the dryness of his mouth and throat audible.

"Hello?" said Leonid. It was always a question.

"I'm here," said Mars.

"Hello, Mars! Did you know that your name is also the name of a planet?"

"I think that's why Tsiolkovski chose it."

"Sometimes I think I've spotted it, the planet, but the window is small. More than likely I've only seen another star."

"Mars would appear red."

"It's a better name for a person than a planet."

"Thank you."

"Mars, Mars, Mars."

"Yes?"

"Did you know that you can hear your own heartbeat in space, after a while? There's no other sound but the clicks of the capsule. The beating emerges like something out of a hole. At first, it's maddening to have a living thing pounding in your head, but soon enough you realize you're only hearing yourself. How's that different from thought? *Beat-beat-beat* becomes your only cognition, and any thoughts you do have are an intrusion. The beat becomes your mind."

"What does this new mind tell you?"

"The only thing it's able: Keep going."

THE KENNEL SEEMED more full of people than dogs. Nadya and Leonid had visited almost every day for years, and besides the woman who fed and washed and walked the animals, there was never anyone else there. But today, a half-dozen white-coated veterinarians were pulling dogs from the cages and prodding them with instruments and for every veterinarian there were two assistants, who might have been veterinarians themselves but did not have the white coats to prove it. The dogs were unusually silent, as if all the activity had stunned them too much to bark. Sometimes a small yip came as a dog received a needle or had its mouth forced open or ear probed. The sound was a cry of pain but also of sadness, Leonid knew. He remembered the hungry cries of the cats in his village, before they were all gathered up to be eaten.

"You're hurting them." Leonid spoke loudly to the whole room.

"It's just a checkup," said the nearest veterinarian, an old man with a straight back, and Leonid knew without asking that the man had been an officer in the war. The old officers all had a way of looking at young men, as if assessing their readiness for battle. But this one was a veterinarian now, and had likely been one in the war, more fit for judging horses than people. He nodded once at Leonid, then returned his attention to Laika, who still managed to look happy, tail fanning frantically, even while she was twisted this way and that by unfamiliar hands.

"Where's Kasha?" asked Nadya.

Leonid spied her tail, arcing up and over, the tip dipping down at her back. Instead of white fur, her body was a pale blue, and it took Leonid a moment to realize she was wearing a vest. The veterinarians tugged it into place as he watched. The vest did not look comfortable, too tight, squeezing Kasha's body, the fur directly above the neckline puffing out like a mane. Leonid had never realized how small she actually was, how much of her apparent size was due to the thickness of her fur.

She tried to run over to Nadya and Leonid at the door, but one of the veterinarians restrained her while another adjusted the vest, tightening it even more. Leonid went to Kasha and knelt.

"Be careful," he said.

"The dog's fine," said one of the veterinarians.

Indeed, Kasha wagged her tail and tried to lick Leonid but could not reach and lapped at the air instead. Nadya stood behind Leonid and rested her fingertips on his shoulder.

"So it's true," said Nadya. "We're really going to send her into space?"

Leonid did not understand what she had said, and her expression revealed nothing. He caressed Kasha, starting above her ear and ending at the scruff of her neck. It was the way his brother had always petted Kasha's mother. She nuzzled against Leonid's arm.

The old veteran veterinarian loped across the room. His chin came to an uncomfortable point, as if the sides of his face were pressed in with a vise. His limbs seemed too long and too thin. Leonid thought he looked very much like the horses to which he once had tended.

"I don't know the plan," he said. "We were just called in today to check the dogs and establish a training regimen. The last time I was here was what, five years ago?" He looked at Nadya until she looked back. "Your launch made all our work for naught. Little Laika here was destined to be the first living thing in space."

"Perhaps also the first to die," said Nadya.

"Excuse me?" said the old veteran.

Leonid sprung to his feet, inserting himself into the space between the veteran and Nadya.

"But she will fly now, yes?" asked Leonid.

"She's too old. A feeling I can relate to! No, this time we'll launch that one there." He pointed at Kasha. "I remember her mother. She was my first choice for launch. Much quieter than even Laika, you know. Very calm. But for some reason the Chief Designer wouldn't allow it. If it can't be Laika to launch, then I'm glad it's Kasha's daughter."

"But we can't launch Kasha," said Leonid. His eyes felt hot. A sick taste rose to the top of his throat. He swallowed. He took a quick breath and swallowed again.

The old veteran laughed. "You go into space yourself and yet worry for a dog! Cosmonauts are a strange breed."

Leonid looked down at all the dogs. Little creatures. Sweet and needy. He whispered their names: Kasha, Laika, Strelka, Chernushka, Ugolyok, and all the others. Nadya gripped him around the biceps and led him from the room. He was whispering the last of the names as she shut the door.

"I'm sorry I didn't tell you," she said. "I think I didn't want to believe it myself."

"Why now?"

"Would another time have made it better?"

Leonid took backward steps until he bumped against the wall on the other side of the hall.

"Did you know that my brother and I saved the original Kasha? The villagers were starving and wanted to eat her. There had been no meat in so long. We hid her in our home and she knew not to bark. That's why the veterinarians here loved her so much, for her restraint. No matter what they did to her, she never complained. I think she would have been better off had she bitten someone now and again."

Leonid pushed himself off the wall and hurried away. Nadya trotted after him.

"Where are you going?" she asked.

"Perhaps it's time to give the Chief Designer a nip to the hand."

AFTER THE GENERAL DESIGNER left, the Chief Designer could not concentrate on the reports stacked all around his desk. The stack nearest the edge he pushed off and watched as the individual pages fluttered free from their folders and to the floor, mixing and matching with papers from other reports. If only the right pieces would land together, he might finally rid himself of reports forever.

Another commotion arose in the waiting room, Mishin and Bushuyev speaking loud, quick phrases, another voice responding, nearing the door, and then the door opened. The Chief Designer expected a return visit from the General Designer, but instead it was Leonid followed by Nadya. The Chief Designer felt himself relax. He did not think he could handle another conflict today. At least the reports never talked back.

His relief left him as quickly as it came, though, when he saw the look on Leonid's face. That mouth, trained for years to greet everyone it came across with a grin, a grin that could hush crying babies and swoon the wives of even the most charming men, instead glowered. Beside him, the expressionless Nadya seemed elated in comparison.

Mishin and Bushuyev stood on the other side of the doorway. They shrugged at the same time and pulled the door shut.

"You don't seem happy to see me, Leonid," said the Chief Designer.

"You can't do this. You must not. Choose another dog, but not Kasha."

The Chief Designer had been unsure of how Leonid would react to the news. That was why he had not told him yet. But while news did not escape Star City, it was impossible to keep it from spreading within. The only secret that had ever seemed to keep was that of the twins' very existence.

"It isn't the same Kasha as from your home."

"I don't care!" Leonid shouted and slammed his fist against the door behind him. The hush that followed reminded the Chief Designer of the moment after a launch when the rumble of the rocket finally faded to nothing.

The Chief Designer stood but did not round the desk. He held his face in his palm and rubbed his thumb up and down the scar on his head. Sometimes he thought the scar was growing in length, stretching with age. His wife had told him he was silly for thinking such a thing. He would have liked to see his wife.

"What can I do, Leonid?" he asked.

"Choose another dog." Leonid stepped forward. "But not Kasha, please. Don't take her away from me. She's all that's left."

"Khrushchev chose her."

"And Tsiolkovski chose us," said Nadya, "but you went along with him. There are only so many times you can pass responsibility to someone else."

The Chief Designer lowered his hand from his face and looked at her. Guilt had always flowed through his veins like blood, but never once had the guilt been placed on him from the outside. Especially not from Nadya.

"You owe us at least one thing, yes?" said Nadya. "Make it this. Find a way to save Kasha."

The Chief Designer crouched beside his desk and leafed through the papers he had knocked to the floor. A dozen pages on the failure of the ablative heat shield in the latest tests. Several more on painting larger red stars on the sides of rockets. He was glad to see that this particular item had been copied to the General Designer as well. Could he be the answer? Could the Chief Designer bear to work with that ass of a man?

He found what he was looking for and stood.

"There might be a way," said the Chief Designer. "And if that doesn't work, there might be another."

He handed a photograph to Leonid.

"What's this?" asked Leonid.

"It's Khrushchev's dog."

The picture showed a tiny animal, eyes taking up a significant portion of its face, long hair frizzing from its ears. The hand that held it in the photograph looked like it belonged to a giant in comparison to the dog's waspy torso and wiry legs.

"This is a dog?" said Nadya. "It looks like a well-groomed squirrel."

"That's its name: Byelka."

"What a horrible accident of breeding."

The Chief Designer looked at the piece of paper that had accompanied the photograph.

"It's a Russkiy Toy," he said.

"How will this dog help us?" asked Nadya. "Will we launch it instead?"

"We have to launch both," said the Chief Designer. "On my end, I'll try to find a way to bring it back along with Kasha. But I'm not sure I can. You know I've been trying to bring back all of you . . . all of your siblings with every launch. In case I can't prepare the capsule to return the dogs, though, I need your help."

"What can we possibly do?" asked Leonid.

"Find me the twins of these dogs. I'll have Mishin and Bushuyev assist you. They helped capture the original batch of strays, and know the best streets to search in Moscow."

"This doesn't seem like a simple task," said Nadya.

"I don't recall having ever faced a task that was simple."

"There's a whole room of veterinarians here right now. Let them help us."

"It has to be only those who know . . . only the twins and then Mishin and Bushuyev."

"What about Mars?" asked Leonid.

"Mars is . . . busy. And this is only a contingency. I hope that we never need to use it. I hope that Kasha will become the first living thing we return from space."

"I hope she never leaves the ground," said Leonid. He glared into a corner of the room.

Nadya reached back and opened the door. She gripped Leonid by the shoulder and led him out.

"Thank you, Chief Designer," she said.

He nodded. "Please send Mishin and Bushuyev in on your way out."

He heard the outer door open and shut. God, he was tired. He opened his eyes to discover Mishin and Bushuyev in front of him. The Chief Designer shuffled through the papers on his desk until he found the report on the heat shield.

"I don't have time to read this," he said. "Tell me what it says."

"Nothing new," said one of them.

"What will it take to get a report on the heat shield that does tell me something new?"

"A miracle," said the other.

"That's all you can offer? A prayer? To what god?"

The Chief Designer felt heat rise to his face. He flung the report toward the wall beside his desk. The papers fluttered apart and drifted down. He had wanted the report to smack against the wall. He wanted the satisfaction of the impact. He let out an inarticulate scream, like the roar of a bear.

"I'll beat all of you with a stick. I'll beat you until nobody will be able to recognize your face for how bad I've beaten it." The Chief Designer was standing, leaning across his desk toward Mishin and Bushuyev, thrusting his fist into the air to punctuate every word.

"I'm fifty years old," said Mishin or Bushuyev—one was fifty and the other only thirty-seven, but the Chief Designer always forgot which was which. "This is not the time to be threatening me with a stick."

The Chief Designer focused his eyes—his vision had tunneled with rage—and took two deep breaths. He hurried around his desk as quickly as his aching knees could move him and pulled Mishin and Bushuyev into an embrace.

"Forgive me, forgive me," he said. "No offense intended. I was overreacting."

He had so few friends, so few people to rely on. Why did he lose his temper with them? The General Designer had been here not long ago. There was a man worth threatening. The Chief Designer released Mishin and Bushuyev from the hug. One of them stooped to gather the papers from the floor, as if the Chief Designer's outburst had never occurred.

"Giorgi will start the centrifuge in an hour," said the other.

An hour to tackle all the reports that had been stacked again upon the Chief Designer's desk. Another countdown. He had told the General Designer that gravity was the only competition. But perhaps time was the most formidable foe of all.

THE LAST NIP of chilly morning air had been chased off. Leonid passed through the line of trees beside the dormitory to the narrow quadrangle beyond, a long strip of celadon grass, sere, crunching beneath his old training boots. He doubted that the grass would come back after each harsh winter, but it always sprouted green again. Walkways had been paved across the quadrangle at regular intervals, though there was nothing on the other side, just trees thickening into forest. Like everything else at Star City, the paths were part of some future plan. Leonid surmised that half of being a visionary was the willingness to pave paths to nowhere.

The Chief Designer was like that, leaping ahead without checking to see where he might land, never looking back, as if he could not bear the image of what was behind him. Leonid had heard some of the Chief Designer's history. Siberia, the gulag. He could see as clearly as anyone the scar on the Chief Designer's head. He had witnessed more than most how the Chief Designer gritted his teeth, the real ones on top against the artificial ones on the bottom. The fake teeth, worn half away, had to be replaced once a year. Was it enough that the Chief Designer felt guilt, that it ground him down, that it had him awake and working hours before every dawn?

Tsiolkovski had told them over and over again that all their sacrifices were for the good of the Motherland. The loss of their homes, the long hours of training, the endless studying, the separation from their twins, and eventually the twins' deaths. Before he left, Tsiolkovski would orate speeches like sermons. Or tell stories like a grandfather. Whatever he said, it seemed impossible not to believe, whatever he ordered, impossible not to follow. That was how Leonid had always forgiven the Chief Designer, swept up like the rest of them in Tsiolkovski's fervor. With Tsiolkovski gone, though, Leonid's belief waned, and he saw in Tsiolkovski nothing more than the old gods dethroned by the Soviets, a comforting belief with no basis in reality. There was no Motherland, just the people who lived on top of it. Every sacrifice had been for a lie. All these lies to ensure the survival of another, grander lie. Leonid was tired of pretending.

Nadya had followed him outside, but now wandered on her own toward the far end of the quadrangle. Whenever she came to one of the paved paths, she paused before it, looking down as if at a creek, and then jumped across. Far as she could jump, certainly farther than Leonid, she could not quite make it to the other side. Perhaps if she had taken a running start, but she never seemed bothered by coming up short. Leonid could not understand the rules of her game, assuming there were rules at all.

The dry grass crackled behind him. Ignatius entered his peripheral vision, head craned up at the sky, hands thrust in the pockets of her leather jacket. She stopped at Leonid's side.

"It's too hot for this," she said.

"Take it off."

"Your proposition lacks subtlety."

"You never seemed concerned with propriety."

Ignatius lifted her arms without removing her hands from the pockets, spreading the jacket like the wings of a crow, the fur collar a tuft of feathers. She turned one of the wings to her face and inspected the faded red lining.

"It's a kind of uniform, yes?" she said. "It suits what I do."

"Harassing me?"

"I was speaking of my job. Harassing you is a hobby."

Nadya leapt over the last path, far down the quadrangle. She was shrunk by the distance, just a blur of motion against the trees. She stood there, glancing around, as if she did not know what to do now that the task of leaping paths was complete.

"She's like a child sometimes," said Ignatius.

"It was never intended that she become an adult."

"Children are at once much easier and much more difficult to control."

"What, we're children to you? And to the Chief Designer?"

"Yes, but to each of us in our own way. The Chief Designer loves you all like flesh and blood. I, on the other hand, am just a nanny. Yes, I may care for you, but I don't care for you enough to take care of you without getting paid."

"A rather bourgeois sentiment coming from an instrument of the Party."

"Payment isn't always in the form of money."

"What then?"

"The Chief Designer works for pride. Mars out of regret. Nadya because she knows nothing else. And you? You work for duty. Duty to your brother, to your grandmother, to Tsiolkovski, maybe even to the Chief Designer."

"Duty? Half of those you listed are dead, one abandoned us long ago, and the last is responsible for the death of the first. I'm the one who is owed, not the other way around."

"Kasha, then."

Leonid looked at her. Her lips turned up in the faintest of smiles, eyes narrowed, an expression between mirth and stern serious-ness. It was the look she always used to silence him, as if she knew more than him and always would. Nanny, indeed.

Leonid waved his hand, brushing her expression aside. Today it would not work.

"It doesn't seem that she has much longer to be with us," he said. "If duty is what drives me, then I'm soon to be without motivation of any sort."

He turned back to the dormitory and took a step in that direction. Ignatius's hand darted from her pocket and gripped him by the sleeve. Still holding him, she orbited to his front, inches from his face. All the mirth had drained from her expression.

"Whatever you're thinking, know one thing: If the Chief Designer is exposed, it's not just him that will suffer. It's you and Nadya, Mars, Yuri, Valentina. Mishin and Bushuyev. Everyone in the whole damn program." She gestured to several figures walking down the path toward the centrifuge. "It'll be like Stalin all over again, except directed specifically against the only people you know."

"Exposed for what?" asked Leonid. His mind raced back over their conversation. He had said too much, admitting the deepest secret of the space program to Ignatius. He had been upset, and she disarmed him with feigned kindness, tricked him into confiding in her. She hadn't even needed to drug him like the Americans in London. Ignatius had expressed no surprise, though. Even before Leonid had admitted anything, she mentioned his brother. She knew. She had known all along. A wash of panic swept through his stomach.

She smiled again. "Leonid. I'm not an idiot. Just as you know that my job entails more than Glavlit, more than writing articles for newspapers, so, too, I know that there's more to the space program than the public, even Khrushchev, will ever suspect."

"What will you do about it?"

"The same as I've always done. Ensure that the articles I write celebrate Soviet glory. I'm not a threat to you. The Chief Designer is scared of me, and I suppose he should be. But it's in my best interest that he succeed because it's in the best interest of the Party."

"How long have you known?"

"There was no specific day, but one can't remain near something without coming to understand the inner workings." She released his arm.

Nadya, still distant, retraced her path, walking backward, like a film played in reverse. She took a short, comical hop at one of the paths. Stumbling back, she seemed about to fall, but quickly righted herself. She shuffled backward through the dry grass.

"What about her?" asked Leonid. "Do you understand Nadya? I've spent more time with her than anyone but would never claim to know what goes on inside her head."

"She's an exception. I've found that the best things are always exceptions."

"And me?"

"You, Leonid, are the rising of the sun. The chiming of a clock. The churning tides."

"Predictable?"

"But who's complaining?"

Nadya hopped backward again.

THE CENTRIFUGE SWUNG into its first loping revolution. The metal bulb that held Giorgi capped the end of a tapering tube, several meters across even at its narrow end, the fat end secured to a great metal cylinder at the axis. The whole contraption had been painted the same sickly green they used for rockets. The Chief Designer never knew where that paint had come from, or who had chosen it. One day he'd walked to the assembly facility, and found the first R-7 already painted. And then it turned up coating equipment at

Star City. The centrifuge even looked a little like a rocket lain on its side. Grinding gears in the rectangular base pinched out a low whine. The pitch lifted and faded and then went silent, replaced with a toneless rush of air.

The Chief Designer watched from the observation room, separated by a pane of glass that shuddered when the centrifuge's capsule hurled by. He flinched a little each time, expecting the glass to shatter. The worry was not unfounded. During the centrifuge's first test, the original window had burst apart, propelling a shard all the way through the operator's wrist. The new glass, the Chief Designer had been guaranteed, would not shatter even under the force of a bullet.

Mishin and Bushuyev sat at the console today, one of them incrementally twisting the black knob that controlled the speed of the spin and the other monitoring Giorgi's vital signs, which were spit out on several strips of paper, squiggled lines that meant near nothing to the Chief Designer. A mechanical beep marked each beat of Giorgi's heart. The beat stayed constant even as the g-forces reached what must have been an uncomfortable level. The metal of the centrifuge groaned, as if to make up for Giorgi's silence.

The Chief Designer leaned down and spoke into the microphone, "You're doing well, Giorgi."

The speaker filled with a heavy pulled breath.

Giorgi said, "Mishin, Bushuyev? Is that all you have?"

One of them twisted the knob a quarter turn to the right. The change in speed did not seem like much to the Chief Designer, but as when launching a rocket, he was not in the thing itself, where he was sure the experience was different. He wondered what other jobs were like his, where one never experienced the final product. Even generals had once been soldiers themselves.

"Much better," said Giorgi. The words sounded forced, but the lines on his readouts bounced in a steady pattern.

Another revolution and another. The door to the observation room clicked shut, and Ignatius was standing over the console, next to the Chief Designer.

"I didn't hear you enter," said the Chief Designer.

"I didn't wish to distract you."

"And yet here you are."

Several more revolutions, the centrifuge stretching into a green blur. The Chief Designer and Ignatius watched in silence, their heads turning in unison to follow the motion of the capsule. Ignatius shook her head once as if she were dizzy.

"I'm taking Nadya and Leonid," she said. "They'll go on a planetarium tour. The major cities. Also to two or three towns where mobile planetariums have been set up. Have you seen the mobile planetariums? They're quite brilliant. Everything fits into a truck."

"I need Nadya and Leonid here," said the Chief Designer.

"All they ever do is care for the dogs, and now you have a team of veterinarians on hand all day and night."

"They have other duties."

"If I'm not mistaken, Leonid is currently sitting on a bench in the quadrangle. While I'm sure this is essential to Star City's operations, surely someone else can take over for a few weeks."

"Is he not entitled to a moment of rest?"

"You said he has duties."

The Chief Designer took the few steps to the back of the observation room. Ignatius followed.

"I don't believe you're actually a writer," said the Chief Designer, "but with the way you twist words, you should be."

"I could write stories like Tsiolkovski. Adventures in outer space."

"You shouldn't joke about his stories. Most of us in Star City are here because we read them in our youth."

"I don't joke, Chief Designer. I read them, as well. Why do you think this assignment was given to me?"

"Certainly not for your personality."

"Who's joking now?"

The Chief Designer tapped a finger on his scar, the widest, deepest part in the middle.

"There's no way I can stop you from taking Nadya and Leonid?"

"You could try, but I have all the leverage and you have none."

"There's very little that I do have. And now you take away two of the only people I can rely on."

"Just for a short time."

"Time is another thing that I lack."

Ignatius reached into the pocket of her coat and pulled out a small square of paper. She held it up and inspected the front, appraising it like a jewel, and then flipped it in her fingers to face the Chief Designer. It was a photograph of Khrushchev's dog, tiny and brown, the hair hanging off its ears twice as long as the ears themselves.

"If one were to need a dog quite similar to this one," said Ignatius, "wouldn't it help to search in several cities instead of just Moscow? Nadya and Leonid will only be busy for a few hours at the planetariums. I don't care what else they do while we travel."

He inspected her as he might a new component for a rocket, trying to ascertain from her appearance alone exactly how the complex machinery inside might work. "You're helping me?"

"I'm talking, Chief Designer. Only talking."

"Thank—"

"Stop. There's nothing else to say."

She reached into her coat's other pocket and pulled out a stack of papers that had been rolled into a tube. Unrolling them, she handed the papers to the Chief Designer. They were marked at the top with the insignia of OKB-52. A brief abstract in the middle of the first page described what was to follow. The Chief Designer started to skim it, got halfway through, and then stopped to start over at the beginning. It was a report on the status of the General Designer's ablative heat shield. Flipping through the pages, the Chief Designer found what he was looking for, a simple line graph that showed the shield's performance through a range of temperatures. He tracked his finger along the x-axis of the graph until he found a particular number. If the graph was accurate, and if he was reading it correctly, then the General Designer's heat shield worked. It could return a capsule safely through the atmosphere.

"Where did you get this?" asked the Chief Designer. He retraced the graph with his finger.

"Why do you always ask questions you know I won't answer?" She looked up and to a corner of the room. "What's that noise?"

A high-pitched tone came from the direction of the centrifuge, modulating up and down.

"Is something broken?" asked Ignatius.

Mishin and Bushuyev laughed. The Chief Designer stepped to the console and turned a silver knob next to the speaker. The tone increased in volume.

"Giorgi's whistling," said the Chief Designer. "He should barely be able to breathe, but he whistles to show us that he's fine."

"I don't recognize the tune."

"I think it's 'Korobeiniki.' At least how 'Korobeiniki' would sound if you had a train parked on your chest while you whistled it."

"I think I prefer this version," said Ignatius.

A timer on the console dinged. Mishin and Bushuyev adjusted knobs on the console, clicked metal switches from up to down.

New creaks and moans came from the machine as it swept by, each revolution slower than the last. The capsule crept around the circumference on the final turn, lurching to a stop in front of the gate. Giorgi whistled through the end of the tune, and then coughed into the microphone.

"We're done?" he asked.

"For today," said the Chief Designer into the microphone, "unless you have another verse."

## Georgiu-Dezh, Russia—1964

The last time Leonid was in Georgiu-Dezh, some fifteen years ago, it had been called Liski. He did not remember anything specific about the city, just a sense of its enormity. But now, as the train neared the station, he realized his memory was incorrect.

The train tracks had cut through cultivated fields, grains whipping in the wind, straight lines of sugar beet stalks. Once, a field of sunflowers appeared, each angled in the same direction, lit up as if they were giving the light and the sun receiving it. The Chief Designer and everyone at Star City thought themselves special, but these flowers had reached the sky long ago. Sometimes a silo poked up in the distance, gray and indistinct, like a primitive rocket. Sometimes the steep peaked roof of a barn showed above the stalks of grain.

Georgiu-Dezh's buildings rose barely higher than that, a few stories at most. The bulk of the town consisted of houses crammed right up against each other, some even sharing chimneys. The train slowed. A horse drew a carriage away from the train station. A carriage! The roads were paved with loose stones, if they were paved at all. The only structures of any significance were a factory, several kilometers away, its stacks lofting like monuments, heaving out black smoke, and an old *sobor*, white-walled, the four onion domes on the corners shimmering blue, the one in the center gold.

Leonid had expected a small version of Moscow, but this, this was barely a city at all, just a group of people who all happened to settle in the same place.

The wheels pinched out a final screech, and the train halted in front of a long platform, the wood of the planks gray with age. A boxy ticket booth made of the same wood sprouted from the platform. A long, low warehouse stretched parallel to the tracks, sections of its roof patched with mismatched shingles. Leonid shut his eyes, trying to bring the reality of this place, Georgiu-Dezh, into harmony with his memory of Liski. That was a boy's memory, a boy who had never been outside his tiny mountain village, who had never seen any human thing taller than a hut. Then came Moscow, shattering his idea of scale. And then when he watched Nadya launch, the other Nadya, the power of the rocket diminished even a mighty city to a speck.

Several men clustered on the platform, shifting back and forth, glancing at the door of one train car, then the next, then the next. They wore fine suits, or what passed for fine in a town such as this, the kind of suit bought on their one trip to Moscow years ago, now too small in the waist, too heavy for the weather, the color faded.

The first passengers disembarked, locals who headed straight-away through the gates into the outskirts of the city. Then came visitors, taking two or three deliberate steps away from the train before pausing, looking around as if for a familiar landmark, finding none, and only then moving on. Last came the families, parents herding packs of half-wild children, like trying to contain an explosion.

A hand on his shoulder drew Leonid's attention away from the window. He had almost forgotten that Ignatius was there, and Nadya, too. The whole trip had passed in near silence.

"Let's go," said Ignatius, "before they start loading the next set of passengers."

Leonid had no bags, just the coat to his uniform, which he flipped on and shrugged over his shoulders. The medals clinked together. He had forgotten some of their names and made up his own, like The Soviet Order of Exploding Stars and Little Metal Lenin Face. He followed Ignatius and Nadya outside.

The same several men were still on the platform, glancing from car to car with frantic energy. When Nadya stepped through the door, they let out a collective sigh. They were the greeting party, probably the mayor and a party representative and then other city officials with unclear titles. Leonid drew himself away from the window. He was the last person off the train, save the conductor, who leaned out the side of the engine, fanning himself with his cap.

Nadya, Ignatius, and Leonid lined up facing the greeters, the oldest of whom snapped a quick salute. Surely an old soldier, one who had seen real fighting. Leonid had learned to recognize combat veterans by the sad but respectful way they looked at his uniform. Their eyes were always drawn down to the fabric, as if it were woven from memory itself. This particular veteran focused on the epaulets, always looking just to either side of Leonid's face.

The shortest of the men, wearing a too-small felt bowler, stepped forward and spread his arms.

"Greetings," he said, "and welcome to Georgiu-Dezh! I'm Mayor Osinov. And this is . . ."

The Mayor listed off names that Leonid forgot even as he heard them. Instead, he named the men as he had his medals; there was Bear Beard and The Bespectacled Twig and Browncoat, the old soldier. Out of respect for his position, Leonid let the mayor just be *Mayor*.

But god, the Mayor was a talker. After the introductions, he babbled on, not allowing Ignatius time to introduce herself. He explained the lodging situation for the evening and now seemed to be regaling them with the whole history of the city, even prehistory, starting with the nomadic tribes that used to live here during the Ice Age. The Mayor spoke an excited sentence that ended with ". . . mastodon!" He took a breath. Ignatius jumped forward.

"Thank you so much for greeting us in person. The official dinner's tonight, yes? After our cosmonauts visit the planetarium?" She shook each man's hand in turn. "For now, could you please take us to our rooms? I'm afraid Leonid never sleeps on trains. Though he's too proud to admit it, he could probably use a nap."

She forced out an artificial laugh. Leonid did not trust such a laugh, but it seemed enough for the greeters, who joined her in laughing, all but the Mayor, who frowned, obviously ready to share more stories that he would now have to wait all the way until evening to tell.

Leonid took two strong strides forward, stopping directly before the Mayor. He shook the Mayor's hand.

"Thank you, Mayor," said Leonid. "I look forward to spending time with you at dinner this evening."

The Mayor beamed, stammering in response, "Yes, yes. Of course. Yes."

One of the men, Bear Beard, ushered Nadya, Ignatius, and Leonid in the direction of the hotel, leaving the other three men to linger on the platform. Ignatius halted and turned back.

"Excuse me," she shouted over the clamor of the train yard. "Does this city have many stray dogs?"

THE HOTEL ROOM was barely nicer than the dormitories at Star City, which the cosmonauts referred to as *the gulag*, at least when the

Chief Designer and the engineers of his generation were not around. Many of the engineers had spent time in actual gulags, and the rest had seen friends and family sent there, never to return. It was a joke in poor taste, yes, but the cosmonauts were doomed to the same fate. It was about more than just the shoddy construction and limited amenities of the dormitories.

Leonid sat on the creaking bed, loosening his tie and unbuttoning his collar. The room sweltered. The window was open, but no breeze entered, just the creeping heat. Leonid slipped off his jacket and discarded it on the other side of the bed. The battered armoire in the corner had no hangers inside.

Ignatius had deposited Leonid and Nadya in the hotel and then left, saying she would be back in an hour. Had it been an hour already? Leonid wore a watch but had neglected to wind it for months. Since the day of his brother's launch. He wished he had brought a book. Giorgi was always recommending things to read, to Leonid and all the other cosmonauts, but no one ever took his advice. Besides the many manuals written by the engineers for training, the cosmonauts never read anything. None of them except Giorgi, and he seemed able to do everything all at once. Did Liski have a bookstore? Wait, the city was now called what? Did Georgiu-Dezh have a bookstore? Did the town called Liski have a bookstore that had since closed, so that one of the names had a bookstore but the other did not?

Leonid stood and walked to the window for the dozenth time. He was on the second floor. Below him was a narrow lane, sunwashed sky above. And before him, a stone wall, so close it seemed he could reach across and touch it. It was farther away than it seemed.

The door opened, and Nadya came in without knocking. She

joined Leonid by the window. To someone seeing them from behind, it would appear as if they were gazing out at a great scene beyond, as if the window overlooked a breathtaking vista.

"It's better than my view," said Nadya.

"You've found a grayer wall than this?"

"My window faces the city. But it's not really a city. It's a town pretending to be a city. The buildings are covered with city-like façades, and the people wear clothes copied from Moscow. It's like a child aping older siblings."

"I was the eldest, if only by minutes."

"Who did you copy?"

"The men of the village, I suppose."

"Maybe our individual personalities are just the areas in which we failed to perfectly copy someone else, all individuality a mistake."

"But if we mistake the mistakes of the previous generation, then perhaps we right them. Maybe we're exactly like the people that the people we tried to emulate tried to emulate."

Nadya left his side and sat on the end of the bed, directly on top of his jacket.

"These beds are terrible," she said.

"It doesn't help that you're sitting on my medals."

"I have more than you." She ran her hand along the line of them. They clicked together with a pathetic, tinny sound. She shifted on the bed, but did not move off Leonid's jacket. She grasped one of her medals in particular. "This one is from the French."

"Ignatius lets you wear it?"

"I doubt there's anyone who can identify all of them. I received a ribbon once as a child. If I still had it, I would wear it, too."

The door opened and Ignatius entered without knocking.

"Yes, please," said Leonid, "come in! Come in!"

"It's time to go." She glanced around the room, pausing at the open armoire. "Where's your jacket?"

Nadya raised herself off the bed just enough to slide the jacket out from under her. She held it up for Ignatius to see. Ignatius took the jacket, shook it once like fluffing a pillow, and tossed it across the room to Leonid. The medals clicked together.

UP CLOSE, GEORGIU-DEZH'S *sobor* rose to an impressive height, the main golden dome visible only from the underside, its point implied but unseen. The four smaller domes were set half as high in the ordinal directions. A gray base surrounded the whole church like a fortification. The walls above it shone so white in the sun that Leonid had to squint when he faced them. Out front stood a statue of Lenin, upturned hand held out as if in offering. Leonid had seen old men in a Paris park posed the same way, feeding stale bits of bread to birds from their palms.

A panel truck, left over from the war and as old as Leonid at least, was parked in front of the church. The drab army green had been painted over with a mural taking up the whole side. The mural depicted, in the flat style typical of propaganda posters, a rocket launching into space, arcing back toward the center of the frame. From the bottom corner emerged the figure of a woman, lifting the smaller figure of a man to the heavens in the red wake of the rocket.

Nadya regarded the truck from a distance, and then stepped close, tracing the lines of the illustration only centimeters away with her eyes.

"Giorgi's paintings are better," she said.

Ignatius ran her hand along the surface of the truck. "These things are produced in factories. A line of painters, each with a single brush and an individual color. The first painter paints his marks, and then the next. The whole process takes only minutes."

She flicked her fingernail against the metal siding. The interior of the truck resounded with a long, lone ping.

"I don't understand art," she said.

The back doors of the truck sprung open from the inside, and a woman's face poked out, perfectly parallel to the ground.

"What was that?" asked the woman.

"We're here," said Ignatius.

The woman's head pulled straight back into the truck. A moment later she scrambled out into the open. Her hair was a plaited mess, strands tangled so intricately it almost seemed intentional. Her coat, dusty gray, bore wrinkles all across it, as if it had only just then been unballed from the back of a closet.

"Is it already time?" she asked. "I slept in the truck last night."

"It's almost evening," said Ignatius. "Apparently you slept all night and day."

"Astronomers use the term *night* how you use *day*, and likewise the inverse. My work begins when the sun sets. My day is marked by stars."

The astronomer looked behind Ignatius to where Nadya and Leonid stood, and took in a deep breath. Her mouth dropped more and more open. She stumbled forward, bumping into Ignatius and then around her. The astronomer raised her hand, fingers outstretched in an unnatural way, like in the ancient portraits Leonid had seen in the Louvre. The astronomer rested her hand against Nadya's face, letting her fingers conform to the contours of her chin and cheek. The astronomer smiled, showing a set of yellowed teeth.

"And now the stars have come to me," she said. "Tell me, what did you see?"

Nadya grasped the astronomer's wrist between the tip of her finger and the fat of her thumb and drew the astronomer's hand down.

"I saw the same as you," said Nadya, "only closer."

Ignatius smiled at that.

"Come, astronomer," she said. "It's nearing dark. Introduce us to your planetarium before the crowds arrive."

The sun had dipped low enough to shoot the sky through with orange. The white walls of the church went from blinding to warm, like hot glowing coals. The domes, shimmering before like agitated water, now seemed coated in melted glass.

"Yes, yes, of course," said the astronomer.

She scuttled back to the truck, and turned a hand crank sprouting from the frame beside the back doors. The clacks and clanks of chains echoed from inside. The whole muraled side of the truck, hinged at the top, began to flip open. The astronomer kept cranking until the panel was at a forty-five degree angle above vertical, like an awning hung upside down. The underside of the panel was painted flat black. Leonid thought that the effect was not much different from the factory-produced image on the opposite side.

The astronomer began to unload items from the back of the truck. She set up a telescope—similar to the one Giorgi would pull out on clear evenings at Star City, but even larger—perched atop a tripod of thick wood. Next came a short stick, which Leonid guessed was simply a pointer. And lastly, the astronomer lifted out a small black dome and set it on the ground under the middle of the open panel. A cable ran from the back of the device to the truck, where it disappeared through the wall into the cab. The only thing left in the back was a bedroll, still crumpled from the astronomer's afternoon somnolence.

"There!" exclaimed the astronomer, clapping her hands as if crashing cymbals. "All done."

"That's it?" asked Ignatius.

"What more do you want?"

"I had expected something . . . more elaborate."

Nadya looked through the telescope's eyepiece, but did not adjust the focus. All she could have seen was the blurry sky, now sunk to purple. She turned the telescope to face Ignatius.

"What are you doing?" asked Ignatius.

"Your surprise is a rare and precious thing. I want to see it up close."

Leonid laughed, and then kept laughing and could not stop. The others watched him until he quieted.

"Shut it, Leonid," said Ignatius, her face stuck halfway between scowl and smile.

Leonid convulsed with a few final laughs, but held them silent and inside. He kept staring at Ignatius and kept smiling until she turned away.

"What's next?" asked Ignatius.

The astronomer answered, "Now we wait for dark."

THE FIRST of the crowds arrived even before the sun finished setting. These were farmers and their families, come into town specifically for the demonstration. They wore clothes the color of the earth, the same color as their deep-tanned skin. Each had donned one article or accessory that looked fancy and brand new, as if they had divided the household's one nice outfit among the whole family. A bright white shirt here, a necktie there, a scarf, a sash, a watch colored artificially gold. These farming families stayed huddled close together. The youngest among them, children with the gnarled hands of the elderly, stared up at the church and the other tall buildings and never lowered their gazes to the familiar ground.

Next came the residents of the town itself, factory workers and the Party-appointed managers who supervised them. Leonid was surprised to see that they dressed barely better than the farmers, in simple, shapeless clothes, the kind he remembered from his own childhood in Bohdan. The people of Moscow had adopted fashions more like those in London and Paris, not quite so flashy, but nowhere near as subdued as here. Standing all together outside the church, these people seemed a gathering of monks.

The crowd continued to grow, the first trickle of people inflating to a steady flow, as if each side street were a branch of a river delta emptying into a sea around the old church. A sea of tired faces, but Leonid noticed excitement, too. And not just from the children, more and more of whom were being hoisted onto a parent's shoulders for a better view. The people buzzed, like the engineers in the bunker before a launch. Leonid saw his own face throughout the crowd on cheap pins and buttons, the *znachki* that had been popular since Nadya's launch. One little girl had a dozen versions of Leonid's face stuck to her threadbare blouse. Plenty of the adults in the audience had similar displays, some with pins for each cosmonaut, arranged like the mural Giorgi had painted at Star City.

The astronomer reached into the truck and pulled out a microphone. A wire ran from it back into the truck. Two speakers were mounted from the underside of the open panel.

"Good evening," said the astronomer. The speakers squealed. She reached back into the truck and twisted a knob and the feedback silenced.

More children were hoisted onto more shoulders, joining the statue of Lenin as the highest things this side of the church. *Little monuments,* Leonid thought. How many people were here? Two hundred? Leonid would ask Ignatius after the event.

"We're here this evening," said the astronomer, "to explore the cosmos. Soviet science has exposed the whole universe to us, and now we can bring it to you, the Soviet people. We can fit all of creation into this truck, our planetarium."

She reached back to the truck and flipped a switch next to the knob that had controlled the volume. The domed device on the ground emitted light through pinprick holes, casting constellations onto the black-painted underside of the open panel. Like the opposite of a film screen, Leonid thought. A spattering of applause came from the crowd, soft chatter.

"We now know," continued the astronomer, "that the stars are not dots of light on the firmament, but suns like our own, impossibly distant. But not as impossible as we once thought. I'm joined today by two people who have reached for the very stars and touched them. In exploring the cosmos this evening, we'll be joined by two of our great Soviet heroes, two of our cosmonauts, the first and also the most recent."

The applause came in earnest, and Leonid raised his hand into a hearty wave. He did not need to think about it, the wave just happened. He wondered if his arm would start waving on its own anytime he heard clapping. Pavlov's cosmonaut.

Ignatius nudged Nadya, who shuffled forward and waved, too. The motion was never natural with her. Or maybe it was completely natural, while Leonid's was absolutely false. It just appeared, to anyone looking, to be the other way around. Regardless, Nadya's awkwardness had never hurt her. In fact, it seemed to endear her all the more to the public.

Leonid lowered his arm and stepped back and Nadya did the same. The applause trickled out.

The astronomer reached into the truck and flipped another switch. The dome started turning, shifting the fake stars projected on the black screen.

"Ancient people," she said, "used to invent gods to explain the movement of the stars. They could only see themselves as the stationary point around which the whole universe spun. It took but a few simple observations to disprove this, to show that it's the movement of the Earth that makes the stars seem to shift so rapidly. Yes, the stars move, too, and so fast you can hardly imagine, but they're so very, very far away that their motion is imperceptible except when measured over a long, long time. Think of how nearby trees seem to rush past the window of a train, while a distant mountain barely moves at all. Stars are millions of times more distant than that mountain."

A blue-gray dot, larger than the other simulated stars, crept up from the right corner of the screen. When the dot reached the center, a click came from the projector, and its motion ceased. The astronomer whipped her pointer up, rapping it against the metal screen.

"This is Saturn, one of nine planets that orbit around our sun. Tonight, I'll be showing you the real Saturn through our telescope"—she tapped the telescope with her pointer—"and we'll even be able to see the planet's majestic ring system. There are many of you this evening, so while I show each of you in turn, I'll ask that my comrade cosmonauts answer your questions."

She instructed those who wished to look through the telescope to form a line, and then handed the microphone to Nadya. Nadya inspected the microphone as if it were an unfamiliar thing. She held it up, pressing it against her lips.

"Hello," she said, almost swallowing the microphone. Her voice boomed from the speakers, followed by a brief electric whine. She handed the microphone to Leonid.

"What would you like to know?"

Hands shot up throughout the crowd.

People asked the usual questions: What was it like in outer space? What does weightlessness feel like? How is that food you eat that comes from tubes? Were you scared? To this last question, the answer was carefully scripted: *Absolutely not.*

Leonid addressed most of the questions, holding the microphone over to Nadya from time to time. Her answers were always brief, almost curt.

Leonid pointed to an older woman—from a farm by the look of her—standing in the middle of the crowd. She had kept her hand raised the whole time, even when Nadya and Leonid were answering the questions of others.

"I read the newspaper," said the woman. She paused, as if that were all she planned to say. Leonid started to respond, but she continued, "I've read every article about you cosmonauts."

She paused again. This time Leonid waited. The child peering through the telescope exclaimed into the silence, "I can see Saturn's moons!" A ripple of laughter passed through the crowd.

The old woman continued, "I lost both my sons in the war."

"I'm sorry," said Leonid. "I lost my father." This was both true and part of the fake history the Chief Designer and Tsiolkovski had crafted for him.

"Then how can you say in interviews that there's no god? That there's no heaven? When they used to let us come to church here, the priest always told us about heaven. My mother always told me that if I was good I'd go to heaven. And that's how I raised my boys. What's the point of being good if what you say is true?"

"Science has explained things better than religion ever did," said Leonid, quoting directly from the list of potential questions and answers Ignatius had made him memorize.

"But where are my boys?" asked the woman, her voice heavy with pleading. "They were good, good boys. Where do the good ones go?"

There was another line Leonid was supposed to say at this point, but it caught in his throat. He stammered. His brother, the good one, literally gone to the heavens. He imagined that this woman was his own grandmother, begging for answers from the soldiers after Tsiolkovski had taken him and his brother away. He said several more disconnected syllables, unable to string them into words.

Nadya slipped the microphone from Leonid's hand.

"If good only occurs because of a desire for reward and a fear of punishment," she said, "then good isn't worth much. Your boys were good, yes, and you spent good time with them. But they're gone. Not even the saints painted on the *sobor* walls will be seen again. Except as paintings. Good is not staring at paintings wishing for them to come to life. Good is action or deed or sacrifice. Good is actually living life, not longing for a lost past. Not pining for a false future.

"If your god did exist, he would be coincidental, just happening to align with your own innate goodness. This god appeals to you because he exemplifies your idea of good, the same good your boys possessed, not because god created the idea. You create an external cause, god, when the whole time the cause was within you. You passed your own goodness onto your boys, and they in turn passed it on to others."

The woman, whose hand had remained aloft the whole time, lowered it, a motion like a collapsing building.

"I don't even have a painting of my boys," she said. "Since they took down Stalin's portrait, there are no paintings on the farm at all."

"Perhaps there should be," said Nadya.

As soon as she uttered the last word, Ignatius was there, snatching away the microphone. Ignatius thanked the crowd and explained that Nadya and Leonid had been traveling all day and needed to retire. The crowd applauded, a subdued wave of sound cresting from front to back. In the silence that followed, a little girl at the telescope asked, "How many moons does Saturn have?"

"We've discovered nine so far," said the astronomer, "though there are likely quite a few more. Look hard, and maybe you'll be the one to find them."

THE SUN HAD NOT yet found a way to creep through the narrow lane and into the hotel window when a knock came on Leonid's door. He lay in bed hoping it would not come again but knowing that it would. *Knock knock knock knock.*

He rolled onto his back and shucked off the sheets. His legs were pale, the muscles soft. There had been no training since before the launch. While he had always rued the morning runs on the dorm's treadmill, seeing how quickly his body lost its shape made him appreciate them. Maybe he would run this morning. *Knock knock knock knock.* Dropping his legs over the side of the high bed, Leonid slid to a standing position. No, there would be no running.

The old armoire stood in the corner of the room, overlapping part of the window. Pocks and dings speckled the dark wood, scratches like streaking meteors. The hinges chirped as Leonid opened the door. Inside, his uniform draped over the rod. The note from the Americans, with the address in Odessa, had slipped halfway out of the uniform's inside pocket. He didn't know why he had kept it or why he hid it in a place so close to his heart. There would never be a chance for him to go, but it felt like a possibility, an alternative in a life that had never before presented him with alternatives. He pushed the note all the way back into the pocket. Dangling next to the uniform was a robe, dingy white with pink trim, a color Leonid suspected had once been crimson. He slipped the robe off the rod, in the process spilling his tie to the floor. He pushed the tail of the tie back inside with his big toe and shut the armoire. The hinges chirped.

Leonid opened the door to the hallway, still cinching the robe around him. Ignatius leaned against the frame, dressed in casual clothes, a pair of sunglasses on the top of her head like a tiara.

"Did I wake you?" she said.

"I thought we didn't leave until this afternoon. Unless I slept all night and through the morning."

Ignatius crouched down and tugged at the hem of Leonid's robe, closing an open V that revealed his thigh almost all the way up to the hip.

"Can you try not to be half-naked when you answer the door?" said Ignatius.

"What time is it?"

"The clock in my room doesn't work."

"You wear a watch."

She held up her arm and inspected it. A large watch, one designed for a man, always took up the whole of her wrist. A blue face set in a silver frame, red star at the top and the white outline of a submarine at the bottom. It was the naval version of a watch Leonid had seen many of the army officers wear at Star City. Leonid doubted that Ignatius had ever seen the inside of a submarine.

"It's six," said Ignatius.

Leonid inspected her clothes, a blouse of provincial style, similar to what the women wore to the planetarium last night. Her hair was pulled up and secured with pins. Her eyeliner, usually dark and flared at the corners, had been applied in a more subdued fashion.

Leonid scratched his head. The hair stuck out in all directions. Ignatius grinned.

"What do you want?" asked Leonid.

"I'm here for what you want."

"You don't seem to have breakfast with you."

"I thought we might tour the city. See what dogs there are to see."

Leonid felt the grogginess flow from his face like a blush in reverse.

"Dogs?"

"A city like this is sure to have quite a variety."

"I'll get dressed," said Leonid.

"Perhaps a bit of bathing first. We've been traveling for two days."

Leonid pinched a lock of his hair and rubbed it between thumb and finger. It was slick with grease.

"And don't wear your uniform," said Ignatius.

"It's all I brought with me."

"Check the top drawer of the dresser."

Leonid stepped back into the room and opened the dresser, a piece of furniture in no way matching the armoire except in the damage to its surface. A change of clothes lay neatly folded there, plain pants and a simple shirt. A pair of worn brown boots, though worn in by whom he was not sure. Atop a brimmed hat, the kind a farmer might wear, rested a pair of sunglasses, sleek and modern and out of place with the rest of the outfit.

Leonid held the sunglasses up to Ignatius. "The sun is barely out yet."

"But it will be," she said.

LEONID THOUGHT THEY LOOKED a ridiculous trio, strutting down the unfamiliar streets in their unfamiliar clothes, outfits that while they looked like what the locals wore, seemed too new, too much like a costume. Nadya wore clothes almost exactly the same as Ignatius, skirt and blouse in bland colors. All three had on sunglasses, like masks meant to hide the obvious fakeness of their personas. But no one looked at them twice.

That felt strange in itself. Nadya was still among the most famous people in the world. It was impossible for her to go anywhere in public without attracting stares. In Paris, a stranger had come up to her, taken a knee, offered flowers, and proposed. Nadya had laughed, obviously not the response the man had been hoping for. Ignatius led him away, around a corner. She returned with the bouquet and carried it with her for the rest of the day.

Leonid could not decide if being ignored made him happy or disturbed. It was peaceful, yes, but also unfamiliar. The familiar, he had learned, was comfortable in a way that peace was not.

There were few people on the streets at this hour, anyway. The early risers strolled down the middle of roads, as if daring a car to come along. Nothing was open yet, so it was unclear where these people might be going. Perhaps just for a morning walk to shake off their tired, shuffled steps before the factories opened.

"What are we going to do if we actually find a dog?" asked Nadya.

Ignatius stopped. Nadya and Leonid took a few more steps before they noticed Ignatius was no longer beside them.

"I hadn't thought of that," said Ignatius.

Leonid pinched his shirt and pulled the fabric forward. "You remembered disguises, but didn't think to bring a leash?"

"I have many responsibilities," said Ignatius, "but until now animal care has not been among them. You two keep searching. I'll go find something with which to secure a dog."

"How will you find us?" asked Nadya.

"It will be easier to find you than to find a dog, I think."

With that, Ignatius turned and walked back the way they had come, rounding the corner in the direction of the hotel.

Nadya planted her hands on her hips and looked up and down the street. "If you were a dog, where would you be?"

Leonid raised his face and closed his eyes and revolved slowly in place. "We'll know by the smell."

NADYA CAUGHT the scent first, just a whiff of rotten meat and a nutty overtone of excrement. They walked in what they thought was the direction of the odor, but it diminished. They returned to their starting point, reacquired the smell, and headed in the opposite direction. The odor grew stronger, as if the air itself putrefied. Through a lane between two old houses, their stone walls coated with black ooze, Nadya and Leonid found the source.

The land sloped down to what had once been a creek, now stagnant with garbage. Decades if not centuries of refuse, heaped several feet high in some places, had turned the whole creek bed into a junkyard. The windows on the backs of all the houses at the top of the hill were boarded up or filled in with brick. Wood-paneled outbuildings, barely more than lean-tos, bent like crippled sentries behind each house. From some of them, underneath the rear panels, a gooey slick of human waste ran down the hill in rivulets.

Leonid planted his heels with each step as he descended the

slope. He was glad to be wearing borrowed boots and not the polished shoes of his uniform. He would probably have to discard the
boots down this very hill when they left.

"I thought we were looking for dogs," said Nadya, "not dis-
eases."

"Back in the village," said Leonid, "Kasha, the original Kasha,
rooted through any pile of trash she came across. If we want to
find another dog like her, then I can't think of a better place to
look."

Nadya followed Leonid down the hill, taking cautious steps,
not as if she was concerned about slipping but like she wanted to
delay arriving at the bottom.

"If nothing else," she said, "we can find a rat and bleach it."

Leonid's feet sank into the mud at the bottom. The boots fit
loose, and he worried they would come off. He lifted his feet up
and down in place. The wet suck of each step sounded like someone vomiting. Leonid whistled, a sound like a chirping bird that
Giorgi had taught Leonid's brother how to make, so Leonid had to
learn it, too. A tin can plunked down the garbage pile to his left.
Another item, something brown and rotting, tumbled from the
pile in the same area. A large dog peered its head around a ridge of
garbage. Its fur was pure black, the exact opposite of Kasha's. It
saw Leonid, curled its lip as if to snarl, but then seemed to change
its mind. Turning its head, it barked once in the other direction.
Several more dogs emerged from amid the trash, mutts of gray and
brown, skinny more than they were sleek. The nearest, a tan-and-
white hound with long fur that went wavy at the ends, held a
cracked teacup in its mouth. The ghost of a face printed on the
cup's side still showed.

"Can you tell which one of us it is?" asked Nadya, leaning down
for a closer look.

"Mars, maybe? Hopefully none of mine have faded so much so soon."

Leonid walked down the path, surveying the mutts. They moved like fish through the sea of garbage. The tan-and-white dog dropped the teacup and followed him, and Nadya after that. The mud released his boots with wet smacks. Nadya walked on her toes. The dog was the only one that seemed to have no problem with the muck, though the long hair hanging from his legs was stained black.

"He has sad eyes," said Nadya.

She now walked alongside the dog, regarding him the way she did the animals back in Star City, the only time her usual icy expression cracked. The dog had lost most of its tail. The nub jerked back and forth, a vigorous nod.

"We can't take him with us," said Leonid.

Nadya scratched the dog behind the ears as they walked.

"Besides," said Leonid, "the last dog I brought with me to Star City is the reason we are now wading through garbage in search of another."

"Is it fair?" asked Nadya.

"Is what fair?"

"To find another dog to die in the place of Kasha. Who are we to spare one animal and condemn another?"

"It's a dumb death either way."

"You didn't answer my question."

Leonid stopped. He kicked at a brick sticking up out of the mud.

"It's like relativity," he said.

"You're an astrophysicist now?"

"Leading up to the launch, I was assigned more time with Giorgi. When he's not painting or writing poetry, he likes to read up on science. Do you know relativity?"

"You're not the only one who talks to Giorgi."

"It's good to know he lectures the rest of you, too." Leonid started walking again. "It's like how in relativity my perspective seems to dictate the very laws of the universe. As does your perspective and everyone else's. To me, the speed of light is constant, but also to you, even if we travel in opposite directions and observe the same light. Light travels in as many ways as there are eyes to see it, but at the same time travels constantly for all."

"This has what to do with dogs?"

"Relativity is both supremely individualistic and perfectly socialist. My perspective is essential, but only to me. I sometimes think that's what Marx didn't understand. Community is a myth, a convenient, perhaps essential one, but what community can there be if no two people see light the same way? So the idea of community is what lets us rationalize our selfishness as something noble, when in fact we're stuck with only our own internal logic. The math of the logic is universal. We're all looking at the same numbers, but the equation is unique for each of us."

"You *have* been talking to Giorgi. You're even starting to sound like him. But I still don't understand you."

Leonid turned and waded into the pile of garbage. He bent down and plucked up discarded items one at a time, inspecting each, and then setting them back down with care, as if he was arranging curios on a shelf.

"I'll choose the dog I like more," he said, "and I'll let the other one die. That's how the light moves from my perspective. And then I'll try to convince myself that the light moves the same for everyone else. Otherwise I would be guilty. At least if I imagine a community, we're all guilty together."

Nadya joined Leonid amid the garbage, sorting through the trash and adding to Leonid's curated collection of junk.

"Do you think the Chief Designer chose his favorite?" she asked.

"The opposite, I think. He's a man without community, one who must carry the full weight of all his guilt. He sent his favorites to die so he wouldn't feel guilty for choosing."

"So I . . ."

"You're his favorite out of all of us. Your injury saved him in a way. It saved him from having to make the decision himself. I sometimes wonder if he could have recovered from the loss of the first Vostok had it been you inside and not your sister."

Nadya cradled an object in her hands. It was clumped with mud and shapeless.

"And me," said Leonid, "I'm just the last of what was left behind."

The tan-and-white mutt edged close, snatching a splinter of blackened wood from where Leonid had balanced it. The dog sprinted away down the muddy path, other dogs emerging to bark as it passed. None of the dogs looked like Kasha. Not at all.

LEONID WALKED BAREFOOT, having chucked his boots down the hill after they had climbed back to the top. There had been no sign of Ignatius since she left in search of a leash, and not even a glimpse of a dog that could pass for Kasha, much less Khrushchev's Byelka, that little rodent of a dog, surely too frail to survive on its own, its only natural habitat a lap.

Every lane or alley they came to, he and Nadya marched down, a parade through the city's forgotten streets. The back sides of buildings blossomed with cracks in the masonry and sprouted black growths like ugly flowers. It was as if each building were actually two, one face clean and one filthy. The stray dogs stuck to the filthy side of things. Leonid had always assumed that dogs just liked trash for trash's sake, but now he suspected it was privacy they craved. He and Nadya had come across not one other person in all the alleys.

Back on one of the main streets, they passed a woman leading a boy, only five or six years old, by the hand. The woman seemed too young to be the mother, but too old to be a sibling. Leonid's own family had consisted of he and his brother, separated in age only by minutes, and he found it hard to imagine two people so far apart in age being brother and sister. He decided to think of the woman as the mother.

The child pointed at Leonid's feet and started to say something but the mother hushed him. The boy's own shoes were worn and obviously repaired in places. Leonid paused, raised one foot, and wiggled his toes. The boy giggled. The mother glowered, inspecting Leonid's face, as if trying to see around the sunglasses to the person behind the lenses. For a moment she seemed to recognize Leonid, but that expression crumpled back into pinched lips and slitted eyes. She pulled the boy along by his hand.

"There you are!" Ignatius's voice came from behind them.

She crossed the street, leading a gray dog behind her on a leash that looked to be made from torn and knotted bedsheets. Every few steps the dog would stop, straining against the leash until Ignatius's persistent tugging got it moving again. Leonid could tell from far away that it was an old dog, the pale color of its fur once something more vibrant. Its eyes drooped and its jowls sagged from a boxy snout.

Ignatius stopped and pulled the dog forward into the space before Nadya and Leonid.

"Look what I found," said Ignatius.

"Are you showing us the leash or the dog?" asked Leonid.

"The dog, of course. The first dog I came across after I found the leash was white."

"Did you come across another dog, then?" said Nadya. "Because this one is gray."

Leonid leaned down and held the back of his hand to the dog's nose to sniff. It huffed in a few snotty-sounding breaths and then licked his hand, leaving a sticky strand of mucus when it pulled away. Leonid scratched the dog's cheek, and the dog nuzzled against his hand.

"She's sweet, at least," said Leonid.

"He," said Ignatius.

"How would you know that?" asked Nadya.

"Don't be crude."

The dog hacked. The dark of its eyes was filmed over with white. When it licked its lips—a motion that seemed slowed down, the tongue some sort of limping mollusk—only a few blackened teeth could be seen still stubbornly rooted in discolored gums.

"This dog must be near dead," said Leonid.

"Isn't that a good thing?" asked Ignatius. "Don't we want a dog that's going to die soon, anyway?"

"A greater concern," said Nadya, "is that this dog looks nothing like Kasha."

"Of course he does."

"For one, Kasha is female."

"Who will be inspecting its genitals?"

"You did, apparently."

"It rolled on its back!"

"And he would never do that at Star City? But gender aside, he's the wrong color. He's too large by a considerable margin. His face has the wrong shape. His hair is short and stiff, and his tail does not curl the same way."

Ignatius looked down at the dog, appraising it. It had lain down, its flesh flowing out across the ground as if the dog were melting.

"I don't see the big difference," said Ignatius.

"I assume you didn't have pets as a child," said Leonid.

"There was a war when I grew up," she snapped. "If we had an animal we ate it."

The dog raised its head like a creaky, rusted machine.

Leonid said, "I didn't mean . . ."

"You're right," said Ignatius. "This fellow looks nothing like Kasha."

She bent down and loosened the noose of the collar she had fashioned at the end of her makeshift leash, slipping the loop over the head of the dog. He grunted.

"Go on," said Ignatius, shoving the dog on the rump.

The dog rocked in place, like a heap of the gelatinous, rehydrated food they made cosmonauts eat. Otherwise, the dog did not move at all. Ignatius sniffed the air.

"Is that smell you or the dog?" she asked. "And where are your shoes, Leonid?"

"They didn't suit me."

Ignatius consulted her watch. It looked out of place on her wrist, clashing with the drab colors of her costume.

"The train leaves in ninety minutes," she said. "I suggest we head back to the hotel so you can bathe before we depart. Otherwise they'll make us ride with the cargo."

Leonid glanced around as they walked, hoping to catch a white flash of fur in one of the lanes between buildings. But nothing in Georgiu-Dezh was white enough, not even the distant *sobor* walls, not even with the sun glaring right against them.

The small tract of land planted with the season's vegetables made it all the way through spring without showing a single sprig. The deep brown, almost black dirt of the valley had dried out to pale gray. Even the fir trees on the hillsides were losing their needles, layering the whole woods with a brittle, brown carpet. The two Leonids used to run barefoot through the forest, but now one wrong step and a needle would pierce the thin skin on the sides of their feet. What needles remained on the trees were clumped together and few, just a reminder of how the forest had once looked. The straight black trunks rose to an explosion of bare branches.

The Leonids sat on the roof of Grandmother's cottage and looked for images in the branches' tangled shapes. The younger Leonid saw fantastical things, many-spired castles and airplanes with a dozen wings and animals that could not possibly exist. The older Leonid mainly saw hands.

"Do you know what the branches remind me of most of all?" asked the younger Leonid.

"What?" asked the older.

"It's the shape of hunger. Whenever I get very hungry, when we haven't eaten much in a few days, I feel that my stomach looks tangled inside."

The older Leonid's stomach offered a faint growl at the mention of eating. He could not usually see the same things his brother saw in the trees, or in the shape of the stars at night, but hunger he understood, and it did feel very much like a ball of sticks poking at his insides.

"We'll have something to eat soon enough," said the older Leonid.

This is what Grandmother had told them days ago. To her credit, she had not specified how soon *soon* would be.

From the direction opposite the forest, the sound of voices carried from the center of the village. The Leonids crept to the peak of the roof and looked. Through the now-bare trees, they could see a dozen villagers clustered together, some of them with sacks in their hands or slung over their backs.

The older Leonid had never realized how close Grandmother's cottage was to the rest of the village. The slope of the hill and the trees had always hidden each location from view of the other. The path that led to the village twisted far to the left and then back, so the walk was longer than the actual distance between the two points. But now, through the naked trees, it was close enough that he could hear the sound of the villagers' voices if not their words.

Those voices were raised, the villagers with the sacks appearing to lecture those without. Or maybe the other way around. One man clung to a sack-laden woman by her arm until she shrugged him off and walked away, climbing the hill toward the train station. About half the villagers followed her.

The Leonids scrambled to the back of the roof, sliding on their rear ends to the edge so their feet dangled. They pushed off the roof, launching their bodies to berm. The older Leonid landed on his feet, stumbled forward, and fell to one knee. His brother landed directly into a somersault, springing to his feet at the end of one revolution. They sprinted straight through the trees and down the steep hill. At the village proper, they darted behind the row of cottages and followed the dry creek bed to the road on the other side.

With the brush shriveled to almost nothing, it was hard to stay hidden as the Leonids followed the villagers. The ruts in the dirt road, once carved as if into stone, had crumbled in on themselves. The villagers' shoes stirred up plumes of dust, each footfall emitting a low, gray shock wave. None of them spoke. On days the train would come, the banter would not stop even as the villagers loaded carts and hauled them back to the village. But the train had not visited in so long that Leonid barely remembered its sound, the rumble it sent through the mountain and the greeting hoot of its horn. He wondered if maybe one silence caused the other.

Near the train station, the Leonids hid behind a tall kalyna, the only shrub in the valley still showing green. The white flowers had just recently given way to red berries. The boys ate two or three from time to time, a tart flavor that puckered the whole mouth, but any more than that made one sick. Kasha had once eaten a whole branch-full and spent two days vomiting and shitting herself. The berries were a food that would leave one hungrier in the end than before they were eaten.

The villagers went to the other side of the small building beside the tracks, what everyone in the village called a station, though it was no more than a closet where a few unidentifiable items were kept for use by the train's engineer. The building, neglected by the village even before the train stopped coming, now teetered to the left, the bottom of the right wall pulled up and away from the platform. Rusty, bent nails filled the gap like fangs.

The Leonids left the shade of the kalyna and ran to the building and sneaked around its side. The villagers were not there. There was no sign of them within the deep forest opposite the station. The door to the building was still locked shut. The younger Leonid stepped all the way onto the platform, looked right, then left, and then jumped back.

"They're moving up the tracks," he said, pointing in the direction of the pass.

The older Leonid peeked around the building. The villagers were already a few dozen meters away, walking in a line. They moved strangely, measuring their strides to the crossties. He had done the same many times, but the gaps fit the legs of a boy better than they did an adult. The villagers' steps seemed too short, as if they did not actually want to get to where they were going.

The Leonids emerged from behind the building, crossed the platform and then the tracks, and jumped down on the other side, where the ground was several feet lower. If the villagers had looked back, they would have seen the twin domes of the Leonids' heads hovering just above the level of the tracks, but no one turned.

Even at their plodding pace, the villagers pulled farther and farther away from the Leonids, who with every step had to contend with dry brush and loose soil, twigs clawing at their arms and stones grinding at their palms as they braced themselves against the embankment. The younger Leonid pushed a long branch out of his way, and when he released it, it snapped back, the tip gashing the older Leonid across the arm. The older Leonid let out a yelp before he could clamp his mouth shut. Hot tears welled up in his eyes in response to the sting. Blood dripped from the wound, marking three long streaks down his forearm.

The younger Leonid stood on his toes to raise his eyes above the level of the embankment.

"I don't think they heard you," he said.

"How about I hear you apologize?"

"You know I'm sorry." He pulled himself up the embankment and onto the tracks. "They're far enough away not to notice us."

He reached down and offered a hand to his brother. The older Leonid went to raise his injured arm, but winced, and raised the other instead. He dug his toes into shallow pits in the pebbly soil of the embankment and hoisted himself over the edge. Ahead, the villagers were barely dashes rising above the convergence of the rails.

"We'll lose them if we don't hurry," said the older Leonid.

"All we have to do is follow the same path that they're following." The younger Leonid walked on the rail, arms spread for balance.

"Where do you think they're going?"

"The tracks only go one place. Outside the valley. Maybe they're leaving."

"If they're leaving, then they plan to return. Their sacks are empty."

"Maybe they're going to bring back food?"

The older Leonid did not answer, quickening his pace, taking the crossties two at a time. His brother struggled to keep up while still balancing on the rail. For all they had explored the forest of the valley, they had never followed the tracks this far. The angle grew steeper as the tracks approached the pass, a dimple in the even rim of the valley's trees.

The pass was the only way into the valley that did not require difficult, dangerous climbing. In all other directions, the forest gave out to sheer rock. The Leonids often wondered to each other who had discovered the valley in the first place, and once discovered, why they chose to stay. Were they hiding from the rest of the world? If so, why had they allowed the railroad to be built? Did they just stay for the good soil, so fertile it always produced many times more than the villagers needed for themselves? Not anymore, though. The soldiers came and took away the last decent crops.

Now the only things to come from the ground were a few pathetic root vegetables that reminded Leonid of scrawny muscles.

The angle of the tracks had become steep enough that the Leonids were using the ties like a staircase. They were gaining on the villagers, who could have looked back and seen them at any time. The villagers' shoulders hunched forward, their steps barely rising high enough to reach the next foothold, as if the empty sacks were actually filled to the top with buckwheat.

Ahead of them, the gap in the trees grew, revealing the crest of the pass. The villagers quickened their pace, as if hurrying to the top would somehow make the descent easier. For a moment, each of them stood on the apex before disappearing by inches on the other side, as if they were sinking into the ground. When the last villager was out of sight, the Leonids hurried to the crest.

Shouts stabbed through the quiet. It was the first noise they had heard beyond the breeze and their own whispers. The older Leonid realized that not even birdsong had accompanied their climb. Where were the birds? And how long had they been absent? The shouts were clear, but Leonid could not understand them. There were softer voices, too, and from these he could make out a few words, but then the shouting came louder and faster and from several mouths all at once. None of it made any sense, just random phrases, familiar syllables that should have connected with others but wound up misarranged instead.

"It's Russian," said the younger Leonid.

The older Leonid listened and managed to pick out a few words he knew. The Russians were shouting for the villagers to turn back, but now the villagers were shouting in response. Their families were starving, they said, there was no food. If they did not find food, everyone in the valley would die. The villagers shouted in

Ukrainian, and the Russians in Russian. Leonid knew that neither side understood the other.

As the twins reached the top of the pass, one final shout in Russian, louder than those before it, and then a series of pops like wood being chopped, at first one and then a cluster and then tapering back out. The older Leonid crawled to the crest, peeking over when one of the villagers bounded up and almost stepped right on top of him. The man jumped back when he saw the twins. One final pop from the other side of the pass and the man lurched forward, falling halfway back into the valley.

He squeezed the older Leonid by the shoulder. "Run," he said.

"Mr. Yevtushenko?" asked the younger Leonid.

Mr. Yevtushenko, like his father before him, made small wooden toys for the children in the village. His hands had thick knuckles and the fingers curled in on themselves.

"Just run," said Mr. Yevtushenko. He winced, then vomited on the older Leonid's hand. Leonid jumped to his feet and backed away, wiping the milky pink sputum on his pants. The younger Leonid pulled him by his other hand, and then they were bounding down the mountain, taking steps like giants, almost out of control.

The climb had seemed to take forever, but the descent happened out of time. The older Leonid leaned on the building at the train station, wondering what had happened to the mountain and how he had gotten here and why his lungs burned and his heart felt ready to burst. His brother still stood on the tracks, looking up at where they had been, but it was too far away, too high to see from where they were.

THE LEONIDS RETURNED to the village slick with sweat and gasping for breath. They doubled over in the small square, beneath the bare tree planted in the center. The younger Leonid sucked up a lungful of air and forced out a shout, "Everyone!" No one stirred in the cottages. He shouted again. This time Mrs. Tarasenko opened her door and came out.

"What is it, boys?" she asked.

The younger Leonid shouted again.

Another door and another villager, but no more.

The younger Leonid shoved his brother. "Go, go."

The older Leonid loped to the opposite side of the square and knocked on doors, calling for everyone to come out. His calls were weak and the effort left him light-headed.

"Come to the square!" The younger Leonid seemed to have found a new wellspring of energy. He sprinted down the row of cottages and shouted full from his throat.

The villagers emerged one by one and crept toward the square. They all moved as if awoken from naps. One of the women carried a rifle. Kasha poked her head from around the Tarasenko cottage. Her fur looked like snow against the gray rocks of the mountain and the black trunks of the bare forest.

"What is it, boys?" repeated Mrs. Tarasenko.

The older Leonid leaned against the tree, still trying to gather a full breath, and the villagers looked to him. He did not know what to say. Among the faces, he saw Mr. Yevtushenko's family, and the families of the other villagers who had trekked to the pass. They bore an expression of curiosity. They had no idea the news to come. Leonid had memories from during the war. Then, when such news was delivered, the families already knew it before a single word was spoken. The sight of a soldier at the door contained the full content of the message. How did it work now, when they were dumb with peace?

Leonid stammered out a few syllables that failed to form into words. His younger brother stepped in front of him.

"We followed the villagers to the pass," said the younger Leonid. "There were Russian soldiers on the other side. Everyone from the village was shot."

The older Leonid saw Mrs. Yevtushenko staring at the blood-stain on his pants, her face shifting through a series of emotions he could not name. He brushed at the stain with his fingers. The spot was still damp, or was it the same sweat that soaked his clothes everywhere else?

"Surely you're mistaken," she said.

"We heard the guns," said the younger Leonid, "and then we saw Mr. . . . we saw one of the villagers fall right before us. As he died he told us to run, and we ran."

"No," said Mrs. Yevtushenko. The word echoed through a dozen other mouths.

"We have to go to the pass," said someone.

The nos were replaced with yeses.

"No." Grandmother walked up the path from her cottage. Hers was the first voice to carry any sense of authority. The murmur of broken conversations silenced.

"They may still be alive," said Mrs. Yevtushenko.

"You know better than that," said Grandmother. "Even if they were alive when the twins left, they're dead now. And if any fool goes to the pass, that fool will be joining them in death."

"We can't just leave them."

"It's the war all over again," said Grandmother, "and that's how a war works. One leaves behind what can't be carried."

Grandmother went to the center of the square and led the Leonids away, squeezing their hands so tight that it hurt. The older

Leonid wanted to protest, to ask her to loosen her grip, but his lungs felt empty, the rest of him hollow, too.

Behind them, the shock of the news must have worn off. First a few and then many of the villagers began to weep.

GRANDMOTHER CLOSED THE DOOR to the cottage, turned, and slapped the younger Leonid hard on the cheek. The older Leonid staggered back as if it was he who had been slapped. The sound reminded him of the gunshots. Every time he managed to breathe in, a sob spasmed through him, squeezing out the air. The younger Leonid stood there, unmoving.

"You shouldn't have followed those people," said Grandmother.

"We always follow the villagers when they go to the train," said the younger Leonid.

"What train! There hasn't been a train in months."

"All the more reason to see if one would come."

She drew her arm back for another slap. The older Leonid winced, backing into the table, clattering it into the wooden chairs. Grandmother started at the sound. She looked up at her hand, still raised beside her. Tears flowed from her eyes as if someone had pulled the handle of a pump inside her.

"What if something were to happen to you?" she said.

"Are we any safer here?" The younger Leonid gestured down at the warped planks that made up the floor. "The last time soldiers came, they murdered Mr. Tarasenko in his own home. Even if the soldiers don't come, there's not enough food."

"I know all this. Of course I know."

"We don't know where the danger will come from." The younger Leonid's voice was raised, louder than his brother had ever heard it except outside. "It might rise up from the ground. It might fall from the sky. It's as likely right here"—he stamped his foot—"as any-where. What's the point in waiting?"

"As you discovered today, the only option we have left is to wait. Otherwise, we'll bring ourselves to the danger that much sooner."

The younger Leonid turned his head and spat. He ripped open the door and left without closing it behind him.

Grandmother closed the door slowly, so slowly that it felt al-most painful to the older Leonid, like a bone being bent and bent until it broke. The door clacked shut. Grandmother walked to the table and hugged Leonid and muttered soft apologies and mean-ingless phrases, and he heard her say the name of his father, so he was not sure to whom she apologized, his father, his brother, or himself. He worried that Grandmother did not completely know the difference.

## Baikonur Cosmodrome—1964

The Chief Designer might not have known the rocket was moving at all if not for the sound of grinding steel. The Proton rested on its side atop three flatbed railcars, screeching slowly along the tracks between the assembly building and the launchpad. Sunlight diffused through a haze of dust all across the steppe, the landscape flooded with yellow broth. He walked behind the rocket, just beside the tracks, pacing his steps so he would not catch up and overtake it, looking up into the nozzles of the six engines. The Proton was not one of his rockets, and the configuration felt strange, like trying to read another language. The engines attached to six tubular blocks spaced around the bottom stage, as if they had been added as an afterthought. As if engines had been neglected in the original design. The Chief Designer did not think it impossible that the General Designer might have forgotten engines.

An army officer approached from the other direction, following the tracks from the launchpad back toward the assembly building. Still several meters away, he leaned his head forward and made a visor of his hand. "Chief Designer," he said. The Chief Designer squinted, recognizing the officer as Marshal Nedelin by the overflowing cluster of medals on his uniform even before he could make out the features of the man's face. Nedelin had fought, it seemed, in every battle in the war. Once, at a state dinner, the Chief Designer sat near him as he consumed three whole steaks, sawing off huge chunks and shoving them into his mouth with a prideful motion. Nedelin had explained that after Stalingrad, where days went by when he did not taste food, he never ate less than all that was offered to him. Still, he was a fit man, no belly even as he pushed well beyond middle age, his spine like an aluminum rod from the base of his back all the way up to his skull.

Marshal Nedelin smiled as he covered the last of the distance to the Chief Designer. The men shook hands, firm, but not like with some military men where it seemed a contest of grips. The Chief Designer would have liked the Marshal very much if it were not for the fact he reported directly to Khrushchev on matters concerning the space program. When Nedelin was around, it was always an evaluation.

"Marshal," said the Chief Designer. "We've not seen each other since the last test of the N1." He winced to himself at the mention of that test, which had been far from a success. Not the worst test ever, not the largest explosion. It was a strange business where success was measured by the relative sizes of explosions.

"Indeed!" said Nedelin. "I apologize for not being able to make the last launch. All my time is spent thinking about the moon, and the General Designer had an engine test that required my attention."

"You know how I feel about his engines. We may have had our problems, but a similar malfunction from the General Designer would prove catastrophic."

"Your concerns have been noted, but I won't lie—that engine of his is a sight to behold. I've seen many, many explosions. Hell, I've created more than a few myself, but I never once thought to control one."

"It's his ability to control it that concerns me."

"And yet you're here for the test."

"I have a small piece of business with the General Designer."

"Would that require you to actually speak with him? Both Khrushchev and I wish that you two would get over whatever led to this feud in the first place."

"Feud? Can't I consider the man to be an ass without it being labeled as a feud?"

Nedelin laughed, a sound that rang in his chest as much as it came from his mouth. Yes, the Chief Designer liked Nedelin. If only more officers were like him.

"If you promise not to fall to blows with him," said Nedelin, "will you join the General Designer and me for dinner this evening? The test isn't until tomorrow, and this place hardly has any diversions except for the company of others."

"Even if that company is a man who hates me?"

"I'll be entertained by it, at least."

It was the Chief Designer's turn to laugh.

"I'll see you this evening, then," he said.

Nedelin pointed backward with his thumb. "Last I saw the General Designer, he was at the south fuel pump. If you hurry, you can catch him."

"There's no need to rush. He won't leave before the rocket arrives."

Nedelin walked on, chuckling to himself. The Proton had pulled several meters away during the conversation. The carrier's wheels squealed against the tracks and a shudder passed up through the rocket. The Chief Designer had made this same walk with rockets of his own. Then, every vibration worried him, every pop and click of the rocket's structure. Now, he appreciated the music of it, how something so rickety could loft to the stars.

A technician came from the other direction, but stopped when she saw the Chief Designer. She turned and jogged back along the tracks. The Chief Designer recognized her. She used to work at OKB-1 in the '50s, poached by the General Designer when he opened OKB-52. She was hardly the only one. Several dozen engineers had gone with her. Whenever the Chief Designer came across any of them at meetings or conferences, they seemed terrified, as if they thought he carried a violent grudge against them. Yes, he did not like the General Designer, and he could think of a million people for whom he would rather work, but he did not fault anyone for advancing their career. In his youth, he had done the same thing, leaving Tsiolkovski to set out on his own. Unlike Tsiolkovski, the Chief Designer was one who could forgive.

The only noise across the whole steppe seemed to be the wheels of the train. When they quieted, even for a moment, it was like a light had been shut off, the silence as black as how the cosmonauts in orbit described empty space. The Chief Designer found himself closing his eyes until another squeal escaped the wheels. He focused on his steps. The launch tower loomed nearer and nearer, but so large it was difficult to tell exactly how far away it was. Long after he expected to have arrived, it still stood some ways in the distance.

A figure approached him along the tracks, at first just a black tick against the dry earth, moving toward the Chief Designer much more quickly than he moved toward it. The tall, thin man, wearing a full suit despite the heat, could be none other than the General Designer. He hurried to a stop directly in front of the Chief Designer.

"I'm flattered," said the Chief Designer, "that you came to greet me personally."

"I'm quite busy, as you well know."

"Not so busy that you couldn't spare the time to walk half a kilometer to meet someone who was already on his way to meet you."

"What are you doing here?" The General Designer's face, pinched as if he smelled something unpleasant, looked even more ratlike than usual.

"You're forever talking about your engines," said the Chief Designer. "I figured I should see them at work."

"We don't allow tourists at the launchpad." He shifted one foot as if to turn and leave but stayed facing forward.

Another technician passed them, heading to the pad. She wore a rubberized suit and had a breathing mask dangling from her neck. The goggles on top of her head made her look amphibian.

The Chief Designer cupped his hand over his nose and mouth. "Anyway, I don't have a breather."

"I can't hear you through your hand."

"I was simply observing that we don't require breathing masks to work on our rockets."

"That again?" The General Designer spun and started to walk away.

"Wait, General Designer. I apologize, I apologize. It was a poor attempt at humor."

"I expect nothing but poor attempts from you."

"Was that a joke?"

"I'm not a humorous man."

"Then let me take care of my business before you return to yours."

The General Designer twisted his head to look back over his shoulder.

"I have a favor to ask," said the Chief Designer.

For the first time that the Chief Designer could remember, the

General Designer showed an expression other than spite. The tight pinch of his mouth softened, falling into a small O. His eyes, usually squeezed to slits like the tail edge of a wing, opened enough to reveal the color of his irises, a gentle blue. The eyes of a baby, the Chief Designer thought.

"Why would I help you?" asked the General Designer.

"You're not even going to hear the request before you deny it?"

"What do you want?"

"Your heat shield."

"You have a heat shield."

"You have a better one."

The General Designer shifted, rotating more toward the Chief Designer without turning all the way around.

"Yes," said the Chief Designer, "I admit it. Our ablation rate has never been satisfactory. But I've seen the reports on yours."

"Those reports are brand new. Most of my staff have yet to see them."

"I've been at this game longer than you. I have my sources."

The General Designer's face returned to its normal glowering state.

"Don't be angry, comrade," said the Chief Designer, choking out the last word.

"What would I get in return?"

The Chief Designer walked around him so that the two men stood face-to-face.

"My gratitude," said the Chief Designer, "expressed to everyone who matters."

"Khrushchev?" asked the General Designer.

The Chief Designer turned and headed back along the tracks. The squeal of the rocket carrier seemed far away now, but it was still just over his shoulder.

"There's no need to decide right away," said the Chief Designer. "Marshal Nedelin invited me to join you both for dinner."

The General Designer offered a reply, but the Chief Designer was already too distant to hear it.

THE BUNKER NEAR the old R-7 test site had been converted into Baikonur's formal dining room, in that it now had a great round table in the middle set in a simulation of formality, other metals substituted for silver, glass for crystal, dull ceramic plates produced in a dank factory. Red drapery hung from brass rods screwed into the concrete walls. Scarlet curtains, unmatched to the drapes, decorated the slit of the old observation window. A painting of outer space, deep purple with shining stars and swirls of ethereal gases, covered the whole ceiling, giving the impression that the table was falling top-first into the void. The Chief Designer noted with pleasure how much better Giorgi's paintings at Star City were.

Several of the General Designer's top aides also sat at the table, people the Chief Designer had seen before but to whom he had never spoken. After a few greetings when he arrived, the table fell back into silence. That had been about ten minutes ago. Nedelin and the General Designer were late.

A young man, bespectacled and with hair slicked into a neat part, cleared his throat.

"The General Designer always makes us wait," he said, his tone half apologetic, half joking.

"Not to worry. Where else would I have to be?" The Chief Designer gestured around him. "Nothing but dry, cracked land in every direction."

A murmur of amusement passed around the table. Several of the aides visibly relaxed.

"I promise," said the Chief Designer, "the stories the General Designer has told you about me are mostly untrue."

A round of laughter, but it was cut short by the click of the door, a wood-paneled slab that had been installed in place of the bunker's old steel one. The aides at the table stood, and the Chief Designer followed suit. He faced away from the door, and saw only the questioning looks on the aides' faces. He turned.

Ignatius shut the door behind her and smiled. She moved to the seat beside the Chief Designer, shucked her large leather jacket, and hung it over the back. She smiled again, taking time to make eye contact with each person at the table.

"Greetings," she said. "I'm from Glavlit, here to report on the test."

The young man with the glasses responded, "This test is secret."

"Then I guess I'm only here to eat your food."

She pulled out her chair and sat. The others retook their seats as well, though none looked away from Ignatius. The Chief Designer felt a little sorry for the aides. They had an important test tomorrow, and first their boss's rival joined them for dinner and now an agent of the Party. He recognized his younger self in these people. He recognized how they tried to hide their nervousness with little tasks, straightening a knife on the table, taking a sip of water so dainty it could not have done more than moisten the lips. The young man with the glasses adjusted the knot of his tie six times. The Chief Designer wondered if he had been so obvious as a young man, and worse yet, was he still so obvious now. He doubted it. Experience had long since purged the nervous tics out of him, and maybe the trick to not seeming nervous was to accept the truth that you were, not try to hide it. Hidden things had a way of being discovered.

The Chief Designer noticed Ignatius inspecting him the same

way he had been inspecting the aides. She never seemed nervous, but then he had never seen her in a situation in which she did not have control. She barely seemed human. Perhaps part of Tsiolkovski's master race. The Chief Designer pushed thoughts of Tsiolkovski out of his head.

The door clicked open again, and Nedelin and the General Designer entered. Beads of sweat dotted the General Designer's face. He dabbed at them with a handkerchief, but as soon as he pulled it away, new beads emerged. He and Nedelin, continuing a conversation, took seats opposite Ignatius and the Chief Designer.

"... a test cycle on the pump before we can begin fueling," said the General Designer. He looked at the handkerchief in his hands as he spoke.

"As children, we would make rafts and tie long ropes to posts on the banks of the Don and float out to the middle." Nedelin tilted his head and flashed an impish grin for the benefit of the table. "It was best just before harvest, when the crops crept right to the edge of the river like waving cliffs, and the currents then were at their most gentle."

The General Designer continued his previous tack, nodding to himself. "From the time the fuel lines are disconnected, we need two hours before the rocket will be ready for testing. And before a full test we'll want to run several simulations."

"Along the straight stretches of the Don, we could wade out for meters. In winter, it froze solid enough to walk on, though our parents forbade it. Like many things forbidden by our parents, we did it anyway."

"So we'll start the fueling process at five in the morning. The first crews will be at the pad by four."

"I rarely make it home, and I miss the river." Nedelin turned from the General Designer to the rest of the table. "All I asked him was what time the test would occur. Ten minutes later, I'm not sure I have the answer to that question, but I do now feel qualified to construct a rocket all by myself."

The Chief Designer chuckled and Ignatius unleashed a full-throated haw. The aides turned their faces in whatever direction but toward the General Designer, whose cheeks blossomed with red. He looked around the room as if noticing the other people for the first time.

"I'm glad you're here," said Nedelin to the Chief Designer. "This group is always so serious before a test. They won't even join me for a drink." He glanced around the tabletop. "They don't even have a drink to offer."

The General Designer stuttered something in response but failed to form an actual word. This made the Chief Designer laugh again. He had never seen his rival so flustered. He wondered if Nedelin needled the General Designer like this all the time, or if it was just with this particular audience. Nedelin was a tactician, after all, and what better way to gain control over the General Designer than to diminish his esteem just that much.

Ignatius reached into the deep pocket of her leather jacket, which hung from the back of the chair almost all the way to the floor. She pulled out an unmarked bottle filled with clear liquid.

"I'm more than glad to join you for a drink," said Ignatius, "I can't speak for the Chief Designer."

"I know your face, but I don't recall your name," said Nedelin.

"You've never known it, Marshal. I'm an agent of Glavlit."

"Oh? Then I guess I never will. Is there at least a name I can call you?"

"Ignatius."

"A saint! As much as a Jesuit can be a saint."

"Or a saint a soldier." She half-stood from her seat and stretched her arm across the table, offering a glass of vodka to Nedelin. "Who else?" she asked.

The General Designer did not respond, nor did any of his aides. The Chief Designer tapped two fingers on the table. She filled his glass to brimming.

The young man with glasses raised his hand. Ignatius grabbed the nearest glass, from in front of another of the aides, and filled it halfway. She passed it to the left, and it was handed from aide to aide to the General Designer to Nedelin before it reached its destination.

"Only the four of us?" asked Ignatius. "That's all right. I only brought one bottle."

She raised her glass. "To the engineers gathered here, and to all who give themselves to this great Soviet . . . no, this great human project. To our engineers."

She, Nedelin, the Chief Designer, and the young aide raised their glasses, and the rest of those seated at the table scrambled to find an empty glass to raise as well. The staggered response came: "To our engineers."

The Chief Designer had always enjoyed the sound of glasses being set back on a table after a toast. It reminded him of a gunshot before a race, a signal that things could finally begin. He held his glass high and set it down last.

"So, Ignatius," said Nedelin, "why the name of a saint?"

"I prefer to think of him as an educator. Anyway"—she pointed up—"one would need to believe in a god to believe in saints."

"A good state atheist, then?"

"Does that mean you aren't?"

"I don't believe in the old god, comrade, but not because the party told me so. I saw the holy die just as easily as the damned on the battlefield. Easier even. It's more difficult to give up if one doesn't believe in a second chance. It's the same human greed that keeps us alive as makes us believe we can live forever."

"And now we fly our cosmonauts to the front door of heaven, knock, and find it vacant."

"Is that why we fly?"

"The birds have never offered up a reason, why must we?"

The curtain hung in front of the doorway to the kitchen parted, and a line of servers emerged carrying plates full of food. The men were locals, Turkic. When Baikonur had been founded, the Chief Designer had been forbidden from hiring locals for any sensitive position, though what qualified as sensitive had never been defined. The specter of Stalin still loomed, when all the designers had to hide their Jewish engineers from his gaze, when Asian members of their staffs seemed to disappear weekly. And for all his genius, what of Tsiolkovski . . .

The General Designer cleared his throat. "We fly to conquer. There's a realm we have not yet claimed, and we, as a species, must claim it. First, we conquered the idea of a god, and now we lay claim to where we imagined his home to be."

"And I thought I was the military man at the table," said Nedelin.

"We do what it takes to survive," said the Chief Designer. "It isn't about conquering, it's about enduring."

"Do you mean the species or yourself?" said the General Designer.

"The same could be asked of you."

"We got rid of god," said Nedelin, "and yet these two men try to claim his title."

The General Designer grunted and looked down at the table.

"They used to say the same about Tsiolkovski," said the Chief Designer.

A reverent hush overtook the table at the mention of Tsiolkovski's name. The servers arranged the plates, reaching through the narrow gaps between those seated, managing not to bump shoulders or brush sleeves. The Chief Designer admired their coordination, the machinery of it. Never once did two plates clink against one another. The server nearest him set down a dish with pickles and another with sliced pumpernickel and pork fat. Three large bowls, arranged evenly around the table, contained cold cucumber salad, the other ingredients completely drowned in thick white *smetanka*. Then came the individual bowls of cold borscht. No one even had time to raise a spoon for the soup before another wave of servers arrived with the main course, some sort of poached river fish crisscrossed on top with whole sprigs of dill.

Nedelin raised his glass. "To Tsiolkovski. Maybe a man, maybe a saint, maybe a god, maybe all three. To Tsiolkovski."

Everyone around the table lifted glasses, full or not. "To Tsiolkovski."

After the toast, the General Designer waved off a server with a pitcher of water and extended his arm across the table, empty glass held in the tips of his knobby fingers.

He said, "Ignatius, was it? A drink if you would, and for any of my associates who would like one, as well. If you have enough."

"Of course." Ignatius reached into the other pocket of her coat and pulled out a second bottle of vodka. "I made sure to bring enough for everyone."

THE CHIEF DESIGNER, Ignatius, and Nedelin opted to walk the two kilometers from the dining room back to the dormitories. Night had set in, moonless and starry. The dirt road showed ahead of them only as a patch of black slightly smoother than the black all around it. In the distance, the lights of the dormitories clustered above the horizon like flaming engines.

Ignatius took a swig from what remained in the bottle. Everyone at the table had ended up taking some, but none of the General Designer's aides took much. Ignatius passed the bottle to Nedelin, who tipped it back, gulping down half the remaining vodka. He passed the bottle to the Chief Designer, who willingly finished it off.

"What to do with the bottle," he said.

"Aren't you in the business of launching things?" said Nedelin. "Send it on its way."

The Chief Designer clutched the bottle by its neck and hurled it into the darkness. It thudded in the dirt and then bounced into something hard. He imagined the shattering was the sound of the stars overhead.

The alcohol flowed as excess heat in his blood. His limbs felt weightless. He thought hard about each step as he took it.

"What actually brings you here?" asked Nedelin.

Ignatius had lagged behind, still within earshot but not offering much in the way of conversation. She gave no indication that she was listening but the Chief Designer knew she was.

"I was hoping to collaborate, for once," he said.

"You must be truly desperate," said Nedelin.

"I'm just wiser. Five years ago, the General Designer had nothing to offer, but now he does."

"So you'll exploit him."

"He's a resource like any other."

"And you?"

Ignatius stepped between them. "The Chief Designer is a resource, too, but unlike all the others."

Nedelin chuckled.

"Look at the stars," he said. "Whenever I go back to Moscow it's like the whole sky disappears."

The Chief Designer craned his neck, almost stumbling backward. The largest stars shone bright as spotlights, and the fainter stars, so many of them, hazed the firmament. If his vision were not blurred by drink, could he pick out Mars? Like the stars but untwinkling, tinged dusty red.

"In Siberia," he said, "when the skies would actually clear, it was as if there were more stars than space between them. That one there is actually a planet. Mars. You can tell it's a planet because it doesn't shimmer." He pointed up at nothing in particular.

"To continue our conversation from dinner," said Nedelin, "this beauty—we can all agree that the night sky is beautiful?"

"Yes," said the Chief Designer.

"Agreed," said Ignatius.

"Isn't it better if beauty is a natural state with no need of a guiding hand to create it? Because we're a species of painters, we assume that all beauty must be similarly created. But weren't the first paintings just copies of nature? Isn't the sky itself full of every symmetry and color? Why do we feel the need to make the source of our aesthetic have a source? At what point is the source sourceless?"

"Marshal," said the Chief Designer, "I feel I've drunk too much to follow you completely. I didn't know the army trained philosophers."

"In Stalingrad, there were no lights. We burned no fires. Only stars, when the smoke from smoldering rubble did not cloud things up too badly. Being a soldier there was to be suspended between the ugliness of war and the splendor of the sky. And one's only occupation between skirmishes was to think."

The Chief Designer thought of Leonid, locked in the Vostok far above them, a speck coursing through the static backdrop of stars. Leonid spoke in the same sort of poetry as Nedelin.

The three of them had stopped walking, each gazing up at a different section of sky. There were no insects to chirp, no trees where a night bird might perch. The breeze came only as a faint sensation against the skin.

"I apologize," said Nedelin. "I seem to have turned the mood somber."

"Sometimes I feel that somber is the natural mood," said the Chief Designer, "but we manage to turn it light now and again."

They resumed walking. The Chief Designer welcomed the sound of the crunching gravel beneath their feet. The lights of the dormitories never seemed to get nearer when he watched but were always somehow closer when he looked again. Then they arrived.

The dried-up remains of saxauls sprouted from either side of the road where it entered the residential complex, two dormitories simply called Dom 2 and Dom 4. The Chief Designer did not know where Doms 1 and 3 might be, if they existed at all. A single wild apple tree in the center quadrangle had managed to survive. Nedelin said good night without stopping and continued to Dom 2. The Chief Designer and Ignatius were left alone with the few lights still alive in the windows. He remembered a similar evening with his wife after they were first married, before his son was born. It might have been the very night his son was conceived. But this woman was not his wife. Was his wife even his wife anymore? He had not seen her in so long.

"I thought you were with Nadya and Leonid," said the Chief Designer.

"We finished the assignment."

"Did you find one? Did you find a dog like Kasha or Khrushchev's Byelka?"

"Many dogs, but none that matched. Part of me hopes that Khrushchev's little rat is a singular entity. Hell if there are more of them."

"Then you didn't finish the assignment."

"I don't work for you, Chief Designer. I'm happy to help out when I can, but don't confuse me for Mishin or Bushuyev."

"I can never tell where the limits of your caring lie."

"It will be easier for you if you accept that I don't really care at all. I have a role and I perform it and I don't give it much thought beyond that."

"I can never tell if that role is to thwart me or to aid me."

"Neither. My role is to motivate you."

"And the General Designer, too?"

"You're a little easier to deal with, Chief Designer. The General Designer, he has no memory of the gulag. He never suffered like you did, and so he can't understand loss as you do. I get my way with you far more often than I should, because I scare you. Don't misunderstand me. You should be scared. So should the General Designer. I'm not praising him, just pointing out how ignorance works in his favor. At least in the short term."

"And in the long term?"

"One of you will go to Mars, and I'll back whoever can get there first."

"You're here to watch the engine test, then?"

"I end up where I need to be. And I have faith that you will as well."

"Faith?"

"It seems the old gods aren't quite as dead as Nedelin believes. Good night, Chief Designer."

As she walked away, she pulled a third, full bottle of vodka from her jacket pocket and pried out the cork.

BY THE TIME the Chief Designer arose in the morning, the dormitories were already empty. He showered, lingering in the stream of water even though it was cold. The dining hall was dark and abandoned, but he found the remains of a black bread loaf in the kitchen pantry. He searched the drawers, metal things with squeaking brackets, until he found a suitable knife. Gripping the loaf with a cloth napkin, he set the blade on the exposed end and sawed lightly until the serration worked a groove in the crust. The knife was sharp. It did not take much pressure. He went slowly and lightly, trying to finish the slice without crushing the rest of the loaf. It was a small challenge he made for himself, to complete this one task with no unnecessary damage. He poured himself a glass of water and ate the bread plain.

Outside, morning light preceded the rising sun, turning both sky and ground the same orange. Clouds, mere wisps, streaked the sky with a lighter hue. The atmosphere quivered at the horizon. Launch towers poked up in the distance like limbless tree trunks, a sparse forest. The Chief Designer walked toward the tower twinned by the Proton rocket. It was several kilometers away, but he had plenty of time to get to the bunker before the summer heat grew too oppressive.

The Chief Designer hummed a tune as he walked. He did not know the name of the song or the words, but the tune was simple and pleasant. Giorgi often sang it in the evenings. To the Chief Designer, it seemed more appropriate for mornings. Some birds sing at dawn and others at dusk. In Baikonur, of course, no birds sang at all. Or maybe they did. The Baikonur Cosmodrome was actually hundreds of kilometers away from the city of the same name, the title a sleight of hand aimed at the Americans. The Chief Designer knew it had taken but a single flight of the U-2 to uncover the ruse.

The bunker came into sight over a tangle of brown brush. Half buried, the bunker looked like the remains of a devastated castle. Several small figures emerged from the door and hurried toward the rocket. As he got closer, the Chief Designer could see the activity around the rocket itself, a swarm of bug-sized people moving in frantic patterns in front of the pad. When the light came through the latticework of the tower at the proper angle, still more technicians could be seen clinging to the platforms. Ants on the stalk of a plant.

Inside the bunker, technicians played with their control panels. No one seemed to notice when the Chief Designer entered. He cleared his throat, hoping for any sort of acknowledgment. He had planned to wait for the test in the bunker, but now it felt unwelcoming. He left and continued down the dirt road in the direction of the Proton.

He had not made it far when the General Designer almost ran into him, his face toward the ground, walking fast in the other direction. The General Designer smoked a long, thin cigarette, exhaling a continuous line of smoke behind him like a steam trail above a train.

"Sorry, sorry," said the General Designer without looking up, shuffling to the side to move around the Chief Designer.

"Isn't your work in the other direction?" asked the Chief Designer. "And should you really be smoking?"

The General Designer looked up. A slight flush came to his cheeks.

"If you must know," he said, "some combination of my nerves and last night's vodka has necessitated that I seek out a toilet."

The Chief Designer chuckled. "Please, don't let me keep you. Is Nedelin at the launchpad?"

"Yes, yes." The General Designer hurried away. His gait was an awkward shuffle, as if by pressing his buttocks together he could hold the shit inside. It was not so different from his normal walk, thought the Chief Designer. Except that the General Designer never seemed to stop spewing shit from the other end. The Chief Designer tried to banish such thoughts. He was here for a favor, and thinking ill of the man from whom the favor was asked would be of no benefit. And the General Designer, to his credit, had been almost civil. Almost human. Maybe this would work out, after all.

A pebble kicked up into the Chief Designer's shoe, lodging under his heel. He crouched down and tried to fish the pebble out with his finger. His knee ached. The pebble eluded him. He pried off the shoe and dumped it. The pebble, barely bigger than a grain of sand, dropped out. The Chief Designer retied his shoe and lifted himself to standing.

White light flashed ahead of him. The white faded and where the Proton rocket had been there was now only an orange blossom of flame, churning out smoke and radiating waves of heat like a rippling halo. The Chief Designer felt the boom in the air before it crashed into his ears. He covered them with his hands until the sound died enough to tolerate. The ground shook, just a tremble at first, growing into a violent rocking that almost knocked him from his feet. A wave of dust rushed at him, up his nose and into his eyes. The dust cast a meter-high haze over the whole landscape.

Tiny figures, silhouetted by the light, fled in the Chief Designer's direction, but few got far before falling. An acrid stench reached him. Vapors of the rocket fuel. Toxic. He pulled out his handkerchief and held it over his nose and mouth. Was he far enough away? Surely the fumes would disperse. A flock of birds rose up in front of the fireball like shrapnel from a secondary explosion.

The General Designer came from behind him and ran past, still cinching his belt. One half of his shirt remained untucked. The Chief Designer called out to him, told him to wait, but he could not hear his own voice, did not know if he even made a sound. Was his throat damaged by the fumes, or had the sound of the explosion deafened him?

He sprinted after the General Designer, who ran with the gracelessness of one who had never run before, not even at play as a child. The Chief Designer gripped the General Designer by the shoulder, which sent him spinning, almost to the ground.

"Stop!" screamed the Chief Designer.

The General Designer turned and made to run again. The Chief Designer placed one large hand on each of the General Designer's shoulders and squeezed.

"It's too late," said the Chief Designer.

The two men turned to the launchpad. The flames had lessened, no longer churning but still burning bright. The top of the Proton emerged out of the blaze. Without warning, it fell straight down, as if the column underneath had been snatched clean away.

THE CHIEF DESIGNER had thought the steppe dry before, but now in the area scorched by the explosion it was as if the very idea of water had evaporated. Dry brown dirt had been replaced with dryer gray ash. The ground crunched beneath his feet. Whole chunks of soot clung to his shoes.

He learned to avoid the larger piles of ash, many of which had once been human. Sometimes he could even make out the shape of a body splayed across the ground. Other piles had bones poking out. All told, some two hundred people were still unaccounted for, but they would never be identified. No amount of patience could reassemble flakes of ash to resemble the people they had come from. The grimace of one skull looked like any other. Nedelin had been identified by the fused clump of brass that had once been his medals. His uniform and flesh had burned completely away.

Somehow, the tower at the pad still stood. It was charred black almost to the top, crowned by bare metal, shining silver in the afternoon sun. The remnants of the Proton lay in a heap at the base of the tower, long cylindrical sections crossed like spent logs on a hearth. A rocket was not much more than a tube, when it came down to it.

Ignatius jogged across the ash toward the Chief Designer. Her motion seemed too casual, too carefree. The somber scene required slowness. After the rush to save the few survivors, everything had decelerated. The Chief Designer was reminded of people strolling along the banks of a river. It was a specific memory of a specific river, wet mud emanating a murky scent, but he could not recall the time or the place. The people he had seen walking there were strangers.

Ignatius slowed as she approached the Chief Designer and then stopped beside him. She covered her mouth with a fist and released a cough from deep in her lungs.

"This dust," she said. The ash covering her jacket made the leather look several shades lighter.

"Try not to think of where it comes from," said the Chief Designer.

"Now there's an unpleasant thought. Thank you for that."

"What do you want?"

"Not happy to see me? I'll be brief. The General Designer is by the fueling station—at least what remains of it. Now might be an excellent time to repeat your request to him."

"Now might be an excellent time to leave him alone."

"The world has not stopped, Chief Designer. Not even for this. The Americans will keep launching rockets, and now you're our only chance to beat them to the moon. To Mars."

"Surely even the Americans will pause for this."

"They'll never know this happened."

"You can't hide the deaths of hundreds."

"I already have. Tomorrow morning, *Pravda* will report that Nedelin died in a plane crash. The families of the deceased will be told the same. And anyone who knows otherwise will be convinced that if they tell the truth, they might meet a similar fate."

Without realizing it, the Chief Designer had let Ignatius guide him in the direction of the fuel station. The walls of the building were tumbled over in the direction of the blast, pipes and tubes sprouting from charred concrete like the decapitated stems of flowers. The General Designer was there amid the rubble, stooping over and then standing back to his full height, a head taller than everyone around him. The Chief Designer stopped walking.

He asked, "Is there a chance that you arranged this so that the General Designer would assist me?"

"You always think the worst of me," said Ignatius, "though I suppose it would be a lie to claim that this is something I would be incapable of."

"Often you seem less human than these piles of ash."

"Let the two of us never discuss our relative humanity."

The Chief Designer's lips turned up in a reluctant smile.

"I suppose," he said, "that would make the General Designer the most righteous among us."

"One can be intolerable and righteous both."

"I'll speak to him. Thank you, Ignatius."

"Oh god, please don't form the habit of thanking me."

"Only this once."

Ignatius spun on the point of her toe and headed off in a direction that seemed to have no potential destination, just open steppe all the way to the horizon. Somehow the dust did not kick up with her steps.

As the Chief Designer approached the fuel station, the General

Designer noticed him, spoke something to the nearest technician, and met the Chief Designer halfway.

"I suppose this is where you lecture me," said the General Designer. "This is where you remind me that you warned me about the dangers of hypergolic fuels. Do you know how we're assembling the list of names? The names of the dead? We're taking roll. Anyone who we don't find is added to the list. It's a list of the absent. These people are simply no more. A few, yes, we could identify. There were several tangled in the wire fence to the east. Some who made it beyond that were unburned. The fumes got them. To think that you got away only to breathe poison. That was their fate. How long do you think they felt lucky? Did they see their friends swallowed up and think, *Thank god, not me!* And what about me? I had to shit, Chief Designer. If I hadn't drunk that vodka, if I hadn't inherited a weak stomach from my father, I would have been there, too. I wouldn't have to answer your questions or any of the questions yet to come. Can you at least give me this day? Let me come to understand my own regrets before you gloat. I killed a hundred people. Two hundred. Right now, I can't deal with your triumph."

"At any cost," said the Chief Designer.

"What?"

"That's what Tsiolkovski taught us: Succeed at any cost. I understand your current feelings better than you may realize, and about this, I will never gloat. I want to reach Mars first, but if I don't, then someone else must. Right now, you're the only other option. You'll recover from this and you'll push me and we'll push each other."

The General Designer put his hand on his face and pressed his eyes as if he was trying to hold back tears. When he opened his eyes again, they were dry.

He said, "You came here for my heat shield, correct? Not

today, not for many days, but I'll have the information sent to you when I'm able."

"Accidents are unavoidable in our industry. That's what I'll tell Khrushchev."

The General Designer tried to say something, his mouth moving like he was chewing on the words.

"Don't thank me," said the Chief Designer. "I still think you're an ass."

"And I you," said the General Designer, and then he said the Chief Designer's name, his real name, the name no one except his wife and son and Ignatius was supposed to know.

The Chief Designer took a deep breath and tried not to think about what he was inhaling.

## Bohdan, Ukraine—1950

When the creek dried up, the villagers began to ration water from the well. Some hope arrived when a few green shoots rose in the field, but the sprouts quickly turned brown, shriveling back into the earth. A baby died. Not uncommon in the village, but this baby died with no fever, no rash, no symptoms at all. It cried one whole night and then stopped crying. The villagers wrapped the baby in sackcloth and buried it without a coffin. The grave was barely half a meter deep. There was no worry of the little body being dug up by an animal. No one had seen an animal in the forest for months.

The Leonids sat in a circle with the other children, not five meters from where the baby was buried at the base of the old tree in the center of the village. Mykola had brought a ball with him, made of real rubber. It was now cracking and stained with dirt, but when he first got it years ago, the rubber was sleek and shiny. The children rolled the ball to each other. Not a game, really. No one had the energy to get up and kick the ball or throw it. They just shoved it across the short diameter of the circle until another child thought to shove it back.

The next time the ball came to Mykola, he snatched it up and stood. He walked away without saying anything. The other children got up one at a time and headed in the direction of their homes. It was dinnertime, Leonid guessed. Once, at this time every evening, a chorus of parents calling to their children could be heard through the whole valley. Now it remained silent, and everyone went home only out of habit.

The Leonids were the last to stand, along with Oksana, a girl a couple years older who lived at the end of the village nearest Grandmother's cottage. Oksana had ears a little too big for her face, but nobody mocked her for it. She rarely smiled and was not exactly nice. Leonid remembered, though, how she came to Grandmother's the day after the soldiers arrived with news of Father's death. Oksana had brought fresh bread and then stayed to clean the cottage. Leonid rarely talked to her, maybe because after that he always thought of her as an adult, not another one of the children.

They walked together now, assuming the arrangement of a group, though all three were in their own spheres of thought. As they neared Mykola's cottage, he came back out the front door with his shoes in his hands. He beat them together, knocking clumps of dry dirt to the ground and creating a gray cloud in the air around him. He took both boots in one hand and waved the other in front of his face, coughing. Sitting on the step, he slid the shoes back on.

Oksana stopped, and the older Leonid almost collided with her. The younger Leonid, looking over at Mykola, did not see his brother stop and clipped him with his shoulder.

"Watch it," said the older Leonid.

"Why'd you stop?" asked the younger.

"What's that smell?" asked Oksana.

The Leonids looked at her and then looked around, as if the smell was something they could see. But then Leonid smelled it, too, a wet scent, barely more than steam. Even when he smelled it, he could not place it, something familiar but forgotten.

"Meat," said the younger Leonid. "Someone's boiling meat."

"No one's had meat in months," said the older Leonid.

"He's right," said Oksana. "It's definitely meat."

The older Leonid sniffed again, still unconvinced, but then his stomach decided for him, rumbling loud enough that Oksana and his brother turned to look.

"It's coming from Mykola's home," he said.

Mykola was still lacing his left shoe, seemingly unaware of the three children staring at him.

The older Leonid took one step toward him. "Where did your family get meat?"

Mykola stood without tying his shoe. He stayed on the step and pushed the door shut behind him.

"What are you talking about?" he asked.

Leonid took another step toward him. Mykola hopped off the front step and crept away from the cottage.

"Don't deny it. We all smelled meat."

"No one has any meat."

"Except you. Why is that?"

The boys now stood face-to-face. Mykola tried to take a step back, but Leonid stepped with him.

"Grandmother boiled tree bark yesterday. That's what we ate for dinner. Water flavored with wood. And here you are with meat while the rest of us are dying."

At the word *dying* Mykola looked up, his eyes stretched wide.

"No one's going to die," he said.

"Are you dumb?" asked Leonid.

"Don't call me dumb."

Leonid shoved him, and Mykola staggered back.

"I'm not dumb," said Mykola.

"You're an idiot."

"Fuck your mother."

Leonid lunged forward, wrapping his arms around Mykola at the waist and tackling him to the ground. Leonid pinned Mykola down with a forearm across the throat, and punched into Mykola's ribs with his free hand. The punches felt weak to Leonid, his strength sapped by hunger, but Mykola cried out at each blow.

"Where did you get meat?" screamed Leonid.

Then he was lifted off the ground and away from Mykola, Oksana and his brother gripping him under each armpit. How thin he must have been to be carried so easily. Mykola pushed himself up into a sitting position.

"You ass," said Leonid. "Where did you get the meat?"

Mykola cried, though the tears barely came. Everyone was too dried out to waste water on tears.

"It's the cat," said Mykola. "Mother is cooking the cat."

Oksana crouched by Mykola, dusted him off, and then helped him to his feet.

She said, "That cat barely had any muscle."

"Mother says it's better than nothing."

"It is," said Oksana. "It's better than not eating. Go back inside and have your meal."

Mykola's tears came then, real and wet. He held his ribs where Leonid had punched him. As he walked back to his cottage he wiped his eyes with the back of his hand and straightened his posture. He banged the heels of each shoe on the front step and went inside.

"Who would eat a cat?" asked the older Leonid.

Oksana started walking away. "Anybody who's lucky enough to have one."

OKSANA DIED the next week. She contracted a fever, followed by diarrhea and vomiting. What little food could be spared for her she could not keep down. After the fever set in, she moved into one of the abandoned huts, and spent her final days alone so that she would not risk spreading the illness. Even before she took ill, she had been giving most of her food to her sister. When the villagers prepared her for burial, they discovered that under her dress her limbs were thin to the bone, her ribs as prominent as features on a face.

The Leonids stood next to Mykola at the funeral. They greeted each other with nods. There was not much to the ceremony, just a few words spoken by Oksana's mother's friend. No one had known the girl well, it seemed. After the frail body had been lowered into a shallow grave, as several villagers used shovels to push the dirt back into the hole—they did not seem to have the energy to actually shovel—everyone else filed by Oksana's family and offered condolences. Leonid remembered all the funerals he was forced to attend during the war, and how everyone had a story to share about the deceased, how a long line formed before the grieving family. But now, no one said anything more than a couple words, and some simply tousled Oksana's sister's hair and patted her mother on the shoulder. No words at all.

Mykola ended up ahead of the Leonids in the line, and they all stood in front of Oksana's family at the same time. Mykola looked at her sister and her mother and then looked away, vaguely in the direction of the grave. The older Leonid pressed his lips into what he hoped was an understanding smile. The younger Leonid took the hand of Oksana's sister. He knelt before her, but lifted his head to speak to her mother.

"One time the three of us were in a fight, and Oksana broke it up. If she had not done that, we might not be friends today." He spoke as if the event were from the long ago past, as if he had been one of the fighters.

Oksana's mother, who had become silent during the burial, cried anew. Mykola and the Leonids moved on and other villagers took their places. Before they parted ways, Mykola and the older Leonid shook hands. The older Leonid said, "I was so hungry," and Mykola nodded.

Grandmother remained near the grave, keeping herself busy talking to the other villagers while always keeping an eye on Oksana's family. The Leonids walked home without her.

As they walked, the older Leonid thought about what his brother had said. At the time, he interpreted it to be a comforting lie. But now, now he knew the friendship was a prediction.

THE LEONIDS WERE the only ones outside in the village. The windows of all the cottages gaped open, but no noise came from inside, no motion could be seen. It was impossible to tell which ones were occupied and which were vacant. Who was alive and who was dead. Because an empty home tended to stay that way.

They passed beyond the cottages and into the forest, huffing up the straw-lined ground at the base of the mountain. Leonid watched his younger brother's legs, barely more than twigs. And his face like a skull with skin painted on. Some of the younger children, those who had managed to stay alive, had fat bellies, like they had eaten too much. Leonid did not understand how both eating too much and not eating enough could cause the same condition.

Farther up the hill, two villagers crouched on either side of a box. The open side was down, and they were reaching under it, propping up one side with a stick. It was a squirrel trap, the same kind the children of the village made at the end of each summer, when the squirrels were busiest foraging food for winter. But these were adults, and Leonid had not seen a squirrel in months.

The younger Leonid knelt beside the box and lowered his head to peek through the gap.

"If you use a longer stick," he said, "and prop the box from the inside, it's easier for a squirrel to trigger it."

"These are the sticks we have," said the woman, Mrs. Oliynyk. She clipped each word she spoke. Her hair had turned white since the last time Leonid saw her.

The younger Leonid stood and wandered deeper into the forest. The older Leonid did not follow. Just the thought of taking another step made him feel tired. And anyway, he could see his brother through the bare branches. If they could see each other, then they were still as good as together.

The younger Leonid did not go far, bending down and fishing a long, thin branch from the dry needles on the forest floor. He returned to Mrs. Oliynyk.

"Here's a longer stick," he said.

She took it, an expression squeezing her face from all around toward the point of her nose. The older Leonid was not sure if she would use the stick to prop the box or to whip his brother for interfering. Mrs. Kharms slid out from under the trap. She took the stick from Mrs. Oliynyk and ducked back underneath. The woman's fingers did not look much different from the stick they clutched.

"Thank you," said Mrs. Kharms. Her voice sounded trapped.

"There aren't any squirrels," said the older Leonid. "And you need bait. If you have bait, you're better off just eating it yourself."

Mrs. Oliynyk snapped her head to him. "What else are we supposed to do?"

Mrs. Kharms managed to get the box balanced and slowly withdrew her hand.

"Our bait is an old bone," she said. "We're not catching squirrels. We're trying to catch the dog."

"Kasha?" asked the younger Leonid.

"I didn't know it had a name."

Kasha had spent less time in the village lately, but when she did appear, she seemed as healthy as before, like she had some secret source of food. A few of the men in the village had tried to catch her, after the supply of cats was exhausted, but she darted away, a white flash that quickly left her would-be captors behind. The Leonids did not tell any of the villagers that they knew where Kasha went, a small cave, barely more than an indentation at the base of the rocky part of the mountain. They did not know where she might be finding food.

"She," said the younger Leonid.

"What?" asked Mrs. Kharms.

"Kasha is female."

"Stop it!" said Mrs. Oliynyk. She pushed herself up and took stumbling steps down the hill. She slipped on a patch of fallen needles and almost toppled back. Kicking at the ground as if in retaliation, she continued on her way.

"She ate her own cat last week," said Mrs. Kharms.

"You'll never catch Kasha," said the younger Leonid.

"I hope not," she said, patting out a rhythm on the top of the trap as if the box were a drum. "But we have to try. We're alive and part of being alive is trying to stay that way for as long as possible." She stopped drumming. "When one of the other villagers dies, I feel a little glad. I'm not glad that they died, but it means that there will be that much more food for me. Hunger shows us our selfishness."

"Grandmother always gives us larger portions than she takes herself," said the younger Leonid, "so can't it also show the opposite, as well? If someone can give when their body tells them to take, take, take, isn't that good?"

The older Leonid had not noticed that Grandmother took less

food at meals. Whenever the plates were set, he began eating right away, burying his face in the food like a wild animal. Red heat rose in his face, a hollow feeling at the base of his throat to match the one he always had in his stomach. Shame.

"Maybe hunger reveals the good and the bad in us," said Mrs. Kharms. "Maybe it reveals what type of people we are."

"Like Oksana," said the older Leonid.

Mrs. Kharms smiled and looked sad at the same time. "She was a good one." She rested her hand on the younger Leonid's shoulder. "That's one of the joys of being young, that most of your decisions are yet to come. I hope you boys have the chance to make many good decisions."

She drummed each of her fingers on top of the box, four beats. She took ginger steps down the hill and into the village where she disappeared among the cottages.

The younger Leonid kicked under the mouth of the trap and dislodged the stick, pulling his foot out just before the box thumped to the ground.

"What are you doing?" asked the older Leonid.

"What Mrs. Kharms told us to do."

"Ruining her trap?"

"Kasha is a good dog, yes? Then how can it not be good to protect her?"

"People are starving. They'll still try to catch her. This trap isn't the first try, and it won't be the last."

"We're all already in the trap together. The valley itself is the trap."

The younger Leonid walked in a direction away from the village, deeper into the forest. The sun had crested the mountain, and the trees cast latticework shadows, shifting stripes along the bony contours of his body.

"Where are you going?" asked the older Leonid.

"To Kasha's cave."

The older Leonid glanced back to make sure no one was watching. He followed.

GRANDMOTHER RETURNED to the cottage with a small basket half-full of objects that appeared to be mostly edible. She set the basket on the table and removed the items one by one, arranging them according to a system that Leonid did not understand. Objects that looked like tree nuts but shriveled and gray she put in a pile next to a stack of leaves that still had patches of green on them. Next to that, she clustered blades of the bitter grass that still managed to grow in the valley's open areas. Some bark that she would boil into what she called, with a bitter grin, stew.

The older Leonid peeked into the basket, but she pulled it away before he could see anything. He suspected that, like many of the villagers, she had collected bugs, and that they were added to the stew with the tree bark. He decided he would rather not know if that was the case and did not try to look in the basket again. Grandmother placed it on the high shelf over the stove, next to the other empty baskets.

"Did you find anything?" she asked.

The older Leonid pulled a few sere and partially rotted blackberries from his pocket. They felt like pebbles and made a tapping noise as he dropped them on the table.

"And . . ." he said.

Kasha barked. Grandmother started and looked around the cottage, stopping at the bed where the younger Leonid sat, and beside him, Kasha.

"Kasha," she said, looking from the dog to the younger Leonid and back again. "The villagers have been trying to catch her for weeks."

The younger Leonid sprung to his feet. "We can't let them."

Grandmother turned to the older Leonid. He nodded. She reached her fingertips into the pile of nuts on the table and spread them around.

"If the villagers find out," she said, "they'll be furious. Perhaps even dangerous."

"Then we won't let them find out," said the younger Leonid.

"We can keep her here?" asked the older.

"They shouldn't have eaten their cats," said Grandmother. "And the meat of one dog won't make any difference in the long run. It's better to be hungry than full in the belly but empty in the heart."

She clapped her hands. Kasha bounded across the room, stopping at Grandmother's feet. Grandmother scratched Kasha behind the ears.

"Strange that a dog should teach us humanity," she said. "Have I ever told you the story of the man who our village is named after?"

"WHEN BOHDAN ZINOVIY Mykhaylovych Khmelnytsky escaped the Ottomans, he headed swiftly home. There were no trains then, of course, and he had no money, his only possessions his clothes and the sword he had seized and with which he had severed the head of his friend the admiral. Khmelnytsky found work on a boat heading up the Dnieper River, a route that would eventually lead him close to his family estate in Subotiv. He escaped slavery only to once again become an oarsman. The captain of the boat, though a Cossack, had none of the nobility of the Ottoman admiral. This captain whipped the oarsmen when he felt their progress up the river was too slow. No one could ever accuse Khmelnytsky of row-ing slowly, but the captain didn't need a real reason to whip some-one. He was a man who enjoyed the pain of others.

"The first and only lash Khmelnytsky would receive across his broad back came as he helped maneuver the boat around a tangle of drifting branches in the middle of the river. The currents there flowed in unexpected eddies. The captain barked orders, and ev-ery time the crew followed them, they encountered another cur-rent or a fresh snag. The oarsmen grew weary. The captain and his hired hands, a group of brute men who stank of the baked sweat that they seldom washed from their skin, men chosen specifically for their viciousness, never offered to assist at the oars. To Khmel-nytsky, these men were fat and lazy, and worse, incompetent. Any word they spoke impeded the boat's progress. Their orders kept Khmelnytsky far away from his home.

"Bear in mind that he had no idea if his estate at Subotiv still existed, and if it did, if it still belonged to his family. His father was dead. Khmelnytsky himself had been absent for years. He had cousins, but they were still just boys. It would have been no matter at all for a rival to claim the land. Khmelnytsky's family might be dispersed across all Ukraine. He might have no home to return to.

"These were his thoughts when the whip fell. He did not flinch. Blood welled up from the wound and soaked through the back of his shirt. He continued rowing. They were in a particularly quick current, and without his strength at the oar, the boat would slip back down the river. The captain ordered the boat hard to port, an order that would have exposed the side of the boat to the stron-gest current. *No*, called Khmelnytsky, and directed the prow through the oncoming water. He bade the men to row harder, and they rowed harder for him, harder than they ever had for the captain. The boat sliced through the strongest of the current and into the gentler stream near the inner bank of a bend.

"Once the boat was well clear of the current, Khmelnytsky barked his second order, to shore the boat. The captain tried to countermand him, but the oarsmen were exhausted and no one who heard it could disobey the booming voice of Khmelnytsky. The captain raised his whip, but Khmelnytsky sprung to his feet and grabbed the captain's wrist with a hand that had spent years wrapped around the handle of an oar. The captain yelped, a sound like a small animal. Khmelnytsky spoke a single *No* and released the captain's wrist and then helped to finish rowing. That was the last of the captain's whipping.

"The oarsmen rested on the bank, Khmelnytsky off by himself. He heard, though, even from afar, mention of his name. The story of his escape from the Turks, it seemed, had spread quickly through the town at the end of the river. And to that tale, now the oarsmen added their own. At each port some men left and others joined the crew, and each who left took with them Khmelnytsky's name.

"It was in this way that when Khmelnytsky finally arrived at the port near Subotiv, his mother waited for him on the dock. Khmelnytsky's story had outpaced him up the river. His mother had known for days already that he was coming home."

## Star City, Russia—1964

Leonid awoke to sunlight glaring through his window. In his years at Star City he had never slept much past dawn, and during the winter he rose well before the sun. At first he thought he was in another hotel. The preceding month had been an endless string of them, visiting every planetarium in Russia, searching every trash heap in every city for a dog. In a way, he had become used to waking up in unfamiliar surroundings. Now he recognized his own room but at the same time did not. Spots he had always taken for shadows turned out to be water stains on the walls. In one corner, dust piled thick and dark.

The search for dogs had yielded nothing. It seemed there was no other dog as pure white as Kasha. None as small and strange as that little mutant Byelka. Leonid suspected that Byelka would not survive even a single night on the street. The rats would eat him alive. He could have no stray counterpart. The only place to find another like him was the dacha of a party official. The size of one's dog seemed inversely proportional to one's political power.

A knock came on his door, and it opened before Leonid could answer. The lock had never worked. Giorgi bounded in, yanked the sheet off Leonid, and slapped him on the thigh.

"*Arise, ye Russian people!*" Giorgi sang the song from *Alexander Nevsky*. He was always making the other cosmonauts watch old films.

"What time is it?" asked Leonid.

"It's Sunday. Does time even matter?"

"What do you want?"

"It's actually pleasant outside, and I've managed to gather enough people for volleyball. Well, almost enough. We need one more, and that's you."

"What would you have done if I wasn't wearing underwear when you pulled the sheet away?"

"Looked in the other direction." He started singing again. *"Arise, ye Russian people, to glorious battle, to a battle to the death."*

"It's too early for a battle to the death."

Giorgi came around the side of the bed and shoved Leonid to the floor.

"It's nearly noon," he said, "and you're out of bed already."

"Let me put on clothes at least."

"If you insist. Outside in five minutes."

Giorgi slammed the door on his way out of the room.

THE VOLLEYBALL NET spanned a stretch of manicured grass in the long empty quad that ran parallel to the dormitories. Both sides of the quad were lined with trees like a green-walled hallway. Giorgi had jury-rigged posts from a pair of wooden rods that Leonid recognized as belonging to the anechoic chamber, and the net had been woven from old orange restraining harnesses. A crude construction, but it was still nicer than the ratty net they used in the gymnasium.

Whichever side Giorgi was on inevitably won. Not just for volleyball, but for any of the games he organized. Soccer. Hockey. Basketball when the weather was bad and they had to play something indoors. In any one-on-one sport, he dominated, as well. He once smashed a table tennis ball so hard it left a bruise on the Chief Designer's arm after the bounce.

Today, Leonid was on the opposite side of the net from Giorgi, who teamed up with Nadya, Mishin and Bushuyev, and two younger technicians Leonid knew by sight but not name. Leonid's own team consisted of himself and the entire cafeteria staff, each of them still in their white uniforms, stained with the grease of breakfast. Leonid had missed breakfast and regretted it now. He felt weak and slow. Jumping seemed as difficult as the first heaving lift of a rocket. Giorgi rained down spikes, and all Leonid could do was watch. When a spike came directly at him, Leonid made half an effort to pass it, the other half of him concerned with simply getting out of the way. The first set went to Giorgi's team. Then the second. Then the third.

Giorgi cajoled the group into another game, reorganizing the teams so that everyone switched sides except him and Nadya and Leonid. The temperature rose with the sun. The men removed their shirts, except Mishin, or was it Bushuyev, who had grown a pot-belly over the last year. Sweat drenched his shirt, turning the fabric translucent, letting everyone see what was underneath anyway.

In the second game, Giorgi chose to play setter, so instead of him spiking it was usually Nadya. This did not help Leonid much, who still watched the ball whistle by more often than not, and his new team seemed equally unable to keep the ball off the ground. Another three sets all to Giorgi's team. Leonid was not sure if his own team's combined points from the whole match would have been enough to win even a single set. He doubted it.

After the second match, everyone gathered in the shade of the trees lined up along the side of the quad. The cafeteria staff had brought food on ice and unpacked it, spreading out several blankets and arranging a small feast on top of them. Dark bread, cheeses, pickled fish, vegetables—also pickled. Sometimes it seemed that they would pickle anything. They had a patch in the garden dedicated to dill, and by the end of summer the whole plot was bare, picked clean. Leonid was used to the flavor, but now, glossy with sweat and dry in the mouth, he thought it tasted wrong, like something spoiled.

Giorgi pulled one of the blankets and everything on top of it a few meters to the side, from the shade into the sun. Dishes and flatware clinked together. He laid back on the sunny corner of the blanket, still shirtless, skin hale and golden.

"Thank you all," he said. He lifted his head just enough to look at everyone sitting around him, then let it fall back into the grass. "I have two weeks in the Chamber of Silence starting tomorrow. You've allowed me a final afternoon in the sun."

Leonid and Nadya groaned at the same time. The Chamber of Silence, the anechoic chamber, that little box of suffering. Leonid had only had to enter once, and only for a week. The twins who trained to fly into space, though, like Nadya, would spend as long as a month inside. Walls two meters thick. Artificial light. Sensors stuck all over the body. Just a chair and a bed and a desk and whatever equipment the engineers decided to include. And then the meals, shoved through a slit at the bottom of the door with one of the wooden poles that now supported their volleyball net. That was the only noise that ever came in from outside. The scrape of the tray along the two meters of the entryway. Mars, the one who died, would crouch by the door at mealtimes and press his ear into the slit when it opened. Otherwise, not a sound.

"Two weeks?" said Leonid. "What a hell."

"We've all done worse," said Giorgi.

He did not know that the Leonid in front of him had never spent more than seven days in the chamber. The other Leonid was the one who had lasted over a month. Leonid was not allowed to speak to his brother when he emerged from the chamber, but he had seen him from the observation room. He felt that they no longer looked the same. He felt sure that the ruse would be uncovered the moment he was presented as his brother in public.

Giorgi sprang into a seated position then hopped to his feet.

"Who's ready for another game?"

Mishin and Bushuyev grumbled.

"The food hasn't even made it to my belly yet," said Leonid.

"There's only so much sunlight," said Giorgi, "and it won't wait for you to digest."

He grabbed the ball and took it to the net, bouncing it around as he waited for everyone else to join him.

THE TELEVISION MONITOR fish-eyed the interior view of the anechoic chamber, stretching it out toward the corners. Only objects centered perfectly in the camera showed true perspective. As Giorgi moved around the room, his proportions changed. When he reached for something offscreen, his arm seemed to grow as it neared the edge. When he stood, his head elongated into a tube, lips round, nose beaked, eyes like a dopey cat.

Leonid checked in on him a few times a day. This was not required. Technicians manned the observation room all day and night, making notes about Giorgi's heart rate and respiration even as he slept. And it was not as if Leonid could talk to Giorgi. Communication was forbidden. In the morning, one of the technicians would assign Giorgi a set of arbitrary tasks, written on a half sheet of paper, slid through the slit under the door with Giorgi's breakfast.

Today, breakfast consisted of butterbrots with ham and two fried eggs. While Giorgi ate in the chamber, the technicians ate the same thing in the observation room.

The main monitor showed the whole room, distorted corner to

distorted corner, but there were two other monitors, as well. One focused on the bed and one on the desk, which now served as Giorgi's breakfast table. Giorgi took a kettle and set it on the small electric hotplate on the side of the desk. The microphone in the chamber picked up the sizzle as condensation dripped onto the burner. Breakfast included coffee, but one cup was never enough for Giorgi. He drank three or four every morning, though he never touched a drop after that.

Following breakfast, Giorgi slid the tray back through the slit with the wooden rod, which he had returned to the chamber after taking down his makeshift volleyball net. The entryway was sealed at the other end by a second door, and the sound of the metal clanking could be heard through the speakers and from the door itself. Pressurized air hissed out of the chamber as a technician retrieved the tray. She hastily resealed the hatch.

The one space in the room not covered by a camera was the toilet and sink. Giorgi went there, and one technician waited with his hand over the switch to turn off the speakers. If Giorgi took a shit, then the speaker would be turned off until he reappeared on the main camera. If he did anything else—piss, bathe, wash his face, clean his teeth, shave—then the speakers would be left on. Giorgi started singing, some old folk tune, one that the technicians seemed to recognize, but Leonid did not know it. The songs of his own childhood were in a different language.

Water splashed in the sink. Sometimes Giorgi's singing lost its words, turned garbled, or degraded into a hum. The technician turned the volume on the speakers up so loud that the sound hurt Leonid's ears. There, between notes, a small scraping sound. The technician turned the volume back down to a reasonable level. "Shaving," he said, miming the dragging of a razor across his own face. The other technician wrote something on a notepad.

Giorgi reentered the camera's view. He stopped, looked up and directly into the lens, and rubbed his fresh-shaven cheeks. He pressed harder, distorting the shape of his mouth. He flapped his lips open and closed like a fish. The technicians chuckled. Giorgi was the only cosmonaut who made an effort to relieve the dullness of their task. Leonid thought that perhaps the only thing worse than being in the chamber itself would be watching it on television for hours on end.

Giorgi released his face, clapped once, and then dropped directly into a set of push-ups. Leonid left the observation room. Once Giorgi started working out, it could be hours before anything else happened at all.

LEONID ALMOST RAN into the Chief Designer in the hallway.

"How is he?" asked the Chief Designer, looking over Leonid's shoulder at the door to the observation room.

"You're back?" asked Leonid.

"You can see me, can't you?"

There was something different about the Chief Designer. Leonid was reminded of whenever a twin took over for their deceased sibling. Everyone could sense the difference, but of course people changed after being in outer space. Where had the Chief Designer been that could have altered him so?

"Giorgi's fine," said Leonid.

"Good, good. It's almost time, you know."

The Chief Designer was grinning. Leonid did not know that the Chief Designer knew how to grin.

"Time for what?" asked Leonid.

"For our next launch, of course."

Leonid checked up and down the hall. It was empty.

"But we haven't found the other dogs," he whispered.

"Of course, of course. We'll launch the dogs first. But it's also time for our next human cosmonaut. Giorgi is more than ready."

"There's just Giorgi, though, no twin." Leonid still whispered.

"Don't worry yourself, Leonid. Everything's been worked out."

With that he turned and sauntered down the hall. If Leonid had to describe the Chief Designer then, he would have said *jolly*, a word he was sure had never been used to describe anyone in the whole of Star City's history.

## The Kremlin, Moscow, Russia—1964

Every time the Chief Designer visited the Kremlin, he was led through a different tangle of hallways but always ended up in the same room. At least he thought it was the same room. There was a chance that the whole structure comprised similar rooms all furnished with the same long table, the same wood-paneled wainscoting, the same square clock to the right of the door and the same portrait of Marx to the left. Thinking back to other government buildings he had visited, the Chief Designer was unsure that he had not encountered the same arrangement in entirely different cities.

He followed one of Khrushchev's aides down a narrow hallway, lined on one side with high windows and on the other with an ornate colonnade, each post carved with curlicues and flutes and flowers. One tulip pattern, repeated in each column, reminded the Chief Designer of the launchpad for the R-7, the section of column above the flower like the smoke trail of a rocket disappeared through the ceiling.

The aide opened a door at the end of the hallway and then opened a door immediately to the right, through which the Chief Designer found the familiar room. He looked up to confirm it, but he did not need to. He knew the portrait of Marx was there even before he saw it. Khrushchev sat at the far end of the table. There was no one else in the room.

"Tell me, comrade," said Khrushchev before the Chief Designer had taken a seat, "how go preparations?"

"Everything's on schedule, Mr. Khrushchev." The Chief Designer sat.

"For the Revolution, then?"

"We'll have a most impressive celebration."

Khrushchev bent over the table, his pale skin pinched around his eyes. His hair, what was left of it, wispy and white, longed for a comb. Khrushchev's cheeks, usually plump with mirth, seemed instead puffy with fatigue.

"It's a shame about Nedelin," he said.

"He was a great man."

"Did he ever share with you his stories of the war?"

"Yes, a few."

"Tell me, do you think men were braver then? Did the bravest all die in the war, and we're what's left?"

"I believe," said the Chief Designer, speaking slowly, "that those times brought out the bravery in all men. Our people had no choice but to be brave."

"What's the source of our courage today, then?"

"Certainly our cosmonauts."

"Yes, yes! That's my point." Khrushchev straightened his back, gesturing as he spoke, thrusting his finger above him with each phrase. "You know I'm excited for Byelka to fly, but I'm concerned. They tell me that the Americans are ready to launch their next project. Gemini, it's called. While we send two dogs, they'll send two people, Castor and Pollux, if you will."

The Chief Designer smiled at Khrushchev. It was an insincere expression, he knew, one he only used with the Premier. Mishin and Bushuyev sometimes called the Chief Designer *Torgovets* for his ability to push the space program ahead as often with charisma as with science.

"I have a proposition that might get you more excited for the mission."

"Do you, now?" Khrushchev furrowed his brow, but underneath his eyes widened.

"We will rendezvous two ships in outer space. We'll launch the dogs in Vostok, and then launch a cosmonaut in Voskhod, bringing the new ship into close orbit with the first. They will fly in tandem. Imagine the photograph. The first picture taken of a spaceship while in orbit!"

"This can be done?"

"It will be!"

Khrushchev sprang to his feet. "Chief Designer, you always prove me wrong when I doubt you. One day maybe I'll learn."

"It's your job to be diligent."

"Who will be the cosmonaut?"

"We have several in training. All excellent candidates."

"I can't wait to meet whoever it is." He sat back down. "This will be safe for Byelshenka?"

"If he's a brave dog, then I believe there's nothing to fear."

"Nedelin was a brave man."

"Then let's honor his memory with bravery of our own."

Khrushchev rapped his knuckles on the table three times, and a door immediately opened on the opposite side of the room from the door where the Chief Designer had entered. A woman came in bearing an exquisite silver tray. Planted on top of the tray were two crystal glasses and a tall bottle full of brown liquid. A paper label on the bottle said something in English. The woman poured the liquid to the brim of each glass and handed one first to Khrushchev and then to the Chief Designer.

"It's called *bourbon*," said Khrushchev. "Kennedy used to send me a case of the stuff now and again. Johnson sends nothing."

The Chief Designer raised his glass. "To departed friends. May we honor them with our actions."

"To departed friends," echoed Khrushchev.

Two glassfuls later, the Chief Designer left the Kremlin by a different hallway, though he could not tell it apart from the first.

## Star City, Russia—1964

Nadya sipped tea from a cup with a picture of her face on it. Such tea sets had been popular the year after her launch. As Ignatius put it, every home in the Soviet bloc had received one as a gift for the New Year in 1960. While visiting planetariums and looking for dogs, Leonid had seen the sets in every secondhand store he came across, the cheap porcelain chipped and faded, Nadya's face reduced to that of a ghost. The tea set at Star City was apparently made of better stuff, the picture still as crisp as ever. Nadya hummed a simple melody between sips.

Leonid sat opposite Nadya at one of the low tables in the lounge, and beside him sat Ignatius, who revolved a teacup in her fingers, orbiting Nadya's face in and out of view. She was never one to sip, preferring instead to chug down whatever liquid she was served. She pulled out a crumpled pack of cigarettes and tapped the bottom until one poked up. She grabbed it with her teeth directly from the pack.

"You're not supposed to smoke in the building," said Nadya. "It damages the equipment."

"Even the Chief Designer smokes in the building."

"I've never seen him."

"That's because the Chief Designer never smokes around you. When you leave a room, he has no compunction about lighting up, even around the most delicate equipment."

Ignatius reached into the pocket of her leather jacket and

pulled out a match that she had somehow struck before it even emerged. The tip of the cigarette fizzed. She took in a deep drag and puffed out a gray cloud that covered the whole corner of the room.

"I don't like the smell," said Nadya.

"Nor do I," said Ignatius. She puffed again. "Have you seen this, Leonid?"

She held up the cigarette box, smoothing out the creases with her thumb. Leonid had seen the brand, Cosmos, before. The boxes came in any number of bright colors with space-themed illustrations. Fantastical renderings of Vostok, portraits of Nadya like those on the teacups, other cosmonauts, Sputnik, rockets. He had lost count of all the different designs. This one, though, he had not seen before, a new portrait. It looked familiar but off, and he knew it was his brother, or himself, despite the fact that the nose was skewed and his smile never stretched so wide.

"I don't even smoke," he said.

"There are also playing cards and matchboxes. Oh, and I was sent portraits of Kasha and Byelka for approval. Kasha strikes a noble pose! I should have brought it to show you."

"A noble pose might be all that's left of her," said Nadya.

"Please, Nadya. I didn't mean to bring the conversation down. We have months yet."

"One dog for another. I don't care for the exchange whenever it happens."

Ignatius pointed with the smoldering end of her cigarette. "Remember that. It's always an exchange, always one thing for another thing, and if you do it right, then the other thing is of a slightly lesser value than what you get."

"Lesser value?" Nadya held the teacup up in front of her.

Ignatius's carefree expression, the one she always bore,

soured. "When you have two objects of equal value but only need one, what do you do? Choosing in such a situation is a game of chance. And you were all chosen the day you left your homes. Tsiolkovski had a plan, and none of the rest of us ever had the wherewithal to challenge it. The Chief Designer made it worse, for certain, but the whole mess was put in motion while he was nothing more than a junior engineer. His grand ambitions aside, this is a burden he couldn't have borne had Tsiolkovski not paved the road for him in advance."

"I always thought . . ." Leonid was interrupted by a commotion in the hallway. A cluster of technicians sprinted past the open door, talking to each other all at once, a ruckus like one of Giorgi's parties. Then came stragglers, running hard and silent except for panted breaths, white lab coats fanning out behind them. More people wore lab coats at Star City than Leonid thought could possibly need to.

Nadya set down her teacup, and Ignatius ground out her cigarette on a corner of the table, smearing the ash into the wood.

"What happened?" asked Ignatius.

"The chamber," said Nadya. "They're headed in the direction of the chamber."

THE HALLWAY OUTSIDE the observation room was filled to bursting with technicians, white coats rubbing up against white coats. They surged as a single mass at the door, but there were too many of them to get anywhere. Ignatius shouted for them to move, and when no one did she and Nadya began to pull them out of the way, and not gently. Several of the technicians tried to fight back until they saw that it was Nadya who moved them. One stubborn man refused, not budging until Ignatius pinned his arm painfully behind his back and led him aside like a prisoner. Leonid watched from a step behind.

Just inside the door to the observation room, Mishin and Bushuyev stood there like bouncers, pushing away anyone who neared the threshold. Nadya and Ignatius made it to the door, Leonid a step after, even as the ranks of technicians closed up behind them. Leonid kept getting shoved in the back. Flailed elbows found a way to his ribs.

Mishin and Bushuyev saw Nadya, and their set frowns loosened.

"Thank god," said one of them. "Where's the Chief Designer?"

"I don't know," answered Nadya.

Mishin and Bushuyev exchanged a look.

"Come in," said the other one of them, "but be warned. It's an ugly sight."

As soon as Nadya, Ignatius, and Leonid entered the room, Mishin and Bushuyev resumed their posts in the doorway. Beyond them, the technicians had calmed, only a few left struggling to earn a view inside.

Compared to the hallway, the observation room was absolutely hushed. One technician sat at the video monitors. He seemed to be shuttling a recording of the video feed back and forth. The screen was too far away to see what was on it. Sometimes the whole screen filled with white. Several other people stood around the room, arms crossed in waiting. They wore the same white coats as the technicians, but the stethoscopes slung around their necks identified them as doctors.

"What happened?" asked Leonid.

Everyone in the room looked at him and then looked away, in the direction of the two-meter-long tunnel to the anechoic chamber, without answering. A repeating squeak came from inside.

Three technicians, maybe doctors, or a combination of both, wheeled a gurney into the unlit tunnel. One of the wheels wobbled and seemed to be the source of the squeak.

The gurney entered the first slant of light angling from the observation room. Ignatius covered her open mouth and stepped back. A tear streaked from Nadya's left eye. Leonid did not understand. The gurney was marred with black and a dark lump rested upon it. It was the smell that let him understand, fresh-seared meat. It made him hungry for an instant until he realized the source of the smell, the charred thing on the gurney, young Giorgi somehow burnt to near nothing. Nothing human, at least.

Leonid found Giorgi's face and made himself look. It was less black than the rest of him, reddish and bubbled with exploded skin. Where his eyes had been, just indentions and crisp flesh. The end of his nose completely gone. His golden hair an impossible memory. Giorgi's lips, ashy with stripes of pink where they had split, moved in slow syllables. Leonid leaned close and walked with the gurney across the room, listening.

Instead of clearing a path, the technicians in the hallway pressed closer, preventing the gurney from exiting. Mishin and Bushuyev tried to shove through the throng, but got lost in it themselves. The doctors called for people to make way, clear passage, move, but no command had any effect. Ignatius stepped to the doorway and drew a Makarov pistol from somewhere within her leather jacket. She pressed the Makarov to the forehead of one of the technicians, an old woman, white hair in a pouf around her head. A crazed look had reigned the woman's face and the faces of the whole crowd. Now her expression softened and set off a chain reaction of reason. The shoving and shouting stopped, and the crowd spread itself along either side of the hallway until the path was clear.

Leonid remembered watching Nadya's homecoming parade on television. All of Moscow lining the streets. Some of the engineers claimed that when she entered Red Square, the roar of the crowd could be heard as far away as Star City. This parade, though, the only one Giorgi would ever receive, passed in silence.

Ignatius led the way, pistol held loosely in her dangling hand, followed by Mishin and Bushuyev, the gurney and the attendant doctors. Nadya and Leonid brought up the rear. A few of the technicians in the hallway wept, but most stood stock-still like they were part of one of Giorgi's murals, painted there on the hallway wall.

"What did Giorgi say?" asked Nadya.

"He just repeated the same thing over and over," said Leonid. "'It was my fault. It was my fault.'"

THE SOUND of the road whirred up through the floor of the ambulance. Somehow, instead of the doctors, Leonid and Ignatius had ended up riding with Giorgi. Nadya rode up front with the driver. When the Chief Doctor protested, Ignatius told him that she was more qualified than he for such severe trauma. When he protested again, she threatened to injure him in such a way that he would need her services, as well. Leonid did not know if she actually had medical training, but it certainly seemed so. She opened one of the small metal cupboards on the wall of the ambulance and pulled out a large syringe and a glass vial. She drew the clear liquid into the syringe. It looked like nothing more than water, barely enough to wet a parched mouth. Without a flinch, she pushed the needle into Giorgi's neck and expelled the contents.

"This will help with the pain," she said, speaking to Leonid.

Leonid watched his friend, or what was left of him. The drug did seem to help. After several seconds, Giorgi's burned body relaxed, muscles loosening. His hands, fingers curled in like a bird of prey's talons, eased into a more natural shape. Leonid thought of a blossoming flower, but something was not quite right. Whole fingers were missing from Giorgi's hands, burned completely away. Nausea surged from Leonid's bowels to the top of his throat. He covered his mouth and swallowed hard three times.

"Vomiting on him won't help the situation," said Ignatius. "Are you all right?"

"I won't vomit," said Leonid.

"Leonid?" Giorgi's voice was weak, slurred like when he drank all night at one of his parties. "Leonid, is that you?"

"I'm here," said Leonid.

"I can't see. The flash blinded me."

"There's nothing to see now but the back of the ambulance."

"Every time one of you returned from space, you all described the stars the same way. The exact same words. Did you know that? 'They do not sparkle, just a pure point of light.' I wanted to see the stars, if only so I could come up with a better description. The rest of you never had an eye for art."

Giorgi coughed. Against the black of his friend's lips, Leonid could not tell if it was blood or spit that came up. Leonid made himself look, despite the ill feelings it caused. He felt obligated, like the reason he was allowed in the back of the ambulance was to bear witness. The skin all over Giorgi's body had the same parched look as his face, but here and there a crosshatched pattern patched the flesh. The jumpsuit. In the flames, the fabric had melted into his skin.

"Do you remember when I first arrived at Star City?" asked Giorgi. "You were assigned to show me around. You barely knew anything about the place. The worst tour I ever had."

"I'm sorry," said Leonid, though the other Leonid was the one who had given Giorgi the tour.

"Do you remember what you told me at the end?" asked Giorgi.

"Remind me."

"I remember it exactly. 'The worst days are yet to come,' you said, 'but just tell yourself that it must be worth it. We wouldn't be here if it was not worth it.'"

"I said that?"

"You believed it, but I'm not so sure you still believe it when I look at you now. Not that I can see." He laughed, which turned into a cough.

Ignatius leaned over him and pressed a folded-over strip of gauze to Giorgi's lips. It was soaked through with red when she pulled it away.

"Do you remember the weekend when we snuck away to Moscow?" asked Giorgi. "What was the girl's name? The short blonde with the pretty pout?"

"I don't recall."

"Of course you do. It's not as if you had many opportunities to bed a woman. Maybe now, but not then."

"Svetlana?"

"No, no." Giorgi's voice had faded to a whisper, barely louder than the hum of the ambulance.

"Perhaps you should rest your voice."

"Is this even my voice? I sound different. And you, Leonid, you sound the same, but I'm not sure it's you. It's like you're someone different since you returned. Does space change you that much? I always looked forward to going so I could see who I was when I came back. Who else gets the chance to be two people in one life?"

Giorgi started to cough but it caught in his throat. His whole body spasmed. After, his breaths came only in rasps. He tried to say something, but his voice was gone. Ignatius drew more of the liquid from the vial and injected it. Giorgi's breathing slowed.

"We're still here, Giorgi," said Leonid. "The Leonid you knew before and the one you know now. The whole purpose of the new one is to make sure the old one doesn't die."

Giorgi murmured, but it was not a word. The sound seemed to have no human thought behind it.

The ambulance lurched to a stop, rattling the gurney and all the equipment stored on the walls and in the cupboards. Leonid and Ignatius slid forward along the bench. Ignatius banged her fist against the wall at the back of the cabin.

"Careful!" she shouted.

The muffled voice of the driver replied, "We've reached the hospital."

Ignatius looked at Leonid as if she was just then noticing that he was there. She pulled a white coat off a hook by the back door.

"Here," she said. "Put this on. I'd prefer that no one see your uniform. Then help me get this gurney unlatched."

The doors swung open as Leonid slid one arm into a sleeve of the coat. With the coat half-hanging from him, he helped Ignatius lower the gurney to the ground. The doctor waiting there gaped when he saw Giorgi's body.

"*Bozhe moi,*" he said. "What happened?"

Ignatius produced a small folio from her pocket and flipped it open, revealing some sort of identification card. The doctor's eyes grew wider than when he had first seen Giorgi.

"Make him comfortable," said Ignatius, and then she walked in a direction away from the hospital doors.

Nadya still sat in the front seat of the ambulance, watching out the window as if at a passing landscape. The glass of the window made it hard to make out her face. Leonid finished donning the white coat and followed the gurney into the hospital. He waited there as doctors scuttled all around Giorgi, the room too dark, walls painted a green the color of sickness itself, until it became obvious that Giorgi's last words had already been spoken.

NADYA HAD BEEN kicked out of the ambulance and now sat beside Leonid in the waiting room, humming a simple melody to herself. There was nothing left to wait for. The doctor had come out and said he was sorry and explained that the burns were just too much. Giorgi's body had simply stopped working. Leonid was not sure if it was one of the doctors from Star City or one who belonged to the hospital. They all looked alike. Leonid cinched the open front of the white coat he wore to conceal the uniform underneath.

From the other side of a set of metal double doors came a squabble, and then they flew open and the Chief Designer hulked through. Sweat spangled the bald portion of his head. He wore no coat, and his shirt was unbuttoned one button farther than usual. He saw Nadya and Leonid and hurried to them. He creaked down to one knee and looked Leonid in the eye.

"Where is he?" asked the Chief Designer.

Leonid looked away.

"He's gone," said Nadya.

"Into surgery? To a burn specialist?" The Chief Designer offered this as a prayer more than a question.

"Just minutes ago. He succumbed. The doctors said the exact cause several times. What was it?"

Leonid spoke without looking at anyone. "Hypovolemic shock and loss of myocardial contractility. Whatever that means."

Mishin and Bushuyev came through the metal doors, one of

them walking backward, apologizing to a nurse who seemed to be making half an effort to prevent them from entering. They stopped behind the Chief Designer and looked first at Nadya and then at Leonid, back and forth. Finally, Leonid shook his head once.

"What happened?" asked the Chief Designer. His voice was higher than normal and pinched.

"There was the spark," said Mishin or Bushuyev.

"I know that!" snapped the Chief Designer. "I need people to stop telling me things I already know."

He punched his fist into the tiled floor. Leonid thought he heard a crack.

"Leonid and I don't know," said Nadya. "Tell us what happened."

Mishin and Bushuyev looked at each other. The Chief Designer flopped back into a seated position on the floor. He lowered his head and lifted his hand in Mishin and Bushuyev's direction. One of them began:

"Giorgi had about an hour left in the anechoic chamber. He's usually so calm in there, busy maybe, but not nervous. Today he was getting antsy as the clock ticked down. He made himself a cup of tea, and then asked us to flip off the monitors so he could get all those *damn sensors* off him. That's what he said. He said they started itching after the first day and he could not handle it any longer. We flipped off the monitors so he could have a little privacy. We left the speakers on, of course. He was singing, no surprise. And then there was a strange noise, and the technician asked if everything was all right, and then the first scream. The technician turned the monitor back on, but it took so long to warm up, and we could not go inside until we knew what was happening. Not that it would have mattered. When the technician played the recording, we saw that the flames consumed Giorgi immediately. He'd been removing the sensors with a cotton pad soaked in alcohol, to break up the adhesive. In the past, he usually just ripped them off, but maybe he was doing it to pass the time. We'd never seen him so antsy. He finished with the sensors on his chest and stomach and tossed the cotton pad onto the desk. But it skipped to the hotplate and made contact with the burner. Just a little spark, we're sure, too small to be seen on the monitor, but right then the flames flared through the whole room, and when they settled, Giorgi was engulfed. We use a high-oxygen mix in the chamber, for pressurization. The oxygen is what flared. His uniform must have been saturated with it, which is why he kept burning. No one ever considered such a thing. No one even thought of it."

"We don't need excuses," interrupted the Chief Designer.

Mishin and Bushuyev hesitated for a moment, and then the other continued, "Once it was clear the flames were limited only to Giorgi, the technicians rushed in and threw a blanket over him. Until then, Giorgi had remained standing. He was almost calm, patting at his body as if searching for a pack of cigarettes in one of his pockets. He tried to make his way to the bed, but his eyes must have been ruined already, and he just kept bumping into the desk. He knocked that damn hotplate to the floor. Watching the video, we were terrified that would cause another spark and another explosion, but nothing happened. We knew that it had not happened, that there had only been one explosion, but we were still afraid. The technicians came and got us, and word got out, and everyone was there. Thank god for Ignatius, or we would never have gotten him out of the room."

The Chief Designer raised his head. "You didn't mention Ignatius before."

Mishin and Bushuyev did not respond. One of them pulled out a handkerchief and dabbed at the corners of his eyes though it did not seem that he was crying. Minutes went by with no one speaking. A nurse passed from the ward through the waiting room out the double doors to the hospital entrance beyond. That might have been an hour ago or only seconds, thought Leonid. The Chief Designer lumbered up from the floor, a motion as if he were assembling his body from pieces into the shape of a standing man.

"Let's see him," he said.

He walked through the other set of steel doors into the ward without waiting for anyone to show him the way. No one thought to follow.

THE CHIEF DESIGNER peered into each room he passed until he came to one where the patient was completely covered by a white sheet. He entered and pulled the sheet back, revealing the black face of a mummy, dry skin stretched tight, lips shriveled back to reveal charred teeth. He had once taken his son to see a mummy at an Egyptian exhibition in Moscow years before. The mummy had terrified the boy. Only a trip to a whole other museum, one with taxidermied animals posed as if in nature, had finally dispelled the fright.

There was nothing to identify the thing before the Chief Designer as young Giorgi. Whatever had made his face recognizable, that made it recognizable as a face, had burned away. Had it not been still attached to a body, the Chief Designer could have dismissed this face as no more than an old hunk of wood, weathered to black. He touched the face. It felt like plastic. He tried to ignore the smell.

He had seen worse in the gulag. A desiccated corpse had nowhere near the gut-churning effect of a fresh wound. The smell was not so pungent as gangrene. With Giorgi he did not have to watch a body slowly rot away. It had been hot and fast. The Chief Designer massaged the scar on his scalp.

"Giorgi, my friend. I was finally ready for you. What's the story from the Bible? Who has read a Bible in decades? My mother, though, took us to church. There wasn't a church proper, but we met in the basement of an apartment building. One of the men who lived there read passages from the Bible and then explained them, as if such stories required explanation. It was the story of the prodigal son, Giorgi. He was the one who left and came back. I was going to bring you back."

The Chief Designer took labored breaths. The simple act of talking exhausted him, how he imagined the cosmonauts must feel in the centrifuge. He rubbed his eyes.

"I should weep for you, my friend, but it seems I can't. One day, I'll grieve you properly. All of Russia will. You were the last of the original six. The last true cosmonaut. The only one."

He pulled the sheet back over Giorgi's face. His hands trembled. He turned. Ignatius stood in the doorway.

"You're more sentimental than most in Star City would suspect," she said.

"What will you do with the body?" asked the Chief Designer.

"We'll bury him in his hometown. His family will be told that he died in a training accident. Training with planes, mind you. No statues, I'm afraid. Not yet."

"If I don't live to see the day when he can be honored, will you see to it?"

"I'm not that much younger than you, but yes, I'll make sure his statue is a particularly majestic one."

"You make jokes?"

"How else do we cope with this?"

"You can start by reassuring me that all of it hasn't been a mistake."

Ignatius chuckled. "What will you do now?"

"I'm afraid that the only solution is to make my largest mistake yet."

"Which is?"

"There is one fully trained cosmonaut left."

"You wouldn't, would you?"

"Tell me an alternative. Do you know where I was before I came to the hospital? I was at the Kremlin. I announced my plans to Khrushchev. Not just sending his dog to space, but a cosmonaut at the same time. The General Designer's heat shield works. We can save the dogs without needing twins for them. But that wasn't enough for me. I promised a human flight, too."

"It's Nadya, then, who will finally fly her mission."

Ignatius took one step into the room. Two men entered behind her, each wearing a black coat. The Chief Designer realized how difficult it was to tell an undertaker from a security officer. The man on the left carried a long black bag draped over his arm, canvas coated with rubber. He removed the sheet from Giorgi, spread the bag alongside his body, and with the help of the other man lifted the body, light as paper, into the bag's long slit. The zipper ratcheted loud in the room.

MARS HEARD the commotion in the hallway outside the radio room, but he did not go to investigate. He had been living there full-time for a month, only leaving to get food and relieve himself and bathe but seldom that. The Chief Designer had visited less and less, and then Mishin and Bushuyev, too. They still stopped by occasionally to speak a few words to Leonid, but even those had been reduced to mere pleasantries. Leonid, for his part, never had much to say to anyone but Mars. Whenever one of the others spoke to him, he would answer their questions, then echo the questions back, wait for an answer, and comment on it with a single word. *Good. Unfortunate. Interesting.* Then the conversation ended, the duty of both sides fulfilled.

It reminded Mars of the two young engineers, a man and woman whose names he could not remember, who had begun to spend time together, sneaking away to walk on the quad, taking meals at the same time, pressuring the chiefs to put them on the same projects. That initial spark had faded, though. After a few months they made only the motions of a relationship. Yes, the couple still ate at the same time, but where once the meals had been about little touches and whispered, punch-drunk exchanges, they descended into rote silence. They seemed to say just enough to each other as necessary, as if conversation were an unwanted obligation. It was no surprise to anyone, except maybe the couple, when things finally fizzled out completely. It had been over for some time without them even noticing.

Maybe the Chief Designer and the others could not come to grips with a thing that should have ended long ago still going. They had expected days, and instead it was months. They had prepared only so many words, so many thoughts, and their supply was long since exhausted. Leonid refused to die. No, that was not it. Dying simply did not occur to Leonid. That is what Mars had concluded. Death was the thought of death. So far, Leonid had other things to think about.

Mars was lying on the cot when the radio crackled. Usually he was up and waiting, but he had been lost in his own thoughts, the only thoughts, besides Leonid's, he ever had access to anymore.

"Hello?" came Leonid's voice from the speaker. Every day, the sound seemed farther away, even though Mars knew the opposite was true. The orbit decayed. Every moment brought Leonid a hairsbreadth closer to the atmosphere and the same fiery reentry that had claimed Nadya. And Mars's brother.

Mars tumbled getting off the cot and fell against the console, bashing his elbow. He turned on the microphone and spoke through his teeth, gritted against the numbing pain that shot up the length of his arm.

"I'm here," he said.

"Is anyone else with you?" asked Leonid.

"No one else."

"I've been thinking . . ."

"Yes?"

"I've been thinking about why I was fearful before the launch. I knew it meant my death, yes. I knew the dangers, that my death might come before I could actually accomplish anything. I knew I might never beam back a single word, which seems strange now, since I have spoken so many to you. Do you write them down?"

"I didn't think to."

"That's all right. It would make a terrible book, anyway."

"Certainly the book would have been hard to follow."

"I've been thinking that the reason I was scared is not because of what fate awaited me but because of the many familiar things I had to leave behind. All I knew since childhood was Star City. Maybe I was always just a martyr-in-training there, but I knew the people and they knew me. I had a routine. I had a bedroom in which I lived for more years than I can remember. I still know what books are on the shelves. Has anyone cleaned out my room?"

"As far as I know it remains untouched. Leonid, your brother, was supposed to move in, but he refused. He stayed in his old room in the twins' dormitory."

"He was never much of a reader. Or was he? Of all the people I knew at Star City, he was not one of them. I saw him only a few times in all the years. Did you see Mars? Your brother, I mean."

"I didn't see him even on the day he launched. He refused my visit."

"I won't lie. I resent my brother and the fact that he gets to live. Perhaps your brother felt the same."

"Sometimes I think it was simply his way to have the final word in all our boyhood arguments. We spoke through the radio after he launched, but that's something different."

"My point is," said Leonid, "that I had friends in Star City. I had a life that was not so bad. Even knowing it had to end, I enjoyed it. I won't speak of my childhood, but know that it wasn't pleasant. I never expected to escape it. But I did and I found a measure of happiness. My fear, then, was that leaving Star City would be a return to the dark past that preceded it. A silly fear, yes? The only future I have is this little capsule, this egg, hurtling so fast through the dark that no other darkness could possibly catch up."

"So your fear was unfounded?"

"I now know that leaving one place is not the same thing as returning to another."

Static popped the speaker. Mars did not know if Leonid had fallen silent or simply passed out of range.

## *Bohdan, Ukraine—1950*

Even Grandmother had finally grown thin. When she hiked up the hem of her dress before kneeling to pray, her calves, once fat as tree limbs, were withered to twigs. The prayer, too, was something new. One day she knelt out of nowhere and spoke to herself in whispers. Leonid just barely remembered his father doing the same, and knew that Grandmother had as well, but she was one of the few villagers who seemed happy when the Soviets came and dismantled the church. She was one of the few who did not gather at the train station to say goodbye to the priest.

At first, the two Leonids had just watched Grandmother pray. Sometimes they walked outside. At the very least they went to the other side of the cottage. But as the prayers came day after day, first the younger Leonid and then the older joined her, kneeling on the floor, facing the blank wood of the east wall. The older Leonid did not know what he was supposed to pray about. Usually, he just whispered the thoughts in his head, carrying on a conversation with himself. He tried to eavesdrop on Grandmother, but whatever she said never made it beyond her lips. No, he never learned why they prayed, but he knew for sure that he did not want Grandmother to have to pray alone.

As they knelt today, Kasha would not stop being a bother. She nuzzled up into Leonid's crotch as if trying to lift him on her snout. She walked behind and pawed at the bottoms of his bare feet.

When he refused to budge, she moved on to his brother. And when his brother did not move, Kasha tried with Grandmother. She tolerated a few pokes of Kasha's nose to her buttocks before dropping back into a crouch and scratching Kasha behind the ears.

"What is it, dog?"

Kasha streaked to the door, still as fast as ever despite suffering the same starvation that affected everyone.

"Let her outside," said Grandmother.

The Leonids rose and headed to the door. Letting Kasha out had become a ritual of sorts. One of the brothers would go out first, halfway up the path to the rest of the village. From there he could signal back to the other brother if someone headed their way. The brother who stayed with Kasha led her around to the other side of the cabin. With the trees leafless, they worried that the white flash of the dog would be easily spotted against the gray earth even from a distance. Kasha did not need to be led. She seemed to know to head to the back on her own. If anyone came from the direction of the village, Leonid felt sure Kasha would know to hide. The ritual then was for the sake of the brothers. It gave them something to do. A brief, twice-daily distraction from the pain that became more and more pronounced in their guts each morning.

When the older Leonid reached the door, Kasha darted to the other side of the room.

"Do you want to go outside or not?" he said.

Kasha pushed herself into the corner where the cabinet met the wall. None of them had ever seen her cower before.

"What is it, girl?" asked the younger Leonid.

A knock came on the door, and the older Leonid, who still stood right next to it, jumped at the sound. The motion sent a sharp pain through his ankles, knees, and hips, fading into a dull burn in the long muscles of his legs. The door swooped open, almost clipping his shoulder. Mykola burst in.

The younger Leonid stood in front of Kasha, though his skinny legs did little to conceal the dog.

"It's customary to allow someone to answer the door after you knock," said Grandmother.

"There are men coming," said Mykola, panting.

"Soldiers?" asked the older Leonid.

"Mr. Honchar and Mr. Dyachenko. They're half-mad. The Honchar baby died this morning. Dyachenko is the uncle, you know, and his own children died already. They were outside saying they would hunt down anyone who was hoarding food. They didn't hide their suspicions about your cottage. They said that out here by yourself you could have enough food hidden away for everyone, the whole village."

"Does it look like any of us have eaten?" Grandmother held up her arm, and the skin hung like a sheet drying on a line.

Leonid realized how little of her there was left. He wondered if there would come a day when he would discover just her empty skin, all the stuff on the inside wasted away. Already she no longer matched his memory of her, the pleasant roundness of her face replaced by angles.

Mykola said, "They already came through our cottage and flipped all the furniture and threw everything from the cabinet. It didn't matter that there was no place food might be hidden."

"Let them come," said Grandmother. "I won't allow them to enter."

"Honchar has an ax. He threatened Mother with it when she tried to stop him. I think he would have struck her if I hadn't pulled her away."

"That man was barely strong enough to wield an ax even when he was well fed. I'm not worried about that." She looked back at the younger Leonid. "However, I don't think it would be good if they found Kasha."

Kasha poked her snout from behind the younger Leonid's legs. Mykola, across the room, stepped forward.

"She's still alive? I thought surely someone had . . ." The phrase choked off in his throat.

"Will you tell them about her?" asked the older Leonid.

"I can't believe she's still alive."

Mykola was crying, thin tears that did little more than glisten his cheeks. He gripped the older Leonid at the biceps. His fingertips touched on the back side of Leonid's arm.

"We have to protect her," said Mykola. "We can't let the men find her."

Grandmother crossed the room and pulled Mykola's hand from Leonid.

"Did anyone see you come?" asked Grandmother.

"I snuck away while Honchar and Dyachenko were in another home."

"Then take Kasha around back and follow the path up the hill. Do you know the path?"

"We've played there before."

"It leads to a dry creek bed, which cannot be seen from below. Go there and follow the creek toward the pass. Find a place to conceal yourself as best you can and wait. I'll send the twins to find you when it's safe for Kasha to return."

"Will the dog follow me?"

"I'm sure of it. She's a wise animal, and she'll do whatever it takes to protect us."

Mykola looked at Kasha, now emerged from behind the younger Leonid and sitting on her haunches in the center of the room. Mykola's brow furrowed in worry. Grandmother grabbed the boy's chin and directed his gaze to meet her own.

"Do you know that the dog has not eaten since we brought her here? Over a month, and not one lick. She protects us, and she'll protect you."

It was true. Kasha had refused even the small bites of food offered to her. At each meal, such as they were, the boys shared morsels from their own pitiful portions. But the morsels would sit there, on the bare wood of the floor, ignored by the dog completely, until the boys gave up and ate the food themselves. When they tried to feed her from their hands, she would push the offering away with her nose, then hurry off before the food could be offered again.

"That's impossible," said Mykola.

"We've survived on little more than nothing," said Grandmother, "and Kasha is a special dog. Now it's up to you to protect her. Go."

Mykola hesitated.

"Go!" shouted Grandmother.

Mykola started at the shout and hustled straight to the door, still open from when he entered. On the front step, he patted his thigh, beckoning Kasha to follow. She streaked between Mykola's legs and out of sight around the cottage.

"Thank you, Mykola," said the younger Leonid.

Mykola jogged after Kasha.

"Will she be all right?" asked the older Leonid.

"It would take more than a man with an ax to stop her," said Grandmother. "In that way, Kasha and I have something in common."

She grabbed the broom from the corner and leaned against the table, facing the door.

HONCHAR ENTERED WITHOUT even knocking. Grandmother stood from the table, sweeping a single spot on the floor. She did not greet him. His eyes twitched around the room, flitting from spot to spot. His hair, now speckled with gray where only months ago it had been nothing but black, wired from his head in every direction. A streak of snot glistened his mustache underneath one nostril. The ax dangled from his knobby fingers.

"We're here to search your cottage," he said.

Grandmother stopped sweeping and gripped the broomstick at an angle in front of her chest. "No, you're not."

Leonid heard the sound of Dyachenko rooting through the pile of firewood outside. There was not much wood left, certainly not enough to hide anything. In years past, the supply would have been replenished months ago. But who had strength for chopping wood? Who really expected to live long enough to see winter?

"If you have nothing to hide," said Honchar, "then you have nothing to worry about."

"You will not search my home."

Honchar raised the ax. The blade showed chips and spots of rust. It had not met a whetstone in some time.

Grandmother sprung forward. Honchar took a step back, but too slow. As if wielding a sword, Grandmother arced the broomstick forward and connected with Honchar's knuckles. The ax fell from his hand, the dull blade embedding in the worn wood of the floor. Honchar reached with his other hand to retrieve the ax, but Grandmother swung again, this time landing a blow on the top of his shoulder. He yelped and fell to one knee.

"*Suka,*" he said.

Raising the broom over her head, Grandmother stepped toward him. Honchar leapt up and backed into the doorway, colliding with Dyachenko, who had come at the sound of Honchar's cry. The two men fell over each other, heaped at the foot of the front steps.

Grandmother stood in the doorway, looming over them.

"Thank you," she said, "for the ax."

Dyachenko tried to struggle toward her, but Honchar held him back.

"If I hear of you searching another home," said Grandmother, "I won't hold back the next time."

She started to come back inside, but paused just past the threshold. Her lip trembled, and tears blurred her eyes. She turned back to the men outside.

"I'm sorry about your daughter," she said.

She closed the door to Honchar's weeping.

MYKOLA STARTED to come to the cottage almost every day, and on the days he did not visit, the Leonids usually went to visit him. When Oksana had died, the village's children had stopped playing together. It was partly due to worried parents, who feared that the fever would spread. It was partly exhaustion. What child had energy to waste on play?

Then a sort of euphoria spread among the villagers. Parents and children alike had long since passed the point of exhaustion, and in its place came a feeling at once calm and giddy. It even affected Honchar, who returned to his old self as if the incident with the ax had never occurred.

Still, though, Grandmother, the Leonids, and Mykola kept Kasha a secret. Grandmother told them that the current mood was partly delirium. The promise of even Kasha's scant meat might drive the whole village into a craze like Honchar's. The dog, for her part, refused to eat and seemed as well as ever.

Mykola arrived at the cottage earlier than usual. He knocked once and entered without waiting for someone to answer. Grandmother still wore her bedclothes. The younger Leonid rubbed at his face with a parched cloth by the basin. The older Leonid sat cross-legged on the floor, groggy from sleep. The only one to acknowledge Mykola's arrival was Kasha, who scampered over and waited for a pet behind the ears.

"Come, girl," said Mykola, "I have a treat for you."

He took one of the seats by the table and opened his palm. Some sort of berry rested there, shriveled and sickly. He often brought a speck of leftover food to see if Kasha would eat it. Berries, stewed bark, insects, greens, any ort he could smuggle from his family's makeshift meals.

Kasha sniffed at his palm, even nudged the berry with her nose, but she did not eat it. As always, she used her snout to push Mykola's hand back. Then she stared at him until he ate the berry himself. After Mykola swallowed with a big deliberate gulp, Kasha sprinted a lap around the room, stopping again in front of him, panting happily.

"I often think that she's an angel," said Mykola, stroking the dog's back.

"There's no such thing," said the older Leonid.

"The teacher told us there's no such thing as a god, but why does everyone assume that means there can't still be angels? I like the idea of angels much better than the idea of god."

"Last I checked, Kasha doesn't have wings."

"Maybe the wings were made up by the same people who made up god. Maybe an angel can look like anything it wants."

"What does an angel do, then, besides run in circles around a room?"

"It watches us from above, from heaven or whatever's out there. And then sometimes it comes down, like Kasha here, to offer help."

"I thought we were helping her."

"We have nothing left in this valley," interjected Grandmother, "but she's given us some small purpose. Something more than simply waiting to die."

"So you think she's an angel, too?" asked the younger Leonid.

"I don't know about that," answered Grandmother. "I think she's just a dog, though a very special one. One that has learned kindness. No, not an angel. But human? That I might believe."

Mykola petted Kasha. Grandmother stood by the cold stove. The Leonids stayed where they were. All of them gazed at the little white dog in the center of the room, as if searching for something woven into her fur.

From the far distance came a low whine. At first, Leonid thought the sound came from inside his own head, a memory. But the sound grew, entering full-throated into the valley. It was the train coming through the pass. How many months since that had last happened? Could it possibly bring relief? Or was it soldiers again, come to rob the village of what little it had left?

Grandmother looked at the wall as if she could see through it and the kilometer of intervening forest to the train itself.

"Be prepared to hide," she said. "Be prepared to flee."

The pitch of the whine dropped as the train neared the station.

GRANDMOTHER WAITED by the door, cracking it open every few minutes to peek outside. Each time, she closed the door and shook her head. Nothing. An hour passed, maybe more.

The Leonids had scavenged small bits of edible plants the day before, a few stems still with a hint of green in them, and they picked off the less-bitter bits and nibbled. Kasha sat by Grandmother's heels at the door. Mykola tried to tempt Kasha over with some of the twins' breakfast, but she ignored him.

The older Leonid started to think that maybe he had imagined the sound. Could the other three have imagined it, as well? Was it possible to share a delusion? Maybe some other noise had carried through the valley. Maybe now that all the trees of the forest were completely bare, when the wind passed through them it mimicked a train. Mykola's mother had said that if you listened carefully after a person died that you could hear their soul ascending. So maybe the sound was all the lost souls still lingering in the valley. Since the Soviets had abolished heaven, where else would the souls have to go? Maybe they waited for the train like everyone else.

Grandmother opened the door again, but this time she did not close it right away, leaning her head outside. Kasha was next, squeezing halfway through the crack. Then the boys, Mykola followed by the Leonids. From outside, they would have looked like a stack of heads leaned against the doorjamb, dog–boy–boy–boy–old woman.

At first, Leonid did not see anything, nearby or farther on through the bare trees, but then at the other end of the village he spotted the specks of figures moving down the path. They passed the first cottage without stopping, and then the next and the next. They moved through the main cluster of cottages and by the old church and the abandoned schoolhouse. As they got closer, Leonid made out the uniforms, the same as he had seen on the men who shot Mr. Tarasenko. Leading the procession was a man in civilian clothes, a black hat and a black coat.

At the near side of the village, the group paused. The black-clad man pointed to where the path to Grandmother's cottage twisted around the woods, and then set off, leading the soldiers straight for it. They could have looked up at any point and seen the cottage. They could have made out the faces in the doorway. But they seemed unconcerned, engaged in a casual conversation about the valley, if their frequent gestures at the trees and up to the mountain peaks were any indication.

"Should we run?" asked the older Leonid.

"We'll wait," said Grandmother.

"But the soldiers . . ."

"We'll at least make them knock," said Grandmother.

She pulled the boys inside and clapped for Kasha and closed the door behind her.

When the knock finally came and Grandmother opened the door, the only one there was the man in black. In addition to his black hat, he wore a pair of circular spectacles with a thin leather strap that dangled from the sides of the frame. His beard, gray streaked with black, dropped from his chin like roots reaching for soil. Deep lines creased either side of his long nose all the way to the edges of his mouth. His lips trended toward a frown. He could have been fifty or he could have been ninety. Parts of him seemed strong and parts seemed weak. Leonid did not know which parts to trust.

"Will you invite me in?" he asked. His voice was deeper and more resonant than his thin body should have allowed. His Ukrainian was clear but stilted.

"Who are you?" asked Grandmother.

"I am Konstantin Tsiolkovski," he said.

"You say that as if your name should mean something to me."

The older Leonid tugged at Grandmother's dress. "He writes stories. The teacher made us read them."

Those stories were about the only thing Leonid remembered from school. He didn't know all the big Russian words, but he had loved the impossible places the stories represented. He imagined that all the different worlds were other valleys, only a train ride away. He imagined that everyone who was gone from Bohdan lived on in fantastical settings. Grandmother looked down at Leonid, then back at Tsiolkovski.

"What business could a writer possibly have in my home?"

"Your son is only half-right," said Tsiolkovski.

"Grandson."

"My apologies. I do write stories, but first I'm a scientist. I work in rocketry."

Grandmother's expression remained blank.

"A rocket is like a plane, but instead of flying in the air, it flies in outer space. With rockets, we will send Soviet citizens to the stars." His voice was flat, as if he were discussing the weather or a distant relative.

"That's not possible."

"Not today, but soon."

Grandmother looked over Tsiolkovski's shoulder to a patch of cloudy sky, focusing her eyes on as far a point as possible.

"Still," she said, "that doesn't explain why you're here."

"Your sons. Pardon me, grandsons. Twins such as these will be of great benefit to the mission."

"You'll send boys into outer space?"

"We will train the boys to become the men we send into space."

Kasha scampered up to Tsiolkovski and sniffed him. Immediately, her sniff shifted into a snarl. She reared back, crouched, ready to pounce. Mykola jumped forward and held her, stroking her with his free hand. Her body relaxed, but a continuous growl rumbled from between her bared teeth.

"The dog doesn't like you," said Grandmother. "And she likes everyone."

Tsiolkovski scowled at the dog. "Then I am no one. And that is the point. Your grandsons, though, they will be heroes. They will be more famous than even Bohdan Khmelnytsky himself."

"This village has had heroes before, but none of them returned after the war."

"This is not a war. Might it be dangerous? Of course. But we have decided it is better to be brave."

"You're so brave that you find boys to assume the danger for you. Why these two?"

The older Leonid had listened to the conversation, not really comprehending. But now, acknowledged by Grandmother, he realized that he was the subject being discussed. It felt bizarre. Who had ever talked about him before? Probably no one. His father when he was still alive, but Leonid was so small then. He had no memory of that time.

"Just look at them," said Tsiolkovski. "They are perfect specimens of humanity. Pure blood. They will be strong, handsome men. They will be brilliant. They will be leaders in the coming Utopia."

Grandmother looked past Tsiolkovski again, this time to the barren trees and the silent village beyond.

"It used to be ideal here," she said.

"This place is a hundred years behind. And look at it now. Do you think it will survive a hundred more?" He rapped his knuckles on the frame of the door. The wood tapped back a sound that was thin and hollow, not like wood at all.

"What's he talking about?" asked the younger Leonid, tugging again at Grandmother's dress.

Grandmother smiled. "This man can help you. He can take you to a place with real food and new clothes."

"Does that mean you agree?" asked Tsiolkovski.

"You say that as if the choice, in the end, will be mine. Can you promise that they'll be safe?" asked Grandmother.

"No more than you can promise that they will be safe here," said Tsiolkovski.

Grandmother pulled the younger Leonid close and beckoned the other. She bent herself into a hug around both of them. The older Leonid felt wetness on top of his head and realized Grandmother was crying, her face buried in his hair. He could not recall her crying before, not even when news of his father . . .

"Why are you sad?" he asked.

"Quite the opposite," she said. Her voice carried a tone that had been long absent. "You two will leave the village."

"I don't understand. What about you? And Mykola? And Kasha?"

"Hush," said the younger Leonid.

The older Leonid looked at his brother. He felt like he was standing in the center of a secret he did not know the smallest part of. Even the dog seemed to understand. Her growling had silenced. That moment reminded him of the quiet at a funeral as the dirt was replaced in the hole.

Pulling himself out of Grandmother's embrace to look into her face, the younger Leonid asked, "Who'll pray with you?"

"My only prayer is answered. I don't have much else to say to god, if he's even there."

Tsiolkovski held up his hand and snapped his fingers. Two soldiers entered the cottage, squeezing through the doorway on either side of him. One of the soldiers, a female officer, gripped each Leonid by the shoulder, firm but not unfriendly, and led them out the door. Tsiolkovski turned to follow, paused, and turned back.

To the other soldier he said, "And the dog. Filthy as it is, we might have use for it, as well."

The soldier pushed Mykola away and lifted Kasha. The soldier seemed surprised at how light she was, how much of her was made of fur and how little flesh. Kasha, for her part, did not so much as squirm. She was the only one to look back, the last of the three to see the cottage.

As the officer led them away, she bent down and whispered to the twins, "One rare and exceptional deed is worth far more than a thousand commonplace ones."

The older Leonid tried to look up at her, but no matter how he craned his neck, the officer's face stayed out of view. There was something about her, though, that reminded him of Grandmother. He regretted the thought even as he had it.

## Kharkiv, Ukraine—1964

The quadruple props of the Antonov An-12 whirred once and then came the thump of landing. Leonid rode in the cargo compartment at the back of the plane, sitting on a bent metal bench beside Giorgi's casket, Kasha curled asleep in the space beside him. The compartment stank of oil and grease. There were seats up front, where the Chief Designer, Nadya, Mishin and Bushuyev, and other engineers had remained for the whole flight. Even Yuri and Valentina were there. The two of them had left the program so long ago that they seemed like strangers. The broader world had seeped into them. Their life extended beyond the Star City campus.

Ignatius had come back once during the flight with a canteen. Leonid accepted a few sips. He handed back the canteen and she left, never speaking. Every time the plane had hit turbulence, the casket would lift several inches from the floor before slamming back down. Leonid tried to tighten the straps that secured it, but they were as tight as they could go. The last half of the flight he spent leaning on the casket's lid, holding it steady in the rough air.

The Antonov taxied to a stop. From the front cabin came the sounds of the other passengers disembarking. A few minutes later, the rear ramp lowered. The sun shot streaks through the cracks. There were no windows in the cargo bay, only pale yellow lights that flickered every time the pilot had throttled the engines. The sunlight seemed like the first flare of an explosion. Kasha roused and sprinted down the ramp to Nadya, who had been the one to insist on bringing the dog. The Chief Designer for his part did not argue against it.

Six soldiers in full dress uniforms ascended the ramp. The one nearest Leonid saluted him. These men were junior officers, and Leonid, according to the insignias on his own uniform, outranked them. The young officer held his salute until Leonid returned it, and then took position on one corner of the casket. The soldiers hoisted the casket onto their shoulders, an action they had obviously rehearsed many times before. Leonid wondered if that was all they did, whole days spent practicing with empty coffins. The soldiers marched their burden out the back of the plane. Leonid followed.

Outside, the other passengers stood in a line that led to the airport terminal. It was only after reading the name of the airport that Leonid realized they were in Ukraine. He had never known Giorgi was Ukrainian. Giorgi spoke such perfect Russian, no hint of an accent. Leonid had never thought to ask him about his hometown. Or his family. The twins all had stories they told, but they were fabricated. It never occurred to Leonid that someone might have a real life, real stories to tell.

Ukraine! The reality of the soil beneath his feet hit him. He had not been to his own country since Tsiolkovski took him and his brother and the original Kasha from Bohdan. This was the opposite side of the country, and he had been closer to the village on his tour through Eastern Europe, but still, knowing he had crossed the border made this feel like home, no matter how imaginary the line of a border might be.

The soldiers loaded the casket into the back of a Chaika hearse waiting by the tarmac. It was the same kind of car that the cosmonauts often rode in parades, though without the retractable roof.

The back of the car had giant fins like those on the models of space capsules that were shown to the public. Pure decoration. Polished chrome ornamented the car's every seam and angle. A black-clad driver revved the engine and drove away.

Closer to the terminal, a line of black state vehicles idled, their drivers standing by open back doors. Leonid watched everyone else from Star City choose a vehicle and funnel inside. No one entered the last car in line, so Leonid chose it for himself. The driver, an older man but not elderly, bone thin and twitchy, seemed relieved to actually have a passenger. Thankfully, he did not try to strike up a conversation. Kasha slipped into the backseat with Leonid just before the driver closed the door.

Leonid watched out the windshield as the convoy snaked in front of him, undulating as the cars rounded curves, bouncing in sequence over bumps, compressing as the lead car slowed, expanding as it accelerated. To the right, the city sprawled. To the left, dense forest. The road angled just slightly toward the city, growing the buildings with every kilometer. The highway hummed under the tires.

"Is it hard to drive?" asked Leonid.

The driver looked at him in the rearview mirror, thick eyebrows scrunched over sagging lids. His eyes were a gray long since faded from pale blue. Below, a long nose protruded over a mustache that hid the whole of his mouth.

"Drive?" Leonid held his hands in front of him and moved them as if he were steering.

Looking back at the road ahead of him, the driver said something that Leonid could not understand. It sounded like gibberish. Slowly, though, the gibberish turned to words in his head. Ukrainian. He had not spoken it since he was a boy, though sometimes his thoughts still came in his native language.

Leonid asked the question again, this time in Ukrainian. "Is it hard to drive?"

The driver looked at Leonid in the mirror again. His expression shifted from confusion to shock. Apparently, Soviet officers did not speak to him in Ukrainian very often.

"I don't think about it," said the driver. "It's just something I do. You don't drive yourself?"

"Giorgi taught me the basics once, on the roads of . . . the place where we worked. Giorgi is the man in the casket."

"I'm sorry," said the driver. He glanced back again in the mirror. "Surely, though, you can master driving. You've flown a spaceship, after all."

"I'm not sure the two are related," said Leonid.

"Was he also a cosmonaut? This Giorgi?" asked the driver.

"He was a friend, more like a brother."

"I'm sorry," repeated the driver. "If you wish, I can let you drive the car before you leave."

The convoy veered off the road they had been following, made a series of quick turns down side streets, and stopped alongside a cemetery wedged between two concrete tenements. The buildings here were new, but had the same worn look as everything erected by the Soviets, not much different from the headstones sandwiched between them. No aging or decay could affect these buildings because they were old from the start.

Everyone exited the cars and passed through a gateless gap in the cemetery's low iron fence. Kasha waited by the car. One of the drivers attached a leash to her, even though she made no signs of moving. The soldiers, who had ridden in the first car behind the hearse, were already unloading the casket. They marched it through the gate, barely wide enough for them to pass, toward a fresh grave, wet black dirt piled high beside it. Several people, family members dressed for mourning, faces stretched to unusual shapes by sadness, already stood by the grave. An officer that Leonid did not recognize stood beside them. He had a hand on the shoulder of a woman Leonid assumed to be Giorgi's mother. Her face was the same as Giorgi's, broad features, a mouth that would likely launch into a grin on another occasion. Now, though, she wept at the sight of the casket, as did the children, teenagers maybe, beside her.

The soldiers navigated an indirect route through the close-packed graves, sometimes straddling the casket over the top of a gravestone when there wasn't room for them all to pass on one side. By the time they reached the fresh hole, the soldiers struggled under the weight of their burden, muscles trembling as they stooped and set the casket onto the straps of the lowering device.

The officer who had been consoling Giorgi's mother stepped forward and began to speak. Leonid ignored most of what he said, letting the words wash over him like the white noise of the Antonov's engines. He picked up just enough to know that the man spoke as if he had been Giorgi's superior officer, but Leonid had never seen this man at Star City. Ignatius, holding her leather jacket tight around her by the fur collar, stared intently at the officer, mouthing the words along with him. That was the story, then. Giorgi's death, officially, had come in a plane crash. Giorgi had been a test pilot, though of planes, not spaceships. He was being posthumously awarded some sort of minor medal. Honor and the Motherland and honor and pride and superiority and honor. Leonid wanted badly for this man to shut up.

Next, one of Giorgi's relatives, a brother by the looks of him, spoke, or tried to. He managed a few words, and then fell into tears. A few more words, more tears. Most of what he said seemed familiar to Leonid, and he recalled the words were parts of the

Psalms the old village priest had used before the Soviets hauled him away. Even before the famine, there had been enough funerals for Leonid to have learned the usual phrases. Here, though, any reference to the creator was absent. No *lords, thys, gods, almightys.* Just the little poem at the start of each Psalm. *My soul cleaves to the dust. Turn my eyes from looking at vanities.* The brother choked out a few final words, face wet from crying, and someone, maybe a sister, led him from the graveside.

Giorgi's mother stepped forward and touched the coffin, caressing the wood as though it were her son's skin. Leonid thought that it was probably more like skin than Giorgi's own, crisped in the fire, flake and ash. She turned to face the semicircle of mourners. Her eyes were pink but her face dry. She thanked everyone for coming. At her words, behind her, the cemetery's caretakers cranked a handle and the straps supporting the coffin lengthened, lowering Giorgi into the ground. The mourners turned and left. The sound of shovels piercing the dirt reached Leonid as he ducked his head back into the waiting car.

WHEN THE CONVOY stopped again, it was in front of a row of townhomes that still showed scars from the German occupation. Roofs had been rebuilt and windows replaced, but the stone of the walls bore white gashes and dark streaks, gouges and burns. At the sight of so many shiny black cars, several children on the opposite side of the street halted in the middle of a game of Dragon. They stared openly at all the strangers, paying particular attention to anyone in uniform.

Ignatius crossed over to the children. She grinned and spoke to them, and the children laughed at whatever she said. She pulled a handful of candy from her pocket and distributed it, reprimanding a girl who tried to take more than one piece. Everyone but Leonid had already siphoned into the house when Ignatius recrossed the street.

"Do you always carry candy with you?" asked Leonid.

"You never know when you might need a piece," said Ignatius.

"You've never shared with us."

"You never seem hungry." She turned around in place, observing the buildings and the few cars other than those the funeral party had arrived in. Far down the sidewalk, a couple strolled arm in arm. "I like streets like this. I'm from the country, a collective farm. Well, it's collective now. When I was a child, it was just a farm, but everyone in the area worked there anyway. A few buildings with kilometers and kilometers of land. The first time I went to the city—and it was not even a real city, just a town—I knew that was where I had to be. A place where you would every day come across people you didn't know by sight, much less by name. But I like streets like this because it's a little of both. For this one block, you might know everyone, but anonymity is just around the corner."

"Do you ever think about what it's like for Nadya, for whom no such corner exists?"

"It's my job to make sure no such corner exists for any of the cosmonauts. So yes, I think about it often. But there's one difference. Nobody knows Nadya. They just know her face. Her accomplishments. Part of being famous is being anonymous. A hero isn't a person but an act. An ideal to worship. That's what it is. Worship. In a nation without a god, we must provide an outlet for faith. We must show the people that greater heights exist, not on some ethereal plane, but right here on Earth. Or, in Nadya's case or yours, in outer space."

"So we're just symbols, not people?"

"Of course you're people. Just not the people that everyone thinks you are."

Ignatius unwrapped one of the candies from her pocket, a Lobster Neck, the outer shell like streaked brass. The white wrapper crinkled as she kneaded it into a ball between her fingers. She held the candy in her other hand, observing it as if it were a smooth pebble, something she'd stumbled across on a riverbank instead of pulled from her pocket. She opened her mouth and pushed the candy toward it, but stopped, and instead offered the piece to Leonid. He took it and sucked on it without really tasting.

"Do you know the General Designer?" asked Ignatius.

"I know of him, but we've never met."

"At his last rocket test, there was an explosion. Somewhere around a hundred people died."

Leonid gulped down a mouthful of sugar-sweetened spit, almost choking down the candy with it.

"Marshal Nedelin was among those who died."

"I only met him the once," said Leonid. He recalled that meeting, the graciousness of the man, how even Nadya had seemed at ease with him.

"This is a dangerous business." She pulled out another Lobster Neck and plopped it in her mouth. She looked up at the tops of the buildings, where the little architectural flourishes, a superfluous crenellation, a pattern in the bricks, were evidence that the structures predated the Revolution.

"If he'd survived," continued Ignatius, "Giorgi, that is. If Giorgi had survived, he would have flown the next mission. The Chief Designer believes he has a capsule ready for reentry."

"Believes?"

"I have my doubts. How many dead now? And not one success. Not a real success, at least."

Leonid looked at her. She had already admitted that she knew the truth of the twins, but Leonid still felt as though he should

keep the secret. Of course Ignatius knew. There was never a moment when she appeared unprepared, as if the big leather jacket
she wore contained not just candy but all the answers, as well. Ignatius glanced at Leonid and caught his stare and held it for a
moment.

"Now that Giorgi's dead," said Ignatius, "there's only one
trained pilot. The Chief Designer plans for her to finally complete
the mission she couldn't five years ago."

"She'll fly?"

"And I think it unlikely that she'll survive. At least not so likely
that I'd bet on it. The Chief Designer is a dreamer, a noble one, but
sometimes the dream gets in the way of his better judgment. The
whole plan was a mistake. Tsiolkovski's folly. But it was the Chief
Designer who turned Tsiolkovski's perverse science into outright
deception. Twins not as experiments but as expendable."

"Why are you telling me this?"

"Nadya's life can't be put at risk. If she were to die on this flight,
I couldn't cover it up. It would be a scar on the face of the nation."

"Stop the Chief Designer."

"He has Khrushchev behind him, so I'm not in a position to act.
My superiors would prefer that I not cross the First Secretary
himself."

"I'll talk to the Chief Designer."

Leonid turned toward Giorgi's family home, but Ignatius
grabbed him by the shoulder, a firm grip though not unfriendly.
She reached into her pocket, the one on the opposite side of the
jacket from where she'd pulled the candy, and retrieved a piece of
paper folded over several times into a palm-sized square. She
handed the paper to Leonid.

"What is it?" he asked. There was no mark that he could see on
the paper to identify it.

"Nadya's inside the house," said Ignatius. "You have a car. Buy me the time I need to resolve this issue."

"How am I supposed to do that?"

Ignatius crunched through the outer shell of the candy in her mouth and chewed away at the shards. She clapped Leonid on the shoulder and walked away, not toward the house, but toward the street corner she had gestured to earlier, the corner around which she would find only strangers. Leonid unfolded the paper. A stack of rubles, doubled over and bound with twine, fell out. Leonid bent down and picked up the money. All the bills were in denominations of a hundred. He shoved the stack into the inner pocket of his uniform jacket. His knuckles brushed against the piece of paper the Americans had given him. He pulled the note out and read it. He put it back in the pocket. The inside of the paper Ignatius had given him was printed with a map of Ukraine, railways and train stations marked with red pen. He shoved that into his pocket, as well.

WHEN LEONID FOUND HER inside the house, Nadya was standing alone in the corner of an otherwise unoccupied room, humming the same simple melody as always. The room was small, crowded by a dining table too large for the space. No chairs. Nadya held a drink in her hand, but it did not look like she had taken a sip. Several blond strands had slipped free from the bun on her head and draped over one eye. The rest of the guests could be heard in other parts of the house, sharing stories about Giorgi, Leonid assumed. What would the people from Star City say? What lies had been prepared for them to tell Giorgi's family? The honorable death of a soldier. The facts scrubbed smooth to nothing. Ignatius had briefed them before they came, but Leonid paid no attention. If anyone were to ask, he would tell the truth. Not the whole of it, but much of who Giorgi was had nothing to do with his training. The games and songs and paintings. Leonid felt he owed Giorgi's family whatever honesty he could manage. Perhaps he should say nothing, silence the only assurance that what he said was true.

"Nadya," he said. "Have you ever thought about what you would do if you weren't a part of all this?"

"This? *This* is an actual home." Nadya pointed to each corner of the ceiling in turn. "*This* already feels like it's far away from everything we know."

"It's not our home, though."

"And that's always the problem."

"I know a place we could go. A place where not even Ignatius could follow."

"I expect Ignatius to crawl out from underneath my bed each morning."

"She's not as bad as that."

Nadya eyed him. "You want to leave?"

"Yes. Right now. Both of us."

"Where would we go?"

He stepped closer to her. "In London, I met two Americans. Ignatius said they were spies, but I don't care. They gave me an address. Right here in Ukraine. If we go there I think they'll find us. They'll take us to America."

"America? I don't remember much from my visit. Yuri said he would have stayed there if he could have, but what do any of us really know about the place?"

"I know that there I would still have a brother and you a sister. I don't need to know anything more than that."

Nadya pushed herself from the wall. "Did she ever tell you her real name? My sister."

"No, none of us ever shared much that was personal. It was

easier that way, to forget the past rather than hide it. What was her name?"

"If she didn't tell you, it's not my place." Nadya rounded the table toward the door. "Let's go, already. I can't stand any more time spent in this home. I thought I might learn something of Giorgi, but he's not here. If he once was, then he took all of himself when he left."

Leonid lingered after Nadya exited. He took in the ceiling, the floor, the strip of wood along the base of the wall, beveled across the top into a quarter-arc with a semicircular lip below that. Leonid had never known a home like this one. He was unsure how such a strip of wood was even crafted. The work of machines or a patient hand? What was its purpose? He tapped the baseboard with the toe of his shoe, leaving a small black smudge, and then followed Nadya outside.

She waited on the narrow sidewalk, a recent addition to the neighborhood, the poured concrete like pure snow compared to the old stone architecture. The line of black cars a streak of midnight. All the drivers waited inside their vehicles, except for Leonid's, who sat on his hood smoking a cigarette, and another who held Kasha's leash as the dog poked her snout through an iron fence to sniff at the wilted plants on the other side.

Leonid whistled and Kasha's head, ears perked to perfect triangles, jerked in his direction. She strained against the leash, hacking as the collar dug into her neck.

"It's okay," said Leonid. He crouched, holding out his arms.

The driver released the leash, and in a white flash Kasha was in Leonid's embrace. The metal fastener on the leash clattered against the sidewalk. Leonid unhooked the leash from the collar and hung it from the fence.

"We're taking her for a walk," said Leonid, explaining it to the driver who had been tasked with dog-watching. And then to his own driver, "I think I'm ready to try my hand at driving."

THE CAR SPUTTERED forward, and then the engine turned over once and fell silent. Leonid had been trying to master the clutch for twenty minutes, but all he had accomplished so far was to grind the gears down near to nothing. The driver, who had proved to be a patient teacher, could no longer hide his grimace at every incorrect sound the car made. Beads of nervous sweat dotted his brow.

In the backseat, Nadya sat with Kasha. The dog scampered back and forth, from window to window, as if the car was moving and the scenery changed with every moment. Her claws tapped the glass each time she jumped up for a better view.

Leonid restarted the engine, slipped the clutch, and the car lurched another half-meter forward. He could see the other drivers, still in their cars parked ahead of him, watching in their mirrors. At first, there had been laughter, but now their faces, what he could see of them, looked almost bored. His incompetence, it seemed, was only entertaining for so long.

"Would you like if I drove?" asked the driver.

"It would be best if I drove myself," answered Leonid.

The car lurched forward again.

Leonid rested his head on the steering wheel. Much longer and their escape would fail before it even began. The contingent from Star City would be exiting Giorgi's family home at any time. The car's back door unlatched, *thunking* shut immediately after. The driver's side door opened. Leonid raised his head. Nadya stood outside, arm extended as a silent instruction for him to exit the car.

"What?" he asked.

"I'll drive," said Nadya.

"Do you know how?"

"I know I'm at least as skilled as you. Get out."

The driver, who could not have understood the conversation in Russian, still laughed. He understood enough.

"That's why she was the first and you the fifth?" he said. He pointed both fingers up and wiggled them. "To fly to outer space?" The laugh that followed rocked the whole car, and the driver was still shaking with the aftershocks as Leonid, now chuckling himself, ceded the driver's seat to Nadya. Before Leonid could get back into the car, she started the engine, shifted into gear, and pulled the car away from the curb and several meters forward. She revved the engine and waved out the window for Leonid to catch up. He went to the passenger side and opened the door on the surprised driver.

"Friend, we must borrow your car," said Leonid. "You can retrieve it at the train station south of the city." Without counting them, he pulled bills from the stack of rubles Ignatius had provided and gave them to the driver.

The driver did not get out right away, as if he believed Leonid's Ukrainian had somehow been flawed. He looked at Leonid and then at Nadya, and then a coy grin grew under his mustache. "I see, I see," he said. He held up the money. "This is too much."

"For a taxi," said Leonid. "Or you can ask the woman in the leather jacket for assistance. She'll return at some point, I'm sure, and will have no trouble getting you to your car."

"She's a scary one! I think I'd rather walk."

"Before, I'd have agreed with you. But I've learned that what I think I know is often not the truth. You can trust that woman, maybe more than anyone else."

The driver glanced at Nadya and then back at Leonid. This time, he did not grin. "Yes, yes. I see what you mean."

He exited the car. As he walked away, he whistled a tune that reminded Leonid of Giorgi, a simple melody, something that had been hummed in Ukrainian villages for centuries. Leonid got into the car and closed the door, cutting off the song mid-melody.

"Get us away from here," said Leonid. "A couple streets farther up this road is fine."

He spread the map out on his lap as Nadya eased the car onto the road, moving alongside the row of black state vehicles. The car lurched to a stop almost immediately. Leonid braced himself against the dashboard.

He spun to Nadya. "I thought you said you could drive."

She did not acknowledge him, staring instead through the windshield. Mishin and Bushuyev stood in the middle of the road, blocking the car's path. They came to Leonid's window and waited for him to roll it down. The glass squeaked.

"What are you doing?" asked Mishin or Bushuyev.

"When did you learn to drive?" asked the other.

They looked at each other in a silent conference, nodded, and then asked at the same time, "Where are you going?"

"Just for a drive," said Leonid.

"We'll be leaving soon."

"Yes," said Leonid.

"There's no time for a ride."

"This is a ride we should have taken a long time ago," said Nadya.

Mishin and Bushuyev conferred silently once again. Leonid started to roll up the window, but Mishin thrust his arm into the gap before it shut completely.

"We're so close," said Mishin. "Finally, after so long, we're close."

"The moon is the same size in the sky," said Leonid. "Mars is still but a dot. All the sacrifices. All the friends burned up like fuel in a rocket, and we're closer to nothing."

"Do you blame him?" asked Mishin. Bushuyev stood so close behind that it seemed his head sprouted from Mishin's shoulder.

"The Chief Designer?" said Leonid. "I used to believe the things he said about a grander purpose, but now I doubt any of it extends beyond himself."

"He's not an evil man, Leonid," said Mishin. "Misguided, maybe. Blinded, sometimes. But not evil. I wouldn't even be alive if it were not for him."

Bushuyev took a step back, as if Mishin's statement needed space.

"I have a hard time imagining the Chief Designer saving a life," said Nadya. "The score is definitely skewed in the other direction."

"You're too young to remember the purges. Do you know how many colleagues Stalin took from us? He feared the intelligentsia even as he needed scientists. The Chief Designer himself . . . have you not wondered where he got that scar on his head? He spent years in Siberia. He almost died. He witnessed hundreds of people who weren't so lucky to survive. And then Stalin forgave the Chief Designer, or decided he needed him more than he feared him. And so the Chief Designer returned, and he brought me into OKB-1.

"I worked for the Chief Designer for years. He came to me or Bushuyev first with every problem. He chose us first for every task. But while Bushuyev was promoted to Deputy, I was left in a low position, an assistant. How I used to stay awake at night and wonder what I'd done to offend the Chief Designer! Bushuyev and I still did the same things. We attended the same meetings. We had the same skills. I started to doubt myself and hate the Chief Designer. Sometimes the other way around. Finally, after years, I'd had enough. The General Designer had not yet established OKB-52, but I knew him, and even though I thought him an ass, the General Designer respected me. He offered me a position as his Deputy.

No, I didn't like him even then, but I needed respect more than I needed to respect the man who gave it to me. When I told the Chief Designer I intended to leave OKB-1, though, he cried. He actually cried. He pled with me to stay, and promised me that it would be worth it, and apologized over and over. I'd only ever seen him burst with anger before, so this new emotion stunned me, so much that I said I would stay without understanding why I agreed to it.

"Less than a month later, Stalin died. A week after that, I was promoted to Deputy. You see, my grandfather was Jewish. The Chief Designer knew, from his time in the gulag, that one of the quickest ways to draw Stalin's wrath was to be of Jewish descent. Half the prisoners were people Stalin perceived to be enemies. The other half simply had the wrong ancestors. Entire Jewish families disappeared. Any prominent Russian who had any measure of Jewish blood was transferred away, never to be heard from again. We were all vaguely aware of this at the time. One cannot pretend ignorance when the problem is so obvious, but we knew better than to talk about it. As someone who was separated from his Jewishness, it never occurred to me that the problem might apply to me. My own ambition, my own pride, would have gotten me killed.

"The Chief Designer did not promote me during Stalin's lifetime in order to keep me safe. If only he had explained that to me, I wouldn't have had so hard a time of it, but I choose not to focus on the ways he failed me, when he, without having to, risked himself to protect me."

"Why are you telling us this?" asked Nadya.

"I just ask you to remember that the Chief Designer does care for you. He may not know how to state it. His actions may seem contrary to it. But he has always, as long as I have known him, had a plan."

Leonid asked, "If not for his plan, would my brother still be alive today?"

Mishin flinched. "Maybe so."

Leonid felt hot red rise up his neck and into his cheeks. His hand gripped the crank as if he might close the window with Mishin's arm still inside. The crank was made from the cheapest plastic. Could he squeeze hard enough to shatter it? Nadya took his other hand.

"We're leaving," she said.

Bushuyev put a hand on Mishin's shoulder and pulled him away from the car.

"We didn't see you," said Bushuyev.

But he and Mishin both stared at the car until Nadya maneuvered it around the corner.

"Perhaps in America it will be a simple matter to go for a drive," said Nadya. She glanced in the mirror.

"I would kill for anything in my life to be simple," said Leonid.

"No, you wouldn't."

Leonid took deep breaths, a calming technique that the Chief Designer had ordered the cosmonauts, and their twins, to master. Even the air he breathed, thought Leonid, would be a reminder of that man. Maybe escape was a fantasy. Leonid unfolded Ignatius's map and traced his finger along the lines.

# Kaliningrad, Moscow Oblast, Russia—1964

The Chief Designer met his private car at Domodedovo Airport while the rest of the party took a bus back to Star City. He would have liked to have gone with them. The thought of his bed appealed to him, but it was early still, and he felt he owed it to Giorgi to work even harder than before. His stomach protested, a wash of burning bile welling up at the base of his esophagus. He swallowed hard three times, a trick they taught the cosmonauts to fight nausea, but it was not particularly effective. Heartburn and nausea were different conditions, after all. Had Giorgi felt like this all over? In Siberia, the Chief Designer had seen men burn their hands over candle flames. They were so cold that they could not feel the heat until it was too late.

The road paralleled the railway on the route to RKK Energia, his old headquarters before Star City, and still the site of Vostok's—and now Voskhod's—final assembly. If one followed the tracks in the other direction, for thousands of kilometers, they would lead eventually to the Baikonur Cosmodrome. Every capsule, every piece of every rocket, had already traveled such vast distances before it ever made it into space. The tracks veered away from the road.

The old part of the factory appeared first through the trees, tall windows surrounding the whole structure, giving off warped, wavy reflections. The walls were crested with a thin outcropping of brick, a pathetic attempt at decoration. His old office was in the narrow turret on the near corner, concrete and glass stretching high above the complex like the control tower back at the airport. It was still his office, he supposed, but he did not recall the last time he had sat at the desk. He wondered if reports piled up there like they did at Star City. He would have to check.

Here the road intersected the tracks, the car bouncing across the rails, nearly launching the Chief Designer's head into the ceiling. *Thump thump.* A crane car, splotched with red rust like patches of inflamed skin, idled on the tracks. A decade ago, he had requisitioned the funds to build a shelter for the crane, but the request had been denied. At least a tarpaulin would have helped, but he had forgotten about the crane until right now. He knew he would forget about it again as soon as he entered the factory.

His driver parked the car in a weedy patch of dirt by the door to the offices. It was supposed to be the best parking space, the shortest walk in winter from car to front door, but this entrance was the farthest from the factory proper, and a maze of hallways lay between it and any of the destinations the Chief Designer might actually seek out. He exited the car and walked toward the other door, the one that opened directly onto the factory floor, some hundred meters away. He was only halfway there when the rumble started. He felt it first through his feet and then the tall windows rattled in their old frames. He stepped away from the wall, worried that at any moment one of the panes might shake loose. Ripples of heat rose above the factory roof, quivering the trees and clouds beyond. The twin smokestacks of the forge seemed to move as if they were made of the same smoke that burped out of the top of them.

He was late. The heat shield test had already begun. He hurried, almost trotting, trusting his feet even though the ground seemed at any moment ready to shake from under him. The heat hit even before he rounded the building. Then the glow, still half a kilometer away, emerged like a second sun, but too close, rising from within the earth instead of far over the horizon. The Chief Designer squinted against the blaze. One of his RD-107 engines had been mounted horizontally to a reinforced concrete slab, the open end of the nozzle aimed directly at a working mock-up of Voskhod.

It was this engine that had destroyed the Chief Designer's hopes time and again. There had been so many tests that he could identify the exact moment the heat shield would fail by the particular color its surface blazed, as it went from red to orange to cream, and just before it reached white the whole thing would erupt, liquid metal spraying from the structure underneath, solidifying into abstract hunks that still marred the concrete slab like sculpture.

Shielding his eyes, the Chief Designer fumbled along the wall until he found the door to the control room, little more than a sheet metal hut. The technicians, eyes glued to dials and readouts, did not greet him. One console in the corner let out a repetitive beep, like a heart monitor. A teacup tittered on a saucer. The cup had Nadya's face printed on it.

The Chief Designer retrieved a mask from beside the slitted observation window. The mask was patterned after the kind used by welders, but without the lower half, just a glass visor covered with several layers of BoPET, which allowed one to look directly into the flame of the engine, to pick out details that otherwise would have been lost in the blaze. Through the visor, the thrust of the engine always reminded the Chief Designer of Amsel Falls. He and several other engineers had managed to visit the waterfall on their way home from Germany after the war, diverting their convoy, trucks full of V-2 rocket parts and more than a few German scientists, far to the south. It was the only time the Chief Designer had ever left the soil of the Soviet Union. He had wanted something to remember from the trip other than the insides of German bunkers. He could have been executed for that excursion, for risking the precious spoils of war on a personal vacation. But by that point, the Chief Designer was, if not numbed to, at least familiar with the looming threat of execution.

More than just the sight of the falls, though, the engine reminded him of the sound of cascading water. Amsel Falls had struck him then as the loudest thing he had ever heard. The power of it humbled him. Now, the flames of the engine affected him the same way. He sometimes thought he was too proud a man for his own business. He wanted control, and every test, every launch, every single day reminded him that he had none.

The heat shield burned at what seemed like a slow pace, concentric rings of bright flame starting from center and burning the surface layer outward, like sheets of paper flaring away one after the other. The color went from orange to yellow to cream. The rings of flame came faster. This was where heat always won. This was the moment when Nadya, the one who died, would have felt the first shudder of a problem as the capsule reentered the atmosphere. She would have had just enough time to wonder about it before the capsule burst apart, disintegrating to nothing.

The Chief Designer waited for it. He had seen it so often that he did not even hold his breath in hope anymore. But the color endured, creamy instead of virgin white, and the pace of the flames steadied on the surface of the shield. He looked at the clock, counting upward, struggling to make out the numbers through the visor. When he read them, he did not believe. He pulled the mask off to make sure he was reading correctly. He mouthed along with the rising seconds as they ticked off the clock.

It worked. The General Designer's heat shield worked. The Chief Designer forgot he had the mask in his hands and dropped it. The sound of the metal on the concrete floor could barely be heard above the engine. He gripped the shoulder of the technician seated nearest him. The technician started, as if the touch were an explosion at the test site.

"It works," said the Chief Designer.

The technician shook her head, unable to hear him.

He leaned close to her ear and shouted, "It works!"

The technician nodded once, as if this had been the expected result, as if it had not been preceded by a decade of failures. But this technician was young. For all the Chief Designer knew, it was the first test she had been a part of. They cycled new people onto the heat shield project on a monthly basis, so none of them would have the chance to learn the secret that the heat shield had never actually functioned. But now it did. Now they could launch Giorgi and bring him home . . .

Giorgi. No, not Giorgi. It was Nadya's turn again. That was good, was it not? She would have the chance she should have had years ago. The Chief Designer had always secreted the guilty thought that this Nadya, the one trained in spaceflight, would have somehow succeeded where her sister failed. He knew it was not true. He felt ashamed every time he thought it. But now she could prove the point. She could triumph where all else had been lost.

The thought struck him then, surprising in that it had never occurred to him before: No one had ever asked Nadya or any of the cosmonauts what they thought of the whole grand endeavor. The Chief Designer had dreamed so hard of space since he read Tsiolkovski's stories as a young man that he could not believe someone might not share the dream. But the twins were conscripts, not volunteers. Their dreams had never been taken into consideration.

The engine cut off. There, where the flames had been, the mock-up of Voskhod remained.

## Star City, Russia—1964

Leonid's voice faded up from nothing in the speaker, already in the middle of a sentence as he came into range. Lately, it had been like this. Before, he seemed to know exactly when Star City's antenna would snare his signal and waited to speak until then. Now he was always halfway through a thought. Mars wondered if Leonid talked for whole orbits now, or if his timing had been thrown off so much that he just started talking a few seconds too soon. There was no way to tell. Leonid's conversations never seemed to have a proper beginning or end.

Leonid paused in talking, and Mars realized he had not been paying attention. Mars tried to recall what he had heard, but his mind was blank. He rubbed his face and was surprised to find a beard there, as if it had appeared full-grown just then. *Leonid must have a similar beard,* he thought. Razors were not among the supplies stashed in Vostok's few compartments.

"Did you know that clouds look the same on top as they do on bottom?" asked Leonid.

"I've seen the pictures the Americans took," said Mars.

"But the clouds never rain up. Sometimes as I pass over dark patches, beneath which I know the rain falls in torrents, I can't understand why the same is not true on the other side. I expect to hear the rain splatter against the hull of my little ship. A ship should be in water, yes?"

"I'm not sure yours would float."

"I can't remember what water looks like. Even the water I had here—I have long since drunk all of it—didn't look like water. I squeezed some out of the plastic container, but it wouldn't fall. It just globbed up in front of me. Like a marble. We didn't have marbles as children. I didn't even know what they were until Giorgi explained them to me."

"Giorgi is . . . Giorgi died." Mars had refused to attend the funeral, even when the Chief Designer insisted.

"I know. I've been up here forever. Everyone I know is dead."

"Who do you think you're talking to, then?"

"You're up here with me."

"Where the weather is always nice."

"I miss the rain."

"As do I."

"You should go outside."

"And you probably should not."

"I'm no longer sure of that."

BY THE TIME the Chief Designer made it to Star City—forty kilometers that took two hours through the endless construction on Route 103, lined with massive wheeled machines of indeterminate purposes that never seemed to move from their places on the side of the road—the effects of so much travel were catching up with him. The last few kilometers he caught only in glimpses, when his eyes startled open from the bumps on the unfinished blacktop.

Like at RKK Energia, the Chief Designer had the reserved parking space closest to the front door of Star City's main building. Here, the lot was paved and painted with lines, in far better shape than the road that led to it. The car made a spurting noise as the driver shut off the engine. The Chief Designer exited the car and walked to the door.

Inside he was met immediately by Mishin and Bushuyev. They had a knack for always being around when he needed them. Did they wait by the door the whole time he was away? Did one of them watch out a window for the approach of his car? Was there an underling somewhere tasked with keeping tabs on the Chief Designer at all times? Some sort of intercom system that could warn Mishin and Bushuyev of his approach? Did they, in the moment just before he opened the door, skid to a halt at the end of the dead sprint that brought them there?

"Let's see the dogs," said the Chief Designer.

"There's a problem," said Mishin or Bushuyev.

"What is it?"

"Actually, there are two problems," said one of them.

"Several, maybe," said the other.

"Out with it," said the Chief Designer.

"We're not sure which to tell you first."

"If you don't tell me something soon, the only problem you will have is looking for new jobs."

"The heat shield."

"What about it?"

"We just received the test results."

The Chief Designer did not know how the data had arrived before him. He would have to discuss the route with his driver. Obviously, there was a faster way to get from the factory to Star City.

"I was there," said the Chief Designer. "The results were optimal."

"Yes, yes. The General Designer's heat shield performed brilliantly."

"Then what's the problem?"

"The materials. We have the asbestos. We'd been experimenting with that ourselves. But the phenolic resin. The factory didn't produce enough before they shut down operations."

"The factory closed?"

"It was converted to process dairy."

"Thank god we'll all have enough cheese. How much resin were you able to get?"

"We can make one shield, but only if we perform no more tests. A new factory is scheduled to open within the year, but it would be the first state project to ever be completed on time if it did."

"There are two launches just months away. Even if the factory opened on time, it would be too late."

Mishin and Bushuyev exchanged a glance. "We might have a solution. The docking clamp."

"What about it?"

"With both capsules in orbit at the same time, one could dock with the other . . ."

"And the cosmonaut could then bring the dogs aboard the capsule with the heat shield. Yes, that just might work." The Chief Designer found himself fully awake now, almost bursting with energy. "This will be an even greater accomplishment than we planned. Two ships docking in space! You, comrades, are geniuses."

"About the dogs," said Mishin or Bushuyev.

"Yes, yes. What about them?" His mind raced, cycling through all the considerations that this new project required.

"Kasha is gone."

"What do you mean *gone*?" He would need to assign additional engineers to the docking project. There had been problems getting a good seal. Sometimes he cursed the Vostok's spherical shape. So practical and so simple, but it made it hard to attach things to the outside.

"Nadya and Leonid took her."

"Took her where?" But the one capsule would not have to return to Earth, so maintaining balance for reentry was not required and the docking apparatus could be attached permanently to the door.

"They didn't return with us from Ukraine."

"They're with Ignatius?" The other ship, though, would need some sort of detachable clamp. Mishin and Bushuyev had been working on one. They would not have suggested the idea if they did not think it would work. Neither was much for taking risks.

"They left on their own. It's unclear where they might have gone."

"Surely Ignatius knows. She would never let the two of them out of her sight."

"We saw them leave, and Ignatius wasn't with them."

"Are you telling me they ran away?" He imagined the docking clamp releasing from a capsule and tumbling away through open space.

"Yes."

"And you didn't try to stop them?" The Chief Designer's voice inched up in volume with each word, the hard syllables coming gravelly from the back of his throat.

"We tried."

He shouted, "But you failed!"

Mishin took a half step forward and spoke the Chief Designer's name. "You of all people should possess the capacity to forgive a failure."

The Chief Designer's scar throbbed.

"Why would they leave me?" he asked.

"The reasons should be obvious," said Mishin or Bushuyev. "The real question, the one that should comfort you, is why did they stay for so long?"

The Chief Designer would have liked to weep. He felt the sorrow, yes, like cold in his bones, but part of him already looked for a solution. The mission was ready. He would allow sadness later. Always later. What he needed now was a pilot and a dog.

## Kharkiv, Ukraine—1964

Leonid and Nadya had made it to the station in Kharkiv too late to catch the train he had originally intended, the one Ignatius had marked on the map. It would have carried them to Kiev, and there in the throngs of the city they could have disappeared. At least Leonid assumed that was Ignatius's plan. At least that much of her plan was his plan, too. But while Nadya was a trained pilot and he had been taught the basics, neither turned out to be much as navigators. First, it took them more than an hour to find a store where they could purchase new clothes. They changed in the store, and left their uniforms behind. Leonid regretted abandoning his medals, not because he felt he had earned them, but because they were not his to do with as he pleased. The medals belonged to his brother.

Leonid took the map and the money and the note from the Americans, and transferred them to the pocket of his new pants. The fabric was too stiff, sharp folds that prodded him when he climbed back into the car.

If it was possible to make every wrong turn on the way to the station, they had done it. Lefts instead of rights, missed turns, street names that had no corresponding mark on the map. It was only by luck that they discovered the station. Out of nowhere, its shallow brown dome sprung into view, and just the top of the sign that identified it. The building looked more like a church than a station, except of course for the trains.

Leonid ran inside to buy tickets while Nadya found a place to park the car, but it was already an hour too late. The attendant, shuffling a stack of unused tickets as if it were a deck of cards, told him they would have to wait until tomorrow. The attendant stared hard at Leonid's face.

"You look like . . ."

"I get that a lot lately," said Leonid in Ukrainian, and hurried away.

A large map, taller than Leonid and twice as wide as that, hung on the wall opposite the ticket counter. The map had been glued directly to the plaster, paper curling out at the corners. It seemed to show every rail line in the whole country, even a few stations in southern Russia. There were many more here than on the map Ignatius had given him, marked in red like veins. Or was it arteries that carried red blood and veins blue? Giorgi would have known. A train chugged by on the other side of the wall.

He scanned the map of his home country and was saddened to recognize so few of the place names. What had he ever really known of it except the valley? Were there still people he knew there? Did they have newspapers or television? Had they seen his face? If they had, did anyone recognize him? There were no pictures of him from when he was a boy. Well, many were taken when he first came to Star City, but he declined to ever look at them. He did not know if his appearance now bore any resemblance to the boy he once was.

There, in the tiniest font imaginable, tucked in the middle of darker greens that meant mountains, he saw one name he knew. Bohdan, the hero of Ukraine. He tried to remember Grandmother's stories. She repeated them so often he should have known them by heart. But he only remembered a few. The hero, like the town that bore his name, had faded to near nothing.

At the bottom of the map, abutting the Black Sea, where Bohdan Khmelnytsky had oared for the Ottomans, sat Odessa.

Leonid knew nothing about the city except the name. He reached into his back pocket and pulled out the note from the Americans, folded into a square, fraying at the edges and ripping along the creases. He opened the paper gently using his fingertips and re-read the note: *Hope to see you soon! —Your Friends from America.* Could he escape to America? He knew even less about America than he did about Odessa. Defecting was not the escape Ignatius had intended, but no matter how grateful Leonid might have been for her unexpected assistance, he still did not consider her a friend. To her he owed nothing. To Nadya, though . . .

He followed one red line on the map east from Odessa. It marked a jagged path to Kharkiv, to the very station where he stood. He had planned to go to Kiev because it seemed like the best place to start, but it turned out he could get to where he was going directly. Leonid returned to the ticket counter and bought two tickets to Odessa. The train left in less than an hour.

"You can't get to Kiev from there," said the attendant. "At least not easily."

"The destination doesn't matter much."

But it did. For the first time he felt where he was going mattered. Nadya came in, Kasha trotting unleashed beside her. Nadya gazed up, inspecting the architecture in a disinterested way. The paint on the underside of the dome was flaking off, revealing an older version of the same color underneath.

"Tomorrow, we'll be on the other side of the country," Leonid told her.

"And then on to the other side of Earth. If we keep at it, I might finally complete my orbit, after all."

Nadya took Leonid by the hand and led him to the platform. They had an easier time finding the train than they had finding the station.

## Bohdan, Ukraine—1964

The train churned upward into the hills, aiming for the higher peaks that it would never reach. Leonid started to recognize the landscape even though he had seen it before only once. Still, this type of tree—Giorgi would have known the name—was the same as in the forests he knew as a boy. One could recognize a forest without recognizing it in particular.

The sound of the train, a sound he had grown used to in his recent travels, came here in a richer timbre, echoing back upon itself so that each thump was actually a chorus of many. It reminded him of the hopeful, fearful sensation the arrival of the train made when he was a boy. The sound would crest the hill long before the train itself. Like trumpets heralding the arrival of a tsar.

The angle of the climb steepened, pressing Leonid back into the seat, a milder version of the centrifuge at Star City. The seat's padding had been compressed to nothing, just old leather over wooden slats. He had to shift every few minutes to relieve the pressure on one side of his back or the other. He had given up trying to find a comfortable position for his buttocks. The slats underneath pinched and shifted no matter the angle. Beside him, Nadya looked out the window, never moving. He could see the reflection of her open eyes in the glass or he would have thought she was asleep. Kasha, curled on the floor in front of them, slept soundly.

There was no one else in the car with them. Maybe no one else on the whole train, if three cars and an engine could actually be called a train. The only other person they had seen was the conductor, a Kazakh or a Turkman, who did not understand Russian or did an excellent job of pretending not to. The sweaty scent of previous passengers mucked the air.

The train car leveled and then pitched forward. There had been several small descents to interrupt the generally upward progress, but this one was steeper. The view on either side was hemmed in by forest, the distant mountains disappearing like a grand illusion. The sound of the engine hushed and the brakes wailed. The car shuddered for several seconds before settling into a smooth deceleration.

Their stay in Odessa had not extended beyond the train station. On a large map like the one in Kharkiv, Leonid had again seen the name of his home village, Bohdan, this time printed larger, with the red line of a railway leading right to it. He had bought tickets before he even realized what he was doing. America would still be there in a week.

Nadya had not commented when he told her about the detour, as if this new plan had been established from the start. She simply nodded. Leonid worried that he had taken the place of those who had commanded every aspect of her whole life, that he was no better than the Chief Designer. But Leonid would make it up to her. Once they escaped.

Kasha, for her part, dashed aboard the train without prompting, as if she knew it would take her to her roots. It was the little dog's excitement that made the journey real to Leonid. He was going home, assuming the village still existed, that a single villager had survived the famine, that the old huts still stood, else the green of the valley had grown up over them or the rain had never returned and the valley was now nothing but dust.

Leonid's skin pricked with gooseflesh. He wanted to turn

around and leave. He would sprint to the engine and force the conductor to reverse the train, to pull them out of the valley. He had barely escaped with his life, and only then because of his brother. If he had not been a twin, he would have stayed and died with the rest of them. He sometimes imagined the villagers still alive and waiting for him. More often, though, he imagined their tombstones, jagged rocks with names chiseled there by untrained hands. What would he say to Grandmother? But no, she was most certainly dead. Was she? He realized he had never known her age. He thought of her as old because grandparents were old, when she might have been little older than the Chief Designer was now.

The thought of the Chief Designer gave him another pause. That passed quickly, though. In all his fantasies of returning home, of which there had been more than he had admitted to himself, his brother was with him. The Chief Designer had taken that from him, stripping him of hope and innocence and family and . . . the list could go on.

Leonid looked at Nadya. She touched the window with her fingertips, as if caressing the trees beyond. Or was it her reflection she saw, and in it the face of her sister?

A bolt of silence, and then the train leapt to a stop. The empty seats rattled. Kasha slid forward several inches, sticking out a paw to steady herself without opening her eyes. Nadya stood, maneuvered around Leonid's knees, and headed for the exit. Leonid followed, snapping his fingers for Kasha. The dog popped to her feet, bouncing along as if she needed no transition between asleep and awake. His arm started a reflexive wave as he exited the train, but there was no one there to greet them.

The station had been rebuilt. Not that the structure was any larger, but instead of the tumbling wooden shed, now it was made of metal. Leonid could not call the shed new. It had been there long enough to grow red spots of rust. The door did not line up with the lopsided frame.

From down the hill came a rumble, a small truck motoring up the path from the village. Leonid recalled the slow walks to the station when he was a boy, but the truck had almost arrived already. An older man drove, and several teenagers sat in the open back, prodding each other and laughing. The truck pulled up alongside the freight car and the teenagers hopped off. Whiffs of exhaust twined with the green-tinged mountain air.

One of the teenagers slung open the freight car's sliding door, and the others hopped inside. The older man, who on second glance was younger than Leonid had first assumed, stepped out of the truck and leaned on the hood, instructing the teens from time to time on where to set the boxes and sacks they lugged from the train.

Kasha took a few cautious steps away from the platform, sniffing at the air. She darted over to a kalyna by the side of the road, nosing, then licking the berries.

"No," said Leonid. He remembered the berries' bitter taste, and also how sick they had once made the original Kasha when she ate just a few.

The man by the truck inspected Leonid up and down. The man's beard was thick and showed flecks of white. His bushy eyebrows cast shadows that hid his eyes, making it impossible to tell exactly where the man was looking. He made a deliberate act of spitting on the ground. Leonid realized he had said *no* in Russian.

Instead of eating the berries, Kasha shoved her rump into the kalyna's branches and peed. The urine splashed loudly against the dry bed of leaves. Two sacks, thrown by the teens in the freight car, *thumped* to the ground. Kasha finished and scampered back to Leonid's side, twitching her head in every direction, taking quick sniffs. She had never smelled mountains before. Leonid had almost forgotten how different the scent was from the choked air around Moscow.

Nadya walked down the hill. The man leaning on the car watched her. It was probably rare that the village received visitors, especially attractive female ones. But the man's look was not a leer, his brows arched in curiosity. Then he looked at Kasha as if noticing her for the first time. His elbow slipped off the hood. He stumbled forward a few steps.

"Kasha," he whispered.

Kasha's ears perked up.

"Is it you, Kasha?"

She looked at the man for a long moment, nudging up to Leonid's leg. Then her tail broke into a wide wag, and she scampered to the man's feet. He bent down and scratched her as if she were his own dog greeting him after a long trip away, stroking from her head to her rump, following the curl of her tail with his hand as it arced up and over her back.

"But no," said the man. "You're Kasha but you're not. Her tail always hung limp."

This man knew Kasha's mother, the original Kasha. He was a villager who survived. Leonid tried to recognize him, searching his face for a feature that matched one in his memory. The faces he remembered were blurry at best. The man looked up at Leonid, and the two inspected each other, faint recognition growing into certainty. The man spoke first.

He said Leonid's brother's real name, the one he had been born with before Tsiolkovski named them both Leonid.

Leonid felt himself smile. "Close, Mykola."

Mykola said Leonid's real name.

"I didn't expect to see you," said Leonid. "I didn't expect to see anyone."

"And yet you still returned."

Hearing Mykola say it suddenly made it real. Leonid was home. He felt the valley around him, a swirling sensation, as if he were caught in a whirlpool that drained to the valley's lowest point. Or he was the lowest point, the trees in orbit around him. He felt release, too, an old throbbing pain finally relieved, a pain he could only now identify by its absence.

Leonid pointed at the dog. "Meet Kasha, the daughter of the original."

"She looks just the same! Except for the tail, of course." Mykola sat back in the dirt and pulled Kasha onto his lap. His face, what could be seen of it behind the beard, lit up like a child's. "And the original Kasha?"

"She grew old, Mykola. She might have been old already when you knew her. We never knew her age."

"Her life was good, though, yes?" He tickled Kasha behind the ears.

"Very. She was loved and loved in return." Leonid's voice choked off at the end. It seemed he was still not immune to the topic of loss.

"Good. I hadn't thought about her much in recent years. I used to wonder often, though."

Kasha hopped off Mykola's lap and trotted after Nadya. The two of them wandered through the brush at the edge of the road, Nadya picking leaves from saplings. There were no saplings in the village of Leonid's memory.

"And you, Mykola?" asked Leonid. "How've you been?"

"Things got better not long after you and your brother left. The train started coming again, bringing supplies. Then the rains returned. We were able to grow our own food. People had babies again. A few people even moved here from outside the village. Apparently, there were places worse off." Mykola rose and brushed the dirt from the back of his pants. "But how about you? You were the only ones to escape. What did you do?"

They did not know him here, not the adult version. The news of the space race, it seemed, declined to make the long trek to the valley. Mykola the boy had not understood the things Tsiolkovksi had said, and Mykola the man seemed not to remember them.

"I'm a soldier," said Leonid.

"I thought so," said Mykola. "There's something about your posture. It's the same as the men who returned from the war."

"I'm not sure if that's due to being a soldier or to coming home after a long time away."

"And your brother?"

"He is . . ."

"I'm sorry." Mykola strode forward and pulled Leonid into an embrace. He had grown a fat belly in the years Leonid had been away. It was hard to imagine anyone in the village being fat. Leonid wrapped one arm around Mykola's back.

"God, it's good to see you," said Mykola. "Sometimes you don't know what you miss until you see it again."

THE HEART of the village was at once exactly as Leonid remembered and entirely different. The tree still grew in the center of the main square, and near it rose the gravestones, plus new ones he supposed. Which one was Oksana's? He could not remember where it had been placed. No one had carved her name at the time. Did anyone come later to name the nameless? Even stillborn babies deserved that much, a name itself a sort of monument.

The arrangement of cottages was the same as in Leonid's memory, but almost all of them looked rebuilt. The old style of construction, hand-hewn panels and roofs pinched into jagged peaks, had been replaced with manufactured boards and fresh black shingling. Glass windows filled the holes that had once been covered by shutters alone. Instead of dirt, the main path through the village was packed with crushed white stone that shifted beneath Leonid's feet with every step. The gravelly sound bothered Leonid, as if he was walking on bones.

Villagers moved around like actors on a stage, miming the actions they were actually performing. Leonid had not seen a water pump since he left the village. He had not needed firewood for just as long. There was always someone to wash his clothes for him, prepare his meals. Indoor plumbing. The village was like stepping into the forgotten part of history, a collection of the little tasks that would never be included in textbooks, but that for almost everyone who had ever lived made up the bulk of their existence. Wars, after all, were the exception. Like the launching of rockets.

One question had plagued Leonid the whole time he waited with Mykola by the station, during the short ride down the mountain, and now as they walked. The words of the question felt too heavy. His Ukrainian had stopped developing when he left the village. He worried that he spoke it now only at the level of a child. The question required some small degree of eloquence, an arrangement of words that would give weight to it, endow it with the proper seriousness, respect. He forced himself to ask the question, but it came out as only a single word.

"Grandmother?"

Mykola stopped walking. The gravel crunched beneath his feet.

"She lived for many years after you left," said Mykola. "When the train started coming again, she met it every time, even when her knees started to ache. She never complained about that, but anyone watching could see the way she favored them. She also never explained why she met the train, but anyone with a heart knew. She was hoping her boys would return. And you did!"

"Too late."

"I visited her every day."

"Thank you."

"She wasn't sad. She missed you, but she was absolutely convinced that things were better for you outside the valley, even after conditions here improved."

They caught up with Nadya at the far side of the village. She crouched by the side of the stone path and pinched a fallen fir needle between her thumb and finger. Leonid introduced her. Nadya dropped the needle and stood.

"Forgive me for wandering off," she said. "I've spent my whole life in cities, inside buildings. This place is like another planet. I get lost in places like this. The Chief . . . my uncle once said I have the heart of an explorer. That's why . . . that's why he always favored me over the others."

Leonid wasn't sure if Mykola would understand Nadya's Russian, but he turned to Leonid and spoke in Russian himself. "I'm an uncle now! My first nephew was born just last month. By marriage, of course. I didn't have any siblings. I guess I should start by saying I'm married. There's too much history you've missed to share all at once."

"Married!" said Leonid. "Who is she?"

"Lesya. You knew her, but she was only five or six when you left. Oksana's little sister."

"Of course I remember her, though I can't recall her face."

"I doubt the face is much at all like the one you would remember, anyway." He turned back to Nadya. "So, you like our valley?"

"It's glorious. I could imagine living here. Not that I ever plan to settle. The only life I've ever known is one of motion. I could linger here, though, most definitely."

Ahead of them, the path diverted to the right, and then curved back behind an outcropping of trees. On the other side was the plot of land where Leonid and his brother had lived with Grandmother. When he left, the trees were dry and bare, the cottage visible at a glance. Now the green grew so thick that it was as if nothing at all existed on the other side.

"Is it still there?" asked Leonid, pointing through the woods.

"It is. One of the few that hasn't been rebuilt. And it's occupied. I believe you know who lives there."

Leonid tried to think of who from the village might still be alive. One of the other children? He barely remembered them. Sometimes he could not remember if a particular childhood friend had lived or died. For years he had dreams about people from the village dying. Some were dead before he left, others not. Sometimes he believed the dreams more than his memory.

"To be honest," said Mykola, "I haven't seen him in so long, he might have finally died."

"I'm familiar with that feeling." Leonid started down the trail.

"Wait, don't you want to know who it is?"

"I'll know soon enough."

Kasha flashed by. Instead of following the path, she entered the woods, dodging around trees like obstacles on a course. Her mother, the other Kasha, had once done the same. Only this Kasha's tail, always curled up and over, let Leonid tell the two apart. Nadya followed the dog into the woods, brushing her fingertips across the bark of the trees as she passed.

By the time Leonid and Mykola rounded the bend, Kasha and Nadya had already passed through the woods to the other side and sat together in a patch of high grasses. Beyond them, Grand-mother's cottage. Leonid did not recognize it at first, even though it was in the right place and was the right shape and could be none other than the home he had known. He had never expected to see it again, and he could not overcome his expectations so quickly. Finally, it was the pile of firewood beside the front door that convinced him. Knowing that the wood was still stacked in the same spot gave him a feeling of permanence more profound than the unchanging cottage behind it.

"Is it as you remember?" asked Mykola.

"The firewood, yes," said Leonid. "We never had glass windows."

"They still have your kitchen table. I remember it being old even before you left."

Leonid crouched and scratched Kasha behind her ears. A bird sang in a tree. Another bird, more distant, replied. He scanned the canopy. No birds in sight, but a squirrel tightroped down a thin branch and leapt to another limb. Leonid had to search deep into his memory to recall a time when there were squirrels in the valley. Kasha followed the motion of the squirrel with her eyes.

"Does any of this seem familiar, girl?" he said. "Your mother lived here, in these woods and in this cottage. This valley's in your blood."

He rose and headed straight for the cottage's front door. It looked new, but he realized that the door was one thing he had taken for granted. It would always be there to seal them off from the outside, and as long as that was the case, why worry with looking at it?

Nadya rose and followed him, and Mykola eyed her, how one might inspect an old friend's new wife. Let Mykola think what he wanted. Leonid had learned from Ignatius that the best lies were the ones you let other people assume for themselves.

Leonid knocked on the door. An old woman answered. At first, Leonid thought it was Grandmother, but this woman looked nothing like her except in age and wrinkles. Grandmother was dead. Mykola had said Leonid would know who lived in the cottage, but this woman, even after staring at her, he did not recognize at all. She was far too old to have been one of the other children, too old even to be most of the adults Leonid had known. She did not speak, and Leonid realized she inspected him in the same way he inspected her. She smiled.

"Konstantin," she shouted back into the cottage in Russian, "you have visitors."

A voice, airy but with an echo of former power, responded from inside. "I have no business with any of those inbred villagers."

"They're not from the village."

"No one outside the village knows I'm here."

She smiled apologetically at Nadya. "I suspect they didn't come here intending to find you."

"Why must you always speak in riddles, woman?"

"Come in," said the woman. "I'm Varvara."

"Thank you," said Leonid. "I'm—"

She interrupted him. "Oh, I know. At least I have a fifty percent chance of guessing correctly."

Mykola was right. It was Grandmother's old table still sitting in the same spot in the center of the room. A strange place for the table, sort of in the way of everything, but Leonid had never questioned its placement as a boy. At the table sat an old man. The word *old* did not do him justice. He seemed merely a skeleton clothed in skin a size too large. He wore glasses, though his eyes were clouded completely over. What was left of his hair was dry and wiry. He held the hollowed-out horn of some large animal to his ear.

"Who is it?" asked the man.

"Old friends," said Varvara, speaking loudly, aiming her face directly at the open end of the horn.

"When have we had friends?" said the old man.

"I have many friends."

"Only because you stoop to socialize with the villagers. They won't even have a place as sewage workers in the new Utopia."

Varvara shrugged at Leonid and Nadya, and gave another apologetic smile, this time to Mykola, who still stood in the doorway.

"I saw that," said the old man.

So he was not as blind as Leonid assumed.

"I didn't try to hide it," said Varvara.

"Well, come here already," said the old man. "I can't make out faces far away."

Leonid walked to the table and sat in the chair opposite him. Nadya took the third chair. There had once been a fourth, but Leonid did not see it anywhere in the cottage.

"Tsiolkovski," she said.

Leonid gripped the lip of the table with both hands. His fingernails cut into the wood. Nadya set her hand on Leonid's.

"So you know my name. Who doesn't? Knowing my name means nothing."

The corners of the man's eyes drooped even farther and the dour frown had been set in wrinkles as if in stone, but Nadya was right. This man was Tsiolkovski.

"How are you alive?" The question escaped Leonid's mouth before he could think better of it.

Tsiolkovski laughed in an unkind way. "I have good blood. Good blood is what's important. And you, who are you?"

"I'm Leonid." The name he had used most of his life tasted bitter in his mouth.

"I don't know a Leonid."

"In fact you know two, and you gave each of us our name."

Tsiolkovski leaned forward. His eyes were so white all over that Leonid doubted again that the man could see at all.

"So it's you," said Tsiolkovski. "And who's that with you, Nadya? All I can see is a halo of yellow. I assume that's your hair, Nadya."

"It is," said Nadya.

"And in the doorway, all I see is a silhouette. Mars? Valentina? Yuri?"

"I'm Mykola from the village."

"Get out," said Tsiolkovski.

"He's a friend," said Leonid.

"Get out!" screamed Tsiolkovski. "I won't have his kind of filth in my very own house."

"It was my home before you came here." It might still have been his home if Tsiolkovski had not come in the first place. Leonid's brother might still be alive. Or they might both have starved. What was worse, the possibility of death or its certainty? Regardless, this man was culpable. If the Chief Designer had been Leonid's brother's executioner, then Tsiolkovski was the judge who handed down the sentence. Leonid resisted the urge to drag the man from Grandmother's chair and toss him out the door.

"It's all right, Leonid," said Mykola. "We don't visit him for a reason. I'll wait outside."

He stepped backward out of the doorway. Kasha yipped.

"And an animal! I'd hoped he would train you all better than this. Bringing that man and an animal to my house. Of all the absurdities. He probably has you eating with your bare hands. That . . ." Tsiolkovski spoke a name Leonid had never heard before.

"Who are you talking about?" asked Leonid.

"Surely he's still Chief Designer. He was a good man. He could never go into space, of course, what with his balding. He was balding even then."

Leonid felt embarrassed that he had never stopped to consider that the Chief Designer might have a name.

"Cosmonauts can't be bald?" asked Leonid. Tsiolkovski's hair clung to his liver-spotted scalp only in wisps.

"There can be no genetic inferiority in space. When we colonize Mars, only the fittest can go. You and Nadya, you'd be fine breeding stock. As much as the process of breeding is repulsive, it's necessary for now. Until we can find another way. Imagine the children you two would have! Leonid, you were my first choice. I don't know why the Chief Designer saved you until last. You're not balding, are you?"

"Not that I know of." Leonid's anger ebbed. This man was but a cracked shell of the old Tsiolkovski. He was like a child. A bitter one lacking innocence, but a child nonetheless.

"Good, good. Then you should have been first. I trust the Chief Designer, but he was always bad at prioritizing. What was last was always first and what was first always last. That's another reason he can never go to space. He lacks faith. How can one conquer heaven without believing in it? Not the tripe from the church, but there's definitely something up there. It's the only thing that makes sense. There's no heaven at the moment, of course. It's our duty to create it. We must create the angels that will live there. And those angels must be perfect. But I'm afraid you can't take your dog. No animals in heaven. They're lesser, and only the superior are allowed. Imagine how great it will be surrounded by only the superior. Villages like this one won't even exist. We'll leave villages like this behind forever."

Tsiolkovski clacked the hollow horn down on the table.

"Where's my lunch," he demanded.

"You just ate it," said Varvara.

"What?"

She leaned toward his ear. "You already ate."

Tsiolkovski patted his belly, such as it was. Age had sucked his innards into themselves. His chest continued straight to his stomach without the interruption of even a bump. How old was the man? Leonid could not remember, but surely at least a hundred. After a certain point, all ages looked the same.

"So I did," said Tsiolkovski. "What about tea?"

"There's a cup right in front of you," said Varvara.

He patted at the table until his hand found it. He snaked one knuckly finger through the handle and held the cup in front of him without drinking from it. A picture of Nadya was printed on the side. With his other hand, Tsiolkovski returned the hollow horn to his ear.

"Is your brother with you?" asked Tsiolkovski.

"He's gone. Dead." The bitter taste returned to Leonid's mouth.

"Nonsense."

"He went to space."

"I know that, of course."

"He died there." Leonid's voice cracked.

"Nonsense. I spoke to him just yesterday." Tsiolkovski gestured to the far corner of the cottage with the teacup, sloshing tea over his hand and onto the table.

In the corner, an old radio, components stacked a meter high, dominated the space that had once contained Grandmother's dresser. The shiny metal surfaces, silver knobs, and glass-covered meters looked entirely out of place. Like Sputnik in a medieval painting. Like Leonid felt now sitting in his own home.

"I believe you're mistaken," said Nadya.

"Where's my tea?" asked Tsiolkovski.

"In your hand," said Varvara.

"You're mistaken," repeated Nadya.

"Who's that?" asked Tsiolkovski.

"Our guests were just leaving."

"Good riddance. You tell those inbred villagers to stay away from me. God knows what germs they carry."

"I'll tell them."

Varvara led Nadya and Leonid from the table and outside. Leonid looked back. He had a view of the radio through the crack in the door until it closed completely.

"I apologize for my husband," said Varvara.

Looking at her, Leonid saw that she was much younger than Tsiolkovski, maybe by decades. How could she tolerate sharing space with the man's ramblings? He remembered the patience of Grandmother, the wisdom that led villagers to seek her out when they needed advice.

"He must be old now," said Leonid. He prodded a mound of black dirt with his foot, uncovering the wet muck underneath.

"One hundred and eight. I think there's something about this cottage that lends the men who live here long life."

"It didn't work for my brother."

"You really don't know?"

"Know what?"

"Your brother's alive. Even now, he orbits the planet. My husband might be senile, but he's not wrong about that. I've listened to their conversations. Every few days, my husband turns on the radio and speaks to him." She pointed up at the trees. "There's an antenna run throughout the woods, and a transmitter farther along. I wasn't convinced that it was really Leonid he was talking to, not until now. You and your brother have the same voice."

Mykola and Kasha were up the hill, playing together as if the years had not passed, as if Mykola were still a child and this Kasha were her mother. But back then, they did not play together like this. Mykola had been too fatigued by hunger. He played now the way he probably wished he could have played as a child, reclaiming some missed part of his youth.

"That's impossible." Sweat slicked Leonid's palms. His mind raced through all the statistics he knew of Vostok. The exact numbers escaped him, but the amount of air in the tanks was measured in days, not months. Water would have lasted a week, and food less than that, even if his brother rationed it.

"There must be some mistake," said Nadya. "They're all dead. Every one of them." She placed her hand on Leonid's shoulder and squeezed so hard it hurt.

"All but one, it seems," said Varvara.

Leonid backed one step at a time from the cottage, pulling free of Nadya's grip. The land sloped away, threatening to topple him. He had not openly grieved his brother, but now realized that he had processed through grief the same as anyone. Maybe it was that the news came in this place, his and his brother's home. He had come here perhaps for closure, but instead found the feeble sutures that held the wound shut ripped open to reveal his fresh red interior. He tried to speak, but he was panting.

"You two, the Leonids," said Varvara, "it's not surprising that one of you would survive against the odds. You survived this place, the famine and the purges. Konstantin, he wanted you to go first, but the Chief Designer saved you until the end. I think the Chief Designer knew that with time his capsule would improve, and combined with your perseverance, one of you would have the best chance to make it through the harsh reality of space. He held off on his best chance of success, denying himself heaven until he knew he had equipment worthy of his conqueror. But it never was worthy, was it? Or was it that we were not worthy to go there? At least not to go there and return."

It was all too much. Leonid planted his feet and balled his fists. "There's no such place as heaven. My brother escaped the hell of this valley only to be sent somewhere worse. Now you tell me he's alive, when that clearly can't be true. To hell with your husband, and with you, too, for playing along. Though I suppose you're already there."

Leonid spun and walked straight toward the woods that separated the cottage from the village. He wanted to disappear there among the trees. He wanted the fir needles to wrap him like a blanket. He wanted to sink into the earth, deeper and deeper until the liquid rock below boiled him. He was sick of the metaphors of heaven and hell, and wanted to know one of them for real. One piece of reality, that was all he wanted. One thing that was not a trick or a lie. He felt he had deceived even himself by believing that there was something in the valley waiting for him. Instead, he had found only the bastard who had begun all the lies in the first place. Goddamned Tsiolkovski.

Kasha barked. She had left Mykola on the hill and was scratching at the door of the cottage, leaving bright gashes like shooting stars on the gray surface of the wood.

"She hears him," said Varvara.

"Tsiolkovski?" asked Nadya.

"It's about the right time." She spoke to Leonid's back. "Konstantin must have turned on the radio. He speaks to your brother even now."

She opened the door, and Kasha flashed through the crack and inside. Nadya and Varvara followed. Leonid hesitated.

Nadya stopped at the doorway and walked back to Leonid. "Are you coming?"

"I won't let myself fall for another lie."

"What is a lie, Leonid? Mere words. It's even less than words, because they're words with nothing behind them. I'm willing to risk that this is a lie for any small chance that it might be the truth.

"I think that's what you never understood. Risk. Not you, not the Chief Designer, not the other twins, not even Ignatius. You all believe I regret that my sister died in my place. I do, of course. I'm not heartless. But I carry a grudge against her, too. I should have been the first person in space. Whatever small chance there was that someone would survive the trip, that chance was mine. Don't you sometimes feel the same thing for your brother?"

Her eyes, usually set and cold, softened in the corners. The line of her lips turned up, however slightly.

"But it's more than that," she said. "Following you here, seeing you in this place, it's helped me realize something about myself. It wasn't traveling in space that was stolen from me, it was the return. An orbit is a perfect journey. From the moment of the launch, an orbit is designed to bring you home at the end. I'm not sure I'll ever know where home is unless I close the circle. I'll just continue on in a straight line forever, drawing farther and farther away from those few people I care about."

Leonid dug his toe into the bed of brown needles at the edge of the woods. "I'm here in my home, and I can tell you for sure that there's nothing special about returning."

"Don't lie to me, Leonid, and don't lie to yourself. I saw your face as you first saw this cottage."

"We're all liars. We've been trained to lie since the day Tsiolkovski claimed us."

She held out her hand to Leonid.

"You may not like my decision, the risks I will take, but I promise you this: I will never tell you anything but the truth."

Leonid searched her face. For the first time he saw something of Nadya's sister there. The physical features, of course, had always been the same, but now some of the other Nadya's warmth was there, as well. This was the face of the girl who had held and rocked him when he woke in tears those first weeks in Star City. The loss of this face was what he had grieved. If it could return now, years after he thought it gone forever, then it seemed possible that his brother could still return, as well. It seemed possible that if he climbed onto the roof of Grandmother's cottage, he could see his brother coursing among the stars.

Leonid took Nadya's hand.

"I believe you," he said.

It had only been a matter of days since Leonid made his escape, since he claimed domain over his own life, and he was already ceding it back to someone else. But no, he realized that he had always thought of his plan as Nadya's escape. Though he had chosen the destinations, he had gone as much for her as for himself. Nadya was the one who everyone followed. Every cosmonaut and engineer. Every Soviet citizen. The whole world. The future lay where she led it.

Nadya pulled Leonid toward the door. He entered Grandmother's cottage for what he knew would be the final time.

## Bohdan, Ukraine—1950

Grandmother and Mykola stood in the cottage doorway long after the sound of the train had faded from the valley. Now it seemed the quietest place imaginable, as if the very air had departed, as well. Grandmother turned her attention to the boy beside her, not her grandsons, but all that was left of them.

"You're always welcome here," she said.

"Will you be all right?" asked Mykola.

She shifted in place, her worn shoes rasping on the wooden floor.

"Have I ever told you the story of the man who our village is named after? Bohdan Zinoviy Mykhaylovych Khmelnytsky commanded hundreds of men in service to the Polish crown. At this time, the Cossacks were considered inferior forces, used only by Polish generals for menial tasks or as fodder for first charges in battle. Khmelnytsky's small force, however, earned a reputation for ferocity and for turning defeat into victory. At the sight of his flag on the battlefield, the Ottoman forces would retreat before a single arrow was launched. It's no exaggeration to say that the Polish empire lasted as long as it did because of Khmelnytsky. It's ironic then that he also factored into its collapse.

"A hero returning from war expects to be treated as such, but before he arrived back at his home in Subotiv, Khmelnytsky could tell by the black columns of smoke that something was amiss. He could not, however, have predicted the tragedy that awaited him. His home and the outlying buildings of his estate moldered from recent fires. Livestock lay slaughtered in his fields. Beside the first cottage he came to, where one of his cousins lived, he mistook for a pile of dirt the heaped bodies of his kin. At the apex of the pile, like the snow that once capped the mountains surrounding our valley, was Khmelnytsky's eldest son, beaten so badly that Khmelnytsky could only recognize him by the clothes he wore, a shirt that had once belonged to Khmelnytsky himself. Only a few flies had found the bodies. He rooted through the pile, familiar faces made strange by rigor. His other children were not among them. Nor his wife.

"From across the field ran several figures, and he recognized his daughter at the forefront. She wore only her nightclothes, barefoot. The others with her, his other sons and a few of his younger cousins, were also disheveled, but all seemed healthy. He searched among their faces for his wife, but she was not with them, either.

"He hugged his children tight to his chest even as he ordered his attendant to reassemble his soldiers. Could the Ottomans have struck at him in his own home? But no, they were too far away. This was not revenge. He couldn't fathom then what it might be. His daughter—Khmelnytsky would always remember that her eyes were dry, and he would always try to live up to her strength—said that the soldiers who came spoke Polish. She pointed in the direction they had fled.

"Khmelnytsky didn't wait for any of his own soldiers to join him. He mounted his horse and tore across the countryside until he found the tracks left by the men who had killed his son, a sizable force judging by the utter muck made of the trail by their progress. The forest thickened, the trail narrowed, but Khmelnytsky urged the horse on even as branches whipped at mount and rider both. Blood dripped from gashes on Khmelnytsky's cheeks and arms.

"Entering a clearing, he espied another column of smoke. Around it were several tents and a contingent of men and horses, maybe thirty of each. As he neared, he spotted one figure hunched among the tall, gloating Poles. It was his wife, sitting by the fire, leaning into its warmth as if to throw herself to the flames. Khmelnytsky made no attempt to conceal himself, driving down on the encampment full gallop. It took the Poles too long to notice him and far too long to react. Before the sentry had unsheathed his sword Khmelnytsky's blade removed the man's arm. The soldiers, sitting around the fire or dozing against the trunks of trees fell in quick succession. Khmelnytsky's horse kicked up a cloud of dust that hid him as if in the black mists of hell, scattering the logs of the fire and launching sparking embers on high arcs through the sky. The nearest tent ignited.

"Khmelnytsky dismounted and placed his horse between his wife, whose hands and feet were bound, and the soldiers streaming from their tents. The blood from the scratches on Khmelnytsky's face had crusted into red-brown stains in his beard. He seethed, hulking in heaving breaths, his muscles bulged by the rage that consumed him. One of the Poles advanced. Khmelnytsky slashed with his sword, and the Pole tried to parry but the blow was so strong that the sword fell from his hands. Before he could think to stoop and retrieve it, Khmelnytsky delivered the fatal blow. Two more soldiers fell as quickly as the first. The rest turned to flee, the demon before them so terrifying, something born of the leaping flames.

"But turning their backs was a mistake. They could offer no defense to the barrage of slashes that befell them. They all died as cowards, asses to their fears, faces planted in the black dirt."

"I'm not sure I like this story," said Mykola.

"You know," said Grandmother, "I never told the twins the whole story of Khmelnytsky's life. I always stopped here. The real darkness comes after. But I like this ending, with Khmelnytsky returning home. Sad, yes, but also triumphant. He had a home worth defending and found a way to defend it. That's why I was willing to let the twins leave. This cottage, the village, the valley— none of that will be the home they one day return to in triumph. Even if they do return to the valley, somewhere else will be their true home, other people their true family. One can't have two homes. One can't be leaving home and heading toward it both at the same time."

"Will you miss them?"

"Won't you?"

## Star City, Russia—1964

It had been half a decade since the training facilities were last this crowded. A man—the Chief Designer thought his name was Kolya, though he would not swear to it—sat in the Khilov swing, blindfolded, as Mishin and Bushuyev spun it around. Kolya's brow dripped with sweat, the beads practically bursting from his pores. All color had fled his face. The Chief Designer recognized the peculiar pinch of Kolya's mouth.

"Step back," called the Chief Designer across the room.

Mishin and Bushuyev released the swing, one a little sooner than the other, which sent it wobbling as well as spinning. Kolya heaved once, and then spewed his breakfast all over the floor, just at their feet. They backed away, almost into Giorgi's mural on the back wall. The huge head of Nadya stared at the Chief Designer with a stern expression, Leonid with a winning smile.

The Chief Designer clapped his hands together once, and a custodian came in from the hallway. The mop he carried was new, though this was far from the first puddle of vomit. Kolya alone had accounted for two dozen cleanups. The Chief Designer worried that he would blow his entire budget on mops and buckets if things continued the way they were.

On the vibration platform sat Galina. She had seized the control knob from one of the technicians and operated it herself, upping the oscillations past what a cosmonaut would experience even reentering the atmosphere. Her expression was similar to

Kolya's, but the Chief Designer knew it was not due to illness. He had come across her one evening using the platform to achieve orgasm. She had not seen him, and he had never mentioned it. Who was he to judge? He had committed worse acts. But at least he kept his secret. Here Galina was in a room full of people making only the feeblest attempt to hide her pleasure. The Chief Designer looked away.

In the far corner, a frail woman named Zlata ran on the treadmill. She tried hard, but the pace was clearly too quick for her. She stumbled, swiping a hand for the rail. She missed, and the shift in weight pushed her top half forward as the treadmill pulled her tangled feet back. She plummeted face-first and was propelled from the track to the floor. The technician there hung her head, waiting long seconds before offering assistance.

It had been since the first five cosmonauts were but children that the Chief Designer had seen such a complete display of incompetence. It was forgivable in the children, but these were adults, trained pilots. He had requested only the best. He had been promised the elite. He hoped, for the sake of the Soviet Union, that this was not the best the air force had to offer.

A hearty laugh came from behind him.

"Did you see her fall? That was truly comical, comrade."

"Ignatius," said the Chief Designer. "I suppose it's good to see you."

She had not visited Star City since the day Giorgi died, but the Chief Designer almost expected her sudden appearance. A surprise that happens often enough ceases to be surprising.

"I'm certainly better to look at than anything occurring in this room," she said.

The Chief Designer held his forehead and laughed despite

himself. "Wasn't this undertaking enough of a comedy to begin with? We didn't need the addition of clowns."

"Giorgi was the best," said Ignatius.

"I don't expect another Giorgi, but surely the air force has better pilots than this."

"Of course they do, but they have no intention of sending them to you. Do you know how you got Giorgi? Marshal Nedelin. He was the one who secured the best people for the space program. Now that he's gone, the air force has no one to hold them accountable. They use the space program to shuttle off their worst recruits. Everyone here has been declared unfit for flight."

"And I'm supposed to prepare them for space?"

"If it's any comfort, they sent even worse pilots to the General Designer."

"Actually, that's the first small comfort I've had in weeks. I never thought relief would come from you, Ignatius." He rubbed the scar on his head. "Have you heard from them?"

"I haven't seen them since the funeral, same as you."

"Where have you been?"

"You missed me?"

"I thought you'd have answers. Do you know where they went?"

"No."

"Did you tell them to leave?"

"I encouraged them."

"I've never thought that you were on my side, so how is it that you were able to betray me?"

"I protected you from yourself. If Nadya had died, I wouldn't have been able to protect you in the investigations that followed. The Party would have discovered all your secrets."

"I find it hard to believe that you've been protecting me."

"Just because it's difficult to believe doesn't mean it's not true. For example, knowing what I do about you, it's hard to believe that you're a kind and empathetic man."

The Chief Designer found himself grinding his teeth. He relaxed his jaw and rubbed at his cheek. *Kind* was not a word he would ever use to describe himself, and it seemed to grow less apt every day. It was not only these pitiful excuses for pilots he had now. No, he did not know how one of them would ever successfully dock Voskhod with Vostok, but so much of that was controlled from the ground. He only needed one pilot to be just competent enough for the five minutes of the final docking maneuvers. He doubted he would get even that, but doubt was a feeling he was accustomed to.

The real problem was the dogs. Khrushchev's dog they could bring back. If the plan worked, they needed no double. But Kasha. Khrushchev asked about her in every correspondence, as if she, like Byelka, were his. For every hour spent training the new cosmonauts, Mishin and Bushuyev had spent two scouring the streets of Moscow for a dog that looked like Kasha. The Chief Designer knew better than to inquire, but he was sure that some of the dogs they brought in had not come from the streets, but had been pets. They were too clean, too pampered. They had the wrong disposition entirely. Anything unexpected terrified them. It did not matter, anyway. None of them looked the least bit like Kasha. The most similar dog had the same shape as Kasha but deep brown fur. Mishin and Bushuyev had tried to bleach it white, but the closest they could get was tan. The poor dog's skin was so tender after bleaching that it was a week before she would allow anyone to pet her.

"Will they come back?" asked the Chief Designer.

"I believe so," said Ignatius. "And if they do, I'll encourage them to stay. I've seen your latest reports. You're ready for Nadya. I admit that I doubted you would be. I focus so much on failure—it's my job, after all, to prevent it—that I often have a hard time anticipating success. Still, I stand by my decision. When I sent them away, all you had to offer was failure."

No one outside of Star City was supposed to have seen the latest reports. It did not surprise the Chief Designer, though, that Ignatius had seen them. Whether or not he was ready, even he was not sure of that.

"They've already been gone over a month," he said.

"It's their first taste of independence since they were children. But even the most delicious food can only be consumed a dish at a time. Nadya thinks of you as a father."

"That I am most definitely not. Not even to my own son."

"Again, it doesn't matter what you believe. Truth and belief are unrelated."

The custodian walked by them, bucket swaying from his hand, as if what was inside did not repulse him. And perhaps it did not. His constitution was certainly better than Kolya's. The Chief Designer would learn this custodian's name, train him for spaceflight, make of him the next hero of the Soviet Union. This custodian would become the first person to clean in outer space.

"You smile," said Ignatius.

"I just had an amusing thought," said the Chief Designer.

"Will you share?"

He would have liked to, but he did not know how. It had all become so absurd. The only thing he could think of that would be more absurd would be to try to explain the absurdity.

"Chief Designer." The voice came from behind him.

"Yes, yes," he said, not turning.

A small yip sounded. At first the Chief Designer thought Galina was back on the vibration platform, but this yip had come from the wrong direction. He turned.

Leonid stood there, Kasha in his arms, Nadya lurking in the doorway behind him. Her hair had grown longer. Leonid's whiskers threatened to fill out into a beard. And little Kasha. She had not changed at all.

"We're back," said Leonid.

The Chief Designer found himself holding his breath, as if to exhale would blow away the apparition before him. He looked at Ignatius.

"You knew they were back?" he asked Ignatius.

"I was notified that they had boarded a train bound for Moscow."

"So you lied to me."

"I prefer not to deliver good news."

The Chief Designer could not bring himself to look at Leonid, even though he yearned to see him, and even more to see Nadya, the woman who thought of him as a father. He still did not believe it, and he feared looking at her, that the expression on her face would reveal the error of Ignatius's claim.

"What should I do?" the Chief Designer asked Ignatius.

"I would start by sending these other so-called pilots back to where they came from."

The Chief Designer glanced sidelong at his cosmonauts. Kasha, the little white dog, tail wagging, tongue flapped out the side of her mouth, seemed happy to have returned. The other two showed no emotion, Nadya even less so than usual.

"Mishin, Bushuyev," called the Chief Designer.

The two men left Kolya, still doubled over in the Khilov swing, and hurried toward the door. They stopped short at the sight of Leonid and Nadya.

"You can send the other pilots home," said the Chief Designer.

"Thank god," said Mishin or Bushuyev.

They walked around the Chief Designer and greeted first Leonid and then Nadya. The two men smiled, revealing a real sort of happiness, not just at having capable cosmonauts again, but at the return of old friends. The Chief Designer had resented them for having let Leonid and Nadya go. He felt sure that in their place, he would have been able to stop them. But with this reunion, he saw that Mishin and Bushuyev understood family in a way that he never would. For someone who had sent so many of his children permanently away, he had never learned that one aspect of family was parting. Family is not necessarily the place where one is, but where one returns, given the chance.

The Chief Designer looked Nadya in the eye. "Thank you."

"We should talk," said Leonid.

He set Kasha on the floor and left in the direction of the Chief Designer's office.

EVERYTHING IN THE OFFICE felt too large. Leonid sat in one of the guest chairs, the seat wide enough to have held him and his brother both. The desk seemed built for ogres. The chair on the other side like a throne. In it, the Chief Designer looked smaller. Less like a bear and more like a cub. It was not just the chair. Something in the man's expression, in how he looked at Leonid, had changed. He remembered the same look on Grandmother's face just before he and his brother left the valley.

Leonid spoke the Chief Designer's name. The Chief Designer's composure flickered for a moment, but he pulled his face into a grin.

"How did you learn that?" asked the Chief Designer.

"I spoke to Leonid. I spoke to my brother."

This time the Chief Designer's composure failed him. He looked like he might be ill, or burst into tears, or both.

"How?"

"Tsiolkovski. He's communicated with all the cosmonauts."

"From beyond the grave?"

"He's alive."

"Alive?"

"More or less."

"Where is he?"

"I think he would prefer no one to know. Also, he's mostly insane."

"Tsiolkovski always had strange ideas."

"I remembered him as a younger man. Someone in control. I suppose he was old even then, his grip already in the midst of failing him."

"His generation, even mine, we pretend control even when we have none. It was the only way to survive the bad times. After the Revolution and through the war."

"Why didn't you tell me that Leonid was still alive?"

"He's as good as dead, Leonid. Already his life is an impossibility."

"That's different from any life how?"

The Chief Designer smiled again. He had known Leonid for the majority of the man's life, but only now realized that he did not know him well at all.

"Why did you return?" asked the Chief Designer.

"My brother told me."

"Told you what?"

"That after Nadya died, the other Nadya, you gave the remaining cosmonauts a choice. They all chose to fly, even when they knew it would mean dying. I don't free you from blame, but I must blame my brother, as well. He's a damned fool. If you're guilty of something, it's raising him to be one."

"I have lately been thinking that while I gave them a choice, I never asked if it was what they wanted. I have spent the better part of my own life making choices that are contrary to my wants."

"Leonid also told me that you apologized to him."

"I won't lie to you now. I've done no such thing."

"He said he didn't think you knew that your apology reached him. He said that you must have come into the radio room one night when he was out of range. As his orbit brought him over Star City, he heard the ghost of your voice, saying 'I'm sorry' over and over, the sound growing stronger with each repetition. When the signal was finally strong enough for him to answer, you were gone, and Mars greeted him instead."

The Chief Designer recalled that sleepless night. It was only a few days after Nadya and Leonid ran away. He had woken from nightmares. Not an uncommon occurrence, but usually they took him back to the long-ago past, to icy nights on the tundra. This one was set in the present. He was surrounded by everyone he knew: Nadya, Leonid, Mars, Yuri, Valentina, his wife, his son, Mishin, Bushuyev, Giorgi, Nedelin, Tsiolkovski, Khrushchev, Ignatius, even the General Designer. They were all there to congratulate the Chief Designer, but as he thanked them they each burst into flame. The fire consumed them slowly. They did not change to look like Giorgi's body, brittle and blackened. Instead they evaporated, from foot to face, a layer at a time like the heat shield. They kept congratulating him, heaping up the most effusive praise, until their mouths were finally consumed. Nadya was the last one to disappear. The Chief Designer stood in the middle of beige, endless terrain, like Baikonur but lacking even the few features that made up that dull landscape. He felt himself on fire. First his teeth disappeared from his mouth. That was when he woke, a feeling he could not identify clenched in both his gut and his mind. He felt near panicked that there was something he had forgotten to do. Something essential. He cried. He had not cried, not really, since he was a boy. Shrugging on his robe and stepping into a pair of old shoes he used as slippers, he went to the radio room. He had not planned to go there, it just happened. It was as if he were still asleep, still in part of the dream. Until now, he was not entirely sure that he had not been dreaming the whole time.

"What did you say to each other?" asked the Chief Designer.

"What is there to say? He's a stranger now. Do you ever stop to consider how many strangers share your name?"

"It's not so rare a name."

"Perhaps that's why a title is better."

"So you came back to discuss names and titles?"

"Honestly, Chief Designer, it wasn't me who came back. It was Nadya. I simply followed. She wants to fly the mission. And don't think that I didn't try to talk her out of it."

There was a report on the new ablative heat shield on the desk. The Chief Designer turned the pages without reading them, without even looking.

"Things might have been better if you could have convinced her."

"That's how your spaceships work, right?"

"What do you mean?"

"The things fly themselves, and the cosmonaut's just a passive passenger."

"Yes." The Chief Designer smiled.

"It turns out that I never learned what to do when given the controls. I only end up where I'm guided."

"You know, sometimes I envy you that."

"No, you don't."

Leonid stood, knocking the chair back several inches.

"My brother told me the details of the next mission. A docking in space. Can't you try to save him instead of the dogs?"

"His Vostok has no docking clamp. Even if we could meet it in space, the best we could do would be to bounce the two capsules against each other like billiard balls." The Chief Designer wondered who had told the other Leonid about the mission. It must have been Mars, but that didn't really answer the question. Who told Mars? Not that it mattered. The Chief Designer was too used to the truth slipping out.

"I know," said Leonid.

"Then why did you ask?"

"I guess I hoped that you'd surprise me."

"Did I?"

"Yes and no. How soon until the launch?"

"Two weeks."

"Have I ever told you the story of the man my village was named after?"

"I know of the man, of course. He's celebrated in Russian history, as well. But tell me."

"Bohdan Zinoviy Mykhaylovych Khmelnytsky had crushed the Poles in battle after battle. Starting at the mouth of the Dnieper, where he had once returned to Ukrainian soil after years of slavery, he overthrew the Zaporozhian Sich, and then moved upstream, taking Dnepropetrovsk and Kremenchuk and Cherkasy all the way to Kiev. He was welcomed to the capital on Christmas Day, his procession the grandest parade in the city's history. Streets were strung across with garlands and every window burned with candles and bands interspersed themselves with the soldiers, playing the kind of joyous songs as had not been heard in Kiev for a hundred years. Parents offered their sons to Khmelnytsky that he might raise them to be great men.

"At a gathering of Cossack nobles, such as a Cossack might be accused of nobility, Khmelnytsky claimed not just the right to rule the Zaporozhian Cossacks but the whole of Ukraine. He became in fact, if not in name, ruler of what would become our nation. From untried soldier to slave to officer to king, somehow he'd not only survived his trials but used them to shape himself into the man of the moment, a hero and a savior. His battles weren't over, no. The Poles didn't much care for him and attacked at every opportunity, but Khmelnytsky always prevailed. Maybe the best measure of his greatness is that his successors could not hold Ukraine together."

"A great man, yes," said the Chief Designer.

"Grandmother always shared his stories with us, but she left out part of his life. I wouldn't learn of it until much later, in a book Giorgi leant me. I believe it was a book he shouldn't have had in the first place, certainly not one that had been approved by Glavlit. It made me realize that Grandmother's stories were just that: stories. In fact, Khmelnytsky had as many failures as successes. More than that, he had as many moments of cruelty as he did of glory.

"The worst was his hatred of the Jews. He blamed them for every ill that befell him, as if they were the disorganized armies of his subordinates or the ones issuing secret orders to the Poles. During his reign, tens of thousands of Jews were slaughtered. Women, men, children, the elderly. Entire villages disappeared in the wake of Cossack forces, the landscape dotted with charred buildings and mass graves, if the Cossacks even took the time to bury the dead. In some places, there were later found piles of bones, marked with the teeth of the animals that had gnawed away the flesh. And the ways the Jews were slaughtered. Dismemberment, burning, torture, even crucifixion. Any terrible death that man has ever imagined was employed against them. The lucky ones were simply stabbed. In this, Khmelnytsky was as bad as Stalin or Hitler."

"I didn't know that about him. The Soviet accounts are sterilized, of course."

"I stopped revering him after I read that book. And Tsiolkovski, while he may be addled by old age, I think it merely reveals the spite that was always in his heart. A hero is a fragile thing. In the case of the cosmonauts, it took two each for every hero you created. That's what I learned while I was away. I don't forgive you, Chief Designer. That's not required, though, as long as I know what I know now. There's evil in the world, but its face isn't yours, Chief Designer. No, it's not yours at all."

His face. The Chief Designer felt the scar there, an endless ache. Once, the pain had reminded him of the wound. Now, it reminded him of everything since. More than his title, more than his name, he identified himself by the ache.

WHEN THEY HAD cleaned out Giorgi's room in the dorm, they found one whole cabinet stocked full of liquor. Domestic vodka on the lower shelves, the upper filled with imported whiskies and a few beverages no one could identify. Their labels were not printed in any of the languages the staff at Star City knew. The bottles were all unopened, waiting for a celebratory occasion for the corks to be popped. Instead, the Chief Designer had drained several bottles over the course of two weeks, always a glass or two before bed. Without the aid of drink, he lay there, mind racing through potential problems.

These were not new problems. He had a name for each. The chance that the ablative heat shield would burn too quickly or too slowly, igniting the whole capsule and exploding it in the upper atmosphere, scattering shards of metal and Nadya's singed bones across hundreds of kilometers of Russian countryside, he shortened to *The Heat Shield Problem*. The fact that no one had ever attempted to dock two ships in space, that the docking mechanism had only been tested on the ground, that no launch yet had inserted Vostok into the exact planned orbit, that they called the cosmonauts pilots when they were really just passengers but now Nadya needed to be an actual pilot, that failure would mean an investigation, revealing a decade of deceit, and everyone who was involved, and quite likely many who were not, would be tried and executed for treason—the Chief Designer referred to that as *The Docking Problem*. There was the usual list of problems the Chief Designer dealt with for every launch, as well. He could not forget those.

Right now, though, the Chief Designer was occupied by *The Hangover Problem*, and to a greater degree *The Dog Problem*. Byelka, Khrushchev's little rodent of a dog, had been delivered, in a private limousine, to Star City the day before. The technicians had been trying to fit the dog with a vest all morning. This was supposed to be a comfort to the dogs, as well as allowing for the placement of sensors, but apparently to Byelka the vest was the gravest travesty in the history of the universe. When they finally got it on him, he began a period of yowling and sprinting in circles that did not end until hours later. It was so intense, and the dog's biting so vicious, that no one could get close enough to him to remove the vest that was causing the fit in the first place. Eventually, the dog wore itself out, and it collapsed in a corner, motionless. The Chief Designer worried that they had killed the dog before it even made it to the launchpad.

When the dog began again to show signs of life, the Chief Designer ordered it sedated. The veterinarian balked at first, but

Byelka yipped anew, a sound so shrill and piercing as to drive straight through the ear canal to the brain. The veterinarian found a vein in the dog's spindly leg and administered a dose even the Chief Designer could recognize as excessive.

"Load the little bastard," said the Chief Designer, and two technicians put Byelka in a small cage and carried him away.

In the next room, Nadya was being fitted with her pressure suit, baggy and bright orange, topped with a helmet as wide as her torso. A cluster of tubes sprouted from the suit below her right breast, leading to what looked like a metal briefcase she held in her left hand. If anyone asked, the cosmonauts were instructed to say that the case contained life support equipment. Not an outright lie, but the case's primary function was to store waste should a cosmonaut need to relieve herself while in the capsule. Mishin and Bushuyev buzzed around Nadya, adjusting the suit's seals and checking zippers.

"How do I look?" she asked.

"Ridiculous," said the Chief Designer.

The top of the helmet formed a perfect white orb, a planet completely covered in clouds. He tapped his fingers lightly on the crown.

"This won't do," said the Chief Designer. "Someone will mistake her for an American pilot when she exits the capsule. They'll think we've shot down another U-2." He ran his finger along the white space just above the visor. "Paint something here. CCCP."

"Who will we get to paint it?" asked Mishin or Bushuyev.

A moment of silence followed, and the Chief Designer knew they all shared the same thought.

"Whoever. No need to be perfect."

"Just good enough," said Nadya.

There it was, thought the Chief Designer. Nadya had created a motto for the whole Soviet space program: *Just good enough.* At first, it seemed to be a criticism, but what could be more Soviet? Getting by with the essentials, eschewing all else. He realized he had so far failed to live up to that motto, accepting *not quite good enough* as good enough. It was time to set things right. Nadya could do that. She would.

"Finish up here and we'll head out," said the Chief Designer. "The plane leaves in four hours."

In fact, the plane left whenever he wanted it to. He felt, though, that setting this deadline might be the last time he had real control over the launch.

## Baikonur Cosmodrome—1964

Nadya was the twin who was supposed to die. But here she was, seated inside the capsule. Voskhod, not Vostok. Not really so different, essentially the same capsule with more components crammed inside. Designed for two or three cosmonauts but there was only one left to carry. This new capsule had a video camera directed at Nadya from just below her chin, her face, framed by the white helmet of the pressure suit, filling the whole screen. The Chief Designer touched the screen with his fingers. It was not the same. For the first time, a crewed Soviet rocket would launch without Nadya in the control room.

The Chief Designer walked around the console to the periscope. This R-7 looked like a mistake, rising higher above the launchpad than the rockets used to launch Vostok. A cigarette gripped in four metal fingers. Steam rose from the base of the rocket and swirled up and away.

It seemed that the smoke from the launch of Kasha and Byelka had barely cleared before they had begun setting up Nadya's rocket. The first launch had gone smoothly, the old routine of launching Vostok like an exercise in relaxation. They had sedated Byelka before loading him into the capsule, through the awkward docking ring around the hatch. As soon as the first rumble came from the R-7's engines, though, the dog was alert and yipping, the noise so persistent that eventually they had to turn off the speakers in the control room. The roar of liftoff seemed quiet in comparison.

Now the dogs were in orbit, telemetry nominal. The only sound from the dogs was a repeated retching from Byelka. They had not fed him, so the Chief Designer was confident that he had not soiled the capsule too badly. Kasha sometimes let out a bark, as if only to remind everyone that she was still there. The monitors strapped to Kasha, in some cases surgically implanted, returned results from her no different than if she were napping back at Star City.

The Chief Designer returned to the control console and moved Mishin, or was it Bushuyev, away from the radio. There were actually three radios set up, one for each capsule in orbit, including Leonid's, though this last was not turned on. Too many people in the room, lower-level engineers, had no idea at all that another capsule still circled the Earth. The Chief Designer pressed the button on the first radio's microphone and sent his voice to the dogs, now completing their sixth orbit.

"Good girl, Kasha," he said.

The reply came in the form of another retch from Byelka. Kasha growled, just a short sound to express her discontent.

"I'm sorry for your traveling companion, Kasha. You'll have better company soon enough."

A bottle of vodka passed between Mishin and Bushuyev and then to the Chief Designer. He gulped back a mouthful. He felt the burn in the empty sockets of his gums, in his veins, up and along the jagged scar on his head. He thought of himself as a rocket being fueled, that when he pressed the button, it would not be Nadya but himself, the human spaceship, lifting through the white wisps of clouds, over the Kazakh steppe's singular unscenic-ness.

The Chief Designer took the bottle of vodka to Leonid. Leonid had been standing in the darkened corner since before the first launch, not speaking once, refusing with dismissive waves every offer to take a look through the periscope.

Leonid took the bottle and drank from it, first one swallow and then another and then another. Throwing his head back, he trickled the last drops straight into his throat.

"So much for the vodka," said the Chief Designer.

Mishin and Bushuyev laughed, and one of them pulled a fresh bottle from under the console. "Ignatius left extras."

They popped the cork, and the fresh bottle began its rounds. Ignatius had been there as the final preparations were made, but she left before the first launch. She even said goodbye. The Chief Designer could not recall her ever announcing her departure before. He wondered if it meant something. He would be relieved to never see her again. But without knowing if she would return, he would never be able to relax to that idea. What was worse, her actual presence or her looming one?

Leonid slouched. They had trained him to always stand tall. When he was a boy, it seemed like half of everything they said to him was some version of *Straighten up.* The Chief Designer wondered if this was the type of man Leonid would be if Tsiolkovski had never found him. The Chief Designer leaned on the wall next to Leonid in the darkened corner.

"When you were gone, it felt like we'd lost another cosmonaut in space," said the Chief Designer. "I know you don't want my thanks, but you have it. For returning and for having been here in the first place."

Leonid gazed up at the gray ceiling, eyes focused on a point beyond it. "Do you know what I realized? While you may have given a choice to our siblings, you never gave a choice to us, those who stayed behind. You just assumed we were all right with it. I don't mind so much being a part of this, as long as I have the option not to be. Even now, I don't know if the choice was actually mine, but if Nadya and Kasha both fly and return, I guess that's good enough for me. That's as close as I'll get to accomplishment. I didn't choose to return. I chose to stay with them, wherever they went."

"Don't underestimate yourself, Leonid," said the Chief Designer.

"Of course not," said Leonid. "I'm a Soviet hero." He ran his fingers across the bottom of the medals on his chest—a new set to replace those he had abandoned in Kharkiv—as if sounding chimes.

Nadya's voice sparked from the radio, not words but humming, and not her usual atonal tune. This song was different but familiar. Leonid found himself humming along. So was the Chief Designer. And Mishin and Bushuyev. The song was one of Giorgi's, one he had always sung to the plucked accompaniment of the balalaika. Leonid and the Chief Designer smiled first at the radio and then at each other.

"Sometimes," said the Chief Designer, "I feel that she's the hero of my very own life. I felt that way before her first launch, and again now. I'm just watching from the side."

"Now who's the one underestimating?"

The Chief Designer walked to the radio and Leonid followed.

"Hello, Nadya," said the Chief Designer. "Just a little longer."

"Let's go already," said Nadya.

"You've waited years," said Leonid. "Another minute won't kill you."

Leonid cringed at his choice of phrase.

The Chief Designer placed his hand on Leonid's shoulder and squeezed.

"It's time," he said. And then into the microphone, "It's time."

The final countdown passed in silence. The Chief Designer pushed a button, conspicuously red, and the rocket ignited. The petals of the launchpad folded away as the flames leapt up to consume them. The rocket reached the sky and kept climbing.

## Epilogue

After the launch, all the technicians filed out. Only the Chief Designer, Leonid, Mars, and Mishin and Bushuyev remained. Someone had shut off the sickly fluorescent lights overhead. Leonid's face was lit only by the glow of the buttons on the console.

"Leonid, can you hear me?" he asked.

"Who is it?"

"It's your brother."

"Oh, good. I was concerned that I wouldn't get to speak with you again."

"Nadya is up there with you. And Kasha, too."

"Ah! I thought I saw them."

"That's unlikely. There's more space than you imagine."

"What's there to imagine? I've seen it all. I have nothing to do but look out this window. Can you tell the Chief Designer to add a larger window on his next spacecraft?"

"I'm here," said the Chief Designer. "I'll add more and larger windows."

"Good, good."

There was a long moment of only static.

"Will they come back?" asked Leonid from the capsule.

"Who?" asked his brother.

"Nadya and Kasha."

"We'll bring them home," said the Chief Designer.

"Thank god," said Leonid.

"Did you see him?" asked the other Leonid. "Is god up there, after all?"

"Don't be ridiculous. There's no such thing as heaven. All around me is literally nothing. But you know, I like the idea of that. I like that what I have now is the only important thing. Even if it's not much."

"Thank you," said Leonid, the one on the ground. "You've always been a good brother to me."

"I'm very thirsty. Of the things I don't have here, water is what I miss the most. I'm very, very thirsty."

A loud click came through the speaker.

"What was that?" asked the Chief Designer.

"It's time," said Leonid, his voice distorted. He was not talking directly into the microphone. "I'm going outside to stretch."

"You can't," said Leonid. "You'll die."

"Do you still believe I'm really alive? It's time to go. I'm opening the door."

The hiss of rushing air, a whine of feedback, the stark silence of space. At first like falling, and then you float.

# ACKNOWLEDGMENTS

My deepest gratitude goes to the real cosmonauts, engineers, scientists, staff, and dogs of the Soviet space program, who inspire me to strive for big, impossible things.

Thanks to my agent, Annie Bomke. The people at Putnam have been outstanding to work with, especially my editor Sara Minnich, Patricja Okuniewska, and all the editors, designers, marketers, publicists, and administrators who've been part of the book-making process.

Christopher Berinato, Gino Orlandi, and Joseph Schwartzburt read the first draft of this book and gave me the feedback I needed to complete it.

Love and thanks to Catherine Killingsworth, Gino (again), and Kakashi the dog for letting me use Kakashi's description for my little space dog, Kasha.

Thanks to the staff at Gallery Espresso in Savannah, Georgia, where most of this book was written. Thanks to Joni and Chris at The Book Lady Bookstore for being champions of local writers. Love to the whole Savannah coterie: Brian Dean, Sarah Lasseter, Erika Jo Brown, B.J. Love, Alexis Orgera, Ariel Felton, Jenny Dunn, Alison Niebanck, Billie Stirewalt, Brennen Arkins, Beverly Willett, Traci Lombardo, Blake "Allfather" Patrick, Danon Jade McConnell, Chike Cole, Adam Davies, Morgan Harrison, Chad Faries, Maria Dixon, Jason Kendall, Patricia Lockwood, Josh Peacock, Sarah Bates Murray, Christy Hahn, Jessi-Lyn Curry, Insley Smullen, Harrison Scott Key, Shea Caruso, and too many more to name. Thanks to Justin Gary and old friends from my long-ago Atlanta days.

To my rad writer pals for making writing not just an activity but a community: Thomas Calder, John R. Saylor, Aaron Devine, Karen

Russell, Nate Brown, Philip Dean Walker, John Copenhaver, Robert Ker-beck, Bridget Hoida, Bryan Hurt, Lindsay Chudzik, Jonathan Church, Emma Komlos-Hrobsky, Rob Spillman, Sam Ashworth, Gale Marie Thompson, and everyone at BOA Editions. Zach Doss, we miss you.

Thanks to The Writer's Center, my literary home in the D.C. area, and to my colleagues Margaret Meleney, Laura Spencer, Grace Mott, Lau-reen Schipsi, Brandon Johnson, Tessa Wild, and Amy Freeman.

I owe a debt to these authors and editors of books on the Soviet space program: Asif A. Siddiqi (*Sputnik and the Soviet Space Challenge*); Siddiqi and James T. Andrews (*Into the Cosmos*); Eva Maurer, Julia Rich-ers, Monica Rüthers, and Carmen Scheide (*Soviet Space Culture*); Colin Burgess and Rex Hall (*The First Soviet Cosmonaut Team*); Nick Abadzis (*Laika*); Jim Ottaviani, Zander Cannon, and Kevin Cannon (*T-Minus: The Race to the Moon*).

In memory of Jeremy Mullins and Kirk Lawrence. It's been ten years, but you're still the two people who've pushed my creativity the most.

In honor of everyone, human and canine, who died in pursuit of the cosmos.

Thank you to my brother, Josh, my parents, and the whole family for being supportive of life paths as diverse as rocket science and writing.

All my love to Stephanie Grimm, who I think is quite nice.